CHANGING VISION

Julie E. Czerneda

CHANGING VISION

D A W   B O O K S ,   I N C .

DONALD A. WOLLHEIM, FOUNDER

375 Hudson Street, New York, NY 10014

ELIZABETH R. WOLLHEIM

SHEILA E. GILBERT

PUBLISHERS

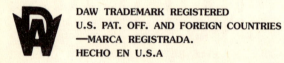

For Jennifer Lynn Czerneda

This has been the hardest one yet to write, which seems only fair. It was an impossible task from the start. I can't possibly distill the love and pride I feel for you into mere words. I've tried several times and failed. Perhaps if I had an immense and lovely lake into which I could toss diamonds . . . or some way to coat the near side of the Moon with sapphires . . . or . . . you can see my problem. The canvas isn't remotely big enough.

So I'll just tell you this, Princess: your Dad and I knew you were something special from the moment you opened your wise blue eyes. You've grown into a spectacular woman: bright, loving, and marvelously brave. May you have joy and adventures as well as warm, comfy moments—and remember, the way home is through our hearts.

Mom

ACKNOWLEDGMENTS

Book four. The most fun yet! I'd need a lot more room to respond to all the kindnesses done to me this year, but I'll do my best.

Thank you, Sheila Gilbert, for your extraordinary efforts to read manuscript during the millennium rollover, despite house construction and visitors. You caught all my lazy and shy spots, improving this story immensely. A special thanks to my alpha reader, Roxanne BB Hubbard, for thoughtful edits and thumping at the right moments.

I'd like to thank the original Lefebvre, Chase, and Sandner for kindly letting me use their names, brave souls. I promised no maiming, but, for the record, your fictional characters have nothing to do with the real you (except any nice bits).

I must single out a particular bunch for their wonderful support and encouragement this past year: my newsgroup. If I'd known all these talented and interesting folks would be there, I'd have jumped in sooner. While I can't possibly fit you all, I'd like to thank Janet BF Chase, Annette Griessman, Jason FFTS Simcoe, Kim McLean, Beverley Meincke, Matt & Karen Cecile, Nicole Hare, Ruth Stuart, Samuel Paik, Iris Peace, David Brukman, Lara Herrera, Liz Bennefeld, Michael Picray, Tim Bowie, Don Bassie, and Alan Mietlowski. And Anne Bishop, who drops in to kindly share the fun and herself.

My sincere thanks to all those who were so very excited for me during my run at the Campbell Award, including James Van Pelt, Nalo Hopkinson, Cindy Huckle, and Lyn McConchie.

My thanks to everyone at DAW Books, especially Sean, Debra, and Amy. I'm very happy to finally acknowledge the most able and thoughtful work of Paula Greenberg, who copy-edits all of my manuscripts, alien names and all. And Luis, you keep getting better. Wow!

Thanks, Jennifer and Scott. Your encouragement and interest makes this a joy for me. (Not to mention your skill at sneaking into my office to see if I'm really working.)

And thank you, Roger. For what this time? For everything.

CONTENTS

Elsewhere

"FIFTY years."

A drop of sweat coalesced on the bald head of the Human standing at the end of the long table, a drop large enough to create its own runnel over his forehead, hesitate in a bushy eyebrow, then push through to land in one eye. The Human blinked involuntarily, but remained stiffly at attention, as if pinned in place by the glare of the lights aimed his way. "You don't appreciate the circumstances, sir. There are . . ."

"Fifty years without a trace, without a sign, without proof, Project Leader Kearn." Out of the shadows, fingernails drummed a staccato on the table, a seven-part rhythm oddly disturbing to those accustomed to a different number of fingers per hand. "Five decades in which this monster of yours—this evil incarnate—hasn't shown itself. In which you've been unable to convince any of our predecessors that the only one in existence didn't die that day." There was a pause as the fingers opened a file. "No one here denies your scholarly accomplishments, Project Leader Kearn. Your research into, ah, yes, into the commonalities of the folklore concerning such creatures—among what I find a frankly astonishing number of species and cultures—has added greatly to our understanding of one another. You are to be commended." The file was snapped closed. "But even you must admit actually hunting for this Esen Monster is a criminal waste of time and resources."

"It's just a matter of time, Hom Slatth," the Human

named Lionel Kearn offered numbly, finding it hard to control his wild impatience. It was Her fault he was embarrassed like this over and over again; Her fault he had to constantly remind these bureaucrats and their lackeys of the danger posed by such utter alienness.

It was Her fault he'd lost his first and only command fifty years ago.

"I'll bring you the evidence," Kearn continued, fighting the tendency of his voice to develop a whining note. Sector Commissioner Slatth, as most Niderons, tended to a regrettable aggression when faced with weakness of any sort—even this smooth and sophisticated diplomat had inflated his nostril hood in instinctive threat several times during Kearn's briefing. And the others here—three Humans, the bagful of Rands spilling off a chair, and a doleful pile of crystal at the end of the table he was supposed to believe was the representative from Picco's Moon—well, none of them were any better. They'd lost patience with him and with his quest even more quickly than the last set.

As he'd done many times before, Kearn consoled himself with the fact that his meandering through Commonwealth space brought him into differing jurisdictions quite regularly, insuring a fresh stream of politicians and the chance to continue his work.

It also meant the same old arguments and resisting the same skepticism. "You've admitted my research has been extensive. I've found shapeshifter legends and horror stories everywhere. There must be more than one creature. And the Esen Monster can't hide what She is," Kearn insisted firmly. "Not forever."

"Forever isn't an issue, Kearn," Slatth almost hissed. "Your funding and career lasting to this particular year's end is. Do we understand one another?"

The pause following Slatth's words lengthened as Kearn fumbled for some meaningful rebuttal. Before he could speak, one of the other Humans from the meeting took advantage of his hesitation. "For all of this," the committee member from Inhaven poked a stylo dismissively at the huge stack of plas disks and other reports Kearn had willingly supplied. "For all of this, Project Leader, I remain unconvinced you are correct in attributing the events you witnessed to some biological entity. How could such a being exist outside of fairy tales? Is it not more likely your so-called monster was a Kraal device: some new weapon tech being tested? You know how paranoid they can be about their military secrets. I've heard rumors of a so-called 'Nightstalker' device— a terrifying biological weapon the five major family clans abandoned as too dangerous, although I believe the term they used was 'inelegant.' Isn't this device more likely than some mythological monster, Hom Kearn?"

"Respectfully, sirs," Kearn couldn't help rolling his eyes and kept his hands at his side with an effort that left him feeling dizzy. "The Kraal have been most supportive of my search. They supplied several of the most detailed eyewitness accounts—"

"My point exactly, Project Leader Kearn," the speaker continued. Sandner, that was his name, a lean older Human who had been a merchant at one time and still claimed to have close ties in the Fringe. *Then why didn't he remember the panic?* Kearn asked himself bitterly. The loss of life, the abandoned ships: it had all begun in the Fringe, moving from its almost unpopulated mining systems to the more concentrated worlds of its boundary with the Commonwealth. *Or did those on humanity's frontier have selective memories of their past?* a suspicion Kearn almost said out loud, before closing his lips over what was wisely kept private.

"All I'm asking is your permission to move through these next three systems," Kearn said instead, blinking another drop of sweat from his eyes. "Some cooperation from local authorities, your approval to open the records I need—that's all."

"And funding." This from Slatth, who pushed a long plas sheet with a detailed supply list into the nearest circle of light on the dark table. There was a rustle as the rest reached for their own copies, followed by discouragingly discordant chimes and other sounds as they started to reread his requests.

Requests? Those were the absolute essentials—the list a pared-down version of the minimum needed to keep his ship, crew, and search underway. Kearn swallowed. This group was going to be tougher than the last two; perhaps they'd already decided against him and were merely trotting out their excuses.

There was no thought in his mind of ending his quest. He would find Esen and the rest of Her kind, even though they could travel through space, hide in any form, or rip apart a starship as casually as he might peel a piece of fruit. He would find them. They would no longer be a threat to the Commonwealth.

Even if he had to do it alone.

1: Office Morning; Warehouse Night

FIFTY years.

A teardrop in an ocean as my species experienced time.

A quarter of a life span for the being whose image smiled back at me from the clutter on my desk. Through his eyes, it had been time enough for maturity, for a new generation to begin, for a swift series of years to bind us as close as the strands of my former Web.

I cleared a space on my desk by the simple expedient of shoving the centermost pile of plas and tapes to the floor, then placed the small, carved box within the opening. Habit made me listen for sounds from the outer office, take a quick look around. I was alone. The rest of the staff of Cameron & Ki Exports would be coming in later; my friend and partner, Paul Ragem—now known as Paul Cameron— usually spent the morning over at the shipcity dickering with traders.

I tapped the side of the box once. Its opaque sides folded open, revealing a small medallion inscribed with our company's logo: our names entwined about a starship, the date added below. Tilting my head, I made myself examine it critically. *Was the silver oval too plain or pleasing in its simplicity?*

Most importantly, would it perform its function? *Only time*, I thought, aware of the irony, *would tell.*

I was still alone, but that privacy wouldn't last. I didn't so much have an office and run a business as I orchestrated within a pit usually filled with a cheerful pack of Humans and other beings, all of whom considered me less an employer than an eccentric and generous aunt they could cajole into almost anything. That their opinion was quite accurate and I had the business acumen of a Quebit was beside the point. The staff were bold and curious at the best of times. It was, oddly enough, a very good environment for someone with secrets.

Such as this medallion, which I opened with no further hesitation.

And what I did next.

I released my hold on this body, discarding Esolesy Ki the Lishcyn but not the Esen of my core, warming the surrounding air slightly with the exothermic result, exulting in the expansion of sensation and relief of effort as my molecular self assumed its true configuration: the teardrop webform of my kind.

My kind. I drifted in the luxury of perfect memory, reliving the time when I had been one of six, that six as much a single entity as different personalities and goals could become.

Enough. The past, however clear to my inner vision, was not what mattered now, nor did I dare risk staying in this form in any place so insecure. Not only did the First Rule of my Web forbid revealing web-form to aliens, with the notable exception of Paul, I had no intention of letting anyone see me struggling to stay in the seat of this chair as a large glob of cobalt-blue jelly. Paul's response the last time had been memorable, to say the least.

I extruded a hair-thin portion of myself, sorting memory as I did so. This was something I'd learned from Ersh, the Senior Assimilator of my former Web and the first of my kind to gain a conscience.

Sorting done, I braced myself, then touched the interior of the medallion with the tip of the pseudopod. Automatically, its tiny lid snapped shut at the contact, neatly nipping exactly the portion of myself I'd planned to sacrifice. I transferred another, immeasurably smaller, portion of mass, carefully memory-free, into energy and used it to twist and re-form my molecules—to cycle—back into the Lishcyn form fast enough to be able to witness the medallion sealing its edges.

I held it up to the light. Beneath the silver was a muted blue glow, almost undetectable. The metal warmed to my touch, but if all worked as it should, the inside would be cooling, its miniature cryounit sucking the last heat from that tiny piece of me. Preserving it. Preserving the memories biochemically stored within.

Fifty years, I repeated to myself as I wrapped Paul's anniversary present in a truly lurid gift wrap I knew he'd like—carpeted with images of quaint little rodents in neckties—it had taken fifty years for me to find this gift.

And to find a way to share with my first friend.

Share. My imagination painted that scent over the wildberry tang of the air-conditioning, a molecular message of trust and willing sacrifice. Once, I had been part of a greater whole, the Web of Ersh. *Share*. Her message on the wind would command us to offer our flesh-borne memories to one another, an exchange as precise as it was physically uncomfortable. *There was*, I thought pragmatically, *a lot to be said for simply writing things down*.

But it was the nature of my kind to form jagged teeth, to consume living flesh, and to assimilate the biochemical information locked within. Literacy was something we'd—acquired—over the millennia.

Today was today. Paul's gift was ready, one I knew perfectly well he and he alone in this area of space could appreciate for what it contained. A vulnerability, to have revealed my true self to an ephemeral those fleeting decades ago; my greatest strength, to have gained him as my friend.

Time to celebrate.

"You should have seen . . . seen his . . . face when he saw the shipment covered in . . . covered in—" the remainder of the words vanished into incoherence; Meony-ro, as usual, laughing so hard at his own stories the complete punch line seldom arrived until well after the flow of wine ended. My eartips twitched in echoing mirth. It was undeniably funnier to watch the otherwise dignified Kraal try to complete a sentence than to hear its ending.

I'd noticed a tendency for many Humans to display unique behavior at social events—one reason I so enjoyed such things. For his kind, Meony-ro took this tendency to an extreme. In the office, he went through his clerical duties with the sort of grim-faced, cold efficiency I could imagine of a soldier on some battlefield. The tattoos on his angular features, marks of loyalty and affiliation now faded to faint scars, were a reminder that Meony-ro could well have been in the Kraal military before his self-imposed exile in the Fringe. Here, one didn't ask. On Minas XII, it was enough that, given access to wine and an audience for his jokes, Meony-ro was the life of the party.

And, as parties went, this one was well underway, I concluded contentedly, looking around for the one guest still missing.

"More spurl, Fem Esolesy Ki?" asked the small, dark Human who approached from my left, Silv Largas, joining us tonight on behalf of Largas Freight, our preferred transport firm. He waved a steaming pitcher encouragingly and, from his tendency to lean forward as he spoke, I thought had probably sampled this batch quite thoroughly.

I slid my cup safely out of reach, flexing an upper lip in a pleasant smile at the same time. Silv immediately beamed in return. With strangers, I usually exercised more subtlety and less spontaneity of expression—many biological heritages included a misunderstanding of the congenial tusk flashing of the Lishcyn, a peaceful species uncommon along the underbelly of the Commonwealth and represented solely by my presence in this part of the Fringe. I rubbed the forks of my tongue fondly over the smooth curve of my left tusk, enjoying the feel of inset carving—an indulgence not quite a planet year old—relaxing in the glow of companionship.

But not enough to risk losing my good sense in a cup of sneakily delicious spurl, I decided, continuing to scan the tightly packed crowd for any sign of Paul. He was late, but then he had planned to visit the shipcity to verify some arrivals before coming here. My gift bumped into my chest whenever I moved, its small box suspended in the beaded neck bag I wore on special occasions.

"My father sends his regards on your anniversary, Fem Esolesy Ki," Silv shouted into my ear, which I flattened in a protective reflex. The Human had stayed nearby, despite my refusal of a refill. I swiveled my big head back to where he stood, his expression somewhat abashed as he realized there had certainly been no need for volume, despite the happy din of music and voices in the office lobby. My current form was fabled for its ability to detect the faintest whisper—a partially accurate fable I did nothing to discourage among my staff or customers. Few would care that I was not only tone-deaf but completely unable to hear into the ultrasonic. "Sorry," he said in an almost whisper.

I flashed a tusk. "No need to be, my dear Silv. Your father bellows at me all the time, does he not? And we remain friends." *And Joel Largas had proved a good friend*, I thought as I gently teased this youngest sprout of that remarkably productive Human. *And more.* The patriarch of the influential and continually growing Largas family was also the grandfather of Paul's own offspring, Luara and Tomas Largas. The twins wouldn't be here tonight. They'd inherited their spacer mother's wanderlust as well as their father's curiosity, leaving home almost twenty standard years ago to pair up as pilot and ships' nav on a freighter. The last Paul had heard, they were plying the profitable inner systems of Omacron space.

As if thinking about the Web my friend had forged for himself among these beings was a summons, I saw a turning of heads and heard cheerful hellos near the main doors, open to the night air. My hand involuntarily crept to my gift, three supple fingers curling around its edge. *Would he like it?*

It seemed unlikely I'd find out any time soon. Not only was the hospitable milling that signaled the tall, slender Human's entrance not moving any closer to where I waited, it began to seem as though Paul was attempting to leave without joining the party. *Something was wrong*, I decided, moving myself. The faces around me grew momentarily puzzled as their owners gave me room.

Paul Cameron, despite his tendency to dress conservatively and stay out of the limelight, was not a Human easily missed, a useful characteristic as I relied on his dark, perennially rumpled hair as a marker to guide me through the mass of taller and shorter beings, all intent on wishing me the best. There was something about the graceful way he carried himself, the way his gray eyes fixed with intensity on anything of interest—as they did once he spotted me. He smiled easily, and usually sincerely, so the falseness of that expression on his face this time was fair warning.

"We have a problem," Paul confirmed quietly, my ears well-tuned to his low voice despite the babble as I drew near. I spared an instant to wonder if he meant our tradition of an open bar when entertaining clients and staff, noticing more than a few individuals hanging around the entryway who were definitely not on my original invitation list. The more the merrier, I believe had been the Human expression Meony-ro had used when taking that responsibility from me at what, I now admitted, had been a weak moment.

More than uninvited guests, I realized almost at once, reading my friend's face with the ease of long practice. His smiles for the well-wishers on every side didn't warm the somber look in his gray eyes, eyes that met and held mine with a clear message.

The kind of trouble we had to handle on our own.

I pressed my cup of well-nursed spurl into the nearest willing appendage. "Excuse us," I said to no one in particular, forcing my sensitive ears up and open in a relaxed gesture despite the almost painful decibel level in the lobby. "Always business. I keep telling the Human: if it's not on a collision course for the bank, it can wait." There was the expected round of chuckles and amused grunts. Paul was widely considered the serious half of our business, despite the respect given to my expertise in evaluating merchandise and predicting trends. *All true.*

Cue and excuse given, Paul didn't waste any time heading back out the doors, not bothering to check I was behind. *In a hurry, then,* I thought uneasily, following as quickly as politeness and the width of my present feet allowed. Fortunately, no one seemed to care that the hosts, and so the erstwhile reasons for the party, were leaving— something I supposed could also be attributed to Meonyro's expanded guest list and our largesse behind the bar. I shunted the appropriate memo to a part of my private memory I would access tomorrow.

Paul led the way around the rear of the squat utilitarian building housing the offices of Cameron & Ki Exports at the edge of the Minas' shipcity. The shipcity itself made up more than two thirds of the area of Fishertown, a reasonable proportion, since almost everyone in Fishertown worked at the shipcity or provided some service to the spacers and their ships, from freighter fleets such as the Largas' to smaller independents. Ours wasn't the best location—we hadn't paid premium price or tax for one of the newly glamorous areas of extra conveniences. Paul had agreed it would arouse suspicion to live beyond our obvious means. Over time, Cameron & Ki Exports had come to turn a decent profit, albeit not a huge one. It was our inclination. And it was safer.

Although, I sighed to myself, considering the stark, practical ugliness of the colonial-era architecture looming ahead, *it would have been nice to dip into the vast store of credits and other currency I'd inherited as last of my Web and at least plant an imported shrub or two*. Minas XII's charming climate, at its best, encouraged a mind-numbing variety of low-to-the-ground bushes and flowers that burrowed into the soil to meet their pollinators.

"In here," the Human said unnecessarily as he waved his right hand before the lock pad of the warehouse side door, our private entrance. "I've put him in the customs-pending vault."

"Put who? And why in the vault?"

"Not here," was his cryptic and most-unhelpful reply, considering we were the only beings currently not inside enjoying the party, the sounds of which still came quite clearly to my ears. Paul tended to err on the side of caution. *He was beginning*, I thought dourly, *to sound more like Ersh every decade.*

We entered the warehouse without turning on the interior lights, a move that seemed more in keeping with potential burglars than owners. Who or what had Paul put in the vault? *What*, I hoped for its sake, since, as storage, the claustrophobic box was far more suitable for a few cases of brandy than anything living and aware.

Paul closed and locked the door behind us, only then activating a hand light. I stood perfectly still until he passed me a second light—the night vision of this form being so poor as to be a joke on several planets and a source of quite real danger on most, if only in terms of collisions with various objects.

"This couldn't wait?" I asked impatiently, although I went after him as he strode to the back corner of the vast, and to me invisible, room. I focused queasily on the dim oval of light aimed in front of my feet, determined not to cycle simply to best him at this trekking about in the perilous dark.

"No, Es. Sorry about the party. But you'll see."

"A few lights would help that," I muttered under my breath.

As it turned out, I didn't need them. My ears involuntarily pricked up and swung forward in response to an almost subvocal moan from somewhere ahead. There were vibrations to the edges of the sound, as though air had passed through a thin layer of moisture. "Paul?" I whispered anxiously. "Who—"

"I don't know his name," my friend said in a heavy voice. "I just know he needs help."

We must have been closer to our destination than my impoverished vision informed me, for suddenly a light came on overhead and, after blinking painfully for a moment, I could see Paul standing in the doorway to the vault itself. He must have left it open: kindness for its occupant and a sensible safety measure, given the regularity with which its cumbersome time lock forgot the date and required the efforts of a locksmith to open during reasonable working hours.

I stepped past him, then halted in the doorway, the fingers of my left hand seeking the comfort of Paul's shoulder in a movement foreign to this form, yet so part of my inner nature by now, I rarely noticed the discrepancy. "I had to bring him to you," Paul said as if in apology. "No one else could help."

The Ganthor male lay facing the door, eyes closed into barely perceptible slits, his snout hanging half over the side of the ramshackle cot Paul must have pulled here from the staff room. He was naked, bearing none of the belts or bandoliers usually seen on Ganthor traveling offworld. By the way his thick bristled skin hung in rolls, gathering like so much fabric over each joint of leg and arm, he hadn't eaten properly in weeks. But it was the huge oozing burn stretching from throat to abdomen that should have killed him by now, despite the fact that it showed signs of decent emergency care. Blasterfire, and at close range. *A mercenary.*

No need to ask why Paul hadn't taken the poor being to a hospital. On a Fringe world such as Minas XII, settled by refugees from conflicts fought largely by paid soldiers, there would be little or no sympathy. In fact, there was a high likelihood merely bringing this being here would land us on the wrong side of the authorities, such as they were, explaining Paul's caution. But there was a larger issue.

"Where is his Herd?" I asked very quietly. The Ganthor looked unconscious, and from what I could see, didn't have one of the implanted devices to allow him to vocalize in comspeak, the trade tongue of the Commonwealth and Fringe. The glistening streaks of drying mucus coating his snout and nostrils were signs that, awake, he must have continued desperate attempts to pick up the scent of others of his kind, an expenditure of moisture his damaged body could ill afford.

Paul's voice was strained—I could hear the helpless anger in it. "No one knows—or will admit it. There must have been action in one of the closed zones. He was transferred through two Inhaven freighters I could trace before ending up on one of ours, the *Largas Loyal*. Her Captain said all they were told was that this was a crash survivor needing to go to the nearest facility. He contacted me on approach, and I met the ship."

"None of them wanted his corpse on their ship's manifest," I said, unable to stop the feather of a growl under my words. Even the otherwise easygoing Lishcyn form could be outraged by such behavior toward an injured being. "I'm amazed he survived this long." Amazed, but not surprised: the herd instinct of the Ganthor was incredibly powerful. Somehow, this dying soldier's desperate need to reach his Herd—not to die alone—must have kept him breathing. It was an innate heroism Ganthor mercenaries all too often paid for as dearly as this.

"There are no Ganthor on Minas XII," I said sadly. "I'd know." In fact, almost anyone would. Hiding the presence of a Ganthor Herd, especially one intent on celebrating a victory or commiserating a defeat, was virtually impossible. Not only were they large and noisy, they tended to break things. Other people's things. To be fair, this tendency was not particularly deliberate, merely a consequence of certain aspects of their hardwiring.

As if he could understand, and perhaps he could, the soldier roused.

Roused was too strong a word. The eyes remained almost shut—probably he didn't have the energy, or will, to try and break the dried crust gluing his lids closed. But one hand shifted listlessly, toes uncurling so their percussive surfaces contacted one another. It wasn't a word. It was only a sound, like a heart breaking.

Paul turned to look at me, his hand reaching out and then dropping, utter anguish on his face. "Es, I've never asked this of you before—"

"No need to ask now, my friend," I replied. When I'd first met Paul, he'd been an alien culture and language specialist—part of a Commonwealth First Contact Team. During our time together, he'd continued his exploration of other living intelligences with the same intense and compassionate interest. Paul knew, as well as any being could who lived outside the imperative of the Herd, the only possible comfort of meaning to the dying Ganthor.

And he knew only I could offer it.

Without hesitation, I passed Paul my beaded bag and slipped out of the issa-silk burnoose I'd donned for the party. I walked over to where a long table bore a set of crates marked perishable. Opening one, I found, as I'd expected, the shipment of rootstocks ordered by Atty Fresk, a local florist and plant dealer. *Most of the order was probably for me*, I reassured myself with a twinge of guilt. My Lishcyn-self could provide more than enough mass, especially since my recent discovery of fudge, but I had to be able to return to this form as well. Foresight, I told Ersh in my thoughts, was something I'd learned the hard way. There had been a very uncomfortable ride home in Paul's luggage the last time I hadn't been prepared. So I selected the thickest, juiciest specimen, hoping it wasn't an irreplaceable rarity—something I had no time to check anyway—and put it carefully aside.

I released the tight grip needed to maintain my form as the slightly rotund Lishcyn, feeling the warm pulse of energy released at the same time. Pausing less than a fraction of one of Paul's heartbeats in web-form was enough for me to sense the throbbing of gravity beneath us, the overlapping music of electromagnetism drawn from atom and star. It was also enough to let me detect the byproducts of decay in the air: the Ganthor's breath. I cycled into what I had to become.

As Ganthor, the stench of imminent death was almost more than I could bear. Worse was the overscent of abandonment. I rushed forward, ramming my snout roughly into the side of the soldier, using the bulk of my healthy body to shove at his with complete disregard for any physical pain. His eyes opened at the same time as fresh mucus bubbled joyously from his snout; it was stained pink with blood. My alarm and concern filled the air between us, broadcast without any need to will it so. *Herd-friend*, it sent. *Not alone*, it affirmed.

A rapid series of clicks, comprehensible words, as though he knew time was running out. *The Herd is dead. The Matriarch was betrayed. Abandoned on the battlefield. No Herd.* This last with a scent of pure despair that tore at my soul.

Herd!! I insisted, stamping one foot against the floor in emphasis. I wasn't mature enough as a Ganthor to impress him as a Matriarch, the senior female and undisputed ruler of her Herd's association of males, related and otherwise, and nonreproductive females, related or forcibly adopted. But I was here and all he had. *Join this Herd!!* I ordered him. *Join!!*

I drove my shoulder and thigh against his again, inadvertently collapsing the cot beneath us both and doubtless gaining a bruise or two in the process. His body was mostly gristle and bone. He gave way, admitting his subordinate role within our Herd of two with a scent of pure relief. There was a rush of belonging, of identification blurring and melding into one. I couldn't get close enough to him.

"Es." The sound meant nothing. I refused to open my eyes, clinging to a cooling comfort.

Es!! The clickspeak was muffled, delivered by the rapping of a knuckle on metal and punctuated by a stamp part of me knew better than to ignore. *He's gone.*

I pulled myself away from what had been a member of my Herd, an effort agonizing beyond comprehension to a non-Ganthor, possible solely because I owed greater allegiance to the being standing anxiously to one side. Thankfully, Paul had known better than to try and touch me. Ganthor were foremost a physical species and my present form outmassed the Human's by a significant and dangerous amount.

I cycled, shedding the excess mass as drops of moisture clinging to my fur. To the senses of this form, the Ganthor was simply dead, the passionate responses of Herd and need merely an echo in memory.

"Es. Are you all right?" Paul's voice was soft and a bit anxious. When I looked over at him, I realized why.

My vision was predator-keen, and my eyes met Paul's

down the length of an elegant, smoothly-shaved muzzle. Without meaning to, or wanting to, I'd cycled, not into the form I lived in on this world and in this place, but into the more comforting one of my birth. I didn't need to dredge up memory to hear what Ersh would have said, doubtless something about my being Youngest and so prone to such emotional lapses in judgment.

Right now, I didn't care, feeling myself entitled to a little emotional lapse or two. "I need a few minutes," I answered truthfully, letting my jaw hang in a sigh.

My web-kin Skalet had made a hobby, more accurately an obsession, of military strategy. One of her favorite sayings, particularly when she felt I was being deliberately obtuse, had been: *There is no such thing as coincidence.*

I stared at the lifeless soldier at our feet and wondered how this Ganthor had found his way to us.

2: Office Afternoon

IT was a curiosity that wouldn't be resolved any time soon. It would have helped if Paul and I had started the next morning with anything other than an argument.

"I can't believe you are being so obstinate," he said, not for the first time. "I'm talking about taking a vacation, Es. You're making it sound like—like being sentenced to some penal colony!"

I curled up a lip in a smile I didn't mean. "I'm obstinate? Why can't you accept I don't want to go anywhere right now? You're making the entire concept less appealing by the second, if that were possible."

"It's supposed to be fun!" His voice lowered to the barest whisper. "They spent their bonuses on our tickets, damn it."

Paul's temper was definitely fraying around the edges. This didn't happen very often and I could see the staff leaning our way to be sure and catch the details. Even Meonyro, who had to be nursing a significant penalty for last night's indulgence, was glancing at us instead of answering his com.

For some reason, their interest, usually amusing, seemed an intrusion. I hunched my shoulders in a scowl and stomped away from what was becoming a too-public debate.

Of course, the flapping of my broad, semiwebbed feet on the tiled floor added no dignity whatsoever to what I admitted to myself was a full-fledged retreat.

Paul headed to his own office with far more offended respectability in his rigid Human back than a Lishcyn could ever manage.

I had a door, one I rarely closed. I closed it this time, wanting to make it perfectly clear I was not amused by his badgering. *Vacation*, I grumbled to myself. I'd only just started living on this world. *Why would I want to leave it so soon?* This was definitely one of the more frustrating aspects of dealing with ephemerals, their need to hurry life. I supposed it had a certain logic. Perhaps when I was older and wiser, I'd see it.

What I refused to see, or even contemplate for more than an uneasy moment, was that the passing of time might have dimmed the importance of our mission here for my shorter-lived partner.

It would never dim it for me.

I walked to the wall farthest from the door. It was windowless and coated with drawings made by artists too young to understand why their earnest mistakes were so captivating to adults. The yellowing ones in the upper corners were from Paul's children. Those toward the center were the latest offerings from the golden-haired daughter of our accountant, Normick Re: a series of detailed and truly horrific images of beheadings by snakelike beings. I'd been told this was in tribute to my own gloriously scaled hide and forked tongue.

I wondered about Humans. *Frequently.*

Today, I hardly saw the young ones' gifts, reaching for the camouflaged control that transformed this oh-so-harmless wall into a wide doorway to quite another type of office.

Machines hummed as if in greeting, although I imagined if they really were aware and saw me enter alone, they'd have huddled in corners. It wasn't fair that the exhaustive technological knowledge from innumerable cultures—alive and dead—carried in my mass couldn't translate itself into less clumsy hands. *Clumsy wasn't being fair to the Lishcyn*, I thought distractedly, looking down at the two long-fingered members in question. These three-fingered hands were strong and steady, with a suppleness quite remarkable in something covered in heavy, overlapping fur-based scales. Unfortunately, the technology hidden in this room was necessarily Human, being easiest to obtain and best suited to our needs. A depressingly large number of controls were simply too fine for me to touch without using special tools. *Fiddly, irritating tools.*

Deep down, I harbored a suspicion Paul liked it that way. Nothing overt, but there had been occasions I could have sworn he'd sighed with relief when I'd called him before making an adjustment or repair on my own. I could have been wrong. I knew I often reacted to him, the other member of my Web, with all the insecurity of a Youngest trying to impress the Eldest. As our relative ages translated, Paul was older than I—despite my added five centuries of existence. It shouldn't have mattered, but he had an indefinable maturity I did my utmost to match. I was, after all, now the Eldest of my kind.

Days like this, I thought glumly, *I felt it without any problem at all.*

I went to the various scanners and checked their readings, not bothering to switch from code to the more easily-deciphered visuals. Practice let me make perfect sense of the dancing symbols. Nothing unusual had passed this system since I'd last looked. *It never had.* I went over to the more important section, the data storage and analysis comps. They were chattering away to themselves, sorting incoming information from sources so varied, we constantly had to upgrade the translation and slang prompts in order to keep it comprehensible.

This was the heart of it, I thought, running one fingertip over the cool surface of a small preoccupied machine, one of several dozen. If we were to find others of my kind, it would most likely be through the way these devices collected and digested what was sent them, a consolidation of knowledge similar to what I could do with my living mass—had I another of my kind to share with me.

This knowledge should also give me warning of the type of kindred I would face. If a pattern of death and wanton destruction appeared, it might signal the arrival of a mindless, conscienceless web-being, like the one which ripped through this region fifty years ago. The Humans had named it Death, though not the only species to suffer from its attack. Death had caused the loss of almost all of the Web of Ersh, leaving me the only one of my kind. It was my chosen purpose, and Paul's, to watch for any more such monsters and destroy them before they could harm the otherwise defenseless intelligence inhabiting this part of space.

A noble purpose? I felt a familiar bitterness, expressed in this form as a muscular tightness in my gullet anxious to move what remained of my breakfast to my second stomach, where it assuredly didn't belong for at least another hour. As Youngest and Least in the Web of Ersh, I'd known my role in the greater scheme of things. The Rules and all of the teachings of my Web were based on our purpose as living, immortal repositories of the accomplishments of ephemeral intelligences. We learned and shared with one another everything about each species, from biology to culture, to be remembered in detail and nuance long after their bodies, cities, and legends were dust.

We had proved alarmingly less than immortal. And our noble purpose had been nothing more than atonement for the sins against such life committed by Ersh herself, First of our Web and its founder. She had entered this galaxy as a scourge even more vile and devastating than Death. Her memories of that truth and her acts, vivid as if freshly experienced, were irrevocably part of my flesh after she had forced me and me alone to share them.

At least the others had never known, I consoled myself, scant comfort for having outlasted all of my web-kin. My other, deeper, consolation was the purpose I had set for the future. The Web of Esen would protect what lived, not hoard the past to itself. My Web would guard this pathway from whatever distant space harbored more web-beings, should another try to hunt here.

The Web of Esen, I thought with a rush of melancholy. *Myself.* Which wasn't strictly true. I was a Web of one plus a friend. The only difference was that with the exception of my gift for Paul, there could be no sharing. I never confessed to Paul my hope for more than another enemy, that I had begun all this with a dream of finding others of my kind who were more than appetite, who might share my desire to protect other intelligences. It was an unlikely fantasy I returned to less and less as years went by.

I shook off the past, focusing on what the machines had to say. The equipment here was worth more than the combined assets of Cameron & Ki Exports, with considerably greater wealth represented by the network of distant information gatherers—each hired and paid through separate names and accounts in a mazed economy along the scale of a small world. *Or*, I thought with a tusky grin, *a large crime ring*. Paul had helped me set this up over the last fifty years. It was self-sustaining now, to a large extent, with alarms set to notify us if anything remotely "weblike" appeared in this sector of space.

"Which means I could take that vacation," I sighed out loud, admitting it to the machinery, if not yet to Paul.

I wasn't sure why I felt almost alarmed at the thought of leaving Minas XII. Paul managed it well enough, although the Human maintained an annoying habit of keeping his schedule and plans to himself until the last minute. It had been hard in the early years to have him show up with a packed case and leave with little more than a quick wave; it was harder still waiting for his safe return. Over the years, I'd grown used to his frequent trips, which, as he informed me, consisted of exceedingly boring visits to our customers and little else.

Not that I hadn't urged caution each and every time. Although he avoided systems where Paul Ragem would be known, and it became clear the authorities had closed all of their files on a dead Human innocent of any crimes, I'd tried to have Paul change his appearance. But, as Paul explained with devastating logic, he'd arrived on Minas XII with the Largas family looking as he did, wooed and married one of their daughters looking as he did, and so when, he would ask me with that faint air of impatience, was there a time in our lives when a disguise would have done anything more than prove he had a secret past? Everyone did, out on the Fringe.

I was, I decided, *taking this vacation idea far too seri-*

ously. Perhaps Paul was right, and we both needed a change. In the meantime, it was approaching midday on this side of Minas XII and six traders had commed in with merchandise. Assessing the potential of goods from the surrounding Fringe systems—and farther—was, after all, my contribution to the business. I secured the hidden room and returned to my public desk, intending to call up the first entries. All the while, I made a deliberate attempt to calm myself, having long ago discovered the Lishcyn tendency to brood under emotional stress was linked to an occasionally disastrous tendency to gamble in business.

Paul's face smiled up at me from the area I'd cleared of clutter last night, that clutter now tidily collected into a box on my chair in mute reminder this space was shared by others. *His gift*. I pressed one hand over the beaded bag hanging from my neck, feeling the outline of the small box. Well, I supposed I'd been a bit distracted between the death of the poor Ganthor, the convoluted efforts required to discretely remove the corpse before the opening of the warehouse for business this morning, planning a proper and private funeral, and, to top it all, somehow being civil to those guests who either didn't know us well enough to leave the party or who knew us well enough to linger until dawn. The arrival of daylight had meant very few of us had bothered to go home. I hoped, quite sincerely, there wouldn't be any appointments in person today, or the reputation of Cameron & Ki would definitely suffer.

A long night, and the presentation of the staff's gift to Paul and me had been its only high point, I thought. Four beings worked right in the office; another fifteen in or around the warehouse. Half were Human—not surprising given that Minas XII, like her neighbors, was primarily a Human settlement—but varied widely in type, background, and temperament as that species was prone to do.

The other half were a mixed and changing group of beings. The still uncontrolled environment of this planet, with its storms and temperature changes, suited some body types more than others. It was a common saying in numerous languages that only Humans could survive almost anywhere.

Most of these sayings also mentioned rats, but in a reasonably good-natured way depending on relative trade-surpluses and the local economy.

The staff's gift had been a trip for two to the Panacia Hiveworld, D'Dsel. It wasn't exactly known as a resort destination, but the Panacian system was the only one within affordable range which could boast a population evolved in place—and D'Dsel was that place. This gave it an exotic gloss of biological history to beings tired of the more cosmopolitan and temporary nature of a colony world such as Minas XII.

I knew D'Dsel.

It had been the first place I'd encountered Death.

3: Cliff's Edge Night

BY unspoken agreement, the argument was left behind when Paul and I headed home that night, bringing with us food trays from the party as did everyone else. And, after a tasty, if eclectic, meal, we finally had the time and privacy to complete our personal celebration—although, as usual, the Human was being difficult.

"You go first," he insisted again, grinning.

I'd changed my mind. Paul wasn't growing more mature and Ersh-like over the decades. He was reverting to some early childhood. "This is silly, Human," I pronounced with all of the dignity of an Eldest.

"No, it's not. You're first."

"I don't want to be first."

"You should have thought of that before I flipped the coin."

I growled under my breath. "Fine. I'll go first."

Paul's face grew positively smug as he passed me his gift. Before I could open it, both of us jumped as the building shuddered to its foundations under yet another assault by the gale-force wind. Another normal night at Cliff's Edge, the name of our home perfectly obvious to visitors who climbed nervously out of an aircar to find their limbs dangling over the sheer drop which began steps from the front door. Joel Largas referred to it as Over the Edge: a joke, Paul assured me.

This building would outlast the rock beneath it, I knew, assured not by the guarantees fervently attested to by the best architect on this world—a distinction arrived at by being the only architect on this world when I arrived—but by my flesh-borne knowledge of how such structures reacted to stress. Most of the modifications I'd paid the confused but happy contractors to add were legacies from Mixs, my web-kin who had so delighted in this blend of art and utility.

Knowing the roof would stay overhead and the walls upright did nothing to stop Paul and me from twitching with each unpredictable howl. Often, the wind would lift stones from the cliff's upper rim, flinging them down like hail against the thick exterior with more than enough force to make conversation an effort. Then, there was the real thing: hailstones the local population boasted were the largest seen on a settled planet. What this said about those who would settle here made me shake my head regularly.

One aspect I did like was that on nights like this, more common than not during the storm season itself but rather rare in the midst of what passed—quickly—for summer, we could count on no surprise arrivals. I wasn't paranoid, but I did relax best when surrounded by a cyclone. What this said about me was something I preferred not to consider at all.

"No hints?" I asked in the next, hopefully longer lull, performing the traditional Human ritual of poking at the package before attempting to open it and satisfy my curiosity. Curiosity might not have been the right word. Paul was not beyond humor at my expense during these annual gift exchanges. Since this had involved everything from minor explosions to time-release fluorescent dyes which had turned my fur into a spectrum for weeks, my approach to opening any of his gifts included a fair amount of prudent inspection.

I glanced over to where the Human sat on the edge of his chair—a large overstuffed thing with gruesome carved paws for feet—and didn't see the grin of anticipation I half-expected. Instead, his eyes were serious and fixed on me, as though the opening of this particular gift held special meaning.

He'd aged well, I thought fondly, taking a moment to gaze at my friend, memory slipping effortlessly into the present. The lean, mobile features of his face had subtly altered with time and experience, lineless still but matured into a nobility and compassionate strength the Human would doubtless deny hotly. The curiosity and intelligence hadn't changed—sculpted across his brow and dancing in his bright eyes. If anything, the Paul Cameron incarnation of my friend was even more adventurous and eager to learn than Paul Ragem had been, having grown accustomed to a life unrestricted by the demands of officers and the opinions of peers.

No, the time had been good to my friend. I was pleased. So if his gift to me was a celebration of this, I would open it in that spirit.

And if it contained anything that exploded, shrieked, flew apart, or stained my beautiful new tunic, I would plan a suitable revenge.

The box, while fairly light, covered my lap—what there was of it. When Paul and I were at home, in private like this, I indulged myself with my birth-form: that of the canid-like Lanivarian. The others of my kin had had no such preferences, choosing their form based on their needs of the moment. The amorphous web-form made it awkward to do much more with technology than ooze cautiously around it without leaving sticky bits.

But I was the only web-being to have been the product of a union between my kind and another's, the result of my birth-mother Ansky's endless loves and lusts—hopefully unique, as there was no room on any planet for a species which was prolific as well as semi-immortal. There were no Lanivarian components to my structure, as Ersh had exhaustively and painfully tested before accepting Ansky's surprise addition to her Web, but I'd always found an odd comfort in assuming the shape.

I knew myself to be sentimental, too. This was the body I had worn when I first met and was befriended by Paul. Although I'd never asked him, I suspected this was what he really believed I was, regardless of the thousands of other forms he'd seen me assume over the years.

His gift was thin and rigid, devoid of any potentially revealing lumps or ridges. The wrapping was plain, brown, shipping plas, the sort of material we used in the warehouse for the least and most expensive shipments. I poked at it again. "Clothes?" I guessed, raising my snout in his direction and dropping my jaw in a toothy grin. The Lishcyn had a fondness for silks and, as Esolesy Ki, I enjoyed a shamelessly extensive wardrobe.

"You could open it," Paul retorted, the corner of his lips turning up. For some reason, his hands had clenched his knees. He noticed my attention and relaxed a little too deliberately. I hadn't misjudged his interest in this gift.

I chose one end and started pulling apart the plas. As if cued, the com buzzed, its interruption barely perceptible over the renewed howling of the wind. Paul lunged up and hurried to the panel beside the fireplace, holding up one hand to stop me. "I'll get rid of whoever it is," he promised.

I tapped the top of my present with my toes, but waited. More or less patiently. I eyed the bag on the table by the door. I hadn't taken out his gift yet. *What were the odds . . ?*

"What?"

I shifted my ears to Paul, caught by the total outrage contained in the one word. He was holding the remote receiver to his own ear, attempting to hear over the sudden rattle of gale and stone. *No,* I decided, *we'd achieved hail.*

"Cancel it." This with a quick frown in my direction, as though the mysterious call had something to do with me. *Oh, oh,* I thought, carefully composing my features in their most innocent configuration. I hadn't done anything Paul would disapprove of lately, unless one counted the order for organic fertilizer I'd inadvertently shipped with some Rillian sheep. Who knew the sheep were allergic to the slightest trace of methane and would shed their precious fleece in transit? Livestock and such were not our usual trade anyway. I'd only been doing a favor for an acquaintance of Joel Largas; hardly my fault—

"Did you keep it off Port Authority's records?"

That bit of the one-sided conversation put a totally new face on matters, and I felt a new expression wrinkle my snout: worry. The caller had to be one of Paul's offworld contacts, a ship's captain, an officer, or crew. Such had brought us trouble already this week. "It better not be another Ganthor," I advised him, fighting a tendency to snarl.

Paul waved impatiently, obviously having difficulty catching something being said. I took it as reassurance and made myself settle back, running my slender toes very lightly across the top of my neglected gift. I had an intense dislike of interruptions, particularly ones that arrived when I had every right to expect some peace and privacy. I'd have to speak to Paul about whom he gave permission to reach us here.

"We'll meet you in the morning." This with an abrupt drop in volume as Paul no longer had to compete with Nature. "Bring whatever you have with you." A pause and another look toward me, this time a considering one. "Yes, she'll be there, too."

"She," I repeated as he ended the link and came back to his seat. "Meaning me."

"You know Chase."

I couldn't help snarling under my breath. I knew Captain Janet Chase: a Human female who thought Paul's devotion to a shaggy-scaled hunk of Lishcyn a serious drawback to a closer relationship. Chase had been more determined than most of Paul's acquaintances, a trait which I would have appreciated had I not been the hunk of Lishcyn in question.

Had there been others I didn't know about? I asked myself suddenly, examining Paul's now-composed face as if there'd be some clue written in flesh and bone. He'd seemed happy. He had contact with his kind, his own apartment near the shipcity when that contact required privacy. *Was it enough?* "Does she still want a temp-contract?" I worked at a casual tone. "Or has she found some other interest?"

It didn't fool him. *It never did.* "I'm perfectly capable of managing my own affairs, Esen," Paul answered with predictable impatience, deliberately using the form of my name he saved for our moments alone. "Besides, Chase's call had nothing to do with me. The *Vegas Lass* was boarded and searched insystem by Tly inspectors. They confiscated our shipment for Inhaven Prime."

He didn't bother describing the shipment, aware I'd know. One of the curses of perfect recall was the perpetual clutter of memory with bureaucracy, including every numerical record that passed over my desk. To avoid undue attention, I made a point of asking staff for information I didn't need. Paul, on the other hand, had taken years to lose the habit of checking minute details with me rather than carrying around lists, though he'd politely stopped short of using me as a walking calendar.

So I knew the tonnage and type of cargo filling the holds of Captain Chase's ship this trip as well as any of the comps back at Cameron & Ki: marfle tea, a number of Human-specific antibiotics, some indifferent but pretty porcelains I thought had promise as seasonal goods, the cargo's bulk a purified chemical catalyst called reduxan 630. All were innocuous, mid-to-low-end sellers in most markets, though we'd been taking advantage of a local rarity of the catalyst, a key industrial import on Inhaven Prime since the Tly had blasted its former source, Garson's World, out of existence as a source of that or anything else.

It didn't hurt our business relations with Largas Freight that the founding ship-families had been from Garson's World. Even fifty years later, the company's captains took distressing pleasure in any deal that boded loss to Tly.

I fought melancholy, the mere thought of the tragedy enough to call up web-memories of the Human culture of Garson's, a young, frontier world well on its way to being distinct before its end under the Tly bombardment. I'd had to stop myself from correcting Paul's children as they learned already corrupted versions of folk songs from their grandfather's lost home; it would have been impossible to explain how my memory could be better than the original refugees'.

In turn, Tly had suffered to its core in the aftermath of that ghastly mistake. Evidence later proved the attacks against Tly forces, furiously attributed to Garson's World and the justification for their revenge, had in fact been made by some mysterious creature. It was, of course, mysterious only to those who hadn't encountered my predatory counterpart. Convicted of destroying an innocent population, Tly's government had fallen, its military fleet discredited and stripped of its former role, its reputation damaged beyond repair for generations to come. The Guilds and other organizations had surged into the gap until, today, Tly was ruled by a more-or-less stable assortment of merchants, crafters, and crooks of varying abilities and disposition.

Few of which had kind words for survivors and witnesses of the tragedy, such as Largas Freight or, by association, Cameron & Ki. But nothing overt until now. Profits were profits, after all. I'd noticed Humans could be quite pragmatic about their grudges when necessary. Except I doubted the Tly or Garson's refugees would be so forgiving if they encountered one of my kind again.

Which won't happen, I promised myself and all Humans, as I had done every day since.

"What excuse did they use?" I said, putting my gift carefully on the side table before rising to pace. This form didn't stay put well when disturbed, being more inclined to action than thought. "Chase wouldn't give them cause—she's by the book." Considering the type of freighter captains who voluntarily chose the Fringe to work, this was an exceptional quality indeed. Largas Freight had been delighted to find her. Rumor had it, they'd dug up something or other from her past in order to keep her, but such sour tales were cheap out here where every being had something they preferred to leave behind.

"She didn't want to say much over the com." He turned one hand over expressively.

I nodded. The in-house system couldn't be as well-shielded as we'd have liked—such protection could itself arouse the suspicion of the local authorities, or, worse, the interest of those who assumed ideal security went with something ideally worth liberating from its owners.

"So what about the record?"

Paul grimaced. "No luck there. The Tly insisted on filing a smuggling complaint against the ship and against us.

Minas Port Authority got it translight before Chase came insystem."

I didn't feel the outrage I expected. Lies, undeserved fines, tarnished reputations: these were all quite likely. *There was too much furniture in this room,* I thought distractedly as I paced around it, *and too many connections between us and this life to make any scrutiny, deserved or fabricated, safe.*

"We can't do anything about it tonight, Es," Paul gently reminded me. "Why don't you open your present?"

Present? I shook myself free of darker thoughts until my fur fluffed itself with static, and picked up my bag. "You first," I said, trying to lighten my voice. "For making me wait."

The Human smiled and put out his hand. I held the bag slightly out of reach, then bent so my nose met the warm, delightfully Paul-scented skin of his palm. I took a quick sniff, feeling him twitch as the breath tickled, then backed away. It was a formal gesture, one of identification and trust. "Here." I passed him my gift.

Paul's smile faded into a more thoughtful expression, as though he recognized something special in my gift, as I had in the giving of his. He worked the bag open carefully, pulling out the box. Although the wind chose that moment to attempt to peel a few more layers off the exterior of our house, I could hear his chuckle at the wrapping I'd used.

He unwrapped and opened the box. I sat down on my haunches and rested my chin on his knee, blinking slowly. *Would he understand its significance? Could any being not of the Web?*

The medallion looked woefully small and unimpressive between his fingers. When the Human didn't move, I straightened up, searching his face. His expression was oddly unfamiliar: his gray eyes were hooded, his lips worked as though incapable of forming words at first.

"Es—" my name came suddenly as a soft, drawn-out breath. "Is this what I think it is?"

"What do you think it is, Paul-friend?" I asked reasonably, if unsteadily.

If my voice was prone to fluttering at the edges, I had all the response I could ask for in the suddenly husky tones of his: "You. You've shared . . . this is your mass in here . . . for me, isn't it? As if I were . . . as if I were truly your web-kin."

"Don't eat it," I cautioned him hastily. "You know web-mass is corrosive to your tissue."

Paul smiled, but there was moisture leaking from his eyes. As he seemed to ignore the phenomenon, I didn't mention it. "Is it alive?" he asked in wonder, supporting the medallion in the palm of one hand. The faint blue glow within the silver showed more clearly against his skin.

I considered the question, feeling the bond between that speck of mass and myself as the faintest of drawings; it would be vastly stronger if I were in web-form. "In a sense," I said finally. "It could not survive for long outside the cry-ounit unless I assimilated it. Within the unit, it should last."

"How long?"

"As long as you wish." It was part of my gift as well, this power over some of me.

Paul quickly slipped the slim chain over his head. The medallion disappeared beneath his shirt. *It should*, I thought with pleasure, *nestle over his heart*, Human anatomy being what it was. "What do I do in return?" he asked, only now noticing the moisture from his eyes and wiping it away with one hand.

I hadn't thought of that. A true sharing included a precise exchange of each individual's mass. He'd been the only alien to witness sharing between my web-kin and me, although it hadn't exactly been such, since Skalet had chewed away most of me before running off to fight her battle. Thinking about that moment, I grinned toothily. "I won't ask you to donate the tip of a finger for tradition's sake. I'll settle for your gift."

"Done," Paul said. To his credit, there wasn't a shred of relief in his voice. "You'll have to sit—over there."

Intrigued, I did as he commanded.

The large, flat package was replaced on my lap. This time I didn't delay, ripping open the wrap. If this was his portion of our sharing, I would give it the respect and attention Paul had granted mine.

Which would have been easier had I known what to make of the plain piece of wood the plas had disguised. I ransacked my memories, and those of my kin, searching for any hint about such a gift and its ceremonial meaning. Nothing. It was a well-polished piece, with rounded corners and a smooth finish. The wood itself was a pale yellow, a native species of hardwood, nothing extraordinary except for its ability to grow almost Human-waist high in the valleys of the southern hemisphere. I flared my nostrils. It smelled like—wood. At last, I gave up trying to guess its meaning and looked up in defeat.

"Place your hands on the outer edges, here and there," Paul instructed, a smile hovering around his lips but not quite there, as though he were too anxious about my reaction to let it out. "Press firmly, then let it go."

"Let it go?" I eyed the wood askance, wondering what to expect. But, because Paul had understood my gift, I trusted him with his, and pressed my blunt-clawed toes into what I could now feel were slight indentations in the sides. They felt like ident pads, the sort one used on a personal vault. Keyed to my Lanivarian hands? How had he—

I had no further time nor inclination to wonder about the how, for the wood was now glowing, lifting from my lap and free of my now-limp hands until the slab floated directly before my eyes. Slowly, it tilted in midair until the flat, broad surface faced me. As I took a breath of astonishment, the surface became a flickering screen.

A screen inhabited by a flashing sequence of thirteen thousand and forty-four images, some silent, many with sound. All were faces and forms of Humans, one hundred and ten individuals, differing in most of the ways that species could, yet many cohesive in the line of chin and cheek, mouth and eye, in the creation of smiles or laughter, even in the occasional tear. The voices made a mosaic of languages and tones, greetings, children's serenades, speeches.

The parade slowed, ending with images of one face: toothless, toothed, gawky, graceful, uniformed, and a last vision that merged with the present as the floating screen consumed itself, its particles falling as a golden dust on my knees and feet, letting me see Paul's smile.

It had taken less than a minute.

I looked in awe at the quiet, slender being, this ephemeral who understood what I was so utterly, he had known the greatest gift he could give me.

I cycled into web-form, luxuriating in the freedom to do so in his presence, and lovingly sorted Paul's living history into the most private memories of my flesh.

We had truly shared.

The Web of Esen held two.

Elsewhere

"WE have to dump more of the records to inactive storage, Project Leader Kearn. There's no room left in the system." The officer stood carefully at attention but his gaze slid to the crewwoman at his side as if gathering support. "We've been telling you for weeks."

Kearn ran his hand over his damp scalp, torn between glowering at the captain of the *Russell III* and groveling. "You've both also told me you can't run the pattern analysis on stored data, Captain Lefebvre," he said, settling for what he hoped was a masterful-sounding rebuttal. He felt at a disadvantage at the best of times: Lefebvre's appearance—medium height and weight, though strongly built, medium brown hair, unremarkable features, in short, medium everything—had belied his abilities, which started with a brilliant tactical mind and, as Kearn woefully discovered over the years, seemed to include being on good terms with some being in almost every corner of the Commonwealth.

He'd hoped for a kindred spirit, or at least someone he could control. Like Kearn, Lefebvre hadn't been promoted to larger, more important ships. Unlike Kearn, Lefebvre had never been heard to regret this, or to speak ill of anyone or anything: an obviously intentional effort to hide his thwarted ambitions Kearn rather envied. That didn't mean he trusted Lefebvre. It hadn't taken long for even Kearn to realize that Lefebvre followed his orders—in his own way—because their quest mattered to the Human and he believed in a disciplined ship.

Kearn's fingers drummed on the surface of his desk, a piece of furniture he found obscurely reassuring after the dismal results of his meetings with this sector's bureaucrats.

"We can't run it now," this from the harassed-looking comp-tech at Lefebvre's side, Mesa Timri. Kearn avoided meeting her stern look; something about tall, attractive women made his scalp itch, even if she was thirty years his senior and her rich chocolate skin wrinkled at eye and mouth. Of course, it didn't help that Timri had forgotten more about the operation of the vital research comps than anyone of Kearn's acquaintance had learned in the first place. Her skills were key to sieving valid clues from the background nonsense within the massive collection of rumor, legend, and so-called factual sightings clogging the ship's data banks. She was vital to his search for Esen.

But it was her search, too, Kearn reminded himself. *She'd come to him. She needed him as much as he needed her.* Timri had served on a Tly warship, part of the blockade on Inhaven attacked by the Esen Monster fifty years ago, ship after ship sent drifting into the dark, all life within consumed. She hadn't seen the creature directly; she hadn't needed to—the results had been enough to have her eager to transfer to the *Russell III*.

He wished she'd found him at the beginning, not twenty years into his search when his crew had shrunk to those too apathetic to request transfer. Before, Kearn had had some credibility, sufficient to gain him this ship and obtain, if not the blessing, at least a firm push on his way from his superiors in the Commonwealth. *Oh, he'd heard what they said behind his back, knew what they thought.* It would make his ultimate success even sweeter.

These two were crucial to that success and, unfortunately, knew it as well as Kearn. Rudy Lefebvre had come from a patrol background, with a record of relentless and successful pursuits. As a bonus, he'd unusually high ratings in interspecies communication and was fluent in three of the four most commonly used languages after comspeak. Timri had been climbing the academic ladder in a Tly research facility, blazing new trails with her work on pattern analysis within immense data streams until her clearance and persistence opened up the secured files on Kearn's mission. Once she learned of the *Russell III*, she'd insisted on this posting or nothing, despite the disapproval by just about everyone aware of her potential.

Since then, Kearn had struggled to keep ship and crew intact while continuing the chase. Even he admitted, only to himself, it had been a fruitless, frustrating chase. It was nothing to spend months negotiating for tantalizing pieces of a larger puzzle, only to come away with little more than a new curiosity to write for some Commonwealth academic journal. Nothing, to rush translight after a reported sighting, only to find beings who extorted payment for information of absolutely no use at all. *No wonder*, Kearn thought, *he felt besieged on all sides*.

Predictably, Lefebvre and Timri had descended on him the moment he'd arrived back with the bad news about their funding, as if they'd haunted the ship's external vids for their chance. "You have to let us narrow down some of the parameters, sir," Timri suggested. "There's simply no way the systems can do what you're demanding."

"And there's that other issue, sir." This from Lefebvre in a calm, dogged voice that forewarned Kearn he wouldn't stand a chance in this argument.

"What other issue? What are you talking about? I don't have time for guessing games."

"The crew needs shore leave, sir. With some of their pay in their pockets."

"We're days translight from any resort world. There's no time for—"

"With all due respect, sir, any world would be a resort. We've been cooped on the *Russ'* for seventeen months. Shall I quote regs?"

Kearn threw up his hands. *His crew was against him, too.* "Mutiny, Captain Lefebvre?"

The Human looked quite properly horrified. "No, sir. Of course not. But we can't keep this pace, not without losing some good people." Unstated, but loud in the cabin nonetheless, were the words "or we find something soon, so we know we aren't fools following one."

Kearn swallowed, throat dry. No, he couldn't lose any more crew. There had already been transfers and retirements—outright desertions, as he viewed them. *Had no one else a sense of commitment to a cause?*

"We'll find someplace on our route, Captain," he said almost fearfully. "But not for long—I won't delay for long."

He begrudged every moment stolen from their search, knowing it gave his personal demon that much more time to plot against him and the unsuspecting universe.

4: Cliff's Edge Night; Shipcity Morning

PAUL'S gift had given me a moment of pure ecstasy. I hadn't dreamed I'd know such sharing again, if only as this muted imitation. Unfortunately, once my mind cleared of euphoria, Paul's gift rang enough alarm bells to keep me tossing and turning in my grassy bed, completely unable to sleep despite a desperate longing to rest.

Sleep was an alien need, one unknown to my web-form. On the practical side, however, form-memory was absolute, meaning I neglected the requirements of a form I used to my own eventual discomfort. The Lishcyn, for example, expected a solid nine standard hours' snoring within layers of sweet, aromatic, albeit conveniently artificial, grasses—the entire mass kept tidily off the floor in a high-sided box. The bed suited my birth-form, the Lanivarian, as well. I'd grown quite fond of tunneling into a bottom corner, in winter piling so much of the fibrous mass over me, Paul sometimes thought I'd left for work when I was semihibernating.

Nothing so comfortable about tonight. My thoughts refused to let go of a wooden box of memories, keyed to my paws' touch. I gave up any attempt to sleep, accepting the consequence of a second groggy morning with a sigh, and got up, scattering the grasslike fibers to the four corners of my room in protest.

Moving quietly through the darkened house—from past experience I knew the Human would sleep through the hammering of the worst storm but could be startled awake by a footstep—I uprooted an armful of duras plants from my greenhouse, then forced open the side door and pushed my way outside.

Once there, slammed by the gale against a sturdy, rough-textured wall, I cycled rapidly, assimilating plant mass to increase my own.

The howling wind was a feather's touch to my new form, the hail and ricocheting shards of stone tickles to a hide enriched with filaments of graphite and studded with excreted gems. Other sensations were almost negligible, and my thought processes perceptibly slower, but otherwise the Wz'ip was an admirable choice to get a breath of fresh air on a typical Minas XII evening.

Well, to be technical, it was an inrush of wind through a row of bone-braced and nicely-angled exterior vents, but the intent was the same.

Paul's gift continued to exhilarate and trouble my thoughts. *Deliberately?* I considered the notion seriously, wary of underestimating him. The way it anchored him in time was a distinct comfort, my nature being reassured by the continuity and continuation represented by his genetic heritage. The Human species might not be in any immediate danger of extinction, but its isolated populations and their cultures flickered in and out of existence within the archives of my web-memory almost as swiftly as his family's faces had passed on the screen.

No, what kept me from the warm depths of my bed was where Paul had obtained those faces. I knew why the gift had been designed to destroy itself after the giving. I had no need for a permanent version; seeing it had been enough. Paul knew I stored everything I saw or otherwise experienced. *From that point of view*, I told myself, *he'd paid me a compliment of sorts—entrusting his past solely to my memory*.

What a shame I couldn't accept it as such.

It was the way of my kind to hide in plain sight, with the key word being hide. We shunned any possible exposure of our true nature to alien eyes. That had been the Rule which kept Ersh and her Web safe for millennia, until I'd managed to reveal myself within a day of meeting Paul, during my first—and only—mission for my kind. *Ersh*, I remembered rather wistfully, *hadn't been impressed*.

She'd tasted friendship to the Humans in those memories I'd been brave enough to share with the Web, understanding its significance before I had, warning me about further entanglements with ephemeral species.

Yet in the end, it had been my ageless web-kin who had died, and the fragile ephemeral who remained at my side as I fled the unwelcome attention of the Commonwealth and its alarmed Humans. I'd tried to stop Paul from accompanying me, to keep his life intact. He'd followed our friendship instead, a choice I, for one, had never regretted. If he had, on occasion, I'd never known.

We remained safe here because we were hidden, I as Esolesy Ki the Lishcyn trader, Paul Ragem as Paul Cameron, exporter. *Hide*. That Rule hadn't changed with the loss of the others; it had been driven deep into my soul, and I'd insisted Paul learn it.

The wind moved up a notch, ripping apart the clouds overhead to show a tattered-edged wall of stars. I focused my optic cluster on the dimmest of these, pushing my thought processes along, quite grateful to feel little or no emotion beyond a vague regret. If I were Lanivarian, I would have howled.

"What have you done, old friend?" I whistled to the storm, my voice arising from disks which turned within the flow of air moving in and out through the vents. It was a low whistle, easily missed, but I could tune it to a minor key, well-matched to my feelings.

To make my gift, had Paul made contact with his family? Once his mother died, we'd never discussed it again; before that, he'd rebuffed my every attempt to suggest it as too dangerous, an unhappy but absolutely necessary consequence of our life together. But how else could he have gathered so much information?

I sighed, rumbling like so much thunder in the storm's darkness, feeling a little darkness of my own. The gift had only revealed itself to my paw print. It had destroyed itself once received. These were wise precautions against discovery—against identification of the being who formed the apex of this genealogy—by anyone but me.

Would these protections be enough? Only, I acknowledged to the wind, the future would tell us. For if anyone suspected Paul Ragem lived, who might suspect I did as well?

Was his gift worth this risk to us both?

Dawn washed itself clear of the surrounding mountains, a brightening I noticed barely in time to cycle, dumping mass, and hurry back inside. Wz'ip were not known for their quick reactions.

Once inside, I sniffed in appreciation. Paul was cooking some egg dish or other. A shame it was a delicacy a Lishcyn literally couldn't stomach, but I was tied in that form by the business ahead as well as my growing interest in caution. Still, I remembered the smell as a favored meal of some other me.

"You could cycle and have some. I made enough," the Human offered.

I resisted the temptation to glower at him, something the Lishcyn did poorly anyway. The broad-lipped head with its rosettes of hair-trimmed scales wasn't good for much facial expression beyond flashing a tusk or two and a debonair wink. "No, thank you. It's this Esen you are taking to annoy Captain Chase this morning, remember?"

Paul scooped yellow fluff onto his plate, topping it with some seared bread and a dollop of spice before taking his seat at the table. This nook was our favorite spot of the house, especially when the storm blinds could be retracted and the three windowed walls offered their spectacular view, as now. The mounded surfaces of cloud might have been continuations of the white tile floor. Birds, or rather the Minascan insectoid equivalent, flew within insubstantial valleys. The sky above was so clear a blue as to bear a seductive hint of space black at its far edge.

In all, a view that scarcely hinted at the distance one

would drop if careless enough to assume those mounds of white could support any weight at all.

A Lishcyn's multiple stomachs could do interesting things with heights, particularly when those stomachs were arguing about which deserved the first crack at some nourishment. It wasn't advisable to let all five become empty. I hurried to grab my favorite bowl from the counter and begin filling it up with whatever was nearest from the leftovers in the cold cupboard.

"For breakfast?" At Paul's skeptical question, I paid closer attention to what I was doling into the bowl.

"There's nothing wrong with prawlies," I asserted, inwardly wincing at the sight of the highly-spiced, many-legged delicacy I'd distractedly ladled over a pile of Meg Sirsey's Choco Surprise. Some foods required the consumption of alcohol before they were remotely palatable. "Plenty of—protein."

He raised one brow, but let the matter of my food choices go. I settled into the chair across from him and studied my breakfast the way a general might plan an attack: how to get at the chocolate and underlying vegetable matter without alerting the prawlies—or Paul—to my complete intention to avoid them.

Paul's own breakfast sat apparently forgotten as he gazed at me intently. "You think I've been a fool, don't you?" The question was too quiet, startling me. "That's what this is about, isn't it?"

"What what's about?" I said, inadvertently shoveling exactly what I'd tried to miss into my mouth. My salivary glands went into overtime trying to dilute the sudden burst of spice on my palate. I grabbed the very large and absorbent napkin from my lap to stem the outward flood before it dribbled between my stiff lips. Paul passed me the pitcher of water in response to my frantic gesture. I gulped down the liquid, succeeding in at least moving the burning sensation to my first, and largest, stomach, and asked innocently: "Didn't you sleep well?" An interrupted rest frequently made Humans irrational in the morning.

"No." Paul put his cup down, rattling the other dishes on the table. "And I wasn't the only one awake."

I almost asked him how he knew, then realized there was, of course, only one way. "You watched me on the vid." Our home was surrounded by surveillance equipment: essential warning for me to return to the Lishcyn form whenever guests or Paul's family arrived unannounced. We didn't use it to spy on one another—until now. I felt my scales swelling along their edges, the hairs on each itching unbearably as they began to retract out of sight, a sure sign my own temper was rising as my outer hide assumed its defensive configuration. Knowing it was already too late to cycle into a less revealing form, I tried glaring at Paul with honest outrage instead.

It didn't work. He merely returned my look, his gray eyes narrowing in what I belatedly recognized as the rousing of his own rare and formidable temper. "Yes, I watched you. Funny reaction to our celebration—and my gift. What kept you awake, Esen-alit-Quar?" The Human's voice developed an edge I'd never heard before. "Tell me it wasn't some worry I revealed myself as back from the dead just to grab a few holoimages. Tell me you know me better than that—tell me you know I would never risk exposing you even to see those I love—because, by now, you damn well should."

I swallowed twice: once to clear my mouth of drool and then again to move the sickening prawlies farther from any attempt to return to the bowl. My first stomach was notoriously quick to react. "Paul—" I began, then found my stomach completely settled and solitary. Again, I'd cycled involuntarily. *I had to stop doing that.*

"So you don't," the Human said flatly, putting his own interpretation to my change of form. He stood as if to leave, shaking his head at me in utter disgust. I spotted a glint of silver under the edge of his shirt collar. He wore my gift. And concealed it.

Paul noticed my attention and, hooking a finger under the chain, pulled the tiny medallion into the open. He didn't let it drop to hang freely, instead capturing the medallion within a tight fist he thrust toward me. "Do you want to talk about fools?" he said bitterly. "I know you, Es. Well enough to know how much this means as a gift—and appreciate it. And well enough to know you'd miss how dangerous this is for me to wear."

"There's no chance the web-mass will leak—" I began uncertainly.

"I don't mean of itself," he interrupted, planting both hands on the table so he could lean over it and glare down at me. His posture brought up the hackles on my neck, but I restrained my Lanivarian instincts with an effort. Biting Paul wasn't going to improve his temper.

He continued, from the stern line of his eyebrows fully aware of my reaction and willing to dare it. "I warned you the Kraal didn't stop working on a scanner to detect webmass. Or weren't you listening?"

Oh. That. I forgot all about biting, feeling my ears press flat against my skull and a whine try to slide up my throat. "Don't worry," Paul said, but not sympathetically. His fist opened, the palm flipping the medallion over. A device similar to one of the tiny scramblers we used on public com systems had been glued to the back. "This should suffice until I can do something better." Finally, his face softened from anger to something closer to disappointment. I wasn't sure it was an improvement. "I value your gift, Es. Honestly I do. But I wish you'd thought of all the risks you were taking with our secret, instead of mistrusting me. And it is our secret." With this last, a corner of his mouth twitched upward, bringing a sudden, familiar warmth to his face.

So I was forgiven. I couldn't say I enjoyed the feeling. I rose slowly from my chair, distracting myself with the problem of whether to return to the Lishcyn form or continue this conversation as I was. If I cycled, I'd have safely empty stomachs: inanimate matter wasn't retained in the form-memory, hence the puddle of water on the tiles beneath my paws. But I felt closer to understanding Paul in this arrangement of flesh.

"Esen," Paul continued as if he could read my thoughts, "we've misunderstood each other often enough over the years. I'll be fair: more times than not it's been my fault. You're very good at interpreting me; I can't always do the same with you." He paused, putting out one hand as if his Human nature needed touch, but thinking better of it. "This time, Es, you were wrong about me. Can't you admit it?"

I felt my lip trying to curl over a fang, not a caring expression in this form. "I admit I hadn't considered the Kraals' experiment—if it continues at all—or that they could somehow use my gift to find you. Anyway, it's all so unlikely as to be ridiculous. They'd need their scanner right on top of you."

The not-so-ridiculous thing was that Paul was very close in his suspicions. There was someone who could conceivably use the medallion's contents to find him—me—an ability I'd desperately wanted each and every time he'd left Minas XII and my protection. Which was regularly. This being the last thing I wanted the proud Human to suspect, I changed the subject. "I see no point in worrying about some phantom technology. I'm concerned with the First Rule."

"To be hidden is to be safe," Paul said, as if repeating a lesson by rote. "It isn't hard to remember, Es. I do agree."

I let the lip do what it wanted. "Then how did you obtain those images if you didn't contact anyone from your—former life?"

I thought his skin turned pale, as though I'd inadvertently struck him. "I'd have thought it obvious, Es," my friend said in too even a voice, "since you were the one to insist we have the capability to dig into any database in the Commonwealth without being caught."

Oh, dear, I said to myself, belatedly realizing many things, including how readily the system in my office could be turned from its secret search for others of my kind to something more focused. Simply collecting images of individual Humans, who were prone to bureaucracy and redundant records, would have taken almost no effort at all.

As Paul said, we'd had our share of misunderstandings. I looked down my shaved muzzle at him, remembering each and every instance in exquisite detail, knowing he hadn't really been fair to himself: many had been my fault. I tended to jump to conclusions, to assume I knew exactly what he or any being would do simply because I understood their physical natures so thoroughly. *Just like this time*, I confessed in the privacy of my own thoughts.

Paul stifled a yawn suddenly, then held up his medallion on its chain once more, letting it swing lightly. "I really do appreciate the honor you've paid me with this, Es." A wave at the table, with its bowl of deserted leftovers and surely cold eggs. "We have time for another attempt before Chase will be ready. If you are hungry?"

This was like my friend, not to insist on an apology I'd find difficult to frame, to move us along. My stomach growled, and he smiled. "I take it that's a yes?"

"As long as I can dump the prawlies," I agreed, suddenly lighthearted and ready to accept what was given. As I had all those times before, I promised myself to think more carefully before judging his or any being's actions.

A promise I unfortunately failed to keep.

As shipcities went, the one on Minas XII was a patchwork quilt with a rotting hole at its center. There had been no plan or grandiose vision behind its beginning, middle, or future. The world had breathable air and potable water for most theta-class species, including Humans. That made it cheap. And Minas XII lay within a day translight of a growing number of valuable mining settlements, while remaining comfortably distant from existing systems—and their taxes. That made it very appealing to freighters and other entrepreneurs looking for a fresh start.

Minas XII herself dictated the terms. Her storm-ridden climate and jagged, geologically-active surface severely limited the amount of flat, firm ground suited to those trying to land. There were deep irregular valleys, smooth-floored by virtue of not too recent lava flows. The largest of these, branched like some nightmare version of a fallen tree, became the site of Minas' capital and only shipcity, Fishertown.

Why Fishertown? According to locals, the first beings to

land here had chosen the site because the main valley swooped down to the ocean, and the Humans on board, tired of being spacers, had had visions of setting up an industry based on fishing. Had they bothered to investigate before venturing out on Minas' huge waves that fine sunny day, they would have discovered the local aquatic fauna took great exception to any disturbance and were large enough to express that opinion. Later settlers wisely avoided such conflicts, taking the name of Fishertown as a reminder of exactly who was considered prey here. There was an illicit, though somewhat amusing, trade involving luring tourists to the ocean and collecting their insurance.

The real economic boom was in supplying cheap freight service between the Fringe mines and their markets. Each new wave of arrivals had plunked their starships findown on the lava of Fishertown's valley and declared themselves a shipcity. As space to do this without tipping over was limited, captains defended their miniature territories fiercely. The infrastructure to dock and service starships had thus evolved in a "first come, first grab" procedure, in which the best land had been claimed by the earliest, and most desperate, arrivals while the margins were eventually settled by those who saw an opportunity to expand their holdings from secure outsystem power bases. The latter could afford quality equipment and tugs.

From the air, without clouds to hide it, I could see the end result. The core of the broadest part of the valley contained a motley assortment of ships, some permanently (and thankfully) grounded by age and disrepair. A few straight avenues marked where space had been left for docking tugs to bring ships in and out. Over the years we'd been here, those avenues had gradually diminished, creating a prison for ships unable to launch by themselves. The entire area was aptly, if irreverently, referred to as the Dump.

To the north of the Dump, winding up two branches of the main valley of Fishertown's shipcity until the mountainsides closed in and funneled the storm winds too violently for safe flight, lay the area controlled by companies such as the Tellas Conglomerate and Largas Freight. The land wasn't the best, but ships arriving in those landing areas were given first-class welcomes, from modern docking tugs to fully serviced parking and reasonably secure warehousing. At a price. This was still the Fringe, after all.

Surrounding the valley, the land rose in abrupt, ragged-toothed cliffs, but closer to the ocean, there were foothills suitable for construction. Clinging to the lowest of these was a blight of buildings containing those who were able to flee the Dump, if not Fishertown; higher was the strip housing commerce and the minimal amount of industry here: most specializing in the repair and maintenance of ships, or brokers such as ourselves. Highest of all were those elaborate, inset structures housing those who had made fortunes here and expected to keep them. The truly wealthy didn't live on Minas XII at all, but there was no lack of an upper class who believed themselves such.

You'd know it was mostly Human without even seeing one, I thought, as I usually did when we flew in from this direction and I could see the entire mess. Other species tended to cooperate rather well when in small numbers and failed to do so when crowded. Humans seemed to require a critical number massed together—and all the associated problems—before bestirring themselves to organize more than a tolerant anarchy.

Minas XII wasn't populous enough yet, apparently. Aircars were the only mode of transportation able to reach anywhere in Fishertown, although trying to land amid the wrecks in the Dump was considered somewhere between bold and suicidal. Flying over the shipcity itself, technically forbidden by the practices of worlds with kinder climates and more forgiving landscapes, required a keen eye for the arrival and departure of ships which rarely bothered to inform the Port Authority of Minas XII of their intentions.

I also kept an eye, and several sensitive devices, turned to the Sweet Sisters. Despite their name and innocuous snowcaps, the seven nearby volcanoes ringing the shipcity were something I, for one, did not trust at all. Their combined past eruptions had produced Fishertown's conveniently level floor and, as the locals sometimes quipped, their next would be one way to clean up the Dump and start over. I did not find the concept amusing, despite Paul's attempts to explain why Humans did.

"You're quiet." Paul observed as he toggled on the approach warning. Below, the roof over our landing pad retracted in welcome and I readied myself for my least-favorite maneuver, locking into the automated system to land. Suddenly, our aircar swung sickeningly to one side as the vehicle's warding system veered us to avoid colliding head-on with another craft rising up into our level of traffic. "Ah," said Paul. "The mail's in."

The driving habits of the local courier service were one more thing I hadn't grown accustomed to in fifty years. It would have been easier if their drivers didn't have such short life spans and correspondingly brief safety records. "Maybe Chase sent her report?" I ventured hopefully.

Once the aircar was caught by the pad controls, floating down lightly and rapidly, my friend turned to look at me with a frown. "And maybe you two can get along while we deal with this?"

I didn't answer, for a moment toying with the memory of other faces: father, brothers, uncles. There appeared to be a stubborn line to the jaw repeatedly cropping up in the Ragem genome. "Of course," I replied smugly. "It's Port Authority we need to deal with—and the Tly."

Of course I'd behave, I repeated to myself, in a much better mood. I planned to be the perfect, dignified professional. Which left open several dignified ways to annoy Captain Chase, if she chose to annoy me.

Elsewhere

"SO he's annoying. That will never change." Lefebvre leaned back in his chair, aware that talking to himself wasn't a benchmark of sanity, but in the ten-plus years he'd spent on this ship he'd become less worried about such things. The *Russell III* had had four captains before his arrival: three had requested transfer as soon as it wouldn't harm their careers, while one had left the service altogether. He'd spoken to that individual before taking the assignment, finding the Modoren in a bar rolling in herbal teas and quite thoroughly drunk. "And the more fool I," he mused, "concluding the being deserted because its predatory mind-set couldn't stand serving a glorified trivia library."

That conclusion hadn't survived Lefebvre's first moments shipside. Kearn's most trusted officer was another Modoren, a scar-faced, tight-lipped male named Sas. Sas was apparently the only living being, besides Kearn himself, to see this Esen Monster in person. He left no doubt of his conviction they were on a worthy hunt, regardless of method.

"As if that makes it all believable," Lefebvre grunted to himself, putting his hands behind his head. He'd spent too many years in law enforcement to fall for the testimony of a potentially lunatic Modoren and a definitely obsessed Human. *Shapeshifters*. He'd credit that part of the tale when he could see it with his own eyes, not watch some confusing vid or listen to Kearn's horrified whispers.

Oh, something had happened fifty years ago. And some *thing* had undeniably attacked and killed without compunction or remorse, out there in vacuum as well as planetside. "But a being that can become any form it likes?" Lefebvre muttered, reaching out to scroll to a new entry. "Bah. Another devil in the dark—no more real than any other make-believe monster. Pick one and we'd have found just as many species using it to scare their offspring. I'll believe Kearn's a born hero before I'll swallow that one."

He'd arranged his office-cum-cabin on the *Russ'* to suit himself, the renovations dating from the moment he'd realized the depth of Kearn's desperation to have a captain last more than one tour of duty. If he turned his head, he'd be able to see his imported and expensive Latasian jelly-bed in the far corner, with its multiple coverlets and pillows tossed, as usual, into a heap as restless-looking as his sleep. On either side were Dokecian tentacle-cast ceramic tables, not a match but together costing more than a year's pay. The rest of the long L-shaped room's furniture was equally out of reach for an ex-patroller from Botharis.

And all unimportant, for in front of him, busy under his touch, was the one bribe Lefebvre had been after from the start. The rest was camouflage aimed at Kearn's ego. "What else do you have for me today, Timri?" he wondered out loud, tapping the control that sent a very special bit of communication technology tunneling through the *Russell*'s comp-tech's confidential records and reports, sifting names and places with inhuman speed.

"Confirming key words," Lefebvre told the machine. "Largas. Megar Slothe." He paused. "Paul Antoni Ragem."

Ragem. Traitor to his species and to all civilized beings, an infamy kept quiet by government embarrassment and inaction, lost in sealed records if not from the tongues of those who had known him. The Human who had brought the monster on board his own ship, endangering his friends and crewmates; who had sided with the creature against his own kind only to lose his life. A figure long gone and to be forgotten.

"Not by me," Lefebvre reminded himself, momentarily losing sight of the screen to stare through memory at a face he remembered very well indeed. "Not until I know why, Paul. Not until I know it all."

5: Restaurant Morning

BY Human standards, Captain Chase was an attractive individual. Short, but attractive. Arrogant and too sure of herself, grasping and overbearing, but attractive. I showed a polite tusk with an effort and took the seat she offered to me with as much grace as I could.

Paul gave me another of his "behave" looks before inspecting his own chair and sitting down cautiously. The last time we'd been here, my friend had sat in the remains of some being's meal—post-digestive remains. It hadn't been a happy moment. I'd reminded Paul, on the way here, we'd received our meal for free. He'd countered he hadn't been able to eat it anyway. Point taken.

The Circle Club's management might not be particularly fastidious, but I adored the place. There were few truly multispecies restaurants in Fishertown, despite its sizeable non-Human population. Most folded after poisoning or insulting some being or other. Somehow, by the simple tactic of offending everyone without prejudice, this place thrived.

Our table squatted in a back corner, too near the varied fragrances of the kitchen for my delicate first and fifth stomachs, and too distant from the main dining area for my famed hearing to pick up anything truly interesting. Paul had standing reservations here for meetings with his couriers and captains, despite my quite justifiable concern that the setting gave Cameron & Ki Exports all the gloss of a smugglers' ring. I looked wistfully beyond the forced intimacy of the portlight hovering overhead—low enough to endanger all of our foreheads and far too dim to show my vision much detail be-

yond the pale features of my companions and the table's mottled surface—at the brighter, livelier, Chase-less tables beyond. Being so occupied, I completely missed the start of
our conversation and snapped my attention back at the sound
of my name. On her lips.

"—Fem Ki predicted his reaction to threat, I'm sorry to
say." *Huh*, I thought. "Myers almost lost it, but I got him
under control before there was an incident. But he was right,
Paul. They had no grounds for boarding—"

"Pardon me," I interrupted. "Captain Chase, would you
mind going back to the very beginning? This is most excit-
ing and I don't want to miss a thing."

Captain Chase had undergone a vision enhancement procedure, one that allowed her to receive feed from her ship's
internal and external systems when activated. It was not common out on the Fringe, and the unusually large, violet irises
she turned on me were another mark of her origins in wealth-
ier, more settled space. She blinked. "Of course, Fem Ki."
My hearing easily detected the sound of her teeth grinding
together. I showed her my other tusk, suddenly in fine spirits.

My feet invaded so much of the space under the table
Paul could tap a warning on my toes without appearing to
stretch. I flipped an ear innocently at him as he said: "We
don't have all morning, Esolesy Ki. We should go over the
documents Janet brought and see if there's anything to help
us predict Port Authority's stand on all this—before we have
to bribe somone."

"Fine, fine." I waved cheerfully at the passing Octarian,
hoping it was our waiter and not—as happened occasionally—a bemused patron wandering around with a dirty towel
still stuck to its chins. "I don't know about you," I announced
to my companions, "but I find it very hard to read without
a morning libation. And," this to the being who had obediently lumbered to my side and laid its auditory tendrils on
the table, "do you have those really fresh green insects on a
stick? You know the ones I mean?"

Paul's "Es—" came at the same time as Chase's complexion turned an obligingly green tinge itself. *Was I to help it that she had some sort of phobia to food that wriggled?*

Still, there was more to deal with than any pleasure I gained manipulating this poor female, whose only crime was the look in her eyes whenever she glanced from Paul to me. I swiveled my large ears thoughtfully. If I hadn't overheard their argument a year ago—which included "interfering shaggy-scaled hunk" as her kindest (and most anatomically believable) reference to my handsome self—I might have taken that look to be one any uneasy employee might pass between a favored boss and his less-than-predictable partner.

But I had heard and, regrettably for Chase, was physiologically incapable of forgetting a word. I smoothed the pleats of my issa-silk caftan over one broad thigh. *However, I, at least, was civilized.* Paul hadn't signed any contract with this female, although I'd been disappointed by his lack of offense at her insults. To confuse me further, when he found out I'd listened to their argument, he'd been angry with me for a planetary week. *Humans could be incredibly difficult.*

So, I thought, gathering my dignity, *it was up to me to deal with this one.* I passed the sheaf of plas sheets Chase gave me to Paul, not bothering to squint at them in this light, then turned my attention from her past faults to a suspicion I'd had since hearing of the *Lass*'s confrontation. "Was there any hint or sign that the Tly inspectors knew what you carried?" I asked her.

Violet eyes narrowed in thought. "What do you mean?"

We paused while the waiter gingerly placed a bowl of pyati in the middle of our table, a true feat to accomplish without sloshing the steaming liquid or its floating dollops of cream. Then the Octarian reached into a large pouch and rummaged noisily for a moment before bringing forth a cup for Paul, a long, troughlike spoon for Janet Chase, and a tall glass for me. With a satisfied-sounding mumble, the waiter left us.

We sorted out the tableware. The spoon was for me, of course, and the glass a complete mistake: typical Circle Club service. Paul wrapped his hand towel—one hung from the side of each chair in lieu of napkins—around the glass to insulate it. Then we dipped our respective containers into the pyati and, with varying degrees of caution, took a reverent taste. It was, as always, superb. And one of the few beverages safe for almost all patrons, although it acted as a conveniently quick sedative to Carasians—something Ersh had assimilated for me from Ansky's bar-hopping days in more biological detail than I'd required at the time.

I licked cream from one tusk and continued: "Why the *Vegas Lass*? You've surely asked yourself that question—as have we."

"I've no idea." Her eyes narrowed, her tone close to accusation. "Do you?"

"What if they'd obtained your manifest?" I suggested mildly. It was one of many suspicions Paul and I had discussed before coming here this morning. "If so, perhaps the Tly confiscated your cargo not because of some violation, but because it contained exactly what they were after."

"That would be piracy," Chase refuted, keeping her voice down, though I was intrigued to see one of her eyebrows move up. "The inspectors were authorized. I contacted the Office of the Tly Assembly myself before allowing them to grapple and board the *Lass*."

"Nicely done," Paul said with approval and a glance at me.

I'd never denied this Human's abilities as a captain, although I found myself wondering what she'd planned to do in the event the inspectors hadn't been authorized. *Submit a complaint in triplicate before sucking vacuum?* "What class vessel did you say they had?" I asked.

Paul answered absently, having begun flipping through what looked to be over a hundred pages of very fine print. "Tly inspectors use Ultari scouts—fast, small, and cheap— the ones the Ultarians make in the thousands. Most of them even work."

"No," Chase corrected him, her head tilting. She had yellow hair this visit insystem, and wore it in a series of cascading braids that reached to one shoulder. "That was another strange thing about this. They had one of the old military cruisers; it had to predate the disbanding. Sent a chill through the scan-techs, believe me, even if the weaponsbay was sealed."

Paul raised his head and looked at me. "Cargo space," he commented dryly.

"So the question becomes: was the Assembly after the cargo itself or to keep it from Inhaven Prime?" I didn't have to include Chase in policy matters, and did so now less to include her, a spacer, in what was usually discussed planet-side, than to impress Paul with my efforts to be diplomatic. From the attentive look on her face as she sipped more pyati, at least Chase appreciated the courtesy. "Any indication from the forms?" I asked Paul, seeing he'd stopped reading.

"What we have here—" Paul answered grimly, setting his cup on top of the pile of sheets, "is a list of complaints filed by Tly against us, accompanied by a very strongly worded request for punitive action by Minascan Port Authority: im-proper stowage procedures, failure to pay customs, safety vi-olations—" he waved one hand upward.

"Trumped-up nonsense—"

I held up my three fingers to silence the indignant cap-tain. "Of course. But they are trying to tie us up with Port Authority. Again, why? To punish Cameron & Ki, and so Largas Freight? Or to hamper shipping to Inhaven Prime?"

"What about your courier pouch? Did they take that as well?" Paul asked. I angled one ear his way, catching a care-fully light tone in his voice, the one guaranteed to make me nervous.

I reviewed my memories hastily. The Tly were quite wel-come to read the business reports and merchandise offerings I'd put in the pouch—maybe they'd buy something from our latest catalog. *What else could it be?*

Before I could ask the question or, better yet, find some excuse to be rid of our companion and ask Paul himself, Chase pulled a nondescript case from under her chair. It was the sort of carrier spacers everywhere used to bring personal items from ship to planetside accommodations. There were likely identical ones under most tables here. She answered Paul's question as she arranged the case in front of her on the table: "Oh, they took the pouch. And the Quebit manuals filling it."

She flipped open the center flap of her bag, revealing its contents. Most looked familiar: our mail, some bundles wrapped around with red-and-white Largas' tape—signifying ship-to-ship messages too personal, too silly, or too sensitive to trust to other means of communication, and an assorted pile that must be new mail the *Vegas Lass* picked up during her stopover at Panacia.

I laughed before I could help it, but managed to turn my big head aside in time to protect my companions and the table from spraying pyati. *She'd substituted Quebit manuals for our mail?* Quebits took the art of manual writing to such extremes, legend held the first Human scholars who'd tried to decipher their written language had spent a lifetime working through what they'd hoped would be a definitive piece of Quebit culture. No one was quite ready to say it wasn't, but the huge ancient text had proved to be a manual for installing a sewage system within a city. Quebits were methodical beyond a fault.

Clever and vindictive. While I was by no means ready to forgive Chase's past insults, this went a long way toward burying them.

Oddly enough, Paul hadn't so much as smiled. Instead he was staring at the bag of mail as though planning to grab it and run. *What do you know that I don't, my friend?* I asked myself thoughtfully, saving the question for another time.

Meanwhile, Chase didn't seem to have noticed anything unusual about Paul's behavior—a satisfying observation I charitably chose not to take further—instead reaching into the pile of Panacian mail to tug free one piece, a plain data cube such as we routinely used for reports having to travel through more than one system. One of the joys of a multi-species' society was the lack of consistent communication between any given pair of technologies. These simple tap-and-store cubes were about as reliably transferable as a carving on a rock: the language would vary, but at least every species in the Commonwealth had the brute capability of extracting the script.

"I knew how important this would be to Cameron & Ki—to you especially, Fem Ki," Chase said, for once looking directly at me without a frown. Instead, she appeared unusually animated, as if what she held might make up for our past misunderstandings.

Huh, I repeated to myself.

Judging from Paul's speculative look, this wasn't what he'd been concerned about. I sensed he was still anxious. There was nothing overt in his behavior, unless it was how he made a bit too much of the challenge of dipping more pyati into his glass, but I could feel alarm doing a fine job on my insides.

Nonetheless, I chose to be touched by Chase's care for the message—whatever it was—or at least curious. "What is it?" I asked, making the logical assumption she knew enough about it to save me attempting to read it in this light.

"It's an announcement," she said, lowering her voice conspiratorially and leaning forward. *As if anyone could see us, let alone hear us back here*, I thought with amusement, but leaned closer cooperatively, if unnecessarily. Obviously, Chase didn't put much credit in the rumors of my hearing ability—which was just as well. "It's about the Feneden," Chase informed me almost breathlessly. "They've sent a delegation to D'Dsel. My contact's heard they are interested in starting up some trade routes. No one expected anything like this so soon after first contact. It's a fabulous opportunity for Cameron & Ki—"

Unlike other species, a Lishcyn's lower jaw could drop almost free on its lower elastic hinge; mine hit my chest with a clunk and a resultant spray of saliva my companions hastily mopped up with their towels.

Feneden?

An intelligent species *I* didn't know?

Something—*someone*—new in my universe? It had been seventy-four standard years, twenty-six days, and an irrelevant number of minutes since that had last happened, and the revelation had been contained in Ersh's flesh as she shared that discovery, not bellowed in a restaurant by some arrogant Human female. I wasn't sure if I was amazed or appalled.

The latter, I decided numbly. One thing was clear, at least. The searching machines in my office had earned serious re-programming.

If this was true, the cube being toyed with in the Human's slender fingers was the most significant thing to happen in my life in fifty years. *What should I do?*

As if in answer, the cube was captured by a larger hand. "Thanks, Janet," Paul said smoothly. "As you can tell," this with a quelling look at me emphasized by a unnecessarily solid kick under the table, "my partner is overwhelmed by your thoughtfulness."

I used both hands—one would have been too unsteady—to lift my jaw into position. A snap of my head relocked the joint into its more customary and comfortable position. As I did so, I found my ears twisting every which way on my head, creating an annoying and distracting variation in sound as one moment, I was deafened by the clatter of utensils from the kitchen, and the next, felt my stomachs lurch in time with some being's enthusiastic slurping. This form had never been so much trouble before. I could only blink apologetically at my dampened tablemates. "Overwhelmed," I managed to echo. "That's it."

Janet's sudden absorption in her pyati implied she felt much the same. Or perhaps, like me, she was having trouble relating to the other life-forms around her. *What, or rather who, were the Feneden?* Had she not said first contact, I might have assumed the word was a derivative of some lesser-used term or even slang. Such appeared with as much warning as the purple domes of the local fungi after it rained.

Thankfully, my self-absorption had stopped Paul's assault on my feet. He made a show of stowing the cube in a chest pocket. "Our thanks again, Janet," he said with more charm than I thought required. "We'll let you know what happens with this. An incredible opportunity indeed." Then, as she nodded and closed the case, preparing to replace it under her seat and out of the way, my friend reached out again and took a firm grip on the handle. "I'll make sure these are taken care of," he added, taking it away before she could open her mouth to object.

"Captain," I interjected, having no idea what Paul was up to, but presuming he wanted me to help deflect Chase from the apparently vital catalogs and other mail, "has Port Authority contacted you about the Tly's charges since you came insystem?"

"No, Fem Ki." Chase pressed her lips together for an instant, glancing from one of us to the other with an expression that was too carefully polite to be called a scowl. *So much for our moment of closeness*, I thought without much regret. "They fired off that copy of the charges when we dropped out of translight. I'd made an appointment to meet with Trin som Lyt once planetside. Port Authority doesn't make any decisions without her okay; we go way back, as you know. But Paul—Hom Cameron—told me to cancel it, so we could meet first."

At the moment, I could care less about Port Authority's petty bureaucracy, the Tly's piracy, or Captain Chase's reaction to what she obviously viewed as our collusion against her. All were true. All were trivial compared to the word rolling under everything else: *Feneden*. A new species. If it hadn't been for Paul's strange concern for the mail pouch and its contents, I would have left already, pleading the usual: an upset in one or the other stomach. Being the only one of a species had distinct advantages when it came to making excuses to leave a shared table.

This time, Paul beat me to it, tapping the credit slot on the table with a company chip to pay for what little we'd managed to enjoy, and making it clear we were about to cut the meeting short. "Leave it with us, Janet," he said. "I'll have Meony-ro go over these charges immediately—he's our legal expert. By the end of the day, we'll turn all this into a claim against Tly for your time and our losses. You'll see."

Meony-ro? I managed to keep my ears and other body parts perfectly still this time, though what legal expertise Paul thought our clerk had, beyond a rumored familiarity with the wrong side of it, I couldn't imagine. The Kraal was pleasant in a stoic way, and a good worker, if inclined to party with too much enthusiasm and expand my guest list to include his less-than-mannered friends. He was, I recalled, reasonably good at mechanical things. I squinted, wishing for enough light to read Paul's eyes.

I could, however, see him stand, and quickly followed suit. We should have known it wouldn't be that easy.

"So that's it," Captain Chase said, staying seated, her voice about as warm as the eye of an Minascan ice hurricane. "I'm to go back to the *'Lass* as if nothing's happened. I'm to tell my crew—most of whom used to live on a certain world which no longer exists—that I knuckled under to the Tly, let them take our cargo, and came home to knuckle under again to this—" a fierce stab with her finger at the pile of plas sheets between us on the table.

This was the Chase I knew and avoided whenever possible. I took a semi-discreet step backward, putting myself out of the ring of light and the debate. Paul did the opposite, stepping closer to her side and, putting one arm over her shoulders, bending to whisper so only she—and those beings present with extraordinary ears—could hear: "That's exactly what you must do, Janet. I promise we'll get to the bottom of it, but it's not going to be fast and it's not going to be clean. Understand me? There's more going on here than the obvious. Let us do the hunting—for now."

Her voice was an edged whisper in return. I couldn't see her face clearly from this distance and in this miserable excuse for lighting—I'd already bumped into another patron's chair and had to mutter an apology. "Then you'd better be careful, Paul Cameron. What is it the locals say? If you toss a net into unknown waters, have your blaster ready."

He'd *better be careful?* I repeated to myself, somewhat miffed. How easily she ignored my role in everything done by Cameron & Ki.

The light wasn't too dim for me to see her reach up to Paul's neck with one hand and start to pull his face toward hers. I deliberately and politely looked away. Somehow my oversized foot happened to snag the nearest leg of our table, jarring it so approximately half a bowl of cream-coated pyati became a tidal wave to flood the tabletop and most of its surroundings.

"Es!"

6: Conservatory Afternoon

AS I matured—growing up not quite being accurate, since web-form did not perceptibly alter in physical structure with time—as I matured from birth to what passed as adulthood for my kind, I'd frequently experienced what Humans call "trouble." It involved, with depressing consistency, some fairly innocent and usually well-intentioned act on my part followed by some unexpected or expected consequence to that act, wrapped up with someone important to my life being really annoyed with me.

For most of my life, that person had been Ersh. Ersh had been outstandingly effective at drawing guilt out of me that I'd never imagined existed. She didn't argue, rarely shouted, and had all the soul-withering, conscience-racking dignity of a being who had lived long enough to believe, with justification, she had to have seen it all—until I arrived. The little surprises I'd unwittingly awarded her throughout our time together had never been particularly welcome.

Nor, it seemed, was my little accident in the restaurant welcome to my now web-kin, Paul.

I tore a little piece of leaf from the nearest duras plant and tucked it under a scale on my chest. It joined the dozens already so planted. At this rate, I'd soon be invisible within my own greenhouse. *Just another oddly trimmed bit of shrubbery*, I told myself, somewhat relishing the melancholy. *That's Esen.*

Not that I was hiding. Not I. Everyone, Paul included, knew I spent most of my afternoons, when business per-

mitted, working with my plants in the conservatory. The almost barren ecosystem of Fishertown and its environs disappeared within these doors, replaced by the thriving growth
of, at last count, three hundred and seven worlds. There was
no order within the place except what my eye found pleasing and biology found acceptable. Plants obscured every
visible surface, in greens, reds, yellows, purples, and any
other color nature had found worked to turn sunlight into
food or gain the attention of pollinators.

My collection would have been a world-class attraction,
given the lack of competition on Minas XII, had I allowed
any but Paul's family and trusted friends to know what lay
inside the back third of our warehouse. The roof was the
landing pad; the sunlight streaming past branch and leaf
was natural enough, but drawn down through hidden col-
lectors; the water and other nutrients were supposedly purchased and consumed by a local brewery. Perhaps it was
an insignificant secret among so many others, but I'd grown
selfishly attached to my privacy and this place over the
years.

Another piece of leaf went into my disguise. By now,
all the easy scales had their companion greenery, making
me have to twist gingerly to reach my sides. Some of the
first transplants had started to wither and slip free. I clicked
my tonguetips with annoyance and reached for more.

"So, Es. What did you do this time?" The rich, gravelly
voice originated from somewhere behind a wall of cascading vines.

It could belong to only one being. My ears struggled into
a happier position, then settled back into their droop. "Does
it matter?" I countered morosely, tucking in another leaf
and wondering if I should add a flower or two for variety.

Joel Largas shouldered his way through the greenery,
pulling a grav cart behind him loaded with trays of seedlings.
After Paul, this was my favorite Human—something else
I'd have been scolded by Ersh for in the past. I sighed, my
thick lips making very effective blubbery noises as I did so.
I might have known I wouldn't be left to mope on my own.
Since his self-imposed retirement last year, the former spacer

had taken to gardening with a passion. This being the only garden on Minas XII, it had been only reasonable to give him unlimited access. Both Human and plants had benefitted; in all honesty, I did as well. Joel was important to Esolesy Ki, the Lishcyn: a judgment-free companion who cheerfully ignored me when I wanted to be alone but somehow decided on his own when I didn't.

"That's going to take a while," he commented instead of answering my question, gesturing to my accomplishment of having leafed the center third of my chest scales and a little farther.

"I've time." Considering web-life span, barring accidents, that was an understatement. I watched him from the corner of my eye.

Joel Largas was always worth watching. A great-grandfather—likely more than that by now—he remained perfectly capable of charming females of his kind, and a few others, to incoherence in under three standard minutes. I'd seen it done. But there was much more to him than mere physical presence. Resolute and determined, Joel had found himself the leader of a refugee convoy, the last to flee Garson's World before the end. He'd coaxed, cajoled, and outright bullied spacers into action, then brought the whole assortment of private vessels and independent traders, with their human cargoes, safely to Minas XII with no ambition but to find a haven for his family and friends. When that meant creating a freighter company out of what remained of their fleet and almost single-handedly seeing to its success, he'd done that, too.

The grav cart contained a battered stool, which Joel pulled out and put beside where I sat in the moss. He settled himself on it, then began casually plucking leaves from the nearest duras plant and passing them to me, one by one. "Paul's no fool, Es," the Human said, nothing casual in his voice this time, although his blue eyes contained a suspicious twinkle. "You usually trust him to handle his own relationships."

Word spread translight around here, I realized, unsurprised my escapade this morning at the Circle Club was al-

ready known to Joel. In my experience, anything worth
knowing seemed to head to him first, whether my discomfiture or fuel prices. Another leaf. Two more. Then I held
up one foot, balancing awkwardly on a rear not intended
for such a position, and wiggled my broad, webbed toes.
"It could have been an accident," I said, finding the whole
thing funny again.

His abundant growth of curling gray facial hair hid what
might have been a smile. "You have a lot of those around
Captain Chase," Joel observed wryly. "It's no wonder you
make the woman nervous."

I'd like to make her disappear, I told myself, but half-
heartedly as I again lost the humor of it. My true self preferred harmony with those around me, a state of community
in which I was either liked, tolerated, or benignly ignored.
It was safer, for one thing. It was much closer to the arrangement within my Web, for another. Discord, even when it
was my choice, made me uncomfortable for days. "She—"
I tilted my snout so I didn't have to look at him, pretending to talk to myself. "She makes me afraid."

I couldn't see Joel's face, but the hand ready to pluck
another leaf reached instead to my forearm. The pattern of
age spots on the back of his still-strong hand echoed those
of my scales. His grip was firm and warm. "You can't believe she could affect your friendship with Paul. Es, you
and he are—you're family." This last was said with all the
meaning Joel himself placed on the concept. There was
nothing higher, no bond tighter to the head of the Largas
clan.

I flashed a tusk at him, turning my big head so he could
see it. "I know," I said, accepting his answer as my own.
"But the other females—your daughter among them—accepted that. They understood I had no intention of interfering between Paul and his own kind. Chase—speaks to
Paul of being rid of me, of breaking up Cameron & Ki.
It's not malice," I admitted heavily. "She sincerely believes
it best for him."

Joel Largas had learned some interesting terminology in
his long career as a spacer. I flicked my ears back and forth,

adding a few more to memory. When he was finished, he patted my arm again. "Don't worry about Chase," he said finally, his face flushed with outraged anger. "I'll have a talk—"

"No!" I said quickly, standing up and, in the process, shedding leaves like some tree at the approach of winter. "That will only convince her she's right."

"Then I'll speak with Paul," Joel offered, still with that glint of battle in his eyes. I felt warmed to my core as I looked at him and recognized this was the other side of humanity, this caring and willingness to sacrifice for another when there was no gain, no prize. It was what had originally drawn me to Paul's aid, made me break Ersh's Rules and reveal myself.

A seductive, dangerous feeling as well. Despite our deep friendship, Joel Largas was one Human to whom I could never reveal my true self. Fifty years ago, within reach of safety, the Largas' convoy had been attacked by a monster. Joel had been an eyewitness, watching the web-being— though he had no name for it then or now but Death—rip apart the ships of friends, helpless to prevent more carnage as it stalked others for the pleasure of consuming the life within. I'd been told he sobbed in his sleep for years afterward, reliving his frustrated fury and grief.

No Human, including Paul, could possibly tell my web-form from that of any other of my kind; even we required taste or scent to be sure of identity. Should Joel see me as I was, his nightmare would be back. I had no desire to ever inflict that pain.

"I appreciate your willingness to help. And your vocabulary," I told him, deliberately damping all emotions to the best of my ability, but letting a note of amused resignation enter my voice. "Let's face it. I haven't helped the situation. She has cause—"

He wasn't convinced. "I don't want you to be afraid of anyone, Esolesy Ki. That's not right, no matter what little tricks you've played now and then."

"I'm sure my fears are groundless—just my stomachs overreacting to conflict. I should know better than to listen to their complaints by now." *He should believe that*, I thought, remembering several instances from our past in which my participation in an argument had had immediate and embarrassing repercussions. I really wished I could find a form to live in that wasn't ruled by its insides. I went on: "I do trust Paul."

His expression lightened, as I'd hoped. "As I said you should. He's a good man, Es. He's not going to listen to any nonsense."

Well, he did, I told myself bitterly, then was honest enough to wonder if it had been so he could learn the full extent of Chase's feelings on the subject. Wasn't the proof in the result? I began to notice that other, depressingly familiar feeling: guilt. Would Paul have refused her solicitation for lip contact, and its possessiveness, had I kept my feet to myself? I felt my ears sink as I realized I'd probably been wrong about my friend twice in the same morning. *This wasn't going at all well.*

"Where is Paul?" I found myself asking. I'd literally run from the restaurant. There had been something unnerving about the stupefied stare of both Humans, clothing and skin streaked with black pyati and sagging blobs of cream. The stuff had missed me completely, which hadn't seemed to help the situation. So I'd ducked my head in mute apology before hurrying out.

Well, I'd tried to hurry. The lighting, or lack thereof, made my rush to the exit a series of spectacular collisions in the semidarkness with everything possible, including, I winced at the memory, a waiter whose tray arched completely over my head before arriving at the wrong table, a Poptian who wound up wearing its salads, and a group of tourists who scattered from underfoot just in time. I hoped they didn't think I was running from the food.

Joel didn't think it odd that I expected him to know. "Paul? He's busy dropping your luggage shipside. You two are due to lift for D'Dsel tonight, aren't you?" When I stared at him, one hand under my jaw as it threatened to loosen for the second time today, the Human looked suddenly contrite. "Es. I'm sorry. I thought you knew—this must have been part of the surprise with your tickets. Don't tell Paul I let it slip, okay?"

I sat down, very slowly, and picked up a leaf to tuck under another scale, hoping my stomachs would mind their own business.

I hadn't left Minas XII for fifty years. I hadn't encountered an intelligent species I hadn't assimilated at least in part from my web-kin in half again as long.

Joel silently passed me another leaf as I contemplated both its position and what to say to my erstwhile partner. *Planning to surprise me, was he?* I wondered if he thought it some bizarre punishment.

Surely Paul, of all beings, knew I hated surprises.

7: Starship Night

"I THOUGHT you'd like a surprise."

I didn't bother replying to that, too busy trying to judge the best moment to plant my feet on the conveyor belt leading into the *Galaxy Goddess*. It was a ridiculous name for a passenger ship and I felt even more ridiculous wearing this hat. Paul's hand pressed against my shoulder, urging me forward. *Fine for him, with feet sized to fit the device.* I scampered into position, having to tuck one set of toes under the other and grab the handrail for dear life.

"The surprise," I muttered, "is that I'm here at all." Well, to be honest, I'd pretended to innocently fall in with his plans from the moment I'd found him back at the office in fresh clothes and with his anger apparently on hold, ready to spring his surprise on me in front of the assembled staff. It seemed the appropriate move on my part—and there was always the chance the starship would have technical difficulties on the launch field.

Paul laughed, tugging at the tassel that hung by my ear. The hat fit; that was all I could say for it.

At least I wasn't the only one forced to look silly as we approached the *Goddess*. The flamboyant headgear, with its glowing, tasseled fringe and flat, outstretched brim, was part of the package—some Human concoction to embarrass the passengers into a prevacation euphoria. *The free (or rather prepaid) mugs of spurl had been more effective in that regard*, I thought. In case anyone, such as myself, wisely had second thoughts about their upcoming adventure and wanted to bolt at the last minute, we were being shuttled directly inside the starship's ornate port by this automated walkway.

Most of our fellow passengers looked Human, although the huge hats made this conclusion no better than an educated guess. The ship's complement, lined up ahead to greet us as we arrived at the ship's port, was a broader spectrum. Of the thirty or more there, almost all were paying no attention to their living payload but instead were looking to the horizon with expressions, depending on species, ranging from astonishment to terror.

Paul noticed: "I take it this lot hasn't been here before."

I nodded, following the crewbeings' line of sight to see the usual evening bank of storm clouds draped over the shoulders of the Sweet Sisters and heading this way. If you hadn't survived a winter here, those black, heaving, wind-ripped clouds could resemble the end of the world.

Since no one else on the conveyor belt appeared interested in the weather, I felt safe in assuming they were all from Fishertown. As long as the belt brought us under cover within the next half hour, they'd be happy. The daily summer storms didn't kill too many locals, although they did have a negative impact on what tourism Minas XII didn't lose to fishing.

The travel organizers' timing was excellent. Although near the end of the line—I had delayed our arrival as much as possible, but Paul had factored that into his timing—we were greeted, cheerily exhorted to consume more free spurl, and sent to our cabins to await the docking tug and lift before the first tornadic howl wrapped itself around the hull.

"Aren't you glad you came?" Paul asked the moment we were alone, sending his hat across the room to join mine.

"Not particularly," I said bluntly, then repented as he grinned at me. "All right. Now that the hats are off, I'm prepared to endure it." I looked around our accommodations. It didn't take long. Economy Standard—it had been a staff gift, after all. I thought wistfully of the Preferred Deck, with all its luxury and space. We could have afforded it, but only in terms of cost.

I began unpacking the small carryall which had arrived

before us. The rest of our luggage would be stowed in the *Goddess'* cargo hold, along with a limited amount of very high-end goods and secure mail. Passenger ships were preferred couriers, partly because they were too heavily armed for most pirates, but mainly because their profit margins depended on getting their clients to their destinations as quickly as possible. The joke in freighter circles was that if tourists could ever be persuaded to travel in trip boxes, requiring no food, care, or entertainment, everyone would want to convert their starships to the trade. I, for one, shuddered at the mere thought.

There was room to turn around, barely, but I managed to keep out of Paul's way as he performed a task that, by now, was second nature to us both, although it would have caused raised eyebrows—or the corresponding expression—among others on the ship. He climbed with primate agility on the furniture, running an extremely sensitive detector over the ceiling and upper walls. It would take him only seconds to establish if we were being watched or recorded. There was a small, little-known company in the Dump whose specialists stood by their work—these detectors—with their lives. It came with the clientele, most unnoticed by any authorities and relying on their privacy to be sure this pleasant situation continued unabated. Paul had taken careful steps to conceal our identities as customers, including arranging for payment from Commonwealth, not Fringe, accounts, viewing it as unlikely anyone would believe Cameron & Ki had legitimate reasons for such paranoia. *And*, I'd thought wryly at the time, *it diminished the chances of inappropriate business referrals*.

"Clean," the Human pronounced, returning the detector to its hiding place in his shirt, then dropping down to check out the bed opposite my box. It might be Standard accommodations, but suiting a being's sleep needs was only good business sense. "How's yours? Going to be comfortable, Es?"

"It's only a day translight to Panacia," I reminded him. Unpacking done, since I hadn't brought much for such a short time shipside—well, three stunning outfits for the evening's Captain's Supper, but I hadn't been in the mood to make up my mind before coming—I wrestled myself into the pile of pseudo-grass. It was rougher and less fragrant than I was used to, though acceptable. I snuggled in a bit, resting my snout on the padded box side so I could see my companion. Supper would be post-lift, so we had a couple of hours to kill. I didn't know about the Human, who had endless recuperative powers, but I was distinctly aware of two sleepless nights in a row. "Not bad," I decided, my forked tongue spreading in a yawn that muffled the words but probably conveyed the meaning on its own.

Paul lay on his back, still in his coat as though he'd forgotten to take it off, arms behind his head. He appeared content to gaze at the ceiling. I listened to his breathing for a minute or two, then couldn't take it any longer. As I opened my mouth to speak, he anticipated me, saying calmly: "It's okay, Es."

"What's okay?" I said, feeling quite affronted by what sounded like forgiveness in his voice. The Human should have been expecting me to complain vigorously about his bullying me on board. *Certainly scope for a tirade or two.* Then I remembered how I'd felt in the conservatory. *It could be*, I decided reluctantly, *my turn for some sincere groveling*.

Before I could say another word, the Human had rolled his head to look at me. "I meant, it's okay to be nervous about leaving home. It's been a long time."

I closed my mouth, holding in the quick denial that suddenly didn't feel right at all. I blinked at my friend, reading—I thought correctly—a look of understanding sympathy in his face. *Why?* "Minas XII isn't home," I said slowly, as much to myself as to him. "Home is—home is—" I found myself unable to finish. To my kind, home was where the Web gathered as one. It had last been Picco's Moon, where I'd lived with Ersh. Then I relaxed, having an answer that pleased me. "I'm home now. Home is the Web—wherever we are together."

The Human appeared to hesitate, then smiled. "Home

this is, then, Es," he agreed, freeing one hand to wave around our tiny stateroom.

I regarded him carefully, sensing he'd intended to say more than that, but had decided to hold back. Well, it was past time to clear some of the mysteries between us, if only so we could get this haphazard vacation underway. "I'm sorry I spilled pyati on you," I said as sincerely as I could. *That probably wouldn't be enough*, I realized, swallowing. "And on Captain Chase."

Again, he reacted unpredictably, frowning and making a sharp gesture of negation as if I'd embarrassed him. "Don't apologize, Es."

I blinked at him, trying to puzzle this out.

"Skalet didn't speak very well of me in the beginning, did she?" Paul's voice dropped to become almost inaudible. It was a habit when we were in strange surroundings and he had things to say to me no one else should hear, trusting my ears.

His mention of my web-kin made me uneasy, as always. I found myself raising my body temperature to bleed away excess energy, a trained resistance to the reflex to cycle into something less prone to emotional response.

"She did tell you to end our association, didn't she?" Paul prompted, when I didn't respond.

Skalet wanted you safely dead, I answered, but only to myself. Out loud, I whispered so his Human hearing could detect it: "Yes. What is your point with this, Human?"

"You listened to her, but didn't take that advice, Es. You kept your friendship with me, an alien, despite the urging of your own kind." He paused and raised himself up on an elbow to face me more directly. "I don't want an apology from you about the pyati. I owe you one."

"So Joel told you," I said glumly. Largas was quite capable of sidestepping any promise made to me, if he thought it in my best interest.

Paul's brows went up. "Told me what?" he asked, in that tone which expected an answer. *His persistence when curious was*, I recalled, *a trait which hadn't changed since we'd met.*

My fifth stomach gurgled warningly. "Captain Chase—" I found my voice fading to nothing.

"That she'd pretty thoroughly spooked you? No, Joel didn't tell me. I finally figured that out for myself this morning," Paul admitted. "You made an unforgettable exit, you know. I tried to catch up, but you'd snagged the last aircar outside.

"Esen," he continued very quietly, eyes intent. "I'm the one who must apologize to you. I am sorry. I didn't realize how deeply you were being affected by Janet's one-sided campaign—and that's all it was. I should have seen it and reassured you long ago. I'd assumed you know I'd never accept anyone who couldn't understand our friendship." His generous mouth curved upward. "So. Am I forgiven?"

I hadn't expected a relief so intense it threatened my control over this form on every level, although, knowing the proclivities of an overtired and stressed Lishcyn, I might have guessed. I squeezed my eyes, ears, and mouth shut, holding the position until the muscles of my jaw began to throb, then spasm. My temperature soared as I concentrated on convincing my stomachs to behave. There was no point cycling into my birth-form even had I dared risk it on this ship. The Lanivarians were a marvelously civilized culture and a fascinating species on the ground; unless thoroughly tranked and in a trip box, they were miserable spacefarers. I'd reason to know. So I had to fight the inclinations of three of my five stomachs to clear themselves for action while grappling desperately at my own equilibrium. *This was going to be most embarrassing*, I concluded with the conviction of experience. Not to mention potentially nasty in such a small room.

A gentle touch became an anchor, a focus to draw my mind from the confusion within this body. The touch was a stroke along the scale-free, highly sensitive oval of skin under my chin: a holdover from youth, a place that would one day host the wiry thatch of beard marking an older Lishcyn—I was hoping for a distinguished auburn, but there'd been no sign of any growth yet. Aunts quieted unsettled infants by stroking this spot—much the way Human adults rocked their young. I myself was much too old for such treatment, though I found it hard to resist rubbing the area when alone and needing comfort.

As now. I couldn't bring myself to object to the caress, feeling my physical self relax involuntarily, the soothing sensation holding me safely in this form and otherwise keeping my dignity intact. I opened my ears the tiniest crack in time to hear him singing something nonsensical I remembered from Paul's days as a new father, awake night after night with his twins. From other forms, I knew he had a reasonable voice, true in pitch, with a pleasant depth to it. His music was wasted on these ears, if not on my soul.

He must have seen. Without stopping the tiny, slow movements his fingers made under my chin—which was wise, as my stomachs were still barely under control—his song changed to words, equally soft. "Es. Esen. It's all right. I want you to listen to me. Okay? Just listen and try to understand, please.

"This is my fault, not yours. I've shoved too much at you, too quickly: the Ganthor, my gift, that nonsense with Chase, this trip. I'm very sorry. I forget sometimes how it all adds up on you: to be what you aren't, to deal with all of the rest of us. You do it so very well, Es."

It might have been the words. Certainly the stroking was hypnotic. I let my body temperature slip below its fever pitch, no longer having to fight the urge to leave this form, back in charge of its tendencies. *Almost*, I told myself honestly, reasonably sure I was no longer about to redecorate everything in range, including Paul, with my breakfast, hasty snack, lunch, and that wee bite I'd grabbed on the way out of the office.

His voice went on, the barest whisper of sound. I opened my ears further to hear it, twitching free of some of the grass. "Ersh would be proud. I know I'm proud of you."

I gave a deep, shuddering sigh to cue my stomachs to rearrange their contents, feeling them finally respond normally, and yawned again. Then I opened one eye: "It was a pretty great exit, wasn't it?"

"One of your best."

I opened the other eye, but only a crack. "Long day, too."

"A couple of long days," I heard him agree, the voice so faint now he might have been in another room, fingers lifting away. "A rest wouldn't be a bad idea, Es."

Way ahead of you on that, I thought, my eyes and ears closing as I burrowed my head under the prickly but warm fibers, taking with me into sleep the warm glow of being home within my Web.

The *Galaxy Goddess* lifted on schedule, her multitude of passengers asleep or in a pleasant stupor, with only two near-misses as she rose into the stormy skies of Minas XII. Had I known, I would not have been at all surprised that one of those misses was the same courier who'd almost collided with us this morning. As I'd noticed, they didn't tend to lengthy careers.

I might have been surprised to learn the other near-miss was with a private aircar hurrying to the Dump—then again, that destination alone was dangerous enough to insure the driver was unlikely to worry about a close call with one starship.

The same, unfortunately, was true about us.

Images of the Hiveworld swam behind my closed eyelids as I drifted into peace, an uneasy combination of wonder and grief.

Elsewhere

"I'VE decided to take the ship to D'Dsel, Captain Lefebvre," Kearn ordered briskly. "It's time we paid a visit
and found out what they've been hiding from our investigation. And," he tried the smile he'd practiced earlier in
a mirror, an expression filled with confidence and verve,
"it's perfect for the crew's stopover."

"A stopover on the Hiveworld?" Lefebvre sounded incredulous. "Are you serious, sir?"

Smile crumbling, Kearn ran one hand over his head,
feeling the moist slick of sweat. Lotions or sprays never
helped: they left sticky patches behind and their scents
usually fought with the cologne he used liberally every
day. "Are you hard of hearing this morning, Captain?"
he said in a tone he hoped was brusque. "I thought you
wanted a break for the crew. There you go. D'Dsel."

Normally well-groomed, for some reason this morning Lefebvre looked as if he hadn't slept the preceding
night, making the excuse of a bout of sickness. Although
Kearn doubted this and would have accused any other
member of the *Russell*'s crew of indulging in drug or
drink, it was impossible to express any such suspicions
to a face this composed and confident, no matter how
exhausted-looking. Lefebvre's voice had a matching
roughness to it, although he remained flawlessly official.
Kearn would have heard it. He always listened for a hint
of patronage or insult. *Just because he couldn't hear
any*, Kearn reminded himself anxiously, *was no reason
to assume it wasn't there.*

Lefebvre answered wearily, but politely: "It's on our route, sir. But it's not exactly set up for a rest—"

"It will do fine. Just fine. More importantly, it doesn't waste any of the *Russell*'s schedule. If you insist I justify myself to you, Captain," Kearn puffed his cheeks in aggravation, "it's vital we verify the Rememberers have supplied everything they've collected." Kearn scowled. "I hope you aren't suggesting the crew wait for the next feasible option. I can tell you now: that won't be for a long while. And we have to keep them happy and healthy, don't we?"

"No, sir, and yes, sir," Lefebvre answered without so much as a scornful twitch on his lips. "I've heard D'Dsel is—fascinating. But you've been there."

Oh, yes. He'd been to D'Dsel. Kearn's lips tightened into a thin, bitter line. And the Esen Monster had been there with him, in her clever disguise as a harmless, concerned passenger. *He'd been Acting Captain, then, with a ship of his own*. Kearn didn't need the vids from his files to see Esen's doleful face as a Ket; his flesh crawled at the thought of her long fingers probing his skin, pretending to give one of the famed Ket massages but all the while mapping weaknesses in the Human physique. He'd thought Nimal-Ket to be Esen's spy, at first, only later putting the pieces together to learn he'd been duped along with the rest of them.

D'Dsel's Rememberers had cooperated during that first hasty search for the Monster, deeply concerned by the pattern of unexplained deaths on their normally placid world. Since that day, they'd closed all records, saying he'd received all they knew. *As if that was likely to be true*, Kearn thought. The *Russell III* had returned twice more—never receiving a warmer welcome. But then, he hadn't had the persuasive Lefebvre in the captain's seat—or a personal invitation.

Kearn pretended to busy himself with some sheets of plas on his desk. When Lefebvre continued to stand at ease in front of his desk, Kearn looked up with annoyance. "That was all, wasn't it, Captain?"

"If D'Dsel's our last stopover for a while, I'd like to take some leave as well, sir."

"What?" Kearn's hands clenched, with the dismaying result of creasing several important documents. He stared up at his captain, seeing the exhaustion but suspicious of its existence, hearing the politeness, but knowing there had to be contempt beneath it. "I don't see how that's possible, Captain," Kearn protested almost feverishly. "I need you on the *Russell*. Timri's staying. You have to stay. We're going to be combing records, investigating, dealing with Port Authority—"

"Only a couple of days, sir, once we're findown and stable. That's all." Lefebvre rubbed one hand over his eyes, an uncharacteristic gesture. "You should consider a bit of time away from all this yourself, sir, if you don't mind the suggestion."

"You may be willing to play the tourist while the Esen Monster remains a threat to every living thing!" Kearn shouted, launching himself to his feet and still, regrettably, having to look up to glare at Lefebvre. "I know where my duty lies!"

"Yessir." A meaningful pause. "Two days."

Kearn subsided, knowing that mild, firm tone of voice as well as he knew the respectful yet unyielding look on Lefebvre's face. He wasn't exactly sure, as usual, when he'd lost any chance of winning the argument.

"Two days, then," he grumbled, his head down, straightening the crumpled sheets on his desk. "And not a minute more."

The door closed.

Kearn looked up to be sure he was alone, then slowly pulled open the top drawer of his desk. Inside were two objects. The first, an ordinary remote recorder, blinked to show it continued to function normally. Its shelf life was supposedly a hundred years. Kearn had a dozen elsewhere in the ship. *No problems with testimony after the fact*, he assured himself, stroking the tiny servo with one finger. *No lies to protect the reputations of dead friends and obstruct justice.*

The second object was a knife, needle-sharp, gleaming with the expensive and pain-filled promise of a finely crafted weapon. Kearn lifted it out reverently, with repeated anxious glances at the door. It should have locked behind Lefebvre, awaiting Kearn's voice or touch to reopen, but he'd never been convinced of the reliability of automatics.

The workmanship was Kraal, given away by the exquisite etchings on the blade itself and the heavy ornate handle. The sophistication of the designs belied the first impression of gaudy excess. There was no doubt Kearn's sweating hands clutched a work of art as well as death.

As if fearing a watcher, Kearn reached for a sealed courier pouch from the box beside his desk, the box almost overflowing with requests from academics of several species, then used the knife to pierce the pouch and open it. He took care, having nicked himself more than once while using this gift so crudely. But there was no other excuse for him to own such a blade and he was always careful of appearances. *After all*, he thought proudly, *hadn't he fooled them all?* The academics thought him some sort of messiah, spilling valuable, hard-to-obtain research into whatever appendages reached for it. They'd have been horrified by his real quest.

But those who knew his real quest, Kearn thought angrily, *those who should have supported it—they thought him mad.* All except the giver of this gift. That one had known the truth about him, believed then and believed now.

With one last stealthy flick of his eyes to the door, Kearn deftly twisted the handle from the blade, putting the business end safely on the desk. The inside of the handle was almost hollow, except for the tiny gemlike reflections of light from within, sparked from metal and crystal. He'd discovered this secret while fidgeting with the knife, his ever-restless hands prone to finding the limits of anything they held for too long. Kearn remembered his horror when the blade dropped off into his lap, assuming at first he'd been attacked by a remote-controlled weapon, then convinced with almost equal terror he'd broken the irreplaceable, frantically trying to think of excuses in case he ever met the giver in person.

Then, a look inside the handle had reassured him on those points and brought up another: what was it? *Keep this token with you at all times*, the note had said before consuming itself. *It will bring you luck in your hunt.*

Kearn peered inside, wishing he knew more about technology. Knowing the source, he guessed the device hidden inside was some sort of weaponry—perhaps a force blade to replace the real one should it break, even though he couldn't find any controls.

But the knife was lucky, he knew it, if only as a reminder that his quest had support from the outside, a powerful backer. This backer communicated rarely and then only via cryptic messages such as the latest: an invitation urging him to take the *Russell III* to D'Dsel with all speed, for reasons too secret to send. Other than such hints, his mysterious benefactor remained quiescent, yet Kearn knew he could count on aid should he find his target.

Not *should*, he admonished himself, reaffixing blade to handle and watching them join together without a visible seam.

When.

8: Starship Afternoon; Hiveworld Night

FENEDEN.

"Feneden," I repeated out loud, rolling the strange word around in my mouth. "The Feneden. Or is it Fenedenians?" Comspeak had a useful, although sometimes frustrating, pliability when it came to names.

Paul must have heard the not-quite panic in my question. "Refreshing to have you not know something for a change," he said mildly, keeping his attention on the display scrolling under the table's surface, occasionally tapping one finger to bring up detail on something of particular interest.

"It is not," I retorted, then flashed an agreeable tusk. "Well, maybe it is. Feneden. Gives me the most delicious sense of mystery." *Not that I wanted it to continue.* "Did you find any references?" It hadn't seemed necessary or wise to allow remote control of our data-collecting machines back on Minas XII, since any potential sighting of a web-being would trigger a coded signal to Paul. This was a lack I now firmly intended to remedy the moment I returned. *I was,* I confessed to myself, *becoming far too dependent on technology.*

Fortunately, Paul always arranged for some news to reach him as he traveled. He was sorting incoming lists now, hence my impatience, and he grunted a negative.

I looked down the sweeping lobby, looking for distraction. There wasn't much. The *Galaxy Goddess*, like most passenger ships of her class, boasted two of these flamboyant corridors, running in parallel. Expansive portholes lined the supposed outer wall, attracting no one's attention but mine. They were vids, as passengers were protected deep within the bowels of the ship, but the crew pretended they were real windows into space with anyone gullible enough. To the ship's credit, the vid was live-feed from the exterior. I could have sat gazing out there for the entire journey except for two things: it made me far too noticeable among this space-jaded crowd and I was too interested in the puzzle to come.

"I want to know everything you can find," I told my friend, likely not for the first time today. "What do they look like? Are they humanoid? Or something really exotic?"

"What would you prefer?"

I suspected Paul of humoring me, but didn't care. "Tall, elegant, dignified," I said, leaning back and resting my long jaw on my chest. "A few extra limbs would be nice." I lifted my flask in one hand, a pastry in the other, and pointed my chin at the remaining treats on the lunch tray with a sigh of mock dismay.

My ears flicked lazily, mostly to avoid picking up random snips of conversation from the multitude of beings sitting, like us, at one of the tables set in intimate clusters under plas umbrellas, or walking about in straggly groups for exercise. *Maybe*, I said to myself hopefully, *some of them were lost*. On a vessel this size, even the most knowledgeable beings might need to roam the length of the passenger section in hopes of a clue from the ship's decor as to the nearest restaurant or their rooms. Several times, perhaps. That hadn't been my excuse for being late to our table, although it might be related to why it now felt wonderful to sit.

"Tall, elegant, and dignified?" Paul chuckled. "Extra limbs? Sounds like a tree." We were both back to our normal selves—the end result of a sleep that, for me at least, had lasted from liftoff until waking alone well past ship-morning. I'd missed the chance to dress for the Captain's Supper, which was likely just as well.

The Human looked as rested as I felt, a change reflected in his choice of a bright-colored shirt and pants, belted with a sash of such vibrant yellow it made the Engullan crew-being wince each time she showed up to refresh our drinks. In any other crowd, Paul would have been visible from the horizon and glowed from beyond it. Here, he blended in with the many other Humans well into the vacation spirit.

For a moment, just a moment, I thought: *so it's a disguise*. Then I shook off the feeling, preferring to accept an adventure for its own sake.

"Ah, here's something."

I leaned forward, resting my chin lightly on Paul's shoulder so that I could see the screen.

The physical parameters of a new species were of interest to almost everyone, from clothing manufacturers to emergency medical technicians, so it wasn't surprising this was the information now filling the table's screen, part of a news release from Panacia.

I couldn't take my eyes from the slowly rotating image. "Don't take this too much to heart, Esen," I heard Paul say. "They drew it up in a hurry from vids, not data provided by the Fenedens—it does seem to be Feneden, by the way. This could simply represent one age group or possibly one subspecies. Remember the Oastessii. Or the Panacians themselves, for that matter, with their multiple castes."

On one level, I understood him completely. On another, more intimate one, I heard nothing, saw nothing but this form captured and displayed.

Humanoid in plan. Convenient, given the prevalence of that body scheme among other species and the sheer number of the Human version in this quadrant of space.

Sensory organs located on the head, grouped into the features of a distinct face. Not all humanoids were as obliging. The pale, almost translucent-blue skin—what showed of it beyond encompassing and disappointingly plain, drab robes—appeared faintly mottled as though either pebbled in texture or colored that way. There was a shiny red-brown growth from the top, sides, and back of the head, as well as around the neck. Too thick for hair, much finer than any antennae or tentacles I'd encountered. I had no idea what it was.

To my very core I longed for a taste—to learn this new form's biochemistry, its biological patterns, its essence. It was an appetite deeper than hunger, certainly stronger than anything I'd felt from merely looking at another species before. It could have been an instinct, a need to add this new camouflage to my repertoire, but I preferred to think I was being true to my upbringing. Here was a new intelligent species. It was my duty to learn its true nature and preserve its accomplishments forever.

It didn't hurt that the Feneden looked every bit as tall, elegant, and dignified as I could have wished. I sincerely hoped they had a digestive system to match.

"How long to D'Dsel?" I asked, lifting my chin with a soft grunt of apology. My head was too heavy to leave on a Human's shoulder for more than an instant, although he hadn't complained. I thought he looked as fascinated as I felt.

"We'll be there tonight." He turned to grin at me. "Do you want me to tell you where we're staying or surprise you again?"

Ignoring the gibe, I stretched a three-fingered hand to cover the image. "As long as it's close to them," I said longingly.

"Hom Cameron? Is that you?" This sudden, deafening coo made me fold down my ears and attempt not to glare over my shoulder at the Human bearing down on us at a near-trot. Paul cleared the tabletop screen with a casual sweep of his fingers. "Fancy meeting you on the *Goddess*. Ah, Fem Esolesy Ki," this greeting somewhat belated, as Harve Tollen blinked in too-obvious surprise at my presence. "I was not aware you ever traveled."

Tollen was a broker, dealing in artifacts of dubious history and even more dubious authenticity. Once he'd discovered Paul and I couldn't be fooled by his fakes, the logical reaction should have been for the Human to give Cameron & Ki Exports a wide berth. There were plenty of other traders of less experience or scruples, especially in the Dump. Instead, Tollen made a pastime of dropping in without warning to show us his latest acquisitions. While he occasionally tried to slip us a replica, as if to test me, he frequently also brought something truly rare and breathtaking. If he hadn't had the manners and smell of a fish dead for several days, I'd have welcomed his visits.

He certainly wasn't welcome now. I struggled to show some tusk. Paul didn't bother with that much courtesy. "We're on vacation, Harve," he said in a no-nonsense voice. "Not business. You can see us back at the office—"

"Me, too!" Tollen said with an expansive wave, showing off the garish colors of his own shirt—as well as the stains under each thick arm. He stole a chair from the next table, apparently as oblivious to the scowls from its inhabitants as to ours, and dropped into it with a thud that probably resounded to the deck below. "What a coincidence."

There were no such things, I remembered, suddenly chilled. This Human, from all we'd learned, was harmless enough if one kept one's nostrils compressed. But he attracted attention like carrion attracted flies. We were on our own out here, helpless in this metal hull, at the mercy of her crew and chance itself. *Attention was something we didn't need.*

My stomachs, contentedly ruminating over lunch until now, chose that moment to object to the aroma now settling over our table like some invisible smog. I had never been able to determine if it was some flaw in this being's physiology or a cologne he mistakenly thought appealing, although I suspected the latter. It could conceivably be a positive sensation to another form, perhaps even my Lanivarian-self. I made a mental note to look into Tollen's client list for clues and increase the ventilation rates in the office before his next visit.

"We have to pack up," Paul said, wiping his eyes surreptitiously. "Not long till we're insystem at Panacia. The crew will want everyone in their staterooms."

"Plenty of time for that. What are they going to do— drag us out? Let me buy you another of—whatever that is." Tollen waved at a passing crewbeing. "This is great," he continued in an irresistible stream of enthusiasm. "You know, I missed your annual party again. The invitation keeps arriving late. Maybe next year, you can remind your staff?"

"Of course, Hom Tollen," I said. I didn't look at Paul, knowing he could read guilt on any of my faces.

Tollen had a square-jawed, reasonably pleasant face, with small green eyes tucked within smooth doubled rolls of flesh that would be the envy of any Ganthor. To web-memory, this variation on the Human theme suggested his origin was Ruductan XIII, one of the fabulously wealthy inner system worlds. Whether attempting to cheat other beings or trying to impress me, Tollen displayed a breadth of knowledge about things ancient that a Human could only gain from many years of study, unnecessary confirmation of his birth. Such facilities were, as yet, still confined to those worlds which could afford them, including Ruductan and her neighbors.

So why was he out here, wasting time pushing his hours-old antique pots on naive Fringe dwellers? I'd never bothered to wonder before.

As I'd worked on moving my lunch to safety within my fourth stomach, the one I used as temporary nondigestive storage—and, truth be told, a handy spot for carrying valuables—Paul had given up the struggle to leave, accepting Tollen's offer of a refill with practiced, if unwilling, courtesy.

"So, where are you staying insystem?" Tollen asked. "C'Chypp or D'Dsel herself?"

"D'Dsel," Paul said, prompting me to attempt to reach his foot under the table. Unfortunately, mine wouldn't fit between the legs of the table and almost became stuck. I wiggled my toes and freed myself, settling for a disgusted flip of an ear. "But," he added smoothly, "you knew that, Harve. The *Goddess* is only licensed for the shipcities of the Hiveworld itself."

"Yeah, yeah," the other Human laughed. "Just trying to catch you, Hom Cameron. Hey, since we're both on vacation, can I call you Paul?"

"Where are you staying, Hom Tollen?" I asked quickly,

reading Paul's likely response to that, I thought, quite correctly. *Besides, it was one way to know where not to travel.*

Tollen waggled one thick finger near my snout. "'Fraid I can't say, Fem Ki. I've been invited to lend my skills as an antiquarian to a project underway by some members of the Rememberers' caste. Their mandibles to my ears only stuff. Sorry."

I wasn't, although I felt an immediate pity for the poor D'Dsellans forced to assume this position. They were a pheromone-influenced society and, to handle Tollen's ambience, would likely have to wear robes with filters over each orifice and breathing spiracle. Still, I was a little curious. Panacians, as a whole, were breathlessly eager to buy any new technology, and just as eager to avoid working alongside the species which produced it. They weren't exactly xenophobic, but communicated so much more effectively with one another, they felt it inefficient to include non-Panacians in their functional groups. They'd only do so if the non-Panacian was essential, which to my mind didn't quite fit anything I knew of Harve Tollen.

Well, I thought to myself, *if he's planning to cheat them out of something valuable, he's in for a surprise*. Everything I knew of that form and its culture ruled out any likelihood of a Human winning their trust. The best one could do, as Paul had over the years, was to establish a reputation as a worthwhile business contact. Even then, as the expression went, Panacians counted their change.

"So you're not really on vacation, Harve," Paul said cheerfully. "Shame. We left work behind us, didn't we, Esolesy Ki? We're after some well-deserved rest and relaxation."

A noisy group of Humans with children in tow passed by, their excited voices shrill enough to flatten my ears to my head once more. More and more passengers were migrating from the lobby now, carryalls and drinks in hand, responding to the polite urgings of the crew. One was coming in our direction—an unexpected but welcome rescue. "Must be heading insystem," I commented, rising to my feet with a rush of my own anticipation. *The Feneden*. I couldn't wait to see one.

"So, planning to meet with the Feneden?" Tollen's oily voice echoed my thoughts so closely I almost dropped my jaw again. "Word is they're looking for trade deals—as well as some border help."

Humiliated, I glowered at Paul as though it was his fault this odious, uninvited Human knew more about the new species than I.

"Their system's out of our profit range," Paul replied, standing himself and offering a hand to his fellow Human. I was fortunately spared the need to echo the gesture of familiarity and lack of weapons, by virtue of a hand too thick to fit comfortably within a Humans' grasp, but weakly showed both tusks. "As I told you, we're here on vacation."

We waved away the crewbeing, who winced theatrically one last time at Paul's belt before smiling and moving to the next group of passengers. "Our thanks for the drinks, Harve," my friend said. "See you back on Minas XII." This last a command delivered in so pleasant a voice even Tollen couldn't take offense.

"Good luck with your treasure hunt," I added, rewarded by the not-quick enough look of denial on Tollen's face.

On the way back to our cabin, a shuffling process involving too many other beings intent on using my feet as carpeting, Paul looked down and winked at me. "Nicely done, Fem Ki," he said with a grin. "Treasure hunting, is he? I think I'll send a message or two concerning the activities of our friend. No reason Harve should keep all this to himself, now, is there?"

"You are a devious being, Paul Cameron," I told him past the glow of two fully revealed—one gorgeously accessorized—tusks.

That my full Lishcyn smile had the effect of opening up our path and so sparing my feet was completely unintentional.

Panacia. A system unaffected by the settlement of the adjacent Fringe by Human and other mining concerns, secure in its civilization and place within the Commonwealth. Three planets of the fifteen circling its swollen star buzzed with life, beginning with Panacia's Hiveworld, the heavily populated D'Dsel, birthplace of Panacia's insectoid intelligence and our vacation paradise.

A roof over our heads would have helped, I grumbled to myself and felt my second stomach agree. I'd been standing guard over our luggage cases long enough to view with alarm the approach of sunset. It was beginning to look entirely possible I'd see the sunrise as well, so I made sure I had a clear line of sight to the eastern horizon to be safe. My personal and extraordinarily powerful lamp hung in a pouch around my neck—no Lishcyn traveled to night-afflicted worlds unprepared.

D'Dsel the magnificent. D'Dsel the utterly confusing. Both aspects lay before me. Once, this had been the home of my web-kin Mixs. She'd preferred the Panacian form and the buildings she designed with her adopted family—not that they'd ever known she was anything but the reincarnation of the famous Mixs of their past, of which there had been a convenient, and not unrelated, number—to the point where even Ersh accepted this as Mixs' chosen work outside the shared tasks of the Web. A significant amount of what I was gazing upon was doubtless Mixs' fault. I experienced the stirrings of distinctly un-Web-like pride in her tampering with this world.

As far as the eye could see, the landscape was urban: towering buildings and elevated roadways, gardens and plazas. Far from a blending of styles, the look was cultivated, almost organic, as if new building designs blossomed in place, spreading out at their edges like invading plants on virgin soil. I could easily spot the results of the innovative Skenkran framing technology Mixs had introduced to her family and this society. Despite fifty years, it was evident in the dizzying height of walkways and unlikely tilt of towers. *She would have been satisfied*, I thought, then shook my head. *No, she'd have changed it all by now*.

For every completed structure, there were as many or more under deconstruction. Panacians favored any technique that allowed them to disassemble as readily as build. In a species which disdained clothing or personal adornment, buildings grew overnight to reveal the current fashion, roads and parkways were defined by the traffic of the previous month, and anyone who thought they knew the place was truly no better off than the bemused tourists flooding from starships that morning.

Including Paul and me. Delighted as I would have been to cycle into my Panacian self and immerse myself in this vibrant, ever-evolving culture, a Human and Lischcyn arrived and should be seen. Being seen in a hotel or similar facility would have been a distinct improvement over being seen waiting in line outside D'Dsel's shipcity's Port Authority office. There had been, apparently, a failure to communicate and our rooms in the All Sapients' District weren't ours at all.

My forked tongue spread in an involuntary yawn. I stayed out here, admiring the scenery, while Paul was in the building behind me for one simple reason. When it came to arguing with bureaucratic nonsense, he had the stomach for it and I assuredly did not.

More fun here anyway, I thought mischievously, watching the line of Humans and other non-native beings duck in unconscious synchrony every time a hoverbot streaked by—the latest with perhaps the width of my finger to spare above the tallest of us. I didn't budge, feeling the wind flutter the tips of my ears and flex the brim of my unfortunate hat—a grimly cheerful token we were supposed to wear until leaving the facility. I knew the automated personal transports were less likely to crash into any of us than the pavement was to liquefy underfoot within the next minute. The hoverbots flitted throughout the sky, behaving alarmingly unlike the aircars these being were used to seeing: which said a great deal, considering how many were from Minas XII. The group ducked again.

Had they ever watched swarms of tiny winged insects above a pond in the afternoon's heat, or seen them clustered within a ball of warmer air, perhaps they would have understood the Panacians' love of this mode of flight.

Or, I thought, gazing at the nervously aggravated Humans nearest me, *they might only see what was strange and therefore potentially dangerous*. It was a protective response I'd long known existed, if couldn't fully comprehend for many years. Ersh had regularly despaired I'd appreciate the need for secrecy it compelled in us, who were arguably the strangest of all.

She would, I told myself with a momentary wish to be that old, unknowing Esen, *be satisfied with me now*.

There was Paul—*well, given the reliability of my vision in the dimming light, it could have been Paul*. He'd appeared out of a door considerably farther down from the one nearest me, implying a lineup inside as well. As he left the archway, I thought I could make out a smile as he shook the appendage of the other being, a Panacian, who escorted him. *A roof*, I thought with satisfaction, *with lights*—this last with a slight tremor of relief.

It was premature, I discovered, once Paul rejoined me. Apparently, we weren't to stay with our fellow passengers and sort this out.

"No rooms. No roof," I repeated, trying not to sound overly upset as I followed his lead. "Most of our luggage—" *my luggage* "—in storage." The Human was unusually silent, merely motioning me toward the second-to-last walkway. "What's going on?" I asked, one hand straying to the bag on my chest. I didn't really need my lamp yet; the various fountains and the pavement itself were self-illuminated, forcing back the sunset-tinged shadows of the buildings and taller vegetation around us. While I could see where to plant my big feet, it had the unpleasant side effect of plunging door arches and side alleys into an almost terrifying gloom.

As if cued, a pair of hoverbots waltzed overhead, momentarily brightening the area around us with their radiance, thrusting back the shadows and letting me see Paul's face clearly for a moment. He flashed me a smile, as though unwilling to show me the expression his face had carried in the darkness.

I moved closer to Paul, avoiding his feet. "Is something wrong?" I asked quietly.

The hoverbots chose that moment to slip skyward, but not before I saw him shake his head. My ears, opened to their fullest, caught the words he breathed: "I can't be sure. I think we're being watched." Louder, so suddenly I winced my head away from him: "Port Authority couldn't explain the mix-up. Doesn't matter. I've found us a better lodging than the one from the travel company."

"Where?" I asked, trying to twist my ears to listen for following footsteps without being obvious.

"There's a residence for the Ambassador caste at the edge of the All Sapients' District. They're willing to put us up— they don't take in regular tourists, but as the founders of Cameron & Ki Exports, we have sufficient reputation to qualify. I've dealt with some shipments for them in the past. They've sent a 'bot to meet us at the end of this lane."

"D'Dsellans don't take aliens into their homes," I protested, now having a comparison to make of something less likely than being hit by a careless hoverbot.

"This place is an exception," Paul said, pulling me forward when my feet seemed inclined to plant themselves. "Something new. They use it as a training area for individuals going offworld, or who will be working directly with other species for prolonged periods. Should be fine. By tomorrow, our other arrangements should be straightened out and we can pick up the rest of our things." He paused. "Aren't you pleased?"

There were two layers of meaning to that, I realized abruptly, attuned to the inflections of his voice. More exactly, he was reminding me there could be two audiences for my response. Paul himself hoped this closer contact with the Panacians would please me—and it did. That he also wanted my enthusiasm for any eavesdropper was far less pleasant.

"It's an amazing opportunity, Paul," I enthused obediently, deciding to keep my last meal in the fourth stomach despite the hollowness of the others. "I'm very pleased. Thrilled, in fact. You could say I'm—"

A discreet tap on the scales of my arm ended what I admitted might have been a little too much enthusiasm, but the sun was definitely down now and my Lishcyn nature was populating the evening shadows with more than sufficient threat for calm. My friend must have known, because he picked up our pace to bring us to a widening in the walkway.

The area we entered was flooded with light, to my intense relief, the reason being a sizable number of purple-carapaced Builders ripping down the front of the building to our left. They were larger and bulkier than other Panacians—since the effective extinction of the warrior caste—and possessed incredible strength in each of their six limbs. Triple-hinged claws in the upper two pairs gripped an assortment of tools, most spouting flames of one color or another. They paid no attention to us, keeping their gleaming, faceted eyes on their task. As I watched, several clambered easily on the shoulders of others, even more repeating with their free claws locked between neighbors' leg segments until the building was coated to its roof in a living scaffold, each component burning away at the existing wall until it appeared to be vanishing before my eyes.

The coordination of effort and ceaseless, glittering movement were breathtaking. Paul tugged on my arm. "Let's go, Es. Our ride's here."

I looked where he was leading me and hesitated. There were three hoverbots suspended an easy step from the ground: one for each of us, and the other for our luggage. It shouldn't have surprised me. Panacians, especially the more old-fashioned families on D'Dsel herself, did not allow more than one individual per 'bot. They told offworlders it was a safety precaution. In truth, it had significantly more to do with the joys of dancing in a swarm while totally anonymous. These calm, practical beings had their wilder side.

Which didn't mean I relished the idea of being separated, especially with Paul's suspicion we were being watched. I made a pretext of brushing construction dust from Paul's shoulder, the proximity allowing me to sense the medallion. I'd need to be in web-form to find him at any distance, an exposure I couldn't risk except as a last resort. But his wearing my gift reassured me enough to climb into the 'bot with only a slightly anxious: "Is it a long trip?"

Paul leaned in, checking what he could see of the hoverbot's minimal controls. Apparently I wasn't the only one concerned about being separated. "A few minutes, unless you have to wait for a spot," he answered almost absently, then turned his head. At such close quarters I could only see him with one eye, and at that could only glimpse the downturned edge of his mouth. "If we get separated, Es, I'll meet you at the usual place. Don't start hunting around on your own. That's how the tourist wound up going in circles until he passed out in a park—"

"And woke up inside the new steam bath," I finished. "I told you that one, remember? The usual place goes for you, too. I'm more concerned about the luggage anyway. I have three new outfits in there."

He smacked my knee companionably. "That explains the extra mass charges."

The door of the hoverbot closed as Paul backed out, the vehicle immediately leaping upward. The Lishcyn, while not the best with heights, was a reasonably good traveler—especially with the internal antigrav working. I studiously avoided looking straight down, instead enjoying the way my 'bot jigged and danced its way into position within the seemingly random flow of aerial traffic. As all appeared identical, I didn't bother trying to guess which one was Paul's. There wasn't much I could do at this point regardless.

The Human had been right. It wasn't a long trip. Almost before I'd indented the cushioning, the 'bot dropped from the sky, sighing to a stop beside a well-lit balcony.

Interesting effect, I thought to myself, cautiously assessing my stomachs. The 'bot opened and the seat pushed me out. Fortunately it hovered sufficiently over the balcony that I wasn't in immediate danger of free-falling, although I might have gripped the offered claws more firmly than was truly polite.

"Welcome, Fem Esolesy Ki of Cameron & Ki Exports,"

this soft, accent-free comspeak from a slender Panacian of, predictably, the Ambassador caste. She was approximately one third the size of the Builders I'd seen, her carapace a shiny, almost iridescent blue flawed only by an unusual patterning etched into the left side of her abdomen. She was standing in the entranceway to the interior of the building. Two more Panacians stood at my side, one whose upper claw I released with a quick apology.

"I am N'Klet, Fem Ki," the speaker continued. "I have been assigned to welcome you. Please let me know how we can help you enjoy our home." She bowed, an incredibly gracious movement involving not one but two body divisions. The other two echoed her.

I returned the bow, an accomplishment for my Lishcyn-self involving a practiced compromise between a moment of semi-graceful balance and a swift recovery before tipping completely over. "I wish all honor to your home, N'Klet. Is my partner here yet? Hom Cameron?"

Another spoke, with an equally melodious voice. I began to feel like a rusty servo by comparison. "I am C'Tlas, Fem Ki. I have been assigned to your care. Hom Cameron is about to arrive, Fem Ki. We would ask you to move farther into the room now."

That mildly delivered advice seemed wise to follow—I wasn't worried about being swept from the railless balcony by the hoverbots dropping from the heavens, but if Paul was launched from his seat as abruptly as I'd been, the willing claws waiting to catch him could use my absence. I followed C'Tlas from the balcony.

I'd caught the merest glimpse of the exterior of this building, but enough to notice it was taller than most and unusually old. One didn't ask questions about architecture except of the creators of an individual building—it was considered deeply offensive to discuss art without the artist present, leading, I recalled from Mixs' memories, to some interesting semantic twists when debating what to do with the structures of deceased Builders. Perhaps that was where the Panacian belief in reincarnation in each generation had originated. Many of those newly emerged (or, in Mixs' case, those pretending to be new) assumed the name of a famous ancestor of their family, in this culture thus gaining both the identity and the accomplishments of that individual.

It was certainly linked to the presence of the "old Queen," the mummified corpse kept in the basement of every household to figuratively represent the rights and opinions of previous generations. On other Panacian worlds, the old queen was a statuette, often crafted in the likeness of an exalted forebear. On D'Dsel herself, the old queen was literally that.

Still, this building's age was unusual. I recognized the style as being in use over a hundred planet years ago. By Panacian standards, did this mean the school had been housed in what passed for a slum? *Or*, I suddenly concluded with an inner grin, *was this how the Ambassador caste dealt with the confusion of aliens?* It had to be difficult to host meetings when your guests couldn't recognize the building from visit to visit. If my supposition was correct, the Ambassador caste had made some significant advances in dealing with other cultures since my last visit. I was impressed. Of course, that's what they'd been designed to do, from their smaller, starship-sized bodies to the suppleness of their vocal apparatus and quick, adaptive minds. Panacians were as boldly experimental with themselves as with their living space.

This particular living space was just as unique. Compliments were acceptable, if properly phrased. "This is most considerate of your guests, C'Tlas," I said warmly, admiring the huge room with its assortment of furniture. It wasn't pretty, or well-matched. In fact, I doubted there were two pieces of furniture from the same planet, let alone the same manufacturer. But, at a glance, there was something worth sitting, lying, oozing, or squatting on for almost every species known to the Commonwealth. Those missing were the ones who couldn't have breathed the atmosphere here anyway—a practical and perfectly logical omission.

"I serve the Hive in all things," C'Tlas murmured in a pleased tone. "There are sleeping accommodations through the passageway, Fem Ki. Food preparation," she paused as if to frame a delicate topic, "and other biological needs are in different areas. All is within easy reach. Should you require anything we have not provided, you need only ask."

"Exceptional courtesy," this from Paul, whose gray eyes found me before looking around the room. I flashed a tusk at him as the Human entered with N'Klet, who must be his assigned guide, the remaining D'Dsellan in their wake carrying our few bits of luggage.

"Hom Cameron. Fem Ki," said N'Klet. "Welcome to the School of Alien Etiquette. I express the extreme delight of our Queen and family that you so kindly accepted our invitation. Our Queen also wishes me to thank you for your discretion in this important matter."

Invitation? I felt my ears try to touch the ceiling. *Discretion?* It was amazing how two words could so dramatically change one's perception of certain recent events. I looked over at Paul, suddenly convinced I'd been thoroughly manipulated into leaving my work, coming to this place, and becoming involved in something yet to be revealed to me by the one being who knew me well enough to succeed.

A vacation, indeed.

Elsewhere

"FOR once, I agree with Kearn. You can't leave now." Timri folded her hands together neatly as she spoke; she'd explained the nervous habit years ago, in a bar they'd both forgotten, on a night they'd said too much to each other for comfort. She'd wanted to fit in to her father's culture, which frowned on personal excesses such as the expressive hand gesturing of her mother's upbringing. That culture had also frowned on military service, making it necessary for Timri to choose between planet and parent. The planet may have won, but the habit remained decades later.

"It's not up for debate, Timri," Lefebvre replied, unsurprised by her reaction. Sas hadn't been impressed either. *Enjoy yourselves*, he thought, inclined to be amused. *Misery loves company.*

Lefebvre regretted the impulse to stop by the comp station and say good-bye. He could have left, been away for days, and returned before most of the crew, including Timri, noticed—particularly while the *Russell III* sat in the shipcity. They'd become used to his solitary ways, to a captain who wandered through the bridge when it suited him, a physical presence on the ship by virtue of a closed door when it didn't.

"I'll make you a bet," Lefebvre announced impulsively, leaning back on the doorframe with his arms folded. He was out of uniform, barely, having chosen to pull on a nondescript pair of spacer overalls—the type worn by independent traders and used for rough work by almost everyone aboard this ship. If the crew assumed it was so he could cruise the shipcity bars, that was fine by him. "I'll make you a bet," he repeated. "If anything comes up—anything at all—worth finding while I'm gone, I'll punch through that promotion you've been after." He watched the calculating gleam appear in Timri's dark eyes. They both knew Kearn's tendency to sit on promotions in case the encouragement prompted a crewbeing to leave his ship for greener pastures. "He's never going to okay it," Lefebvre reminded her.

"And if nothing comes up?"

His smile changed his face. It should have made it warmer, but somehow the expression turned the lines around eyes and mouth into something dark and bitter, "Then nothing's changed or changes—which is exactly what's going to happen while I take my two days off this scow. You really should try it, Timri. You won't miss a thing."

Timri turned her back to him, her hands lifting to the boards. "I don't intend to."

Lefebvre walked away, a small carryroll in his right hand, and prepared to leave the *Russ'*. As he did, he said to himself: "Neither do I."

9 : School Morning; School Afternoon

PAUL'S obsession with the courier pouch—indeed everything about that final day on Minas XII—had finally started to make sense. *Well*, I admitted, *it didn't so much make sense as it lent itself to a conclusion.*

There had been something for him in the pouch. Something he hadn't wanted anyone else to find.

Not even me.

"More furrit slices, Fem Ki?"

I was thinking furiously, trying to follow what threads I had, and nodded absentmindedly until furrit slices built to a towering height on my platter and I realized what I'd done. "Forgive me, C'Tlas. I wasn't paying attention."

"I'll bring a larger platter," she offered.

I squinted down at the pile of orange-red fruit and sighed. "Thank you," I said, resigned to having to eat more than anyone should. Furrits were tasty enough; they just took a long time in the third stomach of this form—seriously cramping my room for dessert.

What did Paul want me to figure out? What were we doing here? Alone while C'Tlas hunted a way to keep my juicy mountain tidy, I turned my attention back to these and other questions.

There had been no clues during our evening here. The Panacians had swept my Human and me on a tour of their school, introducing us to what had to be every member of this novel extended family with the exception of its core:

the Queen. There had to be one—no cohesive unit of Panacians, closely related or not, functioned without the guiding pheromones of their monarch. Neither Paul nor I required an explanation; meeting the Queen was out of the question. Access to Her Radiance was restricted even among her family.

The introductions themselves had been informative. We shared this portion of the building with a surprisingly small group: thirty-six females of assorted ages, including the three who had greeted us, and six adolescent drones who appeared to be contentedly confined to the kitchen amid absorbent B'Bklar plants—presumably to protect them in the event of pheromonal enticements from other houses. None had been introduced as Her Glory or Sec-ag, those titles reserved for those of accomplishments worthy of note outside the household. Since Panacians were not a humble species, this suggested none of that rank were present at the school—or willing to be known to us. Another oddity to add to a growing list about this place.

Apt students, beyond any doubt. The exchange of pleasantries had been in immaculate comspeak, with exquisitely perfect gestures appropriate to each of our species. While mimicking a Human handshake was typically straightforward for any being with limbs, I had to give them credit for finding a way to flash a tusk. At first, I'd assumed the Panacians had something stuck behind one of their food-handling palps, making it necessary to protrude that palp in my direction. *Most thoughtful*, I thought approvingly—once I'd realized they were attempting to smile at me rather than prying food from their mandibles—and smiled back. Multiple exterior mouth parts were tricky things to read.

In turn, I had the distinct feeling we were an assignment—an alien culture field trip conveniently brought to the students. While I didn't mind, I knew that wasn't why Paul had brought us here.

Opportunity to question my partner about this didn't arise. One moment we were surrounded by groups of curious Panacians, the next we'd been adroitly separated so Paul could be led to his quarters and I to mine. There was a wealth of meaning in the look he tossed back at me, which probably would have been helpful had I interpreted more from it than the usual, "*behave*."

Advice I'd taken, I nodded to myself, tossing a handful of furrit into my mouth and chewing slowly. I'd behaved, weaving my way among beds of all shapes and sizes to the box of real grass they'd prepared for me, although momentarily tempted by a gently bubbling bowl of yellow ooze I knew was the way to really sleep if you happened to be a Whirtle. I'd been unable to stop myself from at least leaning on a spectacular post bed designed for a Skenkran. The hangers for those immense clawed feet looked perfect for my version of that form.

But I'd resisted all temptation to experiment, gaining a good sleep. Now, breakfasting alone except for the helpful services of C'Tlas, I was doing my best to decipher the rapid and mysterious events that had brought these furrits and my shaggy-scaled self to this table.

Paul had itemized most while we were on the *Galaxy Goddess*. I spread furrits out as markers: one for the Ganthor, one for Chase's confrontation with the Tly, an especially thick slice for the pouch of mail and Paul's reaction to it. A second row held a piece for the Feneden and one for the Ambassador School.

Thoughtfully, and slowly, I added one more, representing Paul's gift.

I had, I decided, gazing at the array of fruit for a lengthy and profound moment of deep contemplation, *made a mess of my breakfast*.

To hide the evidence, I began capturing the slippery things and popping them between my teeth as quickly as possible, ears aimed back to listen for the soft footfalls of my hostess. I chomped down on Paul's mail and the Ambassador School. *They might go together*, I told myself pensively. Maybe he'd arranged this, and the mail was confirmation. Maybe it was something to help us get closer to the Feneden, since only the Panacian Ambassador caste would deal with aliens. Then, secrecy was understandable. We had many business rivals, and I couldn't imagine a more tempting morsel to dangle before them.

Too tempting. Cameron & Ki Exports were in the business of staying too small to notice, not trying to corner a spectacular new market.

I added the Ganthor and Tly pieces to my mouthful, suspecting—as did Paul—that those two were somehow related, and not to our benefit. But neither seemed to matter here and now. I swallowed.

I chewed on the Feneden's piece. There was a mystery I sincerely hoped would start resolving itself today. The mere thought of their existence, possibly in this same building, though our hostesses hadn't so much as hinted at that, was enough to cost me my appetite.

Which left Paul's gift forlorn and alone on the table. Gingerly, I put the furrit slice back on the corner of my platter. *There were questions*, I admitted to myself, *I wasn't ready to ask.*

After breakfast, the School of Alien Etiquette learned something they apparently hadn't thought to ask about the Lishcyn. That was all right. *I hadn't known either.*

"You needn't apologize," I kept saying faintly, leaning on a pair of my deceptively fragile-looking hostesses. "I'm the one who should—"

"What happened?" This alarmed cry came from my Human, rushing toward our little procession with N'Klet at his side. He looked considerably more flushed than usual, and wore a robe similar to the one draped around my narrow shoulders, although it was a smaller size. "What's wrong?"

"Fem Ki didn't react well to the steam bath," C'Tlas said quickly as Paul reached us and, for some unknown reason, thought it useful to peel back the lid of my nearer eye and peer into it. My reflex blink was powerful enough to pinch his fingers.

I attempted a toothy smile. "I reacted too well to the steam bath," I corrected, trying to lighten the Panacians' mood of incipient panic. Several were finding it necessary to stop in their tracks and wrap their upper limbs about their thoraxes, a bit extreme, given the object of their grief was up on two feet and essentially mobile. "I'm a little wobbly, that's all."

"Your—ah—stomachs?" Paul asked, the corners of his lips not quite rising. He looked down at my rotund front as if to diagnose me by sight.

"They're fine," I replied with dignity. My Lishcyn-self didn't always embarrass itself that way, and I saw no reason for him to further concern our hostesses. "The bath was a little too warm for me."

C'Tlas took it upon herself to grab my arm firmly, give it a shake, and tell Paul her version: "Fem Ki lost consciousness and slipped beneath the surface. She might have drowned had it not been for those watching. We had to drain the bath to save her."

There was a sharpness to Paul's sudden look at me. He knew if my life was seriously threatened in a form, I couldn't help but cycle from it into something safer or into my web-self.

I winked at him. "It was a very—comfortable—unconsciousness," I explained, grateful this form couldn't blush. The hot water and bubbly steam had created an interesting mix of semisleep and euphoric fantasy, a state completely enthralling to my Lishcyn-self. The Panacians had not found me a cooperative or easy body to rescue. "I've tried to explain to these dear beings: Lishcyns have amphibious heritage. I can doze underwater for some time. Right, Paul?"

His brows lifted, gray-eyed gaze considering me. "Let's avoid the steam baths from now on, Esolesy Ki," my friend suggested. "I'll take over." This was directed to the pair of Panacians bravely trying to take some of my weight on their bent backs, not having shoulders of their own. The Human muttered something dire about diets under his breath as he began helping me to my sleeping quarters. I pretended not to hear. The Panacians remained huddled in a group, discussing something among themselves, providing the first chance we'd had to talk in reasonable privacy since arriving on Panacia.

"This so-called vacation of ours: you set it up to get me here—to meet the Fenedens—didn't you?" I whispered.

His voice was somewhat strained, but improved once I took back most of my weight. Although I was feeling better by the moment, floating had been ever-so-much easier. *And those steamy, seductive bubbles under my scales.* I caught myself drifting again and made myself turn an ear to catch his reply: "—both, actually," he was saying, a wry note of humor coming through. "I knew you'd want to meet them. It was intended to be the highlight of our holiday— but you really didn't help me there. Still, it got us here, where it seems your skills are very much needed, old friend."

"For what? Not trade." The Panacians were hurrying to catch up to us. We didn't have much time.

"I expected to have some trouble arranging a meeting with the Feneden—every trader in this Sector is lining up— but we were granted one almost immediately. Turns out the Fenedens are causing our hostesses some translation problems and the Panacians were looking for some discreet assistance. I don't have details," Paul said quickly, "not yet. But you know how Panacians prefer to deal with knowns— especially when it involves offworld contacts. That's us, apparently. Or me. You haven't been here before, remember?" *Of course I had*, I almost protested, then realized with a start it had been not just another time, but another form. *Sometimes*, I thought to myself, *that sort of thing confused even a perfect memory*.

I shook off the lingering sensations of the steam bath, removing my arm from Paul's shoulder. The Human straightened with an unnecessarily fervent groan of relief. I ignored him, turning in time to almost collide with my six rescuers.

"You have recovered, Fem Ki!" observed C'Tlas. My hearing discerned a quivering under the words, as though the breath she had drawn through her thoracic spiracles to speak had shuddered in passing. I was fully aware her concern was based on her responsibility to the Hive for my care. It was no less real or personal.

"Due to your swift action on my behalf, C'Tlas," I returned, doing my best to bow and feeling Paul grab one arm just as I recognized I wasn't yet as stable as I'd thought. "My thanks."

"And mine," Paul added, patting me heartily on the shoulder once I was safely upright. "I couldn't imagine succeeding in any endeavor without my partner. Especially," he stressed, "anything that involved understanding a new species."

A message for me, I wondered, *or a reminder to the Panacians to keep my necessary self away from household hazards such as alluring bubbles?*

The steambath episode was another of those experiences I promised myself I'd repeat in, oh, another century. There were some things one really should be mature to appreciate, most of these, I'd found, included intoxication and corresponding lapses in judgment. I was capable of the latter on my own.

Such as this one. Lishcyns don't sneak very well, so I was using bold "I belong here" body language as I traveled the deserted hall. Approximately five steps from my assigned quarters, I'd recognized this as one of those brilliant impulses that entitled Paul to use his "behave" look so often.

Not that it mattered, once I realized the door had somehow locked itself behind me.

With a fatalistic shrug, I continued on my way, remembering the requisite turns without difficulty, until I reached the area with lifts to the other floors of the School. The Panacians may have thought to fool us during the tour into thinking we'd seen it all, but I'd noticed we'd been kept to three levels and to lifts without settings to reach anywhere else in the building.

I didn't bother hunting for signs of automated surveillance. Panacians in general abhorred the practice, and D'Dsellans were the most traditional of them all. A reasonable prejudice, since individual Panacians left scent trails wherever they went, leaving abundant information on mood and health for any other Panacian who might be interested. If they wished to know more about your actions, they simply stayed with you.

Of course, by making it virtually impossible to travel any distance on their world without using preprogrammed hoverbots—which did have abundant internal and external sensors in the name of safety—they kept track of visitor movements fairly easily. It was only within their homes and buildings that alien biology allowed concealment, hence the rarity of invitations to visit. Mixs-memory informed me that the oft-used excuse of not liking the physical habits of the messier sort of aliens, such as Humans, was really a way to avoid having to interpret beings who couldn't share their mood with every step.

In a very real sense, I thought, idly tapping a tusk with one finger while considering which lift to try first, *the predominantly Human Commonwealth and its associated non-Human species failed to enter the true awareness of Panacians*. Perhaps the new caste, the Ambassadors, interacted with non-Panacians with a belief in their existence. I knew, from my experiences and those shared by Mixs, that the vast majority on D'Dsel and the other heavily-populated worlds of this system were convinced alien intelligences were somehow nonbiological. I'd read learned papers, naturally kept species-private, postulating everything from non-Panacians being some type of machine to an exhaustive theory that others were from another dimensional reality, only partially impinging on this one. *A personal favorite*.

It was a tribute to their ability to learn and mimic polite behavior that so many other species viewed Panacians as friendly and approachable. Truth be told, it didn't matter in everyday life whether the average Panacian believed in the rest of the universe or not. *I frequently*, I chuckled to myself, *had my own doubts*.

I'd chosen correctly. The door of the third to last lift—there were six in a row—sighed open at my touch, revealing a panel of controls much more extensive than the ones we'd used last night.

Not down, I thought. The lowermost floors would be the Queen's chambers—close to the street level so her offspring could easily be moved by ground transport to one of the mass emergence areas when the time came. There would be controlled air-locks at every entrance from her area, intended to seal in and concentrate her pheromones. These would freely move throughout this building and be packaged for sending by hoverbot or courier to any of her family not within reach. This included starships, making the few unfortunate Panacians serving the Hive offworld prone to mental and emotional stress when they received pheromonal information at inappropriate moments and, worse, arrived home to be months out of sync with their Queen anyway.

What would be inappropriate and potentially dangerous, I reminded myself, *would be any attempt to approach the Queen unless invited and escorted.*

The lift's settings offered eighty-one choices. From my memory of the exterior—from that regrettably brief glance as I'd arrived by hoverbot—the School of Alien Etiquette was located eighteen down from the topmost. So I was on the sixty-third floor. What we'd been shown as the remainder of the School extended two floors below me.

If I assumed everything below that was the Queen's territory—better to overestimate than risk annoying our charming hostesses—that left an intriguing eighteen floors above me to explore.

I used a dessert fork I'd saved from lunch to press the indented button for the top floor, on the principle that running downstairs would be easier if I were caught. Not that every Panacian building contained stairs—some designs incorporated intestinelike slides I rather enjoyed, depending on my form.

The lift headed upward obediently, and I assumed a carefully neutral expression. My present smile, however, warmly intended, was no way to start a conversation with strangers.

I also, somewhat belatedly, began practicing my greeting to my very first, completely new aliens.

A shame, I would realize later, *that I was wrong.*

Elsewhere

IN Lefebvre's experience, Port Authority, regardless of species, world, or the size of the crisis, tended to behave in a manner reminiscent of a Human staring at his or her own navel, awaiting divine revelation—especially when confronted with credentials that, in theory and by treaty, gave outsystem officials access to their records.

The D'Dsellans were no exception.

Lefebvre stifled a yawn, then sat straighter. *Finally.* There was movement behind the frosted door panels: two figures walking past in silhouette, pausing as though trying to see him in the dimly lit and classically unwelcoming waiting room, before limbs reached for a handle. He slouched back down as their shadows faded again, the two apparently deciding actually talking to him in person was a bad idea.

His fingers slipped into the pocket of his coat, pushing deeper within its emptiness until he could feel the inner seam, reaching along that until he touched the other pocket concealed within it. His key was there, safe, ready for use. All he needed was a lock. Which required some cooperation from the other side of those doors.

"Captain Lefebvre?" Another Human had entered the waiting room through the same entrance he'd used, from outside. No Port Jelly uniform here. This individual wore inner system fashions, the type that meant cost was not an issue in his life. They didn't suit him, Lefebvre judged, despite excellent tailoring. The stranger was lean, weathered, with an air of no-nonsense competence; Lefebvre could more easily picture him in a faded pair of spacer coveralls like his, working on an engine—certainly a better match for the faded spacer tan of face and hands. The Human's eyes were keen and his expression that of someone who didn't intend to waste his own precious time. "Sandner," he introduced himself. "Councillor Sandner from Inhaven Prime. What's this about Paul Ragem?"

Sandner. Lefebvre recognized the name, keeping any reaction from his face: one of the committee who'd granted the *Russell III* access to this sector, and not just any member. Kearn had railed for some time about how the Inhaven representative had sabotaged their funding, as well as almost skewing the vote against them. *What was he doing here?* "I'm conducting research," Lefebvre said, deliberately keeping his tone and bearing official, despite the disadvantage of having been caught seated and in obviously nonregulation garb. "As I believe you are aware is the mandate of the *Russell III* and her crew, sir."

"And that research includes sending Port Authority scrambling after genetic records for a dead Human? From a three-day visit, fifty years ago? Do you realize what a waste of resources and time this represents? Let alone—" Sandner, to Lefebvre's surprise, stopped his almost passionate tirade and sat abruptly, looking like a parent confronted by his child's misdeeds at school and a bit embarrassed by it all. "Captain, forgive my outburst. This isn't your fault. I suspected Kearn was off in his own dreamworld, but this—this is simply crazy. Don't you agree?"

Lefebvre's patroller instincts were sending chills down his spine. "It's not my place to question orders, Councillor Sandner," he answered evenly, "only to follow them to the best of my ability. As I was attempting to do here. Am I to assume you have asked D'Dsel's Port Authority not to respond to our request? Is this what I should report to my Project Leader?"

Sandner's startled look was perfect, Lefebvre thought, *perhaps too perfect.* "I have nothing to do with law enforcement in the shipcity," the Councillor said. "If you are experiencing problems, I suggest you take them up with Sec-ag T'Pleck. Her Glory is the System Coordinator for Panacia's Port Authority."

"But you don't support this line of inquiry, sir," Lefebvre dared press the other. "Isn't that why you're here? To persuade the Project Leader to abandon his search?"

"Talk to Kearn about his nonsense? I wouldn't waste a minute on it." Sandner's thin lips stretched into an outright grin. He leaned forward with a conspiratorial wink. "I'm here to meet the Feneden."

"The Feneden." At Lefebvre's blank look, Sandner drew back as if affronted.

"Does Kearn have the newsmags censored on your scow, Captain?" this with what seemed sincere indignation. "Of course, the Feneden! First Contact, Lefebvre! They've come here to meet with the Commonwealth as well as investigate trade possibilities. Councillors from all the affected regions are coming to D'Dsel this week for talks. Where have you been?"

"I'm aware of the existence of the Feneden, Councillor. They are hardly my concern at the moment." Lefebvre gestured to the frosted doors. "Getting the cooperation your committee promised us in our search— that's my concern."

"And that search has somehow expanded to include a dead Human? Good thing Kearn didn't try that on the Committee." Sandner appeared to come to some decision. He stood again, and Lefebvre politely followed suit. "I'd wish you luck in your efforts, Captain, but I still believe the entire business a waste."

"Assuming for a moment it wasn't a waste, sir, where would you look?" Lefebvre asked, suddenly curious if he'd get an answer. Sandner wasn't a typical politician. Nor was Sandner's appraising gaze that of someone as disinterested as he made himself appear to be. "Where would I look—for Kearn's monster? As I tried to tell him, the Kraal were involved up to their tattooed necks. There's where your answers are, although it's likely we'll all be long dead before that bunch admits any involvement." Sandner gave a hearty laugh. "If then."

"And Ragem?"

The laugh stopped. "Persistent, aren't you?"

"I have my orders, sir," Lefebvre said, careful to add a tinge of resignation to his voice.

"Then you'll need permission to break the quarantine on Artos, along with a shovel and a lifetime, Captain, if you expect to find what's left of Paul Ragem—assuming the bone hunters haven't found him first and cemented him to an altar. I can't help you there. Perhaps divine intervention?" Sandner paused. "Tell me. What possible interest can finding Ragem's corpse be to Kearn? Wasn't the poor man slandered enough? Think of his family, if nothing else.

Careful, Lefebvre told himself, definitely wary of underestimating this being. "I'm sure it is not Project Leader Kearn's intention to reopen old wounds, Councillor. Perhaps he has some doubts about the veracity of that—slander—sir."

Sandner looked startled. Lefebvre held his breath, but instead of replying, Sandner said: "Yes, Tomas?" to another Human who'd opened the door and stood waiting to be noticed, a chauffeur by the look of him.

"You asked to be reminded of your meeting, Councillor," Tomas replied. He had a bright, friendly face, the sort that didn't so much suggest intellect as a certain practical knowledge about the world. His red hair looked to have never seen a brush. Still, Lefebvre committed the face and voice to memory, a bit of his patrol training he'd found useful many times.

"Yes, yes. Thanks, Tomas. Pleasure meeting you, Captain Lefebvre," he said with a firm handshake. Rather than letting go immediately, Sandner's grip tightened momentarily as if to underscore what he said next. "You can transfer off that madman's ship, you know. Officers of your ability have—options. Don't waste your talents chasing fairy tales and ghosts."

"Yes, sir. Thank you."

Lefebvre sat back down, watching the door close to leave him alone again in D'Dsel's Port Authority waiting room.

A high level hint to stop looking for Ragem?

Time he looked even harder.

10: School Afternoon

THE lift doors opened. After checking to make sure my best formal silks weren't bunched at the waist again, I took a bold step forward into a promisingly ornate lobby area, ready to make first contact with a new species.

Had anyone else been there, it would have been a perfect entrance.

I looked around almost frantically, all the nerve and calm I'd managed to develop on the ride up here spoiled by the anticlimax.

The lobby spread into four broad, tiled corridors from where I stood, each illuminated in differing intensity as if representing dawn, midmorning, noon, and dusk. It was an interesting conceit and one I didn't remember in a Panacian design before. Still, I thought, it had been fifty years since I'd truly refreshed my knowledge of this culture. Images and reports were nothing compared to being here, as Paul frequently reminded me.

Wherever here *was.*

There were only two lift doors set into the wall behind me, implying—as I'd guessed—some limitations on who could reach this floor. There was a mirrored surface between them, allowing me to admire the fall of harvest-gold silk around my thick legs, generous slits in the fabric showing a decidedly handsome patterning of scales. I wore a bag, unwilling to be without my light, but it was finely beaded with gold thread to coordinate. Just the touch to complete the look of Esen, diplomat-at-large.

Had there been any beings to diplomat with, I grumbled to myself.

It had taken all of my daring to get this far. *It wasn't fair*. At this rate, Paul would step out of the next lift, complete with a swarm of politely offended D'Dsellans, and all I'd have to show for my efforts would be a long, dreary round of apologies.

I flicked my ears toward the nearest corridor. *Perhaps*, I thought, *the Feneden were down there, a little bored, wishing for company. Esen-type company.*

I'd remember that thought later.

I chose the farthest, and brightest, corridor to explore first, careful not to flap my feet on the tiles, talking to myself as I went about the odds of being caught, the odds of being embarrassed, and the odds of causing the poor beings' hearts—or whatever—to fail at the sight of my current form. I ignored myself, driven by a need to learn greater than any curiosity I'd known before.

Of course, they weren't in the nice, safely bright corridor. All I found were locked doors and a series of stands displaying holos of various buildings—likely those standing on this site in the days before the present structure's novel permanence. I retraced my steps and considered my remaining choices.

Gritting my tusks, I picked the dusk-lit corridor for my next exploration, on a whim that said anything I wanted was likely to make itself difficult to obtain. It wasn't easy to convince my Lishcyn-self that keeping my fingers comfortingly on the bag containing my lamp was any substitute for hauling the thing out and sending its broad beam into every dark corner. *Which would*, I scolded myself, *be a touch conspicuous*.

I shivered as I walked, judging this a psychological weakness of this form as it responded with nervous tension to the meager lighting, then realizing it was because the corridor was definitely growing colder with each step I took. I thought wistfully of the hagra-hair cloak in my luggage back at the shipcity and shivered even more.

Six locked doors. More stands with holos. I made myself try one more handle, poised to hurry back to the beckoning glow of light and warmth that marked the lobby and lifts.

The door opened.

So did the door to one of the lifts.

Estimating it would take a fit and motivated Human at least five seconds to run this far—considerably more if he picked the wrong corridor—I stepped casually inside my door.

Thankfully, the light was brighter here, allowing me to see quite clearly. My breath condensed in bursts as it left my nostrils, falling to either side of my snout. I was standing within a large room, its walls and ceiling stroked with ocean colors, its floor carpeted in a slimy, almost moist green substance that gave beneath my webbed toes, releasing a mintlike scent when I took an involuntary step forward. There was furniture, but it hung from varicolored straps attached to the ceiling, suspended at differing levels as though floating in midair.

I stared at the Feneden. Three of them reclined in swinglike chairs, rocking gently as they gazed back at me. Two others stood on either side of a hanging table, as though I'd interrupted a game they'd been playing with small figures spaced over its surface.

The image Paul had found hadn't done them justice. They were uniformly tall and slender, though well within the range of Human sizes. Like Humans, they possessed five-fingered hands, with opposable thumbs. One took a step toward me, a bare, five-toed foot showing briefly beneath the flowing robes. The robes hadn't been well-represented either. Although unornanented and simple, seen this close they had a subtle shimmer, like moonlight on water, and ranged in color from midnight blue to a deep russet.

By many standards, including mine, the Feneden needed no ornamentation, being beautiful beyond description. Even motionless, they exuded grace and elegance. I felt clumsy, this solid form a weight I'd never noticed before.

The nearest one spoke, a torrent of predictably liquid and lovely sounds that meant absolutely nothing to me. I had to hold my jaw in place, stunned by the realization I didn't know their language. I didn't know anything about them.

They were—*new*.

"Psst."

Four seconds. I bent one ear back at Paul, the rest of my attention on the Feneden standing before me. That being cooperatively fell silent, watching me out of her wide-set, slanted eyes. The sex was a supposition on my part, but the upper portion of her robe curved out as if flowing over generous mammary organs, while two of the other Feneden were flatter chested and somewhat larger.

Her eyes were fascinating, a central black pupil surrounded by a warm gold-and-black iris. A sudden red flash across her eyes startled me, then I realized with wonder it had been a nictitating membrane, a third and brightly-colored eyelid blinking from the inside corner of each eye to the outside. My first impression was that the other facial features were indistinguishable from Human standard, then I noticed the nostrils flaring slightly outward at their bases with each inhalation, the lower skin not attached to the cheek.

What I'd taken for hair was a sort of cilia, a thick, soft growth covering the scalp and neck, forming a living collar. Delicate waves passed through the cilia this way and that, producing a rhythmic effect as though a breeze played with grasses in a field. The cilia themselves were a deep red-brown, striking against the paleness of the skin. The skin itself was almost translucent, the blue-white of old ice, with a faintly pebbled texture as though scaled beneath the surface.

Still, close enough in appearance to the being breathing down my neck to be conceivably mistaken as one of his kind. "I found the Feneden," I told him breathlessly.

My somewhat unnecessary announcement brought forth another round of speech from the Feneden who had seemingly appointed herself as hostess. Or defender. I wasn't about to jump to conclusions. The other four had remained exactly where they were and as they were, silent spectators.

The stream of words, rich with upward inflections, began to sound tantalizingly familiar, which wasn't surprising given that I held hundreds of thousands of languages in web-memory. Not a tongue I knew, but similar to several. I concentrated, striving to pull together a relevant syntax, some commonality. After a few more sentences, the Feneden quieted and stood looking at me. I looked helplessly back.

"Paul Cameron." Having named himself, with a palm on his chest, the Human put one hand on my shoulder. "Esolesy Ki." He then moved his hand very slightly in the direction of the Feneden.

Great, I thought in frustration.

This could take a while.

It didn't take as long as I'd feared, primarily because the Panacians hadn't been far behind Paul. C'Tlas and N'Klet arrived sometime after our labored introductions, and before we'd really settled the potential confusion of whether Paul and I were different species or members of the same one.

"Fem Anisco," N'Klet said, bowing deeply at the one Feneden who'd continued her efforts to communicate with us. "Fem Ki, Hom Cameron" this with equally deep bows. *So we were supposed to find our way here*, I concluded, looking at Paul whose tiny nod confirmed he'd seen it. It was nice not to be in the wrong, especially when I was reasonably certain I had been.

Named, the Feneden before me seemed much more of an individual. *Anisco*, I repeated to myself, glancing from her to the other four. Despite the impression of uniformity due to the cilia, which was identical on all of them as far as I could tell, there were significant differences in their facial features—again, a trait closer to Human than many other humanoid species. I would have to compare notes with Paul later to see what his species-specific reactions had been.

With the arrival and greeting of N'Klet, another, presumably male, Feneden slipped down from his swing chair and went to what looked like a storage case, also hanging free. I poked my toes surreptitiously into the floor covering, wondering if there was a prohibition against touching the stuff with anything but feet, or if it was simply a matter of protecting the furniture from the dampness.

The case held an unfamiliar device the Feneden gave to Anisco, who took it and slung it by a strap from one shoulder. She then detached a small, boxlike piece to offer me, keeping another, identical piece, poised near her lips. She waited.

I'd stopped shivering, having needed to dump energy as body heat. This close to the Feneden, I had to resist the instinct to change to web-form and nip off a portion of cilia— or anything else in reach, for that matter. The urge to acquire their genetic makeup was incredibly strong. *Why?* I wondered suddenly, even as I accepted my share of the device.

"Hold it to your ear, Fem Ki," N'Klet advised, two limbs upraised as though eager to insure I followed her directions immediately. "They have assembled a mechanical correlation between their language and comspeak. It isn't ideal, but the Commonwealth linguists have been most impressed." She gave a most uncharacteristic sigh, her faceted eyes glinting as she looked back at the Feneden. "The Feneden are having some—difficulty—learning comspeak." She left unsaid, but understood, that the Commonwealth linguists were feverishly working to decipher the Feneden tongue.

Paul discreetly adjusted the recorder he carried in one hand, something he took everywhere he traveled in order to bring me the details I craved about distant places and beings. Since I was here, I assumed this recording was either for his own curiosity or so he could argue with me about some aspect of my conduct later.

I raised the Feneden's gadget, keeping it safely distant from my sensitive ear, then nodded to Anisco in hopes the gesture would be understood.

Her lips uttered her language, while out of the machine, separated by only the slightest of pauses, came: "What are you?" in a flat, mechanical voice. She transferred the device to her ear and nodded to me.

An improvement over "me Es, you Anisco," I decided,

still frustrated by the slowness of this interface. Questions boiled up in me, questions I had no idea if I could or should ask.

Then, the truth hit me. *I was reacting like an ephemeral,* I realized with a sinking feeling, *forgetting all that I was, how I was supposed to be.* This wasn't how a web-being met a new species. When I'd come here, it should have been to watch unobserved, to secretly collect all the information I could about them, to have the protection of knowledge before any direct interaction. Now I was the focus of their attention—they were learning about me as quickly as I about them. I identified the feeling beginning to twist my insides.

Vulnerability.

Which was nonsense, I scolded myself, flipping one ear to catch the reassuring sounds of Paul's steady breathing to one side, accelerated slightly with excitement. To prove it, I brought the translator to my lips and said slowly: "I am called a Lishcyn, Fem Anisco. My species is from a system very distant from yours and this one."

Eyelids flashed red, twice. "Why are you here, Lishcyn?"

I put my hand on Paul's shoulder. "We are interested in trade with your world."

She didn't understand, I concluded from the way she reached for the main part of her machine and ran her fingers over some controls. Then she brought the device to her lips again.

"Are you a shifter?"

It was only the unexpectedness of the question that kept me from reacting. Paul had stiffened under my hand. The Panacians folded their limbs in a posture that indicated resignation and patience.

"I don't understand the question," I said reasonably, hoping I didn't.

The other Feneden chose this moment to approach us, forming a semicircle behind Anisco. There was no expression to be understood on their faces, unless the increasing rate at which their eyes blinked that disconcerting red meant agitation.

"Are you a shifter?" she asked again.

C'Tlas made an apologetic gesture with one limb. "There's an unidentified problem with the translation machine, Fem Ki," she offered. "We can't seem to clarify this point. Just say no and she'll move on."

I looked at the Feneden, held the device to my lips, and numbly answered: "No. I am not a shifter."

The Feneden took the device from me and began to pass it to Paul. I closed my fingers around the memory of it, knowing the purity of my genetic disguise, trying to assure myself this was, as C'Tlas said, probably a glitch in translation. Perhaps to them, "shifter" meant someone dishonest or not to be trusted.

On the other hand, "shifter" could refer to web-talents and the device about to be given to Paul could be some kind of detector—

I turned, planning to snatch it from Paul, thinking of the bit of me lying beneath his shirt, but the device, for better or worse, was already in his hand and raised to his ear. I could easily hear what she said.

"What are you?"

Paul's answer came out twice, overlapping in comspeak and the machine's interpretation. Anisco nodded, asking: "We have met Human. Why are you here, Human?"

Paul repeated what I'd said, keeping it simple. I knew he was as disturbed as I, but his voice was calm, his body language that of friendly respect: modulations of intent lost on the Feneden, but valuable indicators for the Panacians. N'Klet, I was sure, was an expert at reading Humans. No one else would have been assigned to Paul.

"Are you a shifter?"

Over his denial, I felt my temperature soaring. She must have asked this of the other Humans she'd met. So it was something they asked individuals, not just other species as a whole.

The Feneden appeared to relax, the other four returning to their former positions in the room as if we were no longer of interest, or, perhaps more likely, we were now Anisco's responsibility. Anisco bowed to both of us, a courtesy she might have absorbed from the Panacians, who automatically bowed back. As she dipped her head, I watched with fascination as a series of waves passed through her cilia, forming an intricate pattern wherever the waves met and rebounded.

Paul held out his hand. After a moment's hesitation, Anisco touched his palm with two fingers. I reached out in turn, even if a Lishcyn's idea of a handshake involved a genteel clicking of tusks and some mutual salivating.

She touched my palm, as she had Paul's, then apparently couldn't resist running her cool fingertips over the rosettes of scales forming my skin. I kept perfectly still, even though it tickled unbearably.

In that moment, I thought I finally understood why my Human friend had chosen a career searching for new species, why he so enjoyed everything about other cultures I showed him. This tentative contact, this mutual strangeness overcome, was incredibly exhilarating. It was also completely terrifying to my web-self. For once, I couldn't imagine what Ersh would have said.

As if the mere thought of her had been a key, Ersh-memory, immeasurably older than my own, surged up and I was tossed from the here and now . . .

. . . to a planet rich with life. Feeling the cunning of a hunter. Prey was everywhere, screaming, running, enticing with its pain and fruitless struggle, the taste overwhelming all other sensations. It was impossible to consume enough, to rip through flesh fast enough to feed that insatiable appetite . . .

"We shall dine together and talk of trade."

I heard the words without understanding as I came back to the here and now, feeling Paul's grip tight on my arm. Thankfully, no one else appeared to have noticed my lapse of attention.

Ersh had left me her private memories, stored as frozen flesh. Although by now I had consumed and assimilated this legacy, most of her memories surfaced only when triggered by events.

As now.

I looked into the golden eyes of Anisco the Feneden with complete and utter recognition. There was no problem with the translator. She asked strangers the question that revealed the terrible scars carried by her species, the fear that must have been passed from generation to generation, rearing its ugly head each time they encountered the unknown.

Her ancestors had been a shifter's prey. With a heave of nausea in all my stomachs, I remembered their taste.

Thanks to Ersh.

11: School Night; School Morning

IT had been a long time, as Humans felt years, since I'd knowingly kept a secret from my one friend. This one settled around my hearts like a cancer.

Dining with the Feneden had been a waking nightmare: a bizarre progression of polite, faintly confused small talk, a sequence of Panacian delicacies the Feneden ignored and I'd grimly rammed through to the safety of my fourth stomach, planning to retch it out in the privacy of my room, and—worst of all—seeing Paul's innocent delight fading more and more into concern each time our eyes met.

I rinsed out my mouth, wishing memories could be as easily removed.

I'd known—I'd been forced to share and know—how Ersh had arrived in this galaxy as a barely-aware lump of appetite, seeking only to survive. In my flesh were images and sensations from that time, dull and safe until a starving Ersh had encountered her first non-Web being and consumed it without hesitation. From that moment, the pattern of Ersh's life, and that of her Web, had been set—for once the web-flesh patterned itself after living intelligence, that need for awareness resounded through every choice of form. To cycle into unthinking matter was to feel suicide; to remain there, literally was.

Over millennia came experience and learned skills; with learning, came control and conscience. The Ersh of my own past had been wise, calculating, full of caution, and determined to protect other intelligence from being lost.

That this determination was rooted in what she had done to other species before learning such laudable restraint and compassion, was knowledge I could have cheerfully lived without.

The Ersh of the Feneden's past was something else entirely. I would have heaved again, but there was nothing left inside any of my stomachs. I ignored their contradictory complaints about this; nothing I gave them would stay.

Ersh had stumbled on the Feneden's world and chosen it as her private larder, living among them at times in secrecy, hunting from the darkness, and at times—and whim—becoming a plague to wipe out entire populations. Despite her cruel harvest, the Feneden had survived, grown in number and culture, developed technology. As they did, the hunter became the hunted. Ersh became cautious, protecting her precious web-self from vengeance. *The First Rule of our Web*, I thought cynically.

The monster of the mountains—the *Shifter*—became a story told to children, a cultural archetype, a warning against strangers.

A story Ersh remembered for me in numerous versions, having posed so many times as a Feneden child herself. If I wished, I could dredge up her first memory in Feneden form . . . a memory that included instinctively thrusting her face into the frontal cilia of the Feneden adult who found her, lying naked in the brush where Ersh had cycled to hide herself . . . a memory that included the taste of partially digested food, warm from the adult's stomach, conveyed by gentle cilia between Ersh's new lips—an experience so powerfully satisfying, she decided to stay.

An act of kindness which doomed that Feneden's village and others like it for generations to come.

I twitched an ear, hearing the sound of my supposedly locked door opening, followed by a low, urgent: "Es. Es, where are you?"

That hadn't taken long, I thought with significant self-pity. "In here," I called, unwilling to leave the 'fresher stall with its comforting pulses of water hitting all the right tension areas along my belly. I'd been careful to keep it cool and free of bubbles, though the thought had crossed my mind.

I heard his footsteps; they went on and on until the Human must have paced around the entire sleeping area twice. I set the 'fresher to dry, keeping my ears twisted so the rush of air wouldn't deafen me, so I didn't hear him wander in to what the Panacians politely referred to as the "biological accommodation" until a knuckle rapped on the outside of the stall.

Without a reasonable excuse to stay inside—having passed the point of excruciatingly clean long ago and my scales puffy with moisture—I shut off the air and leaned out to greet the Human.

He put one finger in front of his lips, still concentrating on passing his sensor over the fixtures and walls. *Explaining the multiple footsteps*, I decided, if not why Paul suddenly suspected the Ambassadors of such unPanacian behavior.

As if I'd asked out loud, Paul said quietly, "Panacians are no longer the only species here, are they?"

I curled a lip. "Meaning if I can sneak around, so could the Feneden?"

"Or others," he agreed. "While you were exploring the top floor, I was—" Paul's cheeks might have reddened slightly, or it could have been the warmth of the room. "—exploring elsewhere. This building houses several species—including Iftsen."

My Human's curiosity had bested his manners, too? That deserved two tusks, and I shone them at him, meanwhile climbing out and draping my exceedingly clean self in a more conservative caftan. "Iftsen—funny our tour guides didn't mention they had non-oxy facilities here, given how proud they were about the plumbing," I said curiously, leading the way into the sleeping area and motioning Paul to sit on one of a pair of wooden blocks. For an instant, I was distracted by memories of how the decorative and heavy rectangular objects were actually used: as weights laid over the slumbering forms of Seitsiets, a species with a tendency to generate internal hydrogen during sleep and so prone to float off unless pinned safely in place.

"It's odd," Paul agreed, hands around one upraised knee. His face was animated, as always when he faced some puzzle. "I knew this building was used as a meeting place for alien dignitaries—as well as a school—but it looks as though they've provided long-term quarters here."

"Embassies?" I ventured.

He considered it, then nodded. "Makes sense. The Panacians have always resisted alien construction on D'Dsel, with the unavoidable exception of the shipcity and All Sapients' District. Maybe this is their answer." The Human leaned forward, putting both feet flat on the floor. "Es. The Ambassadors are hoping we can help with the Feneden. How quickly can you learn their language?" His lips tightened. "It might be important to us as well—I didn't like that question about 'shifters' any more than you did."

I know several Feneden languages, I could have told him, but then would have had the awkward task of explaining why those were dialects so old they wouldn't be understood by the modern versions on the top floor. Ersh's last memory of the species was three thousand years older than I. "I need time with them," I said instead, truthfully enough. That I didn't want to have anything to do with the Feneden was equally true.

Of course, Paul read that from my voice or face. *His perceptiveness*, I thought glumly, *was rarely to my advantage*. "You want to tell me what's wrong, Es?" he asked gently.

"No," I told him honestly.

He dropped his voice even lower, making me prick up my ears to hear. "Esen. If there's something about this situation I need to know, don't you think you should tell me?"

I rocked a bit, wishing I'd chosen softer seating or a less determined partner. "There was no mistake in the translation machine," I admitted.

He paled. "You mean—"

"The Feneden have—met—shifters," I said reluctantly

and in a whisper, just in case Paul's gadgets had missed some eavesdropping device. "I recognized their species after all."

Paul closed his eyes for a moment, as if needing the privacy of his own thoughts to consider the ramifications of this, then opened them. They'd darkened, as they did when the Human had made up his mind about something unpleasant. "We have to get you out of here," he said firmly. He rose to his feet. "Now."

"If I run from them," I argued, staying where I was despite my complete agreement and a rather sore behind, "they'll suspect." There was more at stake here than my identity—Paul Cameron had a full life, a family, a great deal to lose. I'd stolen that from him once already; I wouldn't do it again. "I should learn more about them," I added. "At least their language and intentions."

Paul stood silently, looking down at me. I forced a curl out of my lip. "If the deals don't look profitable, Cameron & Ki will go home," I insisted.

"Translight," he emphasized grimly. "I don't like this, Es. It's too much of a coincidence."

I'd thought of nothing else since meeting the Feneden. *Well*, I added to myself, *I'd also given a great deal of thought to cosmic irony and the laughter of uncaring gods.* "I don't believe the Feneden are looking for—real— shifters," I said, searching for ways to reassure him as well as myself. "I suspect the question is a formality, a need to assure peaceful intentions." I pulled myself to my feet. "C'Tlas told me N'Klet has arranged for me to meet with Hom Sidorae in the morning. Apparently, he's brought samples of art they're willing to export. I can work on the language with him."

"I'll be with Anisco and the Panacian linguists, trying to improve the mechanical translator." Paul didn't appear particularly reassured. There were small lines around his eyes, a corresponding tightness to his lips. "Be damned careful, Es," he added.

"You know me, Paul," I said with a debonair wink. "I'm always careful."

* * *

"Careful!" I admonished the Panacian who'd overzealously reached her fourth limb for yet another highly fragile ceramic. "A second trip would be wise," I suggested more calmly, holding the treasure out of reach in case she disagreed.

The Feneden, Sidorae, and I had met in a species-neutral room, one with long tables connected to the floor, not the ceiling. It was just as well, since the tables were filled with an eye-catching display of truly wonderful and varied art forms, most appearing unlikely to survive any rough handling whatsoever. With Sidorae's permission, delivered via another mechanical translator, I'd begun sorting them into transport crates according to which markets best suited each style. Two young Ambassador caste students were helping— a bit too eagerly.

I kept up a rattle of questions for Sidorae, my ears turned so I listened more to the language leaving his lips than the corresponding comspeak droning from the device in my hand. After an hour or so, I was relieved to be at last making clear sense of it. The modern Feneden were using one of the ancient dialects from Ersh-memory—the root words and underlying grammar were recognizable, but many descriptors had been modified into verbs, with changes to endings and tenses. I'd had centuries of practice catching up on language shifts in other species. If it weren't for the unsettling combination of appetite and guilt overlaying every one of Ersh's memories of this form, I would have enjoyed this return to my former life.

The question "was I shifter?" came up, as I'd forewarned Paul, forming part of Sidorae's initial greeting to me and to each of the Panacians. The machine translation into comspeak was accurate, if scanty. I now recognized the Feneden word, *rosaki*, as a derivative of the original: *iroki sak*, demon of shifting shape.

That would be Ersh, I thought sadly. Not a monument she'd cherish, becoming a catch phrase for an insecure culture as it met the rest of the universe. Not a legend I wanted spread to other civilizations either, so I was relieved when

Sidorae refused to elaborate on the term, saying only that it was "important to be polite." I agreed with that.

Ersh-memory, distasteful as most of it was concerning this species, was woefully incomplete. She'd left their world after the Feneden had come close to destroying themselves in a globe-spanning war, an unfortunate coming of age shared by many otherwise intelligent species. I had the genetic makeup of the Feneden, of course, and copious memories of their earliest history—but it wasn't comprehensive, being focused on those accomplishments of interest to a very young Ersh, such as music and the flavors of sweets. *I'd need several years of my own research*, I decided, *to determine what preoccupied adults of this species.*

By the time Sidorae and I had examined almost all of his display, I had to be meticulous in responding to the meanings contained in the comspeak uttered by the machine, no matter how some jarred against what I heard him say. Still, our time had been profitably spent. Cameron & Ki Exports now had some prime merchandise with which to tease our clients; I'd acquired a workable grasp of the modern Feneden tongue, as used by these representatives anyway; and, perhaps most importantly, I'd had a crash course in their culture. The latter I didn't think would have pleased Sidorae, had he known, but it was unavoidable. The art of a culture was always a revelation of its heart, a sampling of its scope and interests. While I couldn't conclude much about the Feneden themselves from these pieces, I did have a better idea of what affected the group represented by Sidorae and the others on Panacia.

They were thieves.

Elsewhere

A FULL day and a half wasted. There had been no records. *Or no records to be had*, Lefebvre reminded himself dourly, following the path of a stray bubble as it launched itself from the inside of his beer glass and wobbled its way to join the froth on the surface. *Another dead end*. He'd had enough to drink to find that funny.

It had been the same story at every other system. No genetic material, not even the quickcopy routinely made by customs. What rested in Lefebvre's concealed pocket was the closest to the real Paul Ragem he'd been able to come without breaking into a Commonwealth data vault: a painstakingly complete collection of genetic markers from every biological relative he'd been able to track down, blended with some scientific hocus pocus and wishful thinking into what might be a key. *Might be.* First, he needed to match it to some Port Authority record for Ragem, some documented sighting. Then, he could be sure he had the right key to unlock where Ragem had been during those last fateful weeks.

Confirmation would have been ideal, but Lefebvre was prepared, as always, to proceed without that reassurance. *After all, why should his search be any easier than Kearn's?*

The beer poured cold and bitter down his throat.

"Hom Captain? 'cuse me. Hom Captain?"

This bar—Lefebvre couldn't recall its name at the moment: something about *Flashy Gills*—was in the All Sapients' District, a narrow ring of non-Panacian development around the ever-changing shipcity itself. As such, its clientele could be any being, of any oxy-breathing species—rooms for the other sort were behind a plas wall, allowing at least visual interaction between those who otherwise couldn't survive each other's company without wearing an environmental suit, or e-rig. There was a hot and heavy game of rummy at the far end, a tentacle showing through a blue fog held a set of fluorescent cards, while the pair of Humans at the facing table glowered at those in their own hands.

So Lefebvre wasn't surprised to be accosted by an Ervickian here. He was slightly surprised to be accosted by an Ervickian in its ept-morph, an age at which barhopping was barely legal even on non-Ervickian worlds. The Human expression, wet behind the ears, applied nicely, the nervous young being standing too close to Lefebvre's side having a steady drip of sweat passing down the slick yellow sides of its head. Two pairs of overly-earnest eyes stared up at him, all four eyeballs on the beady side. The body was a fair match, skin and bones within a too-large Human sweater, an extra hole cut from the chest area so the being could shovel food into its secondary mouth without lifting its garment.

"Captain Lefebvre. My name to Humans is Able Joe. You can remember that, yes?" this with a wink that passed through all four eyes in sequence. Ervickians tended to assume one-brained species were all slightly simple. "I know it's you, Hom Captain. I have an ident right here." Able Joe began waving around a large, purple card. With more coordination than he'd have credited himself with, Lefebvre snatched it before the youngster attracted the wrong sort of attention. It wasn't a particularly upscale bar.

The card was his, all right: a plas version of a notice he posted every time the *Russell III* came insystem. This hadn't been a place he'd expected a response, but Lefebvre had long ago separated his expectations from his quest. A grubby, eight-fingered hand stole it back. "Says here you want information on another Human. Named

Megar Slothe." The words were delivered in a whisper likely overheard by anything in the bar with auditory organs and still conscious.

"Don't waste my time," Lefebvre said, turning his back on the annoying creature. Any Ervickian off its world was a con artist, the species congregating translight wherever a fast credit could be made. Their moral system was, to be kind, pliable.

Able Joe didn't object out loud. Instead a small holocube slid along the bar's surface to kiss Lefebvre's beer glass. Lefebvre glanced down at it, then stared, mesmerized.

The cube contained an image taken, from the look of it, from a store's internal security vid. It showed two beings.

One was Panacian, by her color and size, a member of the Ambassador caste. Even in this still, her proud bearing implied she'd been trained on D'Dsel itself.

It was the second figure that held Lefebvre speechless. Human. Tall, slim, that face he almost knew better than his own, despite not having seen it for over fifty years.

Ragem.

Lefebvre reached for the cube, but Able Joe's hand was there first to snatch it back. Lefebvre tapped his credit chip on the bar, then beckoned the Ervickian to follow him. The little being was quivering with anticipation—or was starving, something Lefebvre would rather not know. The remnants of former meals decorated most of the sweater as it was; Ervickians weren't famed for their table manners. The taller Human led the way to a private booth, tapping his chip on its entry panel.

Once inside, Lefebvre straightened, willing to reveal he was much less drunk than he'd appeared while nursing his beer at the bar. "An interesting image. What makes you think this Human is Megar Slothe?" He felt as taut as a wire about to snap. *It couldn't just fall into his lap like this—or could it?*

"You gonna pay me or what?" Able Joe said, feigning outrage. Lefebvre held up his credit chip but refused to touch it to the being's receiver.

"Prove it."

"Sure. Sure." The youngster's bushy paired eyebrows drooped at the edges. "The vid's from a store my créche operates on Ultari Prime. Every member of my litter carries a copy. We don't forget cheats—everyone knows that about us; you know that, right?—and this Slothe cheated our family in a big way. He's gonna pay." A pause while four eyes examined Lefebvre in the gloom of the booth and the receiver was lifted hopefully. "So, are you? Gonna pay me?"

"Cheated you how?"

"Bought a load of stuff from my créche parent—a starship, supplies, high-tech stuff—all prime, high-end goods. Nothing shabby, y'know? Then there was a cancel sent by remote to reclaim every credit paid. Just about ruined my parent, that did." This with a note of almost sanctimonious pride.

"Slothe sent the cancel?" When the Ervickian's primary mouth remained closed in a stubborn oval, Lefebvre touched his chip to the being's receiver, tipping in a generous amount without result. He repeated his donation.

A gleam from vestigial teeth—the really useful ones resided lower down and Lefebvre was as glad not to see them. "Yeah. My sibs and me, we think so," Able Joe said cheerily. "Who else?"

"That depends. When was this image taken? The exact date—standard time, not local."

The Ervickian held up the holocube, pressing a control to bring up the security vid record. Lefebvre scanned it. An older model but still in use today, being as tamperproof as such things could be.

Lefebvre's lips moved soundlessly as he repeated the date to himself. *A full week*, he calculated numbly. A full week after Paul Ragem had been reportedly killed on Artos—his death activating the emergency warning from the implant under his skin before its signal inexplicably cut off—this vid captured him on Ultari Prime.

Kearn was too blinded by his obsession with monsters and shapeshifters to see what had been under his nose all along. Lefebvre had always suspected Ragem's death as too convenient, especially when Artos became a closed system immediately afterward, preventing any retrieval of a body or investigation.

And Councillor Sandner had gone to such pains to emphasize that point.

The Ervickian might have slipped him a stim shot, from the way Lefebvre felt his heart pounding more heavily and quickly, until his pulse rushed in his ears like ocean waves. *Paul was alive?*

So much for hunting the truth of his final days, digging out scraps of evidence, following leads that vanished in his fingers as rapidly as the whorls of smoke in the bar. *This*, Lefebvre realized, *changed everything*.

With a supreme effort, Lefebvre kept his hands off the small box.

"Do you have a list of the goods he bought?" When Able Joe hesitated, Lefebvre went on persuasively: "Look—I know some things Slothe had with him before he disappeared. That way we can settle if this is the same Human. If it is—" Lefebvre waved his chip suggestively.

An hour later, and three months' pay lighter, Lefebvre left the bar a much happier Human. *And why not?* he told himself, one hand possessively over the cube in his pocket, a cube containing an eccentric and expensive shopping list including a mammoth comp system, a portable greenhouse, and sufficient exotic salad greens to feed—or more likely poison—an army.

Best of all, it contained the sales slip for a starship— a used taxi designated Speedy InterSys Transit No. 365, registered to a Megar Slothe—the very same ship found abandoned by Kearn fifty years ago on the former Inhaven colony, Ag-413.

Lefebvre smiled to himself in a way that made an approaching pair of spacers choose the other side of the walkway. Ag-413 was the location of the final recorded sighting of the Esen Monster, and its supposed destruction by the Kraal.

Now a Kraal Protectorate—perfect Kraal logic: if you've saved a planet, why not keep it?—Ag-413 had also been the source of a mysterious message Kearn received from an unidentified Human, a Human claiming to know all about the monster and possessing the right emergency codes to demand immediate rescue. A rescue, Lefebvre learned, Kearn had delegated to some civilian freighters named Largas with typical cowardice. The Largas crew had maintained they'd found no one, returning to their course and ultimately leaving Commonwealth space for the outskirts of the Fringe, well beyond reach of authority.

Lefebvre felt pieces falling into place all around him. All those years of fruitless searching—he could almost be grateful to Kearn for bringing him here now.

And in his other pocket, an image of the not-so-dead Paul Ragem and his accomplice.

A Panacian who traveled outsystem with a Human? Not common. Not common at all. Even the Ervickians had realized that; Able Joe, tongue well-lubricated by Lefebvre's credit chip, admitting to being the fifth in its créche litter to journey to D'Dsel to try and find her, without success.

They'd been fools to try, Lefebvre judged. Ervickians, like most of the intelligent species encountered by Humans thus far, were constrained in their dealings with others by biology and temperament. Any one species managed to communicate very successfully with a few others, muddled through somehow with several more, and were hopelessly confused or offended by the rest. With each new species encountered for the first time, the Human Commonwealth became even more of a glue to hold the loose, yet expanding, economic association of various species together. Only Humans seemed to possess the right combination of optimism, open-mindedness, and a surely species-specific obstinacy to work with just about any beings if necessary.

Of course, there was that saying, that Humans had thicker skins than Ganthor.

The shipcities that sprang up wherever starships docked, and their associated All Sapients' Districts, were very often hosts to planned or unplanned mediation by whatever Human could be found by the aggrieved non-Humans trying to understand one another. Since these usually involved bar bills or trade disputes, it didn't seem to matter that the Humans involved were occasionally semiconscious.

There were rumors that the more diverse limb of the Commonwealth, months away translight and so effectively its own entity, had abandoned its Human-centered government system altogether and moved toward some sort of pact between trading species. *He'd believe that one when he saw his first shapeshifter in person.*

The truth remained, the Ervickian needed a Human to communicate with the Panacians and help find those who had cheated its parent. Lefebvre and Able Joe hadn't so much formed a partnership as arranged to share information in the future, Able Joe quite clear on the advantage of credits on its chip as opposed to chasing them in the street. Lefebvre left the quivering being with a prepaid menu and a mutual promise to keep in touch.

Not that either of them planned to honor that promise, Lefebvre thought contentedly.

Finders, keepers.

12: School Morning; Sanctum Afternoon

"EVERY piece?" Paul asked, brows lifting almost to his hairline.

I tilted my head up and down in the Human gesture. "Most of it. There were a few items in the collection I'd say were Feneden, but no guarantees how they were obtained."

"And the rest were Iftsen. You're certain we're dealing with theft? They're neighbors, after all." His lips curved up, as if to acknowledge the irony of the Feneden learning they were not the only intelligent species in the universe, simultaneously with the discovery their particular corner of space was the most crowded in the quadrant. Had the Feneden wanted to colonize within a day translight, they would have had to rent something small.

"Sidorae claimed all of it was from his homeworld," I told Paul, "but last night I handled two hundred and forty-four pieces of art from the First Citizens' Gallery of Brakistem, on Iftsen Secondus. I don't recall hearing the Gallery had closed and broken up its collection."

I paused, momentarily deflected from the present to when Lesy had proudly taken me to that same Gallery, to see her work exhibited for the first time. I'd kept private the thought that Ersh likely paid to have our web-kin's sculptures displayed—Lesy was the sort of artist whose passion for her muse vastly exceeded the result. She'd been so happy. Since her death, I'd arranged to buy all of her work and have it stored safely, for no reason I could justify to myself or Ersh's training. "It was pretech," I continued my explanation, "the sort of thing the Iftsen never display for aliens. You know how touchy they are about being—less developed. I doubt they even posted an alert about the theft."

"So the Feneden should feel safe trying to sell it on the open market." Paul snorted. "Harve Tollen. I'd say we've found out why he's on D'Dsel."

"C'Tlas tells me the Feneden haven't made any other arrangements for their merchandise." I chuckled. "Perhaps Harve wasn't able to impress them."

Otherwise, it wasn't a laughing matter. I tilted my head downward, examining the scales on my belly and running a finger across their pattern. Had there been leaves nearby, I'd have started tucking some, right about there.

Paul knew that stance. He came over to where I sat, then crouched in front of me with his hands on my knees for balance. "You've thought of something."

I pressed my thick lips as closely together as they would go, then nodded, meeting his gaze. "Whatever's going on between the Feneden and Iftsen, I don't think it's simply petty theft, Paul. Sidorae asked me about establishing markets; he wanted details about the maximum number of units each could bear without dropping the price. Unless it was all for my benefit—and I don't think so—the Feneden must believe they have access to an almost unlimited supply of Iftsen art, as well as the gall to think they can get away with selling it indefinitely. How?"

Paul thumped my knee. "Why don't we talk to our hostess?"

"The Feneden—and the Iftsen?" C'Tlas' voice was oddly strained. "What makes you ask about their relationship?"

"We anticipate overseeing a great deal of trade between their species, Fem C'Tlas, and wish to be as well informed as possible," Paul explained.

Our meeting with the Panacians was being held in the chamber we'd first entered by hoverbot. Morning sunlight gleamed through the open windows to warm and brighten the room, reflected by predesign from the surfaces of neighboring buildings. N'Klet was there, along with C'Tlas, her pitted carapace perceptibly smoother to my practiced eye. *Damage almost repaired*, I judged. *But damage from what?* She noticed my attention and stepped slightly behind C'Tlas—a subtle avoidance I realized she'd been doing every time I looked directly at her. *Self-conscious or not fond of shaggy-scaled aliens?* Regardless, I made a mental note to be careful not to stare.

"Trade?" N'Klet repeated. Panacians didn't laugh, but they had a body gesture to express incredulity, consisting of stiffening the joints of the upper arms so the elbows swung out and up. It made them look as though they thought they could fly, but had misplaced their wings.

"Forgive our presumption, Fem N'Klet," I said. "It was something Hom Sidorae said to me during our meetings—"

"Are you sure you understood him?" She was still amused. *More than that*, I decided, perhaps inclined to be oversensitive. But she sounded almost mocking, as though it was my ability she doubted.

Oddly on the defensive, I spoke before I considered, one of those traits I seriously needed to outgrow: "Their language is hardly that complex."

Paul closed his eyes in an unguarded wince. *Oh, well*, I told myself fatalistically. *At least I wouldn't have to carry around the annoying translator anymore.*

N'Klet and the others bowed deeply. "Your fame as a linguist had preceded you, Fem Esolesy Ki," N'Klet said. "We'd hoped for a quick breakthrough, but this—this is truly remarkable." She straightened and clicked her slender upper claws as though faintly alarmed. "Indeed, such a feat is difficult to imagine." For once, N'Klet seemed to have no hesitation aiming her faceted eyes my way. I curled up a lip in a weak smile.

"You may not be aware, Fem N'Klet, that we have been preparing for this encounter since our first contact with the Feneden was announced," Paul improvised immediately, a talent I valued highly in him. "There were recordings, other works to consult," he added vaguely, waving his arms about to admirable effect. "This is hardly a sudden breakthrough. Fem Ki has labored for weeks and weeks—months, really—"

The supposed time span of my labors thus established beyond doubt, or at least repeated, the Panacians seemed calmer. "Our gratitude, Fem Ki," C'Tlas said with an air of relief. "At last we have a way to communicate with the Feneden no longer reliant on their machine's limited and often flawed interpretations."

"News worthy of the Queen's notice," N'Klet said, faceted eyes glinting. "I will recommend an audience."

Although she bowed immediately, as did we at the mention of the ruler of this kin-group, C'Tlas and the other D'Dsellans in the room appeared startled. *An appropriate reaction*, I decided, feeling much the same emotion. Aliens were so rarely allowed within a Queen's sanctum that such events—usually involving heads of state from other worlds—predictably made the newsmags on several systems.

Otherwise, Queens were only seen at the Spring Emergence, protected from approach by watchful ranks of their own relatives, while those around them were protected by pheromone-absorbing B'Bklar plants. *Physical proximity to any Queen of unknown motivation*, I remembered Ersh's lecture, *was something to be avoided at all costs.*

Paul's face had settled into the politely intent mask it assumed when he was seriously disturbed. *No need to guess why*, I told myself, feeling an echoing upheaval threatening my breakfast. I quickly swallowed the remnants into my next, and sturdier stomach. My Human might not have the same vulnerability to chemically-influenced mood swings as a web-being in Panacian form, but Queens posed a special, more personal risk to him. Esolesy Ki hadn't visited D'Dsel before, but a certain Commonwealth alien culture and linguistics specialist named Paul Ragem had been in this very city fifty years ago. *And hardly circumspect about it*, I remembered quite vividly. The problem was, only a Queen could recognize him all these years later.

Unlike other systems and species Paul avoided with care,

he'd eventually been able to travel freely on D'Dsel without concern. After all, not only were Panacians typically lax in distinguishing one set of humanoid features from another, but D'Dsellans lived a maximum of thirty standard years. *Except*, I reminded myself, *their Queens*, whose adjusted hormonal systems provided a longevity up to four times that of their kin.

Meaning Paul's identity had been safe, since no Human met a Queen face-to-face. *Until I came with him.* Fortunately, I could rely on Paul getting us out of this with his usual diplomacy. I hoped.

"We appreciate the honor you wish to offer us," I heard my partner say with the utmost sincerity. "But it's not necessary to disturb your Queen—"

At that name, the Panacians bowed again, as did we. "A great honor," I echoed, ignoring Paul's warning look. *Well, it was*, I told myself somewhat petulantly. "One we surely don't deserve," I added.

Apparently, someone else agreed. C'Tlas canted her head at N'Klet in uncharacteristic disapproval as she said: "A personal message of thanks from Sec-ag K'Tak, Her Radiance's Chief Rememberer, would suffice."

N'Klet dismissed this idea with a snap of her claw. "Nonsense, C'Tlas. Fem Ki's accomplishments may save us from war. What could be more worthy of our Queen's attention than that?" She hung one limb possessively around Paul's shoulders. "I will take great joy in introducing you to Her Radiance."

Beyond arm-waving laughter and certain extremes of body posture, there was little a Panacian used to visually express emotion. They didn't need it, having receptors for chemical messages both voluntary and involuntary. Within the limitations of my Lishcyn-self's senses, I studied N'Klet, feeling suddenly very unsure about many things. But I did know the scarred D'Dsellan wasn't excited or grateful, despite her words.

She was determined.

*   *   *

N'Klet's determination meant our protests, something awkward in the extreme to voice without offering profound insult, were completely ignored. Within too short a time and without opportunity to simply remove ourselves, Paul and I were traveling downward in a lift with C'Tlas, who appeared as shocked as we were by this turn of events.

"I really think a message would have sufficed," she repeated, looking to us as if for confirmation.

We both nodded. "More than enough," I assured her fervently.

"Is your Queen in the habit of granting audiences such as this?" Paul ventured, with that tenacious look I knew perfectly well meant his curiosity was rousing. *Unwise*, I decided, but then couldn't recall the Human ever acknowledging the benefits of timely ignorance. *Why*, I thought, *would he start now?*

In response, C'Tlas stopped the lift, but didn't open the doors. "I mean no offense, Hom Cameron, Fem Ki, but my Queen would never grant you audience," she said with unmistakable pride, standing as tall as she could so the top of her head carapace was level with Paul's shoulder and my chin. "You are to see the Queen of the School of Alien Etiquette." She lifted a graceful clawtip in a mute gesture of acceptance. "Her Radiance has been known to admit a variety of worthy beings to her Sanctum."

I'd never heard of a Panacian kin-group tolerating more than one Queen—living, that is. Some basements had quite the collection of mummified Old Queens, all carefully labeled so their descendants knew which ones to consult about various matters. *I could use some consultation*, I thought. "Forgive me, Fem C'Tlas, if my question is too forward," I said, "but I admit to confusion. Are we not to see your Queen?"

Her eyes glinted. "Her Radiance is my Queen only while I am physically within the School," she explained, although the Ambassador had to be aware we'd know how vast a departure from Panacian custom this represented. The situation must have shaken C'Tlas more than I'd realized, or her sense of propriety was so offended she was willing to vent her feelings with anyone, including us. "Most of the students, including N'Klet and myself," she continued, "are Visitors here, as yourselves. Her Radiance grants us dispensation to stay; our own Queens willingly free us from their Influence so we may dwell here for an interval and then return with shared knowledge for our kin-group. It is the New Way." From her overly precise tone, I decided "New" in this context had at least something in common with a Panacian's disgust with careless building design.

I'd known the Ambassador caste was constantly being pushed in new directions to help the Hive better coexist in a multispecies economy, but this was such a drastic change I carefully put a hand under my jaw and exerted significant upward pressure, just in case.

"Why this particular Queen?" Paul asked, then added quickly, "if I may ask."

C'Tlas restarted the lift, then drew her limbs tightly against her body as though distressed. Paul opened his mouth, I presumed to apologize, but she spoke very quietly before he could utter a sound: "I rely on your discretion, Hom Cameron, Fem Ki."

"Of course," we said together.

"Her Radiance breeds true-to-caste. I believe you know enough about our kind to appreciate this is a rare and valued trait. As Ambassadors, it is an honor to be under Her Influence, even briefly."

What it meant, I thought to myself, swallowing hard and watching the echoing comprehension shadow Paul's eyes, *was that we were about to meet not just any Queen, but the one who was presently establishing the future of the Ambassador caste and, through them, the Hive.*

C'Tlas left us standing outside the Queen's Sanctum for, as she put it, a moment of privacy to gain composure for our audience.

There wasn't much chance of that, I thought, minutes later, gazing at the vaulted ceilings, festooned with draperies in the form of exotic flowers, several hanging in languid folds almost to the floor. I didn't envy the beings who had to dust up there.

"When they open the door, Es," Paul insisted for the third time, regaining my attention, "you go in. I'll have some good reason not to join you. Maybe a faint . . ." he pondered out loud.

"A faint." I flipped my ears back and forth disdainfully. "You'll hit your head on the floor. Not to mention send the students into hysterics."

"I'm merely feeling faint," the Human countered, placing the back of his hand somewhat theatrically against his own forehead. I began to suspect his sense of humor of taking over the more rational part of his brain. *It had,* I knew, *happened in the past.* "It could be the start of some illness," Paul insisted. "They shouldn't admit a sick being into Her presence. Or my stomach could be upset." This last with a totally innocent look I didn't believe for a second.

I refused to be amused. "Or the Queen could be so insulted she'll insist on having us brought before Port Authority—and neither of us need that right now, do we? Honestly, Paul," I chided him. "It's going to be very brief and formal. We'll be lucky if She notices we're there."

"And if Her Radiance happens to notice a bit more—?" He left the rest unsaid, raising one brow in a face without the slightest vestige of humor remaining.

"Don't you think it's incredibly humanocentric to think she'd remember your face?" I couldn't help the aggrieved note in my voice. *It wasn't going to be half as much fun to meet the Queen without him.* I winked at him. "Unless you'd rather have me dealing with the D'Dsellans on my own?"

From the wry twist of his lips, Paul found my latest argument more convincing than previous ones. *I'd thought he might.* "Fine," he said, running his hand through his rumpled hair and completely undoing what little success tidying it he'd managed before coming. "But I'll remind you whose idea this was if anything goes wrong."

There wasn't much sign of anything going wrong at first.

After the door opened, there was more bowing, of course, including a rather awkward moment in which we had to bow deeply while walking through the Queen's force field. Paul and I had practiced this maneuver ahead of time, enough to decide I'd better not tip over because he couldn't possibly hold me up. I was successful, if not impressively graceful, perhaps because I was distracted by the tingle of the field. It wasn't meant to stop anything large; it concentrated the Queen's pheromones for transport to her diffuse family. We waited to be noticed.

All of this was a new experience for Paul, and I regretted he was too tense to treat it with the fascination it deserved. Without making it obvious to anyone but me, he stayed slightly behind me, using my bulk as a shield to keep out of the Queen's direct sight. The first moment was the worst. We both relaxed when there was no sudden cry of recognition. *I had*, I thought rather smugly, *been right*.

The Queen was a magnificent being, in her full prime, her carapace a gleaming blue almost too bright to look at directly. I might have met her before, but it was difficult to tell. Among the changes which accompanied sexual maturity were alterations in the shape of the head as well as an enlargement of the abdomen, although this particular Queen's lower anatomy would have been dwarfed by the truly awe-inspiring mass of Ansky's in this form. *An unfair comparison*, I reminded myself. *Members of the Builder caste started larger*.

The Ambassador Queen reclined in splendor atop a dais carefully engineered to whisk away any eggs laid during conversation. Too young to tolerate the physical—more accurately pheromonal—presence of her successor, she nonetheless was Ambassador enough to insist her successor witness and learn. A holo image of the youngster sparkled in the shadows, her curious faceted eyes on us from the moment we entered.

Four drones, bigger, heavier and—to be truthful—more emotionally fragile beings, lay at the Queen's feet. One continuously stroked her legs with a long feather, while another replenished a green liquid contained in a tall vase at her side from a gilded pitcher.

"Fem Esolesy Ki and Hom Paul Cameron. N'Klet has brought you to Us as deserving Our gratitude." The Queen's voice was strong and vibrant, suited to a being who was the undisputed leader of her family, member of the most widespread caste of her kind. There were other Ambassador Queens on D'Dsel, even more on the remaining worlds orbiting Panacia, but this individual, I realized, having been selected to run this School for her caste, could very likely control the decisions made by the rest.

According to C'Tlas, Her influence was even more direct, I thought. As a rule, queens produced a variety of castes within their offspring, the exact proportions of each being determined by the needs of the Hive—those needs in turn communicated through the pheromones of the Rememberer Queens prior to Spring Emergence. When a Queen bred true, producing only offspring of Her caste, it was believed a sign the Hive had a greater need for that caste than any other. The Ambassadors, from what I'd seen, were definitely becoming more predominant among their species.

And this Queen would be the acknowledged mother of most.

We bowed again. Paul and I had been granted time to dress for this audience. He'd wisely brought a jacket styled to suit the D'Dsellan concept of formality, namely any garment with flashy and complex embroidery running down its front. *It looked very bright on him*, I thought charitably, but wisely kept this opinion to myself.

The Lishcyn taste for elegant, simple designs wouldn't impress a D'Dsellan Builder, let alone a Queen, so I'd tossed all five of my beaded bags around my neck, hoping for the best from the combination of clashing patterns and shapes. C'Tlas had nodded her approval. Paul had grinned, making me regret my own tact.

The Queen continued, waving one claw in elegant emphasis: "With your assistance as interpreter, Fem Ki, perhaps we may yet avert this conflict before it escalates into war."

"War, Your Radiance?" I asked, not needing Paul's quick intake of breath in my ear to prompt my alarmed question. "We weren't aware of hostilities." *And if we had been*, I grumbled to myself, *I, for one, wouldn't have set either foot on the* Galaxy Goddess.

A melancholy click, obediently echoed by the other Panacians in the room. The Queen must have exuded a bit of despondency in her scent with the gesture. "Few are," she said. "The Iftsen have claimed our assistance—there is an agreement of long standing between our systems."

"The Treaty of P'Gkot," I said automatically. The Iftsen system had been discovered by Panacian explorers before the arrival of Human ships in this sector. Although their atmospheres were poisonous to one another, Iftsen buildings had fascinated the Panacians, leading to a systems-wide reconstruction phase often referred to by the Rememberer Caste as a golden age.

"You know our past exceptionally well, Fem Ki," the Queen acknowledged with some surprise. *I could just imagine Paul's expression behind my shoulder.* "We are honored. Yes, the Treaty. It binds us to the aid of the Iftsen, should any other species attempt to destroy their magnificent world. You can appreciate our ancestors had no idea there would be so—many— others joining us in space. And we no longer possess the capability to offer any aid beyond that of negotiation." A clever sidestep around the Panacian decision, made in the first year of peaceful contact with other species, to rid their worlds of the too-easily provoked Warrior caste. The continued culling during Spring Emergence was something the Panacians kept very much to themselves. The Queen went on: "Our efforts in that regard have been unsuccessful thus far, as we've had to rely on the Feneden's translator for the truth."

"May I ask the source of this—conflict?" I ventured, torn between the quick exit Paul was hoping for and the need for more information. I was reasonably sure we were being deliberately briefed on something the Panacians wanted us to know, but it was risky asking questions. *Never push the boundaries of good manners*, as Ersh would say: a matter of both courtesy and survival when on a planet not your own.

The Queen tapped the shoulders of the nearest drone. He looked up brightly and elaborated without hesitation. "The Feneden say they don't recognize the Iftsen."

"In what way?" I asked, hearing Paul muttering much the same question under his breath, apparently as confused as I. "You mean the Iftsen claim to their world, Iftsen Secondus?" My web-memory obediently offered up innumerable examples of ephemerals fighting over rocks, planetary or otherwise.

"No," said the drone. "The Feneden don't recognize the existence of the Iftsen themselves. As far as we can determine, the Feneden have been landing on Iftsen Secondus whenever and wherever they wish, completely ignoring the local population. They take what they like from buildings and have begun several mining operations. The Iftsen," he added with immense understatement, "are not happy."

"The Iftsen are a civilized and patient species," the Queen continued, tilting her beautiful head toward us. "But even they must respond to such affronts. Unfortunately, like us, the Iftsen have few options." She sighed suddenly; from the immediately grief stricken postures of the drones and our escort, the Queen's despair was intense. "The Iftsen may feel forced to make an ultimate response."

I cringed. Beside me, Paul might have turned to stone. "What does that mean?" he almost whispered.

"Iftsen Secondus has only one real defense against off-world assault," I answered when the Queen remained silent, curled in her own tangle of shiny blue limbs. "Generations ago, after first contact with the Panacians and others, they built a weapon called The Messenger. It lies concealed within their system's asteroid belt."

"All true, Fem Ki. The Messenger is a terrible device," the Queen whispered. "A planet-killer. The Iftsen believe possessing it deters others from attacking them. It has worked that way in the past—but the Feneden won't listen.

Since they don't believe the Iftsen exist, how can they believe an Iftsen threat?"

"You hope Fem Ki's understanding of their language will help you convince the Feneden otherwise," Paul said slowly. "Of course, we'll help you any way we can."

"We are grateful, Hom Cameron," the Queen replied, tilting her great head. "N'Klet has told me you are an exceptional Human. Approach me. My eyes are not what they used to be, and I would see you more clearly."

I didn't need to glance sideways at Paul to know he was smiling at the Queen as he obeyed and walked forward, all charm and grace; nor did I need to touch his arm to feel his pulse racing and his muscles rock-hard with tension. Instead, on some impulse, I looked to where N'Klet had been standing. She was no longer in the room.

Odd, when she was the one who'd arranged all this.

"Stop there." The drones bolted upright, then stood in front of Her Radiance, their arms interlaced in a posture of defense. I heard an echoing slither of claw against carapace from the escort beside us. The Queen must be broadcasting anxiety or alarm. *Not fear*, I reassured myself, *or we'd already be under attack.* I shunted my stomachs' contents into the fourth.

The Queen was leaning forward over her worried drones, her own claws agape, her faceted eyes fixed on Paul as he stopped midstep, waiting. I looked at her, puzzled, then looked harder. Age and maturity had made a difference, but suddenly I knew her.

I could hear the cosmic gods laughing now. *P'Lka*. The D'Dsellan who had been assigned to keep an eye on the crew of the *Rigus*, fifty years ago. The Panacian who had helped my Ket-self meet with Mixs, while keeping a certain Human occupied.

Her next words, delivered with a hard, threatening edge, were unnecessary confirmation that she remembered that Human all too well.

"Paul Ragem," said the Queen. "Why aren't you dead?"

Elsewhere

"ARE you shifter?"

Kearn felt his hands shaking and he gripped the case he'd brought more tightly to compensate. *I'm a First Contact expert*, he told himself firmly. *Trained to handle such situations.*

That training had been too long ago and he'd had a staff, including Paul Ragem, to step forward in hazardous situations. Kearn realized he was about to faint and decided courtesy was less important than a chair.

"No," he managed to gasp as he searched for one. "I'm not a shifter. I hunt them. I'm a hunter."

The new aliens, the Feneden, stopped pretending to be interested in anything else. This appointment had been arranged by a nameless third party—Kearn had his suspicions—and he'd been conveyed directly to their rooms by hoverbot. During his first few moments, Kearn had been rendered close to speechless by the exotic beauty of these beings, admiring everything about them except their choice of flooring material. Then the question posed by the individual carrying the translator had driven any thought but one from his mind: *these beings knew the Esen Monster.*

There had been other species with tantalizing stories to tell, Kearn told himself, trying not to tremble, trying to be skeptical. But none used a precautionary greeting like this. His pulse hammered in his ears.

The Feneden appeared flustered, confused. They spoke among themselves in trills and convoluted sentences that sounded completely unrelated to any language Kearn understood.

"The device fails at times," the Feneden who'd introduced herself as Anisco expressed her doubts to Kearn, a wave of her hand silencing the other four. "You know of the Shifter here? No others have told us this."

Kearn sat gingerly on a chair suspended from the ceiling, holding himself still with one toe on the slimy floor. "Not here," he declared, feeling most delightfully in charge. "Not as far as I know. But we've been tracking a shifter and her kind for years. I've killed one."

The Feneden conferred among themselves once more, this time with a great deal of agitated hand gesturing. Then Anisco silenced them with a sharp command.

A second Feneden approached him and held out a ball of what might have been food or might have been modeling clay. It was a vivid blue. "Shifter," Anisco proposed, touching the ball with one long, slender finger. The male holding the ball proceeded to quickly reshape it into something vaguely humanoid. "Shifter," she repeated, her voice trembling in her own language, the word machine-steady from the translator. The male reshaped the ball into a winged creature. "Shifter," Anisco said again, looking at Kearn past the bright red flashes of her inner eyelids.

Kearn held out his hand for the clay, feeling the moment wrap itself around him with glory. He flared his nostrils and straightened his spine as much as he could. "Shifter Hunter," he declared, crushing the material between his palms until it oozed out between his fingers, some dropping to the floor.

As one, so did the Feneden, pressing their foreheads into the soft, moist covering, moaning.

Kearn smiled.

13: School Afternoon

THERE were moments of choice in a life, as in cultures. Ersh had taught me so, with abundant illustration, and I'd experienced such moments for myself—mostly since introducing myself to a Human.

There had been one in P'Lka's Sanctum, a moment in which time slowed cooperatively, allowing me to delve into the dreadful consequences of this choice or that, to see clearly what might happen depending on how I acted. I'd felt gripped by an unimaginable comprehension of everything at once.

Or by hysteria, I admitted to myself, given that I'd been frozen in place as the drones dragged Paul away.

The Panacians, taking my lack of reaction for shock—which it was—and innocence—which it wasn't—had fussed over me, assuring me I was in no further danger from the Human. They'd carefully escorted me back to my rooms. And locked the door.

To give the beings credit, they expected me to stop a war and save them from having to join it. Any guilt associated with the Ki half of Cameron & Ki could be put into perspective, or at least aside until later.

Guilt. I was awash in it, floating on waves of anguish that made the merely physical complaints of my stomachs beneath contempt. I'd done exactly what Paul would have wanted me to do and had repeatedly told me to do—play the innocent, let them prove I was anything beyond what they saw. *It didn't help.* The drones had been polite, but their claws were servo-strong. If I closed my eyes, I could see Paul's involuntary flinch as they'd gripped his arms.

What were they doing to him? My common sense, and understanding of the very civil nature of Panacians, assured me Paul was simply sitting in his own room, door locked, awaiting a visit from whatever official the Queen decided should know about her catch. She might wait for a genetic I.D. *No,* I thought. P'Lka knew who she had in her claws.

Would she have cared, I asked myself bitterly, *if it hadn't been for Kearn?* Paul's former captain had spent the last few decades here and elsewhere making a fool of himself chasing my shadow. In the process, he'd ruined his own career, probably to the lasting benefit of the Commonwealth and anyone who might have had to serve under him, but unfortunately he'd succeeded in one thing. Kearn had managed to place the blame for almost everything Death accomplished in its killing spree on Paul and me. As Ersh had taught me, with ephemerals it didn't matter what was true, but what was heard most often.

I'd found Kearn's collection of fantasy and rumor about shapeshifters mildly amusing at first, until I realized it attracted enough funding to keep Kearn hobbling through the galaxy as my personal curse.

Thank Ersh, I thought, *Kearn wasn't here.* Our latest report on the madman had him trolling for his monster and boring university professors near Picco—there was no reason for him to divert to Panacia.

Should I have seen the danger to Paul here? I was usually willing to take what blame I deserved, having had practice, but this time I didn't see what I could have done differently. Few, if any, Panacians troubled themselves to remember the faces or names of aliens. P'Lka must have believed every lie Kearn had told her about Paul Ragem, including the one that Paul had brought Death in the form of my harmless Ket-self to her world, implicating us both in the death of Sec-ag Mixs C'Cklet, my web-kin.

It was the latter which doubtless had burned Paul Ragem's name and face into P'Lka's memory: a murder she could have believed partly her fault.

Still, the odds of a Queen meeting a Human face-to-face were . . . *Well,* I sighed to myself, *maybe they were a bit better when I was involved.*

Choices. I stood up, surveying the room. As Lishcyn, I was stuck here. As a Panacian, I was not. On the thought, I cycled, releasing my hold on this form, hurrying through my web-self into something quite different.

My caftan drifted to the floor and I kicked it aside, taking a few seconds to reacquaint myself with this form. I held out my four upper limbs, twisting them so their deep, metallic blue caught the light. Lovely, logical, graceful—*it had been,* I thought with guilty delight, *too long.*

The door had been locked against thick-fingered Esolesy Ki. With usual Panacian ingenuity, it wasn't locked at all against a tapered claw, finely serrated at its tip. Insert and twist, and I was free.

Paul's quarters were on the same floor. I headed toward them, being careful to walk with the expected poise of an Ambassador. I kept to the G'Rir, the imaginary line right of center; so any Panacian would choose, in order to walk in the steps of those before.

Haste. There was the burn of anxiety through the sensitive organs on my soles. Identity: C'Tlas. The comforting spice of a previous, more leisurely journey down the hall underlay that message. The floors were scoured in nightly ritual, but not before a Rememberer wandered slowly down every corridor, imprinting the passages taken in memory. Such information helped assess the health of the Hive, its activity, and its future.

It also made urban planning a great deal more responsive to those living in it, I recalled from Mixs-memory.

The trail I was leaving behind would taste of apprehension, and worst of all, be that of a stranger. *Clear threat to the Hive instincts.* It wouldn't help that it began in a room where a guest of the house disappeared.

Time to worry about the finer points of my rescue after finding Paul.

The agitation of the Queen must have surged throughout the building, drawing all to her side; I met no one, not even the staff who appeared to live in the kitchen area. Her pheromones of alarmed fury would easily overwhelm all other drives, and I'd braced myself for their impact as well, but the air scrubbers had already been at work—automated compensation for her emotional storm.

Congratulating myself on avoiding detection, I passed the lifts, heading for Paul's rooms, when the nearest door whooshed open beside me. *Timing,* I scolded myself, *was everything,* preparing for flight.

"Pardon me, Fem," came a voice wheezing with excitement. "Can you tell us the way to the rooms of Fem Esolesy Ki? The Feneden tell me she's remarkably good at understanding them even through their translator. We're trying to work on some specific meanings here and—"

This form had exceptional peripheral vision. Without turning my head, I could look full into the sweating, eager face of my very own nightmare—Lionel Kearn. All five Feneden stood behind him in the lift. Three carried objects I was quite sure the Panacians would strenuously object to having in their building, as blasters did a nasty amount of collateral damage if fired indoors.

I raised a lower limb, gesturing helpfully back down the corridor. Then, before he could ask me anything further, I hurried on my way.

Paul didn't utter a word when I opened his door. Instead, he grabbed a bag he'd already packed and motioned me to lead. I swallowed what I'd planned to say, drawing in a deep breath through my spiracles and feeling it reduce the heat building in my limbs. "This way," I told him. "Quickly."

He knew me, part of me exulted, *regardless of form.* Even among web-kin, unless the form-self was in memory, identification required one to be in web-form, or physical contact.

Who else would disobey the Queen and let him out? the more sensible part of me argued.

I hurried Paul to the lift, not bothering to tell him why. He'd learn for himself if we failed to move faster than Kearn and his new friends. *The Feneden and Kearn? A wonderful combination for bedtime stories,* I thought savagely. *How had those two come together—and why now?*

We careened into the lift I wanted, and I hit the control to send it rocketing downward. Suddenly, I bent over, doubling up in pain. I felt Paul's arms go around my shoulders. I tried to stand with his help, then gasped as another torrent of agony swept me to my first knees.

Somehow Paul got me out of the lift when we reached our destination. Dimly, I saw him choose a few more settings to send the lift on its way, before stepping out. I was too preoccupied to care. He half-carried me along a night-darkened corridor, thankfully confident of where we were going.

"Stop. I have to stop," I gasped after a few steps, ready to scream at the startling pain each movement caused. Paul let me slip down against a wall. We were out of sight from the lifts, at least, but in no place of safety. "I don't know what's happening—"

My next breath roared in, out of control, expanding every part of me until I felt like a balloon about to explode. My hold on this form started slipping and I clamped down. Some instinct told me I had to endure this, but I wasn't sure I could.

Paul dug his fingers into my upper shoulder blade and put his foot against my side. I wrenched my head around to stare up at him in horror. Before I could so much as whimper, he pulled as hard as he could and ripped off my upper arm.

"Better?" he gasped, laying down what was in reality only the dulling shell of my limb, complete with joints and glistening inner ligaments.

I did whimper, then, finally comprehending what was underway at the most inconvenient time possible.

I was molting.

Which wasn't possible! I fussed, while suffering exactly how possible it was. By my relative age in this form, I shouldn't go through my first molt for another sixty standard years—or maybe more. *I was too young for this!*

Paul, not privy to my inner arguments as to why this

couldn't be happening, was busy preparing to help me out of yet another painfully constricted part of my outer skin. *Rip.* Off came another limb. The fresh shell beneath was flexible for only the next breath, expanding with the inhalation, then setting itself into my new proportions. *Rip.* While Paul tugged on one of my legs as though it were an overly tight boot, I found myself flexing back and forth at my waists. The splitting of a seam up both thorax and abdomen relieved so much pain, I felt my upper arms jump into a laugh.

By the end, after what felt like an hour but doubtless took only minutes, Paul and I sat side-by-side, backs against the wall, our feet resting on discarded Esen bits, panting companionably. He was drenched with sweat, and both hands bore light gashes from the sharp edges of my old carapace. I was delirious with the feel of my brand-new self, and not interested in moving any time soon.

Which, of course, we had to do.

Paul knew it, too, asking: "All right now?" in that tone that made it a preliminary to "get up."

We helped each other rise to our feet, taking turns and being equally careful of new or damaged body parts. "How did you know?" I asked him, looking down with fascination at what resembled me after being sucked empty by a vampire orchid, complete with a head bearing transparent domes where my faceted eyes should gleam.

"How'd I know what to do?" Paul gave a brief laugh, a slightly wild note to the sound. "During training, I had a Carasian roommate: Reeto. Believe me, this was nothing compared to his molt. Took a case of beer to bribe three other guys to help; at that, we needed to liberate some power tools before we cracked the main claws. 'Course, the next day, Reeto had the gall to tell us he could have done it on his own—he'd let us peel him as a joke."

Humor, I wasn't fooled. Paul commonly used this method to recover his composure. *Of course,* I thought, *my news wouldn't help.*

I drew my Human close, wrapping all four arms around his soft warmth as though my hardening shell could protect us both. "What's this for?" Paul asked, patting what he could reach with a free hand. "You could have managed without me, too. And just because the Queen thinks she recognized—"

"Kearn's here. With the Feneden," I confessed into his ear, as though a whisper was easier.

Had I thought the Human's body soft against my hardness? Under my claws, Paul seemed to solidify, to become metal rather than flesh. Gently, he pushed me away and reached for his bag, his voice deliberate and cool: "Then there is only one way out of here, Esen old bug." This with a wave down the hall.

"The Iftsen," I said, looking toward what was more air lock than door.

"The Iftsen."

Elsewhere

"THERE. How does that feel?"

Lefebvre rolled his head from side to side, gradually becoming aware of more than the voice. *He was lying down,* he realized. *He'd been walking.* Once the implications of that hit him, Lefebvre surged upward in dismay, only to collapse back onto pillows as his head exploded.

"Wahk . . ." his mouth felt full of grit. He ran a tongue over his teeth—they were all in place—and forced his eyelids to open. A tube ran across his focus, confusing him until he realized it was aimed at his lips. He bit down on it and sucked enough moisture to clear his throat. "What happened?"

"Quite the vacation," came an unsympathetic voice—Timri's, Lefebvre identified, trying to see her through the haze in front of his eyes. "I'd say a blister stick, right across your face. Watch it—" This as Lefebvre attempted to move his hands, sending flashes of white-hot agony racing up the outer nerves of his arms. "Looks like you took a few shots on the hands, too—or were stupid enough to grab for it. I take it you don't remember."

His proof! Fighting the pain—the nerve trauma left by a blister stick was meant to be temporarily incapacitating to most life-forms, not cause permanent damage, although right now, Lefebvre couldn't have told the difference—he clawed his way up to his elbow, peering over the side of what he barely could make out as a med room cot. "My things—" he ground out.

"They were pretty thorough." She sounded almost cheerful. "I put a remote searching for your credit chip. Should protect some of your savings, unless they nip through it all before the cancel locks in."

"My clothes?" Lefebvre's vision improved enough to see Timri shake her head sadly. His heart sank.

"They must have had good taste." She pointed to a stool with a pile of clothing. "You can thank Graham later for getting the filthy things off—I wasn't going to touch them."

He let out a shuddering breath and eased himself back down. From the feel of it, he'd been hit across the back of his thighs as well, a blow that probably dropped him to his knees instantly. The last thing he remembered was walking from the bar. The street had been busy enough—not that even quiet D'Dsel's shipcity ever closed down tight. There were too many ships arriving at all hours with planet-starved crews. *Had the Ervickian set him up for the robbery?* It was possible—even likely.

Lefebvre had only himself to blame and did so with a fury. He wasn't usually an easy mark; today's unexpected triumph had probably made him act like some newbie begging to be rolled. *Probably lucky to be this intact,* he told himself, but it wasn't any comfort.

"Rest while you can," Timri said, turning down the lights. "Kearn's reported in—babbling something about these Feneden and how they're going to help. I couldn't get him to make any sense. He'll be boarding any time now, and he won't be happy to find his Captain dragged in from some alleyway by Port Authority. And—" this with the spite of someone who'd had to stay behind and work, "—you stink of beer."

Lefebvre grunted something Timri could interpret however she liked. He closed his eyes as if taking that advice, anxious for her to leave. The moment he heard the door whoosh shut, he fought his way to his feet and staggered over to his discarded clothing. His eyes watered from the searing pain as he desperately ran his hands over the mud-crusted fabric, digging into the various pockets.

The Ervickian's cubes were gone. Lefebvre knelt by the stool, supporting himself on his elbows as his entire body shook uncontrollably, every nerve protesting. *Maybe,* he told himself dully, *I can find Able Joe again, buy another copy.*

Leave the *Russ'?* Not likely, with what Timri said about Kearn.

Fearing the worst, Lefebvre forced his fingers deep inside that one pocket, despite the sensation of poking his hand into fire. *They hadn't found it.* His key. Somehow, he worked it free. Having nowhere safer to hide it, he made himself find some medplas and affixed the tiny scrap with its priceless information to his ribs.

Only then, did Lefebvre gave himself permission to collapse back on the cot and start cursing.

14: School Night; Starship Midnight

THE Iftsen had been favorites of Lesy, for more reasons than their broad-minded gallery policies.

For one thing, they didn't bother with social niceties. Any of them. Paul and I had been able walk right into what probably constituted the official Iftsen Embassy on D'Dsel—having donned the e-rigs hanging in the air lock—and become two more in the crowd without causing any stir whatsoever.

Not that the current crowd was in much shape to notice our arrival, I decided, doing my best to assess the situation through the curling smog of sulfur dioxide and just about anything else noxious an oxy-breather could imagine, all components of what the Iftsen considered fresh air. Technically, they did breathe in oxygen and breathe out carbon dioxide, so by definition were theta-class beings; the Iftsen had merely evolved within a more challenging mix than most. There were very good reasons why certain industries preferred Iftsen workers over any other. When they could get the Iftsen to pay attention, that is.

Which was one of the other things Lesy had loved. To the Iftsen, life appeared to be one long drawn-out party. Paul and I stepped over bodies rolling on the floor, dodged what might have been a fight but was more likely an argumentative dance, and finally wedged ourselves as far from the air lock as possible.

Paul touched his helmet to mine, gray eyes reflecting silver from its interior light. "This ought to slow them down anyway." *Them,* I assumed, *including just about everyone else in the School.* His voice was muffled, but clear enough. We'd agreed to avoid the com systems in the e-rigs, just in case.

I nodded, trying to spot the First Citizen. There was always one Iftsen stuck with the job of remaining sensible and in charge while the others cavorted.

"How's the molt?" Paul asked, poking a finger in the general vicinity of my abdomen. The extra two arms on his suit stuck out, courtesy of having the former contents of Paul's carrysack shoved into them. It gave him a certain rakish look for a Panacian, somewhat appropriate given our hosts.

"Fine," I said, feeling no more than a pleasantly weary tingle, as though I'd stretched all of my muscles at once. *Which,* I supposed, *I had.*

An Iftsen rocked past, waving a gallant pseudolimb in our direction. Judging by its protruding forehead, it was presently male—a variable state among this species—and Nabreda. Due to the fragmented geography of their world, and their own good nature, the Iftsen had managed to preserve several side branches of their species, unlike the evolutionary carnage of my Human companion's lineage. Some Iftsen branches were more stunted than others, as the expression went, and several subspecies spent most of their time dodging into holes in the ground whenever startled.

None of that lot here, I concluded, losing count again when a stack on a nearby couch dispersed into seven frill-faced Mobera instead of the three I'd assumed.

There was, of course, an identifiable Iftsen body plan. I'd worn the form myself, thoroughly enjoying the full-bodied taste of their atmosphere filtering through my bladder. As for their appearance, well, I'd once heard an Iftsen described with remarkable accuracy, if not much respect, as a lump of dough thrown against a wall. Regardless of subspecies, an Iftsen had a perfectly flattened front and back, while his, her, or the transitional its other edges protruded sideways or up in soft irregular lumps more dependent on mood than structure. Their appendages were equally variable in size, function, and number; much like Quebits, they could produce these at will. Since they also produced a variety of sexual appendages in a similarly unpredictable manner, Humans quickly learned to forgo their ritual of shaking hands.

Helpfully, to those species who relied on faces for conversation, the Iftsen did have heads, topped with a forehead—characteristically lumpy or frilled, depending on subspecies—concluded with a pointy chin, and the middle filled in with an eye, three nostrils, and a very tiny mouth. Less than helpfully, these heads also manifested themselves at various locations along the body's sides and top. I could see three Iftsen from where I stood, and two of them had new head buds growing under what were presently pseudo armpits.

All this was wrapped in a thick, corrosion-resistant skin which flaked off almost constantly, so the floor and any furniture was covered in crinkled disks of yellow-brown.

I'd heard Ersh, who avoided value judgments, refer to the Iftsen as the ugliest things to ever learn to think for themselves. She also sent one of us to Iftsen Secondus regularly, as if afraid to miss memorizing even the slightest achievement of their varied and rich cultures. I stood among them, for a moment savoring web-memories of epic songs and organic towers, art forms whose beginnings were buried in time and whose creation wouldn't end as long as an Iftsen breathed.

"There." Paul had spotted the First Citizen, a forlorn-looking individual adding selections to a table of sweets and various other intoxicants. We made our way through the revelers, having to wait our turn to reach the table itself.

"First Citizen?" I asked, switching on my e-rig's external speaker.

There was something about the role that sucked the cheerfulness right out of an Iftsen. This one was no exception. "What do you want?" she sighed in comspeak, looking wistfully past us to where an assortment of her kind were apparently trying to see how many of themselves they could pile up before reaching the ceiling. I turned away quickly, reasonably sure that wasn't all they were doing.

"We have to speak to you. It's an urgent matter, First Citizen."

"You'll get more attention in the morning," she warned, one thin pseudolimb sliding almost unconsciously toward a plate of chocolate-covered berries. One of those and they'd have to hurry to sober up another First Citizen before this party ended, I thought, and said quickly:

"We need you to hide us from the Feneden."

The sounds of music, gurgling laughter, and bodies in enthusiastic contact began to stop in concentric rings leading out from us until the entire room was as still as a grave.

Paul leaned his helmet against mine. "Subtle," the dryness of his tone coming through quite clearly. "Why didn't I think of that?"

The Iftsen didn't bother building starships. The Panacians had visited them first, after all, and in space-proven vehicles. Why duplicate effort? So I sat, facing Paul, in a third or fourthhand Panacian freighter, trying to make the best of things.

He was, predictably, not making that easy. "Stowage. We're in stowage."

"We couldn't be up there," I waved a claw overhead to indicate the rest of the ship, "without keeping the e-rigs on." *I, for one, didn't care for that option.* "This will do nicely. You'll see."

"What I'm seeing is the result of trying to talk sense with sixteen drunk Iftsen," he retorted. "Okay," this when I drew air through my spiracles to continue arguing, "okay. I concede this was probably the only way we could have left the School unnoticed."

I doubted the departure of the Iftsen had gone unnoticed. They'd had their own aircar, specially outfitted to protect them from D'Dsel's acid-starved air, docked directly to their floor of the School. Even drunk, the Iftsen—particularly the quite-sober First Citizen—had been anxious to avoid confrontation with the Feneden. *To their credit, the option of tossing us back out the air lock hadn't seemed to occur to them.* All of them had rushed us to the aircar, safely within our e-rigs, and packed themselves in tightly to make sure we had room. It could have been a discreet trip to the ship-city, but the two Iftsen at the controls took turns flying in great loops through swarms of hoverbots, gurgling happily as the Panacian craft dodged out of their way.

Once at the shipcity and snugged up to the Iftsen's freighter, the *Didjeridoo,* Paul and I had been given the entire lower deck to ourselves and told to expect lift by morning. Given the pace of events through the last few hours, most reasonable beings would sit and wait. *Of course, reason and a Human didn't always inhabit the same space,* I told myself, watching Paul bounce up again the instant our hosts left us alone.

The Human tossed the e-rig he'd worn onto the table between us and reached into one of the sleeves. He began pulling out its contents, starting with a dark woven shirt he took the time to don before continuing his bizarre unpacking. The shirt wasn't something I'd seen him wear before; it rose up to his chin and had a hood, just now hanging loose down his back. I tilted my head, focusing both eyes. The fabric was uncomfortable to view directly, especially when he moved his arms and muscle shifted underneath. I recognized the technology: it was a masker, a garment used by night-hunters or worse.

I cleaned my feeding palps, a nervous, secretive movement. "Paul?" I ventured cautiously.

His lean features were set in a expression I also recognized: equal parts "don't ask" and "won't answer." Not surprisingly, he hadn't smiled since the Queen's audience. *Typical ephemeral shortsightedness,* I concluded, knowing better than to try and point this out to the Human. Surely, he knew as well as I that P'Lka's accusation wasn't the threat it would have been from another being. It was unthinkable the inward-focused and highly private Hive would allow a Queen to expose herself or her concerns to outsiders; worse, to have her name become embroiled in an interspecies' scandal—as would happen if P'Lka tried to contest the Commonwealth's ponderous evidence of Paul's "death" based solely on her memory of his much younger, very alien face. Once we were outsystem from Panacia, P'Lka had few options, beyond canceling her family's contracts with Cameron & Ki Exports. *Fortunately,* I thought, *hiring assassins wasn't something a D'Dsellan would do.*

Kearn was a different menace altogether. If he found out Paul Ragem lived and learned our new identities, we would have to start again. Perhaps that was what compressed my Human's lips and made him intent on his task: sliding various small objects into a pouch wrapped around his flat middle under the masker shirt.

"Kearn was with the Feneden," I reminded my friend, searching his face. "Knowing him, he'll be so distracted he won't bother to see the Ambassadors. Since you've escaped, P'Lka won't embarrass herself to contact him about you—"

Paul's eyes burned into mine. "We can't make decisions based on guesswork, Esen." He pulled out one last device, checking it with unusual care before sliding it inside his shirt.

A biodisrupter. Its sole function was to kill other living beings. There was no stun setting, no way to merely cause a flesh wound. What Paul cradled next to his heart and my gift was death.

Or its threat. "That's not energized," I said, gesturing relief with all four limbs. "Is it?" I found myself insisting.

His fingers brushed over the weapon's hiding place, as if tempted to remove it, then fell away. "There are times, Es—" Paul began, his gray eyes almost black with distress. "I won't lie to you. Yes, it's energized. I could kill someone with it. I don't want to—but I may have to, before we are safe. Can you understand that?"

I curled my limbs around myself, rocking back and forth despondently. "The Web of Esen protects all intelligent life—you are of that Web," I reminded him numbly. "You know that's not our way."

"In this one thing, Esen-alit-Quar," Paul said ever-so-gently, "our ways differ. I will do what I must to protect you." Then he forced a smile. "Enough gloom. I'm just going out to pick up the mail before lift—hardly life and death."

"The mail?" I asked, rolling my head almost completely on its side as though the shift in perspective might make better sense of him. "What mail? It's the middle of the night! What's so important—"

He touched one of my clawtips. "The mail," he said again, as if that was some kind of explanation. "Don't let this scow leave before I'm back—it might need a push." This time his smile was genuine. "And no heroics, old bug. One sniff of your beautiful self, and the entire planet will know where we are. So stay put."

"In stowage," I tried to mimic his scornful tone from before in an effort to lighten the mood. *I didn't like any of this.*

Abruptly, Paul reached out and held my head so that his face filled each and every facet of my eyes. "Promise me, Esen. You'll lift with this ship, no matter what. If I'm not back before she goes, you go and wait for me on Iftsen Secondus."

"I—"

"Promise."

I clicked my mandibles together in something much too crude for a D'Dsellan of my apparent breeding. "I promise."

His face brightened. "Good. I'll see you soon." With that, Paul slipped the hood over his head and face, turning from my friend into something immediately darker and more deadly. He strode to the smaller port inset in the main stowage doors and let himself out. Before the port finished closing itself, I caught a glimpse of him, more shadow than substance, as he ran down the night-dimmed ramp.

"I promise I will never abandon you, Paul Ragem," I finished to myself, and prepared to wait.

Elsewhere

"SHIFTER."

"Yes, yes. Isn't it amazing? Isn't it wonderful? All these years—hundreds of systems, thousands of worlds—and here they are. Right here." *If Kearn became much happier,* Lefebvre thought critically, *he'd order him sedated.* He'd never expected a successful Kearn could be more difficult to endure than Kearn the failure.

It didn't help Lefebvre's disposition that this meeting was taking place while blister burn continued to roar at random through the nerves of his face, hands, and legs. Kearn had been warmly concerned—until he'd launched into his story about the Feneden and effectively forgot all about his captain's misadventures.

Which was just as well, Lefebvre told himself. Without proof, he wasn't about to bring up the subject of Paul Ragem. Kearn smelled blood—or at least whatever might pass for it in the large amorphous blob of jelly he'd described as the monster's natural form. The proof was as obvious as the newly polished rank insignia on Kearn's collar. Lefebvre hadn't seen Kearn in his Commonwealth uniform since his first day on board, the Human preferring what he considered a more scholarly look, almost living in a brown-toned jacket with overly large pockets kept stuffed with important-looking sheets and extra stylos. Not today. Other than a slight stretching of the fabric around his middle, Kearn looked ready for inspection.

His speech was snappier as well. "They have some

specific needs—dietary and climate. I've given all that to Timri—she's recalling the crew from their stopovers. They can get quarters ready for the Feneden by noon, can't they? Fem Anisco was very eager not to inconvenience me—us—and agreed to as early a start as possible."

"Start? To what, sir?" Lefebvre wondered if he wanted the answer. He knew he didn't want to be the one facing the crew when they began staggering back to the ship from whatever bar or bed they'd found. *There'd be a desertion or two for sure, this time.*

"Our search—we are heading to Fened Prime, Captain Lefebvre. The ancestral home of the Esen Monster!"

He had to be on something, Lefebvre thought. Before he could draw breath to object, Kearn pressed a crumpled piece of plas into his hand, saying: "These are some supplies—the Feneden didn't know where to get them, but you do, don't you, Captain? You know your way around every shipcity—surely there are dealers, traders with surplus. I'll leave it all in your capable hands."

Stunned, Lefebvre could only raise an eyebrow. "You want me to go back out to the shipcity, sir, tonight? Now?" *It couldn't be this easy.*

"You're up to it, aren't you?" Kearn demanded in a tone that said Lefebvre had better answer yes.

"Of course, sir."

"Keep an eye out for robbers this time, Captain. Honestly, that's the sort of mistake I'd expect from a newbie, not you. You have to be bold with these Port scum. You can't look like a target."

"Yes, sir. Good advice. I'll be more careful."

In fact, Lefebvre decided as he walked away, wincing with each step, he planned to look very carefully indeed for a certain robber.

And a certain Ervickian.

15: Freighter Night; Shipcity Night

THE stowage area of the Iftsen freighter was 432 paces long and 102.5 paces wide—if I didn't count the cramped spaces under the overhead cargo racks. Those were mostly empty. I'd already climbed up and investigated any crates without seals, finding only personal effects, presents for the family, and a few jugs of chocolate syrup bound to cause some excitement back home. I spent some time pondering how to explain to a Human such as Paul what chocolate tasted like in the Iftsen atmosphere, but gave up. Not only was it inaccurate to relate what the Iftsen called taste to the similarly-named, but physiologically different, sense in Humans, the Iftsen didn't actually consume chocolate. They combusted it in their respiratory bladder. *With quite the pleasurable aftereffect.*

Paul wasn't back yet.

Once in a while, I could detect thumping and other unusual sounds coming from the deck above. Since my Panacian ears were quite ordinary, and the deck thick, I refused to speculate what the Iftsen were doing. I'd hoped they were becoming sober, but on second thought knew the hope came from my sensible Panacian-self. The *Didjeridoo*'s crew would report to stations in the morning, there were no tasks to be done beforehand, hence, to the Iftsen, it was perfectly reasonable to divorce themselves from whatever else was happening on or off the planet and have some fun.

I could, I thought with some disgust, *fall dead and rot down here before they'd notice. If then.*

If I could find some living mass to increase my own, I could be up there and cheerfully oblivious, too, instead of alone in the drafty stowage and worrying about just about everything possible.

I examined the notion fondly, but without any real intention of following it. For one thing, there wasn't any living mass down here, unless I could catch the rat I'd surprised behind some crates. For another, I had no desire to abandon Ersh's teachings—not now, when they were all I had—and she'd drilled her conservative, safe approach firmly into me: *if the current form can manage, use it.*

I was currently Panacian, *and a lovely one at that,* I decided, admiring anew my freshly-minted carapace. I was also, as Paul had rightly noted, conspicuously unknown to others of this kind. There were literally no strangers on the Hiveworld. Every new adult Panacian was anointed with his or her Queen's scent at the Spring Emergence, the scent ceremoniously reapplied after each molt.

Mixs had become expert at hiding among the resting cocoons, waiting her chance to cycle and simply walk out with the others to where the Queens waited. In the guise of reincarnation, she'd dared reclaim her name and house time after time. She'd brought me for visits, carefully scenting me with samples stolen from remote families whose Queens were unlikely to travel to the cities.

Something else I was unlikely to find in the stowage compartment, I grumbled to myself. At the moment, my footprints left no trace of a Queen's claiming scent, a glaring omission informing any Panacians who happened to cross my path that I didn't belong—anywhere. Hiding my lack of scent in boots, I knew, would simply not work. There were strict laws against public obscenity on D'Dsel.

All of which brought me pacing back to the port which had closed behind Paul, confining me here. I glowered at it, then checked the chrono above again. He'd been gone for almost two hours.

This so-important mail of his had to be in another courier

pouch, most likely sitting in the vault of another starship. *Not necessarily a close neighbor,* I thought. D'Dsel's ship-city was the largest this close to the Fringe, its immaculately maintained shipways fluctuating ceaselessly as docking tugs moved incoming and outgoing vessels either to their assigned dock or into position for lift. At a rough estimate, there would be several thousand larger freighters and passenger ships fins down and open for business, with triple that number of smaller traders making quick stopovers in search of profitable crumbs.

All of the docked ships would have ramps run out to the nearest shipway, creating a city more temporary than anything the Panacians themselves built—a charming feature to my Panacian-self, although the shipcity's overall design was exceedingly dull and fixed. *Matching offworld tech had its downside.*

I couldn't begin to guess which ship was Paul's destination. Several here likely carried goods for Cameron & Ki—once a shipment left our primary carrier at a distribution point, it could be taken up by any number of registered short- or long-haul companies. Largas Freight came here, but the bulk of their routes went deeper into the Fringe, carving new territory rather than competing for a share within established systems. Joel's choice was one I'd long suspected had less to do with profit than with avoiding well-intentioned but cumbersome Commonwealth bureaucracy.

I put my claws on the door, idly testing if it was firmly shut. For a being who had been content to spend twenty years waiting for a hand to regrow—the result of combining the unexpected fragility of my crystalline Tumbler form with an admittedly desperate effort to climb back into my room without being spotted by Skalet—I was discomfited to find each and every minute crawling like parasitic worms under my carapace. *Living with Humans,* I sighed to myself, *had a way of doing that.*

Suddenly, the waiting was over—*not,* I realized with dread, *for the better*—as the entire ship resounded with an alarm. Seconds later, I felt the heavy shudder through my feet and grabbed for the door handle. In lieu of a quake, there was only one possible explanation: the *Didjeridoo* had just been picked up by a tug.

The Iftsen, it appeared, were in more of a hurry than we'd been told.

I could have marshaled several good reasons for what I did next—given time to think of them—but reasonable thought had very little to do with the alacrity with which I switched off the safety lock on the port, hauled open the door, and flung myself out into the air.

Although reasonable thought might have prepared me for the discovery, as I continued to fall, that the ship's ramp had already been withdrawn.

This early, an hour before dawn, was when the tidy Panacians insisted cleaner servos run through every nook and cranny of their cities, following the solemn passage of the Rememberers, an insistence enforced by Port Authority on D'Dsel. As a result, it was probably the cleanest shipcity in the settled galaxy, although from what I'd seen, not too clean for rats and other wildlife to make a living.

I hadn't, I thought gratefully, *broken anything except my pride.* My body had been soft enough from my recent molt not to crack when I'd hit the pavement, although I had some painful dents in my thorax and abdomen likely to remain until I molted again. As a consequence, I'd be wearing the evidence of my stupidity in this form for many years to come, unless I paid for some reconstructive surgery. *I was probably better off keeping the dents as a lesson,* I scolded myself. I'd been lucky not to be caught under the grinding treads of the tug itself.

All that remained of our meeting place now was an empty stretch of darkened pavement, littered with packing and other debris the servos were consuming with machine enthusiasm. I heard bottles being crunched and wondered if the partying Iftsen were aware of their own departure.

Servos were one thing—the variety of sweepers, suckers, and odd ones with spikes moved around me without interest in living litter. The inhabitants of the shipcity were another matter altogether. Even had I known where to start looking for Paul in this maze, I would have stuck to shadows. It didn't matter that this was a civilized jungle consisting of starships and all the trappings of technology—in the bowels of night, the shipcity had its own assortment of hunters and hunted. *Explanation enough,* I supposed, *for Paul's desire to be armed,* if not his choice of weaponry.

Not that I was worried for myself. It was just best—more of Ersh's wisdom—to avoid situations where one's relative invulnerability might actually be tested. And I disliked angry voices.

Such as those accompanying the two figures moving toward me along the shipway, stepping in and out of the circles of ramp lights at a very rapid walk for the Human male, and—I trailed the polishing inner edge of my lower arm over my eyes in case they were fogging in the predawn damp—what was a flat-out run for his Ervickian companion.

I began stepping back toward the hiding place I'd noted earlier—one of the servicing columns festooned like some giant tree with pipes for everything from atmosphere replenishment to fuel, an unimaginable luxury to one used to Minas XII's approach to service—slowly, so my own motion shouldn't be obvious, careful to hold my limbs to avoid reflecting glints of betraying light. I slipped under the cover of a cable broader than my shoulders, ducking as low to the ground as possible before trying to look out. After all, the Human might be Paul, in which case I wanted to gauge his mood before confronting him with my creative interpretation of my promise. *Best to ease into such things.*

Within seconds, they were close enough that I could make out what was being said, not just its furious tone. "I'm beginning to think you planned this, too. You'd better not be lying to me, Able Joe, or your crèche will be emptier by one."

I didn't need the deep voice to tell me this Human wasn't mine; I could see that for myself in the lights cast by neighboring ships as the pair stopped right in front of my hiding place. *Perfect,* I told myself. *Just perfect.*

The Human stood, fists on his hips, looking around the

gap where the Iftsen freighter had stood. I increased my body temperature, resisting an impulse to change into something less conspicuous, or at least something that could scamper away unnoticed. The Ervickian, a young one, was kicking the tiny servos out of his way as he circled the Human, as though pretending to search for something. *If it was a starship,* I smiled to myself, *he was definitely out of luck.*

The Human was younger than Paul, I decided, studying him, maybe by twenty standard years, though his face appeared older. An artifice of the night and his equally dark mood, perhaps, since otherwise I would have judged it a face that should smile easily: not handsome, as Humans went, but with blunt, open features. His frame was considerably shorter than Paul's yet more massive, without exceeding Human norms. When the Human reached out to grab the Ervickian's ear, possibly exasperated by the being's pointless and noisy torment of the servos, he winced and let go almost immediately, as though his hand was damaged. *What was so important here?*

As I wondered feverishly, the Ervickian cringed and I heard it say quite plainly: "Slothe and his accomplice boarded the *Didjeridoo.* My source was reliable. Did you remember that? I told you—I don't get messages from that Kraal and ignore them, see."

Kraal? I dumped the disturbing but not surprising tidbit into memory—the conspiracy-loving Kraal were prone to having spies in every shipcity, even peaceful ones such as D'Dsel—focusing instead on that name.

Slothe. On any other night, after any other sequence of events, I might not have made the connection between the word and the alias Paul had used on Ultari Prime. Of course, it didn't hurt that my memory immediately showed me the face of a certain despicable Ervickian shopkeeper, a face with a definite resemblance around its four beady eyes to the shining example of its race in front of me now.

Oh, dear, I sighed to myself. Perhaps getting my credits back hadn't been the wisest move—satisfying as it had been at the time. I should have known the being would take

it personally; I had, having witnessed Paul's poignant reaction when our brand-new starship turned out to be an ancient taxi.

Of course, Paul's reaction would be even more memorable when he found out about this. *If,* I added. There was
a distinct advantage to selective memory sharing with my
Human web-kin. I found myself hoping he'd take a long
time to retrieve his mail.

The Human stood with his feet wide apart, as though
needing the stability. "Listen, my repulsive little friend," his
voice sounded remarkably as though forced through gritted
teeth. "I'm supposed to be filling my ship's hold, not standing in an empty dock."

The Ervickian threw its hands into the air. "You worry
too much. I told you: my crèche has copies of what was
stolen. As for your shopping: my friends back at the *'Gills*
have doubtless found all you needed. Did you forget all
this?" The concern sounded sincere—Ervickians predictably
assumed other species were missing half a brain. *Which
would be a more reasonable prejudice,* I reminded myself,
if Ervickians ever used both of theirs. "Wasn't it lucky for
you?" Able Joe continued happily.

"What? Finding you again?" Definite menace now. "Let's
hope it's luckier than last time."

The smaller being danced back out of range, hands pro-
tectively over its second mouth as though used to low blows.
"How many times can I tell you, Hom Captain? Able Joe's
no cheat—I didn't send any rats on your trail. You found
those on your own."

Captain? I pushed my head out a little farther, curious
in spite of myself. Any being with a ship could claim that
title, but there was something in the way this Human carried himself that suggested the rank was more than self-
assumed. Sure enough, the Human wore some type of
uniform under that shapeless coat.

"I'd like to find them again," the captain growled as if
to himself. *Not a happy individual,* I thought, *and not one
to have for an enemy.*

The Ervickian I could see chasing rumors of Megar

Slothe, especially if it thought there was a chance to gain credits out of it. *What was this Human's interest?*

A question I had no intention of asking, relieved when the Human said: "Enough of this. We've been misled or we've missed him. Either way, I have to report in. Let's get back to the bar and see if your so-called friends have salvaged anything of tonight."

The two of them started retracing their steps. On one claw, I was relieved they were going. I'd had visions of Paul marching into the two of them, although to give my Human his due, I doubted he'd be that careless. *That was usually my job.*

On the other claw (or three), I remained curious. *Were these two some threat to Paul or just fortune hunters?* I made a mental note to quietly replace the credits I'd canceled from the Ervickian's crèche at my first opportunity.

They disappeared from sight. I waited another long moment before straightening, two more before walking out to where they'd stood. I carefully retraced some of their steps, my feet tasting nothing but the inorganic background of pavement and solvent, plas and metal.

My peripheral vision caught a flash of movement, giving me enough warning to duck as the Ervickian launched himself at me from his concealment beneath the neighboring starship's ramp. My Panacian-self, while stiff-bodied, had two very flexible body joints; ducking put me considerably lower than my attacker expected. He flew completely over my head, landing with a doubled grunt on top of a group of servos cleaning up a pile of some moist, oozing material. He wasn't hurt, as far as I could tell, but didn't look particularly comfortable either.

I wasn't planning to stay and find out, but as I turned to run, two powerful arms wrapped around me from behind, pinning all four upper limbs to my sides and lifting me partly off my feet. *No guesses who,* I thought with disgust.

"It's her! The one in the vid! The one from our store! The cheat! The cheat!" The Ervickian scrambled to its feet, rushing toward me with a very nasty look in all its eyes and its eight-fingered hands out as though to tear me limb from limb. *That might have been helpful earlier tonight,* I found myself thinking, but was unlikely to do more than break his nails now that I'd hardened.

To my surprise, the Human turned so his shoulder was between us. "Back off," he warned his companion. "I've got her." This with an unnecessary squeeze, as though to remind me of my own capture.

I drew a very deep breath through all my spiracles at once. "Hoodlums!" I bellowed. "Murderers!" The volume a Panacian could achieve with air-filled tracheae had to be heard to be believed. "Robbers!"

It was a very effective strategy, sending the Ervickian running down the shipway as fast as he could shuffle and the Human desperately trying to find some way to shut me up without hurting his apparently already sore hands. As my vocal organs were located behind four sets of feeding mandibles—serrated feeding mandibles—he wasn't doing very well. He cursed almost as loudly as I was shouting, then started shaking me.

This wasn't pleasant, but wasn't much of a deterrent to this form either—especially when I realized he was carefully controlling the force he used. I began to enjoy myself, and drew in air for another set of loud pleas for hopefully nonexistent help.

Which I didn't make, having the business end of a stunner suddenly pressed against the dome of my right eye. The Human took advantage of my sudden silence to say in a ragged, desperate voice: "Please stop shouting. I don't want to hurt you. I'm looking for someone—"

"Then maybe I'll do," said a voice I hardly recognized as Paul's. The stunner fell away as my captor obviously felt its value somewhat limited compared to the biodisrupter caressing his cheek. "Don't turn around."

My captor obeyed, standing perfectly still, face-to-face with me. This close, I could see the fine lines pain, and the effort of fighting it, had drawn around his eyes and lips. There was a narrow, feather-edged band of red slashing from his hairline and down to follow a cheekbone—*blister burn,* I realized, wincing in sympathy. It didn't seem to matter. There was a hot gleam in his eyes as he looked back at me and mouthed a word that might have been "Ragem."

I stepped beyond his reach, then couldn't help wrapping my limbs around my thorax. *This was,* I decided, *one of those times when being rescued was probably the worst thing that could happen.*

Paul stood behind the stranger, his face hidden in the masker hood, the hand holding the deadly weapon servo-steady. Then, it started to shake, something that made me—and from the look on his face, Paul's captive—understandably anxious. "What did he do to you?" Paul demanded. "Are you all right?"

At first, I assumed he was reading the distress in my posture—for his species, Paul was superb at interpreting body language—and straightened to reassure him, a movement which involved my dented body parts. I clicked several mouth parts, the equivalent to a Human's wince.

Paul swore and pushed the Human violently to the pavement. The Human didn't struggle—no sane being did when threatened by what my friend carried.

"Oh," I said with sudden understanding. I looked down at my damaged carapace and would have blushed in several other forms. *Or regurgitated.* The physiological signs of embarrassment were typically demeaning. "No. He didn't do this. I—had a little accident earlier. I'm fine. In fact," I added slowly, "he protected me from his partner."

The Human at my feet lifted his face to gaze up at me, his expression—what I could see of it—oddly puzzled. *What had he expected,* I thought irritably to myself. *That I'd demand his head or other body parts?*

"You're sure," Paul persisted, tipping his own head from side to side as though trying to figure out what kind of accident I could have had since he'd left by examining the pattern of bumps. "That looks—awful."

Such honesty, I didn't need. I waved all four upper arms in proof. "Yes. I'm fine! Can we get out of here?"

Paul nudged our prisoner with his toe. "We'll have to do something to make sure he's not on our tails," he said, in a return to that cold, ruthless voice. I'd have been alarmed, but I could see my friend putting away the deadly biodisrupter, exchanging it for the stunner he'd taken from the Human's hand.

The Human continued to stare up at me, such implacable determination in his eyes I couldn't have looked away if I'd tried. He spoke, but his words were directed at the one he couldn't see: "Paul Antoni Ragem. The Traitor. Kill me, if that's what you've become, but the time for secrets is over. Someone else will track you down—" he slumped as Paul fired the stunner.

Paul immediately knelt beside him, turning the limp Human over so he could see the face. "Thought so," he said grimly.

"You know him?" I asked, bending myself to try unsuccessfully to match this face to a memory. *There were,* I thought practically, *too many Humans to meet even in my lifetime.*

Paul pulled off his hood, his face reassuringly normal as he looked at me: annoyed and slightly frustrated. "This is Rudy Lefebvre. Captain Lefebvre."

I knew the name. *Kearn's captain.* I curled involuntarily into a tight ball of misery. "First the Feneden. Now this. How is Kearn getting so close to us all of a sudden? What's happening? We were safe!"

"And you were going with the Iftsen," Paul reminded me unnecessarily. He glanced around, adding the stunner to the arsenal in his shirt. We were alone, the servos chattering whimsy to themselves as they adjusted their paths to avoid us and Lefebvre's crumpled body. "We'll have to leave him here. He'll be all right." Paul went over to a large carrysack he must have tossed to one side when he saw me being shaken by Lefebvre.

"But—" I stopped, unable to say it out loud.

Paul's teeth caught some of the nearby light as he smiled at me. "Stop worrying. Lefebvre was guessing—fishing for your reaction. He didn't see me. He doesn't know you. There's no evidence. The best thing we can do is leave him to try and explain to Kearn what—ah." The soft exclamation accompanied his pulling a large bottle from the sack. He opened it and began pouring its contents over Lefebvre's clothing. I straightened and stood, backing up so the alcohol fumes wouldn't scald my spiracles. "Sorry about this," Paul said to the unconscious Human, before holding the bottle to Lefebvre's lips and pouring some of the drink into his mouth until Lefebvre gagged and swallowed by reflex.

"Let's go. And while we do," Paul said to me sternly, taking his carrysack under one arm and putting the other firmly around my shoulders to urge me in his chosen direction, "I'll give you a choice, old bug. You can start by explaining how—after I leave you safe and sound on a ship—that ship's not here and you still are. Or, you can tell me how, marvelous hider that you are, you wind up in the clutches of our enemy. Or," he paused and sighed theatrically.

"Maybe you'd best begin with this little accident."

Not my first choice, I thought glumly.

Elsewhere

"WHAT do you mean, he's not back yet?" Kearn knew something would happen. It always did. Just when everything was starting to go his way, when things were finally moving in the right direction, someone deliberately and maliciously sabotaged him. This time it was Lefebvre. "Find him!"

Timri didn't look pleased, but then again, no one on the *Russell III* was in a good mood. The crew they'd managed to find had returned grudgingly, noisily, and, in one case, with unfortunate consequences inside the air lock, most heading straight to the med room for anti-intoxicants or to their cabins to sleep.

"Do you really want me to call Port Authority, sir?" she said with an effort, rubbing grit from her eyes. Much more of this, and none of them would be in a fit state to take the *Russ'* offworld tomorrow—*today,* she corrected herself, with a dismayed glance at the chrono behind Kearn's desk. "The Jellies who brought the Captain here after he was attacked probably haven't finished their report yet."

Kearn, well-used to the results of looking the fool to the local authorities, almost cringed. "Yes. Yes. Good point, Comp-tech. Send someone—"

Security Officer Sas, a silent mound of dirty white fur until now, made a hissing sound through his yellowed fangs. "To look where?" he demanded, the hiss and spit moderated into comspeak through the implant in his throat. "There's no return address on the goods that arrived for the Feneden. The beings who delivered them say they don't know Captain Lefebvre—they were sent to fill the list by some third party they didn't know either."

"Quite conveniently," Timri added, "to be paid by us."

"They would not have left the supplies otherwise," Sas hissed, continuing the argument they'd brought into his quarters.

"At least we know Captain Lefebvre was on the job," Kearn said, cheered by this reminder that the fussier needs of his much-anticipated passengers would be met, if not by the implication of Lefebvre dealing in the shadier areas of the marketplace. "But he knows I can't have him being late and holding up the ship. Remind me to put him on report when he shows. He's probably at some bar, becoming useless."

Timri was frowning. "Or he could be lying in a pool of blood somewhere. Sir, may I remind you—the Captain was attacked once already."

Kearn's hands sought the front of his desk drawer, as if seeking comfort from what lay within it. "Of course. There's that." He schooled his face to show concern.

"Drunken Humans get robbed," Sas growled without sympathy. "The Captain should have attended his duties to the Hunt, not his pleasures. Now he makes us late. We must keep our schedule, sir. Let Port Authority locate this deserter. If he turns up, you can discipline him later. In the meantime, by regulation, you should assume the post of Acting Captain."

Acting Captain. While Kearn couldn't quite imagine Lefebvre as a deserter—or himself successfully disciplining the strong-willed captain, he did know opportunity when it struck.

And with the support of the Feneden added to that of his backer, Kearn thought happily, *maybe he could stay captain this time. Or at least find a new, respectful one.*

Maybe, this was all for the best.

16: Starship Morning; Starship Night

"THIS was the best you could do," I complained, but Paul wasn't listening anymore, a circumstance having more to do with my present location than any lack of sympathy on his part.

I was in a bag.

It was a large, clean bag—Paul's carrysack, in fact—and well-padded with clothing. The Human had thoughtfully left an inconspicuous gap in the top fastener and carried this ensemble of Esen, clothing, and bag with irreproachable care.

It was still a very undignified way to arrive on a ship. Paul's insistence that it was also much safer—given we'd attracted so much attention, including the nastier sort such as Kraal—somehow didn't seem appropriate from an individual who'd risked further exposure to bring what I could feel underpod to be my Lishcyn-self's favorite outfit.

On the plus side, I thought, pulling tiny fragments of lint out of a seam, *my current self wasn't easily bored.* Quebits tended to be of-the-moment, busy creatures.

I really hated being a Quebit.

Although this ship could likely use a few of my sort. I extruded an extra ear to analyze the message contained in the faint squeal of mechanics in the lift. *Probably hadn't received proper maintenance in decades, if then.* I knew precisely how to clean and lubricate those moving parts, and harbored dark suspicions of pitted bearings. I poked at the top of the bag suggestively with an upperpod only to have Paul tap quite firmly, and dismissively, back.

I sighed and returned to the lint.

Our transport was the independent trader *Narcissus,* and the entire ship's complement was rolled up into the solitary, heaving bulk of a communal Cin named Marvin. Captain Marvin at that.

I considered the entire situation. "Oh, dear."

"You've said that already," Paul admonished, waving his finger at me. "It's not helpful, Esen."

I was being helpful, if not sounding it, putting the last bits of soil and pot shards into the maw of the cabin's recycler. Paul had arranged for a cartload of live plants to meet us on the *Narcissus.* Having assimilated most of the plant mass in order to escape Quebit-form for something much more comfortable—namely my sturdy, familiar, Lishcyn-self—I was determined not to leave any evidence lying around.

Once finished, I sat down on the bunk—Paul might be a paying passenger, but on this tiny ship that meant the unused crew quarters—and sighed again. "A Cin. You know only a small percentage of them are even borderline sane. Most can't agree on a working definition of reality within themselves, let alone walk in a straight line." I pointed to the nearest bulkhead. "And this ship! Let me tell you, as a former Quebit, this scrap heap wouldn't be safe on the ground, let alone translight."

"There weren't many choices heading in the right direction," he commented mildly. "Few ships are routing through Tly space, thanks to the enthusiasm of their inspectors. Besides, Captain Marvin appears remarkably in agreement with themselves at the moment."

"Small mercies," I said. The Cin were one of two known communal intelligences in this part of space, the Rand being the other. Ersh remembered a few more, but as an evolutionary strategy, communals were prone to becoming static and self-absorbed, falling victim to any sudden change in their environment, such as a virus or climatic catastrophe, without appearing to notice the threat until it was too late to act.

Rands were physically individuals, requiring close contact with at least twenty others to function. The Cin were a variable assortment of individual cognitions, all housed within one roughly humanoid body. A large, humanoid body.

I could become Rand and had as part of my training. It was awkward, because one felt an insatiable need to bundle with other Rands, who didn't always invite strangers into their intimate clusters. Ansky, my birth-mother, was predictably the most comfortable of the web-kin in the form. Mind you, she'd stayed Rand long enough to produce several generations of offspring who adored her, sting and all, so her bundle of joy was of her own making.

The Cin were a different matter. It was one form I had never attempted to assume, although theoretically I could, since the essence of its shape and biology were in my web-memory. Ersh herself had forbidden it. All she would say on the subject was that one personality was all a being should have to deal with in a lifetime.

So I had serious doubts about the quality of our transportation. Paul, on the other hand, seemed to find my concerns amusing—as if having lifted from D'Dsel, all our worries were somehow over.

"Es, old friend," he said lazily. "Relax before you upset your stomachs. As far as the Captain and D'Dsel Port Authority are concerned, you aren't even here. And as of today, I'm Mitchell Kane, with no trace of Paul Cameron or Paul Ragem in sight. We're safe."

"For now. As long as I stay in this cabin—or at least avoid the Cin—and you don't step in front of a vid. Then what?"

My friend, who'd reclined on one elbow to watch me clean up then restore Esolesy Ki, sat up and leaned forward, eyes intent and warm. "We're going to be all right."

I brushed imaginary dust from the edge of the bunk over my head, distracted for a moment to wonder why such a small transport would be outfitted to carry so many crew. Then I considered its age and nodded to myself. Must be a former troop transport—something left over from one of the small, pseudo-elegant conflicts of the Kraal in which it wasn't who won or lost, but who used the most elaborate tricks, that mattered.

Thinking of tricks, I looked into my friend's eyes and wondered something else. "Did you leave the Iftsen ship to get mail, Paul my friend, or these?" I ran a three-fingered hand down the silk covering my wide, scaled thigh. "And why did you take so long? You might have missed me." *He'd gambled,* I thought, mystified. *Paul never gambled.* "You knew I wouldn't leave D'Dsel if the Iftsen pulled out before you were back," I accused him, suddenly sure I was right. "You didn't believe me."

"Not for an instant," he said, not looking the least perturbed to be found out.

"Then why did you leave me there at all?" I controlled the urge to snatch the remaining plants and cycle into something larger. "You lied to me."

Paul shook his head. "No, I didn't. I thought the *Didjeridoo* would stay docked until I came back for you. You had to wait somewhere safe. You know you couldn't travel on D'Dsel as a Panacian and we didn't have time for other . . . options. However—" his eyes softened as he smiled, "if there's anything I count on in this life, Esen, it's that you would never abandon me, promise or no promise. Although I hadn't expected you to leap into midair on my behalf."

Somehow, Paul made my painful mistake sound almost admirable. I flashed a tusk weakly. *Fine with me.*

"And here's the mail," the Human continued, flipping open an outer pocket on the carrysack and pulling out a small pouch. "I'd arranged for it to be dropped in the locker with our extra baggage from the *Goddess.*" He tossed the pouch on the bunk beside him, leaving his fingers on it.

I hesitated, looking at the pouch as though it was about to grow fangs and launch itself at the scaleless patch under my chin. Lishcyns weren't fond of fanged life, being passive by nature and prey by ecology. I hesitated, then deliberately met the intense gaze of my companion, the other part of my Web and my life. *There were some things,* I decided calmly, *I didn't want to know.*

Perhaps Paul read that in my face. I might have imagined disappointment flickering across his, as though he'd hoped to use my curiosity to open a subject difficult to broach. If so, I wasn't planning to help. *We had enough problems.*

Starting with our next move. "The Iftsen," I said firmly. "Could they have left prematurely to avoid Kearn?"

Paul laughed. "Wise beings, if so." Then he sobered. "I don't know. There's nothing in the newsmags about their situation with the Feneden, but those are mostly humanocentric as well as out-of-date the moment they're distributed anyway. I've kept away from our own data system while things are—a little unusual—here." *Ever the master of understatement.* "But from what little the Queen told us, I wouldn't be surprised to find that situation is coming to a head and fast." The Human paused, looking quizzical. "Why? Does that concern you?"

I half rose to my feet. "Concern me? Of course, it concerns me! The Iftsen could very well exterminate the Feneden in self-defense."

Evenly: "They're thieves. You said so yourself."

"I don't believe this," I snapped, furious enough to add a rude gesture with my forked tongues. "Do you know how many billions live on Fened Prime? Do you have any idea of the repercussions on the Iftsen if they take that step, even to save themselves? It is the duty of the Web of Esen to protect intelligent life, Paul!"

A twist of his lips—the one I knew as satisfaction. "Just thought I'd ask, old friend."

He was testing me, I realized with a shock, sinking back down and staring at a face I thought I knew better than any of my own. *As my web-kin had done.* Checking my belief in the Rules, in the fundamental purpose of our lives: the assessment of the Youngest and Least, Esen-alit-Quar, had gone on with monotonous regularity and the occasional sharp rebuke.

Their reasons, I had understood.

What were his?

Paul, perhaps sensing my growing discomfort, chose to change the subject. "The *Narcissus* will be outsystem of Panacia shortly. I told Captain Marvin I would give them our course. So, Iftsen Secondus or Fened Prime?"

I rarely felt the differences between Paul's life and mine acutely. At unpredictable moments, I experienced an awareness of being both older in years and yet younger in self— usually following events when I would have preferred the reverse. Less frequently, as now, I faced the unyielding reality of our life spans. Within my flesh were memories that began long before his species walked upright; I could comfortably devote a hundred years to learning a new art form or language. Paul's time was far more—precious. *Did I have the right to risk him?*

"Kearn's on our trail," I began, keeping my voice matter-of-fact. "And there may be a war—"

"Don't, Es."

I arranged my features at their most innocent. "Don't—?"

Paul frowned and stabbed his finger at me. "I know that look. Don't even think of leaving me out of this."

"Can you breathe on Iftsen Secondus?" I asked reasonably.

"That's not the issue and you know it," he snapped. "I'm not some pet you tuck out of harm's way, Esen."

My "Paul!" was sincerely horrified. *Pet?* "Is that what you think . . . ?" My words trailed off into confusion, volatile first and third stomachs grumbling loud enough to be audible outside my body.

He had the grace to blush, then pulled out his medallion. "Part of Esen's Web. I know. But an equal part, Es. If there's anything you and I can do to resolve this situation without bloodshed—we're doing it together."

I gazed at my friend, seeing his determination and courage—traits which I'd found alternated between virtue and inconvenience depending on circumstance. "Of course," I assured him. "Together."

*And, if there was any risk to him, that was another prom-
ise he should know I couldn't keep.*

A shame I didn't think of that sooner.

"We've gone insystem. Wake up, Es."

I grunted something threatening, but managed to open
an eye. Despite burying my head in as many blankets and
pillows as I could find without robbing those on Paul's bed,
it had taken me hours to fall asleep on the flat, exposed
surface Humans considered a safe place to sleep. After two
nights like this, my Lishcyn-self, to be kind, was as charming as week-old curdled milk. Paul, faced with my company or the confusion of Captain Marvin's many selves,
had spent a great deal of time on the bridge of the *Narcissus.*

Then, what Paul's urgent whisper hadn't said brought me
fully awake. "Insystem?" I repeated, looking up at a darker
shadow I presumed was his face. "Iftsen Secondus?"

"I don't know."

"Haven't you asked the Captain?" *Instead of waking me
up,* I added to myself, preparing to tunnel back down—or
at least pull the pillows back over my head.

There was one of those pauses. "The door's locked."

"Maybe it's stuck," I suggested around my yawning
tongues. "Nobody puts a lock on the crew's quarters."

"Tell the Cin."

I shoved my coverings out of my way, sitting cautiously.
Although I knew the ship's lighting system was functioning, the night-dims weren't enough to trigger a response
from my present eyes. I hesitated to lose mass I might need
later, just to see Paul's face and the other side of a locked
door.

Then I was squinting. At first I thought Paul had found
a control for the light, then I realized the lights had been
upped by remote.

While I worked my tired brain around all this, Paul went
to the door and stood, pressing his ear flat to its surface.
His hands were empty, but I knew he had brought his
weapons on board. "I don't like this," he muttered, almost

to himself, then turned to look at me. "Or this." Paul reached into his pocket then tossed me a flattened black strip. It landed beside me on the bed. I didn't touch it, recognizing the remnants of a tracer.

"It was in my extra clothing," Paul said, his voice flat. "Maybe from Minas XII. Or it could be a recent plant. Remind me to complain about storage security, if we're ever back on D'Dsel. While you're at it, remind me to pay a visit to the idiot who sold me that scanner." He rubbed one hand over his face, then said abruptly: "You'd better hide, Esen. Do it now."

Hiding I was good at, I thought, trying not to be alarmed, *the result of an extended childhood spent avoiding my Elders.*

My Human and I had made and discarded plans of one sort or another, most concerned with ways to find out why the Feneden were refusing to acknowledge the Iftsen. This particular situation hadn't come up—it hadn't needed to, since our life on Minas XII involved my routinely having to disappear at inconvenient moments.

Shame to waste the mass, though, I sighed, releasing my hold on the Lishcyn-form.

I paused in web-form, shedding drops of water from the perfection of my outer surface, senses extended beyond the dissonant complaints of the *Narcissus'* engines to the thrumming depths of gravity tempting me this way and that.

I turned a speck of web-mass into energy and rearranged my molecular structure into that of a species almost as amorphous as my true self: the Ycl. To my new vision, extended well into the infrared, Paul blazed like a beacon.

Beacon was a poor choice of words. I oozed underneath the nearest bunk, flattening myself into what I hoped looked like a stain on the floor—*given the tastes I was adsorbing under here, that should be believable enough.* The Ycl, while admirable in many ways, had regrettable appetites that would likely keep their world quarantined for quite some time. A useful form, particularly for its stealth and predator's sensitivity to sound, but one in which I didn't dare become famished—at least not near any being I'd regret having for lunch.

I could have used a set of vocal cords, however, in order to tell my partner—from the sounds above, now busily repacking his case and otherwise attempting to conceal any sign he wasn't alone in his captivity—that he'd been right to suspect we weren't where we were supposed to be.

My web-self had thoroughly sampled the energy fields around the *Narcissus* and beyond, deciphering the complexities of electromagnetism and gravity as a Human would hum to a melody played by an orchestra.

There wasn't a planet or even a star nearby.

Just the well-tuned power signature of a Tly battle cruiser.

Elsewhere

TORTURE would have been so much easier, Lefebvre thought wearily. He could have fought, reviled his tormentors, gained a moral victory from however long he'd resisted. He might have even held out until they believed his protestations of ignorance—not that he considered himself a hero, but surely time wasn't on anyone's side. *Surely he'd been missed by now.*

His fingers traced the pattern left behind by the dispenser in the skin of his forearm, marks of his betrayal. Torture, at least among Humans, had been abandoned as a means of obtaining information except on entertainment vids, where a villain's threat of physical or mental pain still captivated a certain naive audience. In reality, there were drugs to unlock the tightest lips. The only defense was to prime the individual with a self-destruct—a suicide keyed to the presence of certain foreign substances in the blood.

Significantly less than legal, unless government sanctioned. And, understandably, not an option most career spacers considered.

Lefebvre ground the palms of his hands into his eyes until he saw spots, trying to ease the residual headache. They'd politely offered him painkillers after he'd told them everything they'd wanted to know, given him clean coveralls to replace the uniform that smelled like some distillery—all perfectly professional, nothing personal.

He took it all very personally, from being interrogated under drugs to being held without explanation in this cell, and would have welcomed any chance to express his feelings. There was nothing worth punching in what Lefebvre recognized as a ship's brig and likely no opportunities in the near future. He'd known from the deepening vibration when they'd shifted to translight.

So close! Lefebvre lunged to his feet and, unsteadily at first, began pacing. After all the years of searching, of dead ends and blind alleys, he'd had Ragem within reach. The Panacian had been the one on the vid—no doubt about that—and it was a Human who'd come to her aid. Had it been Ragem, himself? *No way to be sure,* Lefebvre admitted, his assailant had been too careful. But Lefebvre knew, thanks to the Ervickian's information, that Ragem had been using the alias Megar Slothe. The Panacian had known it, too, he'd swear to that. If the Human hadn't been Ragem himself, Lefebvre was certain the two of them knew where Paul could be found.

All of which, he reminded himself with disgust, *was now known to his captors as well.* They'd been Human—that much he'd been able to tell, though they'd hidden their identities as individuals behind med-tech hoods and germ-free robes.

Was he being kidnapped by Ragem and his allies? Or by others chasing the Human for reasons of their own?

Lefebvre had a feeling neither group would place any value on his continued existence. *But if Ragem was on this ship,* he thought with an unsteadying rush of anticipation, *he'd find him.*

And ask the questions he'd hoarded all these years, starting with: *Why?*

17: Warship Morning

FROM my web-kin, I possessed a flesh-born legacy beyond price, an awareness of the life around me in the most exquisite detail, a heritage to protect that was vastly more than my life experiences alone.

From the only other one of my kind I'd encountered, Death, I'd gained a legacy of loss, an awareness of my own mortality, and a sickening heritage of hate I seemed unable to avoid no matter where I went.

Such as now. We were on a Tly ship—not just any Tly ship, but one built originally for war and kept, as far as I could tell, much readier for that use than any informant had revealed. Thanks to Death, this society had consumed itself with guilt until all that remained was hollow, driven, and lawless.

I'd come on board simply enough: the Ycl was an ambush hunter, well able to cling as an inconspicuous layer under objects such as Paul's carrysack. They'd brought us from the *Narcissus* together, the weight of the bag puzzling the Tly guard assigned to carry it.

Captain Marvin had watched us exit their ship, hands writhing about as though they argued with one another. The debate had obviously not ended in their passenger's favor for, when Paul attempted one quick appeal as he was pushed toward the air lock, the Cin had turned their broad back on him.

I would remember.

The Tly warship had been renamed *The Black Watch,* a cheery reference, I presumed, to her supposed function of preventing smuggling. In other words, she carried Tly inspectors whose mission in life, according to Joel Largas, was to aggravate all shipping moving through Tly space and confiscate what they considered contraband—or, to call it what it was, the beginnings of legalized piracy.

The *'Watch* had stopped Captain Chase and the *Vegas Lass*. Under other circumstances, I would have enjoyed a look inside the ship's holds to see how much of her so-called contraband carried Cameron & Ki labeling.

But cargo was hardly my concern. Paul was.

After boarding *The Black Watch*, we'd been separated: Paul being led down a corridor Skalet-memory told me led to the outer decks of the ship, likely on his way to a cell in her brig. Officers and crew on a Tly vector-class cruiser were housed within the safety of its core. That's where Paul's carrysack, and its passenger, were heading. I clung with every cell, thinking inconspicuous and optimistic thoughts, hoping not to be dropped too heavily to the floor when we reached our destination. It wouldn't hurt, but it could attract unwanted attention if my edges jarred free and I landed on someone's foot.

We arrived. The Tly guard deposited the carrysack with reassuring care on top of a long table. I tasted food residue as well as the bitter tang of a caustic cleanser. *A galley, but which one?* There would have been three in the old days: one for the captain and senior officers, one for the remaining officers, and the largest for the crew, sometimes shared with any troops on board. We hadn't passed very many individuals on our way here, implying the *'Watch* carried less than her potential complement of two thousand plus.

"This was all he had on the *Narcissus,* sir," reported the guard to someone beyond the visual range of this form. "In the way of personal belongings, that is. The Captain said Kane ordered a crate of houseplants." This last was included with every indication of doubt.

"Houseplants, you say," repeated a very precise, very careful voice, male yet pitched almost in a falsetto, like a child's. "Odd."

"Yessir. But we didn't find any sign of them."

"Is that, in your estimation, suspicious?"

"No, sir. The Captain of the *Narcissus*—well, sir. A Cin, sir? I wouldn't myself put much reliability into their testimony on the matter. It could have been another passenger altogether, frankly, sir, or the Cin's imaginations."

The voice appeared to consider this. "Thank you— Guardsman Turner, isn't it? Manuel Turner?"

"Why, yessir. Thank you, sir."

"That will be all, Manuel. Please have the med-techs contact me when the prisoner has received his treatment."

What treatment? I drove my temperature up, holding form with a discipline Ersh herself might have envied, knowing that my only hope of helping Paul lay in self-control. This was no place or time for my usual impulsive approach.

The guard named Manuel left. Footsteps approached. *There.*

If I had had eyelids, I would have blinked. From the voice, I'd deduced Human, male, middle-aged. From the diction, I'd assumed educated, civilian, mannered.

This Human was male. I'd been right there. But the body illuminating itself to me in heat and reflected light was gigantic, at the extreme range for most populations of this species, especially among the lightly-built Tly. He was unusually proportioned as well, with arms reaching almost to his knees and hands three times the size of Paul's. His face beneath a shock of white hair was placid and almost dull, until I observed his blue eyes. I'd seldom seen eyes as coldly intelligent as these.

Great, I grumbled to myself. *Just what I deserved for an opponent: a giant genius.* I caught myself longing for Kearn.

The giant wore a Tly inspector's uniform, custom-tailored with a high collar, as if in a vain attempt to disguise a neck thicker than Paul's thigh. This inspector had not boarded the *'Lass,* I decided. Captain Chase would have definitely mentioned this being.

He reached one of those mammoth hands toward the carrysack. I began to think furiously, and futilely, of a way to casually plop to the floor when he lifted the bag. Before it came to that, the com panel chirped: "Inspector Logan. We have a problem."

The hand retreated, taking its shadow with it. I would have sighed if I could. As Logan walked over to the panel, I relaxed my adhesion to the bag and oozed off the table to the floor. *Just my luck.* This was the captain's galley and the floor was carpeted in lush proto-grass—a not-quite living material that felt wonderful to Human feet and formed an endless-seeming obstacle course to me. Grimly, I thinned myself as much as possible and began forcing my way through the dense network of fibers toward the kitchen entrance to this room, making sure to stay beneath the long table. Meanwhile, I listened intently.

"The new subject you brought—he's not going to be as straightforward to deal with as the other one."

Other one? I wrapped a filmy pseudopod around a chair leg as I paused to listen and rest.

"May I inquire as to the reason, Med-tech Burroughs?" I still found the giant's voice chillingly incongruous. In my expert opinion, it was both higher-pitched and softer than should have issued from those outsized body parts. It was either an affectation or the result of some internal defect. No matter which, although the words were polite, there was nothing about the voice itself that was pleasant.

"This one's had the full set of anti-measures, sir. We've nothing that will get answers without killing him first."

Skalet-memory rolled up, dispassionate in its experience, letting me decipher their cryptic terms into meanings too terrible for Esen alone. They had planned to use truth drugs on Paul; they couldn't, because Paul's body had been altered to suicide automatically in response.

When had Paul done this to himself? I compressed myself into a dense little ball of dismay.

I did know why: to keep our secrets.

To protect me.

"Thank you for your report," Logan said in his soft, terrible voice. "Please have my guest transferred to the waiting area. And, Med-tech Burroughs?"

The voice from the comp sounded cautious, perhaps expecting to be blamed for failure. "Yes, sir?"

"Please insure there is a trauma bed and the appropriate staff available at all times until you hear otherwise."

"But that's only done during battle sims—sir."

I could see Logan's feet. He tapped the right one, just once, as if this was the only physical expression of a vast impatience he would allow himself. His voice, as before, was carefully precise and even. "I do not wish to lose this particular guest. We will be proceeding with less traditional methods. Your services may thus be required at some point, Med-tech Burroughs. Urgently. I trust you and your staff will be ready?"

"Yes, sir. I apologize for the misunderstanding, Inspector. We will be at your disposal."

"Thank you."

I didn't need Skalet's dark knowledge to interpret this exchange for me. Many otherwise intelligent cultures devoted time and effort to learning how to take one another apart as slowly and painfully as possible. Humans were not alone in that despicable accomplishment. *They were,* I thought bitterly, *among the more proficient.*

I could hear Inspector Logan beginning to go through the contents of Paul's carrysack. I had no idea what he'd make of the combination of Lishcyn-sized silks and biodisrupter, but the longer he puzzled over it the better. I did know that Paul dropped the mail pouch and its contents into the cabin's recycler before he was taken from the *Narcissus.*

No time to think of him now, I admonished myself, peeling my pseudopod from the chair leg and pushing my tissues through the sticky morass of carpet. My goal was ahead of me. I had to pass unnoticed into the kitchen.

What I'd do after that, I refused to consider.

Elsewhere

"THEY wouldn't have cleared the *Russell III* for launch, otherwise, sir."

Kearn caught his fingers drumming on his desktop and clenched them together fiercely. Almost of their own accord, his hands broke free from one another and began rubbing over the skin of his smooth head, as if searching for nonexistent hair to punish. "I don't want her snooping around, Timri. You know the Ambassador caste are no more than spies for the Hive. I don't see why we had to allow N'Klet on board at all."

"Sec-ag T'Pleck insisted, sir," Timri said louder, as if for some reason the comp-tech thought Kearn was hard of hearing.

He heard perfectly well. He felt oppressed, as if the ventilators weren't working properly and his office was short of air. Her attitude wasn't helping. "What is N'Klet doing now?" he worried out loud. "What is she up to?"

"She's waiting to talk to you, sir. As she has since coming on board."

"Then she can keep waiting! I'm Acting Captain and very busy. Lefebvre's desertion has left everything to me—at a very difficult time—at a moment of crisis!"

Timri shifted but remained silent. Kearn looked up at her suspiciously, wishing she'd sit down instead of making him crane his neck. *Probably deliberate.*

The Feneden—the glorious Fem Anisco herself—had urged him, tactfully and with respect, not to speak to any Panacian, especially those from the School. The poor beings were clearly being persecuted by the Panacians, who were out to take advantage of their ignorance of the Commonwealth and the alien civilizations around them. Anisco had confessed they feared Kearn, the Shifter Hunter, would be influenced against them.

Kearn had no intention of listening to lies about his newfound friends, so it was with complete dismay he learned that Timri had taken advantage of the nap he'd desperately needed to allow N'Klet on the *Russell III.*

All he could do was pretend she wasn't there—which he had done for over a day now—destroying any messages and refusing to see the upstart D'Dsellan.

"How are the Feneden?" he asked, feeling less alone the moment he spoke the name. At last, true believers had joined his quest. Kearn shivered. *Although they'd brought shattering confirmation of his worst nightmares about the Esen.*

So far, only he and Timri knew the Feneden's legend of the Shifter: the monster of many shapes who appeared as a stranger to consume the unwary. At first, Timri had refuted any connection, having witnessed the destruction caused by the Esen Monster in space and convinced it had nothing in common with another old tale. Then the Feneden had showed them both an illustration from one of the ancient texts they had brought as sample goods: an illustration of a cobalt-blue teardrop, its surface split into a gaping maw, lined with horrific fangs and stuffed with the heads of still screaming victims.

Then Timri had agreed.

"The Feneden haven't left their quarters, sir. I've stationed someone at their door at all times. In case they have requirements," Timri added smoothly, before Kearn could protest her posting what amounted to a guard on his special friends.

"Very good," he said, as if she wanted his approval. Although Kearn had officially appointed himself Acting Captain the moment the *Russell III* lifted from D'Dsel, leaving Lefebvre planetside, he knew perfectly well the crew had unofficially appointed Timri. It was tacitly understood that Kearn could remain Acting Captain as long as he didn't try to run the ship. Sas, who might otherwise have supported Kearn's authority in some things, had taken to his quarters—inconveniently and violently allergic to their new guests. Apparently, the Feneden gave him a rash. As the Modoren aged, Kearn had noticed, more things did.

Timri could run the ship, Kearn told himself, just as glad to avoid dealing with the minutiae of crew assignments and complaints. *Until they reached Fened Prime and he began the glorious task of gathering evidence.*

Evidence to prove once and for all the existence of the Esen Monster.

18: Galley Morning

MY former Web had existed as six distinct personalities, separate most of our lives yet connected by the sharing of web-mass and memory. I felt the loss of the others as an amputation might feel to those with permanent limbs—only a ghost remained of what had been mine, a memory of ability and substance.

My memories were, however, perfect. At a whim, I could be embarrassed—and moved—by Ansky's parade of love affairs, know her passion to understand the interactions between thinking organisms; I could gaze in awe at Mixs' designs and feel her cold, clear patterns of thought; I could hear and almost share Lesy's laughter. Underlying what they had been and what I was, I carried within my flesh memories of Ersh, first of us all.

But what I needed now were the least comforting memories, those of Skalet. She had found her niche with those species compelled to war and struggle, a specialty suited to her logical and detached mind. Until her death, she had lived among the Kraal, earning and enjoying a reputation as one of their greatest military theorists. I had been Skalet's punishment whenever Ersh felt our web-kin in danger of straying too far from our great purpose. She'd be summoned by Ersh to teach me this or that about our Rules, under the guise of drilling some of her vast store of knowledge about strategy and planning into my frivolous young mind.

I would never know which of us resented those lessons more; I certainly learned how to hide well. Fortunately, Skalet didn't seem to be called to account as frequently once I hit my four hundredth birthday, either because she adhered better to the Rules or Ersh had other things for me to learn.

At the moment, I was hiding quite well, and not accomplishing much by it. I'd managed to enter the kitchen undetected and stretch myself underneath the cupboards. *What would Skalet do now?* I wondered.

I had two problems, one related to the other. I couldn't stay Ycl much longer without feeding. And I couldn't leave this form without gaining mass.

Well, I reminded myself, *I could become a Quebit again.* And likely end up living happily as a mechanic on *The Black Watch,* which, while appealing on one level, wouldn't help Paul in the least.

Thinking of Paul sent a tide of despair along my body, a longing that was growing significantly more like hunger with each exertion. Moving myself through the carpet had used up almost all my stored energy.

So I needed mass—preferably before my Ycl-self found something moving, warm, and prone to screaming. While my web-self assuredly didn't have the moving, warm, or screaming requirement, it had to be living mass if I was going to make more of myself from it. The kitchen had seemed the most logical place to look.

Except that all of its counters were spotless and empty, and the cupboards contained nothing but dishes, cleaning supplies, and a selection of mediocre wines probably left here in hopes of being forgotten.

I sighed and pressed a little harder against the cupboard. *Waiting was something else Ersh had tried to teach me,* I thought wistfully. I deliberately avoided thinking about Paul—or the other prisoner in the hands of Inspector Logan. If ever there was a time when I must remember who and what I was, it was now.

Since all I dared do was wait.

Elsewhere

THEY'D brought someone else. Motionless on his cot, Lefebvre strained to hear more than overlapping footsteps and a curt order from a guard. A low voice responded. Lefebvre couldn't catch any words, but the tone seemed unusually calm for a prisoner.

His cell, low-ceilinged and possessing a curved outer wall as if to deliberately remind inmates of their proximity to the outer hull and hard vacuum, had two doorways, side-by-side. The first, save for its massive locking mechanism, might have been any portal in the ship. The second was for servos only, being too narrow for a Human to pass through and—if Lefebvre's recollection of the specs for such things served—rigged with force blades set to react to Human tissue. He didn't plan to find out.

But its opening gave a view, of sorts, into the corridor. If he stood to one side, he could see three cells to the left of his, one directly across. Lefebvre didn't look to the right. That way, the corridor turned to the emergency med area—where he'd babbled away everything that mattered to him at the prick of four needles.

The monitoring vids along the walls seemed superfluous.

Lefebvre waited until all was quiet, then went to the servo door. "Psst," he hissed softly between his teeth. "Who's there?"

"Kane. Mitchell Kane. Do you know what's going on here?" the voice was the one he'd heard, still low, still calm—not the calm of indifference or bravery, Lefebvre suddenly decided, but the calm of someone totally in control of their reactions. The kind of control developed with practice. "What are the Tly up to—kidnapping honest traders?" There was just the right hint of honest outrage in the voice.

"What makes you think these are the Tly?" Lefebvre asked, trying to see into the other cell. The voice came from the one directly across from him. *Why wasn't his fellow prisoner standing where he could see and be seen?*

A matching tone of surprise from the voice: "They identified themselves. I see no reason they'd lie about it. This ship is *The Black Watch*, assigned to the Tly inspectors in this quadrant. They boarded us to look for contraband. Personally, I think they were shopping." This last piece of information was delivered with a wry chuckle that brought an involuntary twitch to Lefebvre's lips. "So, why are you stuck here, Hom—?"

Lefebvre looked up at the vid in his cell; the Tly hadn't bothered disguising the things. "Why am I here, Hom Kane?" he repeated. "I'd dearly love the answer to that. And I'm sure so would the Commonwealth! Kidnapping and interrogating a Captain on active service is going to be noticed—you can be sure of that!" Lefebvre closed his mouth, abruptly afraid he'd sounded almost desperate. *Kearn would file a missing being report,* he told himself, refusing to doubt it. *Or Timri.* Despite their personal differences, they were all officers who knew their duty to one another. *Weren't they?*

"Interrogating?" There was a pause, and Lefebvre steeled himself for meaningless sympathy, mortified he'd revealed so much to this stranger, but Mitchell Kane simply asked: "They keep it clean?" There were those who used the truth drugs to expose more than information, uncaring how that damaged both mind and personality.

"I'm all right. It was all very professional," Lefebvre answered bitterly. "Very thorough."

"What are they after, Captain? I told you, I'm just a trader. I don't know any military secrets."

Lefebvre shook his head. "Neither do—neither did I. They didn't ask about such things, Hom Kane. Mitchell. They—" he choked on the words, then tried again. "I couldn't—"

"Don't say anymore. You don't have to tell me." The voice roughened with compassion. "Listen, Captain. The drugs get to anyone. There was nothing you could do, hear me? They get to anyone. It's not your fault."

Lefebvre drove his fist against the wall without gaining more than a burst of agony to match the blood on his knuckles. He pressed his hands against either side of the servo door opening. "I don't know why," he said, unable to say what in the calm, faceless voice made him keep talking. "Why would they want to know everything about me? Everything . . ." He paused, breathing raggedly, then went on almost desperately, "I couldn't stop, Kane. I couldn't shut myself up. I heard myself telling them all of it, everything I'd kept safe. I couldn't spew it out fast enough!" Lefebvre choked on bile. "I'd have died first," he gasped, finished.

"You didn't have that choice," the voice returned, still compassionate but now with a steely edge, as though the other understood all too well. "The only shame here belongs to those who gave you the drugs. I want you to remember that." A pause. "What's your name, Captain?"

"Lefebvre. Captain Rudy Lefebvre of the Research Ship *Russell III.* I was on D'Dsel—I must have been grabbed from the shipcity." *How* had *he come here?* Lefebvre asked himself, reliving that night. *Had the Panacian and her Human companion arranged this—to get him offworld and learn what he knew?* If so, they'd succeeded. He felt himself shaking with the aftermath of the drugs and an anger deeper than any he'd known before.

"Be very careful, Captain Lefebvre," the low voice said, as if its owner could see through the walls between them and knew how close to losing control he was. "What seems a small, accessible target may well be the tip of something much larger and more deadly. Choose your enemies wisely."

Lefebvre drew in a deep breath, then another, feeling steadier by the moment. "Well, Hom Kane, I don't seem to have done that very well," he said, attempting to lighten his tone. "What about you?"

"I have never chosen my enemies, Captain Lefebvre," the other prisoner said, his voice oddly regretful. "They chose me."

19: Galley Afternoon; Cabin Night

I'D been desperate.

I didn't think that would be sufficient excuse for Paul, who was very fond of small creatures, but I was prepared to argue the relative value of one fat and lazy rezt against his life and potentially the billions on Fened Prime.

The rezt, a vermin-hunter evolved on one of the worlds colonized by the Human Tly, were fairly common fixtures on their ships. The creatures were kept as pets—usually at a safe distance, being mostly teeth and attitude wrapped in an otherwise appealing fur coat.

This particular rezt had wandered into the galley's kitchen on the heels of the cook, staying behind while that individual went in search of her assistant.

There wasn't much rational thought involved. I'd barely managed to restrain my famished Ycl-self from attacking the Human. If the rezt hadn't been available—*well, some things just didn't bear thinking about.*

I'd allowed my Ycl-self to feed, knowing I wouldn't be able to safely return to this useful, deadly form unless it was satisfied. *Not that I could have stopped myself,* I admitted honestly, remembering the glorious taste.

So now I lay, an unobtrusive coating on the underside of a table in the galley, feeling an interesting combination of guilt and comfort as I watched the cook look for her pet. *At least the pet wasn't looking for her,* I reminded myself.

The Human left the room, doubtless to convince others

of how a rezt managed to activate the door controls. *Finally,* I thought, extending a filmy pseudopod to see over the top of the table.

Perfect! There must be quite the celebratory feast planned for later. I thought I'd detected the aroma of fresh-cut flowers. Each of the ten tables in the galley bore a helmet-shaped vase bursting with colorful petals and lush stems.

Given what the Tly might want to celebrate, I headed for the nearest vase as fast as I could ooze.

I could really use some clothes. Very few intelligent species found themselves comfortable trotting about in public without some sort of adornment. Ersh had a theory that most ephemerals were so new to self-consciousness, they covered their bodies to remind themselves they were the thinkers on their planets. She elected to prove her case by pointing out that her preferred form, the Tumbler, had matured beyond that need. I'd gained myself a trip to Lesy by using the same argument to run around naked in any form I chose. *Ah, to be that young again.*

Lesy delighted in clothing, jewelry, and whatever else she could drape around, hang, or wrap over her current flesh. From her, the lesson "you have to dress appropriately to the current species' culture" became more along the lines of "and isn't this one fun?" I'd often been confused by how Lesy could seem so impatient with the most serious things yet be so serious about what the other web-kin took lightly. Ersh hadn't so much explained, as added to the puzzle when she'd replied to my complaint about Lesy's approach to life, delivered with the impatient dignity of all my two hundred years of experience. Lesy, Ersh had told me, was the only one of us who dreamed.

I understood more about Lesy once I assimilated the memories Ersh had bequeathed me. Lesy had been the first of Ersh's offspring to survive. There were no details, but deep in my flesh, I knew the struggle facing a web-being who had to divide, to relinquish mass to another. I think Ersh had been unable, that first time, to give Lesy all she needed. There would never be a way to prove it, but I thought Ersh had instinctively shunted what she herself found difficult to her offspring, keeping herself fit and ready to survive, leaving such irrationalities as dreams behind.

I shook myself free of such thoughts; no matter how vivid the memory, I was alone now, and had to deal with my current crisis as only Esen could. *Or would,* I thought, amusing myself.

I tucked the tablecloth more tightly under my arms. A second cloth held the plant material I hadn't needed in order to assume this form. So far, I'd been able to move unseen through the ship—a pleasing circumstance I owed to the fact the ship itself was almost deserted.

In fact, most of the areas I passed through were closed up, doors tagged with perm-seals dated almost fifty years ago. It was as though there were two ships here at once: the ghost of the mighty *Tly Defender*—the name still inscribed on doorplates and cutlery—and the reality of *The Black Watch.* The entire crew's section was tagged and dimly lit; by that, it was likely those now running the ship used only the officers' deck. Which was fine by me.

I picked a cabin at random and twisted the seal free. It was a standard four-person room, with retractable bunks, a fresher, and a central table with benches. I went directly to the drawers on one wall, hoping for something better than the tablecloth.

As I did, I passed in front of the mirrored surface of the stall and stopped.

My Human-self had grown a little, I decided, examining the body in front of me critically. Nothing else had changed perceptibly in fifty years. I tugged my fingers through unruly reddish-brown hair, blinked eyes that were occasionally green and usually an indeterminate hazel, and pulled my lips back from even, small teeth. The skin was on the pale side—partly because I'd last used this form during a winter with Ansky—and the spots I seemed to gain on the snub nose were faded. A straight, healthy body.

I sighed. *What a shame this form showed my relative age so clearly.* The reflection gazing back at me might be as old as eleven. Twelve would be pushing my luck with any being who knew Humans well.

Too young, was the reaction I feared from Paul, who had never seen me like this and never would, if I had my way. He might know I'd lived almost six centuries, though I was young for my kind; that knowledge would pale under the biological programming sure to kick in if he ever met the Human-Esen.

I left my reflection to search the drawers, pleased to discover they were filled with clothing and personal effects. I hesitated, slender fingers caught on fabric as I sensed an incongruity. Why hadn't the crew packed their things? Why leave in such a hurry? It didn't make sense.

Unless the *'Defender* had been one of the ships that had destroyed Garson's World. The Tly had claimed to have decommissioned all six immediately. If they'd lied, and Humans could, the crew might have been hustled away to keep quiet—possibly thankful to leave anything connected with this ship and that deed behind. But those who served her now had to know. *This was a murderer's ship.*

I pulled out a small white shirt, likely to be a dress on me, and began to smile.

Elsewhere

"HOM Kane." Lefebvre kept his voice to the barest whisper, as if the cells had heard enough sound to last them a lifetime. "Mitchell." He sucked in a breath, seeking control. "Answer me, please."

"I'm here." The faint voice was hoarse. *It had to be,* Lefebvre thought. No one could scream like that, as long as that, without almost ripping apart the cords in the throat.

He turned from the servo door and, putting his back against the cold wall, slid down to sit on the floor. He leaned to one side to keep an ear to the opening. "I wasn't sure," Lefebvre admitted. What he didn't say filled the air between them as loudly as any of the curses and threats Lefebvre had shouted—trying to stop them, trying to drown out the sounds of pain until they'd come in and stunned him. All very professional.

"Don't worry—" a careful pause, then more strongly: "They don't plan to kill me. The med-techs were quite clear on that point."

Lefebvre dropped his head back against the wall and cursed to himself.

"Are you all right?"

"Me?" Lefebvre was surprised into a humorless laugh. "I'm fine. They put me to sleep for the worst of it." Then he listened to the waiting silence and cursed himself this time. "Remember what you told me?" he said, keeping his voice matter-of-fact. "It's not your fault. The shame—the shame is theirs."

"I'll keep that in mind," returned the voice, with a reassuring warmth. "Since I have another appointment with
the polite and painful Inspector Logan tonight."

"What does he want, Mitchell?" Lefebvre asked desperately. "What's worth all this?"

The voice sounded as though Mitchell smiled. "A
friend, Rudy."

"A friend." Lefebvre closed his eyes tightly, but nothing seemed to stop the echoes in his mind. He was
numbly grateful now for the relative kindness of the
drug—he may have revealed his secrets, but at least he
hadn't had to prove himself like this. He hadn't imagined
what it would be like. *No one could.*

"Rudy?"

"I didn't leave," he said, surprised to feel himself growing angry at the patient, unseen being.

"I may need you to do something for me—if things
go badly."

Lefebvre couldn't hold it any longer. "What can I do
in here?" he raged, uncaring who heard him. "Tell me
that, Mitchell. What use am I? To you or anyone?" He
was aghast at himself but couldn't stop; it was as though
the truth drugs still infested his blood. "You have this
friend to die for—who have I got that will even care?
Kearn? He's probably made himself Captain and said
good riddance! My cause? Do you think Ragem even
knows I'm alive?"

"I know," Mitchell's voice said calmly, warmly, like a
hand reaching across the empty corridor. "And I care.
This isn't over, Rudy. You and I are not alone. We aren't
going to die here." An attempt to chuckle that ended in
a ghastly, pain-racked cough. "Well, not for a while."

"You're crazy," Lefebvre said darkly, pulling his knees
tightly to his chest and wrapping his arms around them,
as if holding himself together. "I'm crazy, talking to an
invisible crazy man. An invisible crazy man with a death
wish."

"If we're both crazy," replied the voice, "perhaps we're
friends."

Lefebvre swallowed what he'd been about to say, the impulse stayed by a rush of emotion he hadn't expected and didn't understand. "As a friend," he said slowly, cautiously, like someone venturing on to an unknown thickness of ice, "do you think you could tell Logan something—anything?" *Lie, if you have to,* he added to himself, wary of the vids. *Please?*

"I don't dare," the voice said, hoarse as it was, conveying commitment and respect, as well as a tinge of regret. "If I ever answer him, even one word—I'm not sure how I could stop. I'm sorry, my friend."

They were both silent for a moment, then Lefebvre heard the voice ask softly: "So, who is this Ragem?"

20: Warship Night

I'D outdone myself this time, I decided cheerfully. The very first crewbeings I'd encountered had run away, shrieking at the top of their lungs.

This was not a typically Human response to their children—but, I looked down at myself with satisfaction—*I was not your typical child.*

I'd pieced together cast-off clothing to create a shabby nondescript outfit, something that emphasized how small I was, how young. I'd chosen white, then found the perfect accessory: a beaded belt such as was once given as harvest gifts on Garson's World. A bit of creative damage completed the costume, such as shredding the sleeves and adding some bright red stains to cloth and my skin courtesy of a bottle of some liqueur I'd found.

The Tly, as I knew very well, were among the most superstitious of Humans. The stories of missing ships and the mass guilt following the tragic attack on Garson's World had only fueled their fixation with the dead. You couldn't travel on Tly without seeing evidence of charms and potions for sale on every corner. Most citizens were convinced they had to protect themselves from vengeful spirits, or at least thought it wise to be prepared.

So no one on this bloodstained ship should take the impossible appearance of a child from Garson's World as anything less.

I had a plan, now that I had the means. Skalet- and Mixs-memory contained the information I'd need to tamper with the *'Watch.* The door in front of me should open into the environmental control room.

I gathered up all of my courage—having remembered at the last minute that I wasn't actually the bravest creature and this form had no defenses whatsoever—and knocked on the door.

The door whooshed open before I could seriously re-think my actions and I stepped in, moving quickly to one side. Then I simply stared at them.

There were two females and one male at their stations, dressed in the same simplified version of the old Tly military uniform as the guard, Manuel. They stared back at me. None of us so much as blinked.

This wasn't going well, I decided. I shifted my cloth-wrapped bundle of plants on my shoulder and did the first thing that came to mind.

I sang.

It was too old a song to have originated on Garson's World—colonists had brought it—but they'd adapted the ancient melody to their needs. It was a simple thing, a rhyme comparing love to the sowing and reaping of hops.

After a verse or two, tears were running down all of their cheeks, but they still hadn't budged.

Now what? I wondered. Frustrated beyond caution, I took a step toward them.

That did it. All three leaped to their feet and surged past me out the door, one screaming at the top of his lungs.

There was something intensely satisfying about a plan that not only worked, I congratulated myself, *but was fun.*

Once my ghostly self had removed the crew, it took hardly any effort to lower the temperature, raise the humidity, and decrease the effectiveness of the carbon dioxide scrubbers. Nothing major: I wanted the atmosphere inside the ship to become unsettling, not dangerous. But I made sure my tampering wouldn't be easy to find or correct.

For a moment, I rested my hands on the controls, so familiar to my memory. This type of ship had been known to my web-kin; I understood its workings exactly as well as they had. *What if this had been newer?* Abruptly, I saw Paul's urgings to have me travel with him, to see the universe beyond Minas XII, in a completely different light. Had he realized I needed to upgrade my knowledge? That I was wasting invaluable opportunities watching my machines watch the stars? He'd brought me everything he could record, but it was a pebble compared to the mountains of information the Web collected and shared. How much had I already missed? How much did I need to learn?

How could I do it all, when there was only me left?

A droplet hit the back of my hand. I looked up, thinking moisture had already condensed on the cooling metal, then saw it had been a tear.

I couldn't, I told myself, hearing Ersh in the harsh, sensible truth of it. *I could only do my best.*

Starting with haunting *The Black Watch.*

Elsewhere

KEARN stared at the message in his hands, noticing the trembling of his fingers as a distant phenomenon, unrelated to the way his breath wheezed in and out through his lips, or the way his heart was trying to pound its way into his mouth, bringing the taste of his supper with it.

"You've confirmed—this."

"Yessir. It came in on a secured beam. Codes read intact." Com-tech Resdick stood near the door, as if he'd taken a step or two in that direction while Kearn was reading. "Will there be a reply, sir?"

"No."

"Sir?"

Kearn waved one hand irritably: "All right, then. Yes. But later. Can't you give me a moment of peace? I have important matters to think about—I can't waste my time talking to you."

Resdick nodded and left. *He missed salutes,* Kearn thought. *There was something so—reassuring—about a salute.* Of course, Paul Ragem had been expert at giving the bare minimum, a subtle flick of his fingers that showed his scorn while never stepping beyond the bounds of acceptable behavior in front of others. Until *Ragem allied himself with the Esen Monster and joined her reign of terror.* Kearn pulled his thoughts to the present with an effort, not sure why he'd remembered a dead man.

The message was from the Commonwealth—the Deputy Minister of Research, in fact. It was the one

Kearn had always feared. A recall. Some trumped-to-gether nonsense about his responsibility for Captain Lefebvre, reported attacked and now officially listed as missing on D'Dsel. As if it was Kearn's fault the Human had chosen to desert his ship.

They were stopping his search.

When he was closer than ever?

Kearn checked the lock on his door, then pulled out the Kraal knife. With uncharacteristic force, he plunged the tip through the message and into his desk.

They'd have to catch him first.

21: Flight Deck Night

BY the time the lights automatically dimmed in the corridors to mark shipnight, I'd made my way through six decks, terrorized over forty crew, and witnessed three unfortunate physiological reactions. Floors could be cleaned. I wasn't exactly proud of my efforts, but they were beginning to accumulate nicely.

A particularly effective moment had been when I'd located a node in the intership com system and sang into it, making sure to break off with a suggestive sob. The next node I tried had been deactivated. *Well, if I couldn't use it, neither could they.*

The changes I'd made to the ship's internal systems accumulated as well. The walls were damp to the touch, the air perceptibly chill, and the amount of carbon dioxide close to levels that should affect Human ability to think clearly. This last was a minor concern to me, as I felt thinking clearly was likely to matter, so I took the precaution of grabbing an emergency air supply and using it whenever I felt my respiration increasing.

It was almost time to dare the brig corridor and find Paul.

Almost. Despite my impatience, I knew if I were to save my friend, it wouldn't be enough to free him. I needed a way to get us off this ship and away. In entertainment vids, this was apparently a trivial task for any hero worth watching. In reality, I knew this was the most difficult task of all.

A vector-class cruiser couldn't land on a planet's surface. It was a distance killer, functioning as a mobile base of operations in times of war. The *Tly Defender* would have carried hundreds of shuttles and doorcrashers—the one-way stealth gliders used to deliver whatever the military wanted dropped, from biologics to Ganthor troops. *The Black Watch,* I found as I haunted the flight deck, currently carried three shuttles, one antique aircar being restored, and fourteen lifepods, the latter obviously an afterthought to ferry the skeleton crew to safety if necessary.

None of these would do. The shuttles had translight capability, but were locked into launching grids controlled from the bridge. *Somewhat ambitious for a ghost child.* The lifepods would only drift and yell for help.

I didn't think about Paul. He would survive and wait for me to save him. *Anything else was not acceptable.*

The flight deck was the largest on the ship and completely open, wrapping around the circumference of the huge ship so its edges bent downward at the limits of my field of view, perspectives marked by lines of structural pillars curving up to the shadowed ceiling. I wished for slippers—as a costume choice, bare feet were a definite detriment on the cold metal floors—but kept moving, looking for anything helpful.

Then, over the curve of the far horizon, I saw it. When I was close enough to know what I was seeing, I stood gaping at my find in disbelief.

They'd stacked the cargo stolen from traders here; crates made a wall taller than I, stretching to the limits of what I could see of the deck. A lot of it had been food, judging by the smell and long runnels of white-streaked green liquid reaching out in all directions. The crates had been tossed together, not stacked. Most of their contents had to be damaged by the treatment. There was a fortune here, treated like so much garbage.

I thought of my porcelains, indifferent or not, and was horrified at the waste.

Why?

Why steal all of this, only to destroy it? Why hide it, if destruction was the goal?

Inspector Logan. I might have been jumping to ephemeral conclusions, but this seemed like his style—to take, because he could. To destroy, because it suited him.

I went closer, trying to see if I could identify any of the shipments. I pushed aside a pile of packing plas, seeking a label on the nearest crate. It wasn't ours—but it was destined for Inhaven Prime.

Perhaps they all were, I thought. This was by no means all of the shipping heading for Inhaven—but it could represent a significant amount. I couldn't tell without going through every crate, but if the Tly—if Inspector Logan, because I couldn't help putting him at the center of whatever plot this was—wanted to harm the Inhaven economy, there were key goods, strategic needs which could be stopped. Chase's shipment of reduxan 630, for example. If other reduxan shipments had been intercepted by Logan, it could cripple several industries. I could replay in web-memory thousands of cultures conquered from within by such methods.

Just what I needed, I thought with significant self-pity. *Another war to stop.*

There was that nagging little detail of escape in the way. I kept looking.

Covered shapes formed a line beyond the dumped cargo. I hurried to the nearest, believing that anything well kept in this place had to be important, and tugged the plas sheet from it with one grab.

Not all of the *Tly Defender*'s armament had been removed, as the Tly claimed. I put out my hand and touched the flat black side of a doorcrasher—the size used for troop deployment, not weapons. I took a quick count without moving. There were enough here to send down several waves— empty spaces evoking those already used.

I felt my hands begin to shake. *The Black Watch* didn't carry enough shuttles to retrieve any number of troops.

Or was it convenient? I thought of the Ganthor, dying

against me, his click speech warning of betrayal and abandonment.

The Tly—or more specifically Inspector Logan—were beginning to have a great deal to explain.

The minor detail of escape kept getting in the way.

Then, under a split-open bag of rancid meat, I found something that might do. I could almost guarantee Paul wouldn't like it, but I didn't see other choices leaping my way.

I began my preparations.

Elsewhere

"MITCHELL." Lefebvre stood in front of the servo door, staring across the corridor as if he could will the other to stir. "Are you asleep?"

"I wouldn't call it sleeping," the voice answered quietly, as if husbanding his strength. "What's the matter? Did they decide to feed us at last?"

"Something's up with the environmental controls." Lefebvre sniffed again, ran his hand along a damp wall for unnecessary confirmation. He knew starships—the system wasn't failing, it had been reset to these parameters. *Sabotage?* he wondered with a bite of hope. "Your—" he remembered the vids in time to stop and say instead: "Haven't smelled air this foul since the bar on D'Dsel."

"It's an older ship. Are you sure?" This a shade too casual. *So Mitchell felt it, too.*

Lefebvre nodded to himself. "Humidity's up; temp's below norm. Something's not right with the oxygen/carbon dioxide balance either. Tipped. Odd combination."

"These things happen. I'm sure they'll fix it."

"If they don't get on it," Lefebvre commented, "the crew's likely to get a bit groggy. Might even start hallucinating."

"Then let's hope everyone is careful."

Lefebvre was sure he hadn't imagined the stress on "everyone." Did Mitchell have a contact among the crew? Was this friend he protected with his life here?

He chewed his lip pensively, staring at the vids, then sat down on the cot.

Lefebvre knew how to wait. The only concern he had now was how soon Logan would be back for his appointment with Mitchell. How much more could Mitchell Kane's body endure, even with the med's help? That cough could be a sign of some internal damage they hadn't bothered to repair. There could be more.

If Mitchell had a friend on board, Lefebvre told himself, *that friend better hurry.*

22: Chartroom Night

I HAD to hurry, now that I had the components of our escape ready. There was no telling what the crew was up to, but I was sure the rumors of my otherworldly presence must have spread through the officers' deck by now. Whether they were discounted or not, there would be some action taken—a search or, better yet, a meeting. Both would keep more Tly crew occupied and out of my way.

The rumors were certainly helping among the lower ranks, as I found when I walked into the secondary chartroom. *Or it could have been the air.*

"The Child! The Child!" gibbered the poor Human who'd been cleaning the floor, before dropping in a dead faint.

He landed in a contorted heap, gasping for breath. The muscles of my Human-self were woefully inadequate when it came to trying to rearrange his bulk into something more comfortable. Finally, I tucked some dry cleaning rags under his head and hoped for the best.

The chartroom, memory suggested, should have access to internal records. I examined several comp boards before locating the right one, making myself move with care. *The last time I'd rushed had resulted in dents.* This time, the consequences of a mistake were doubtless more permanent.

Anything detailed would likely be encrypted, if only to some officer's ident. What I sought should be more accessible—*aha!* I cued the internal power schematics to show the outer decks. As I'd suspected, most were on minimal, perhaps sealed as well. The greatest usages were clustered

on the officers' deck, the bridge, a few connecting corridors, and one section of the brig.

And the closest med room to that section.

I cleared the display, keeping myself focused on my task.
I called up the vid displays, hoping for something useful.
The machine requested my ident, flashing a threatening red
bar across its screen as I hesitated. Immediately I canceled,
hoping I'd been fast enough.

Time to leave, I decided. I didn't know if the Tly were
sufficiently gullible to believe in ghosts who tried to access
their security comps, but I wasn't planning to chance it.

Not when I had to make my way through almost one
quarter of this ship to reach Paul.

Elsewhere

THE scoring from the blister stick on his palms was almost gone. Lefebvre turned his hands over, flexing the fingers, involuntarily clenching them into tight fists on his knees. Otherwise, he was motionless, breathing in short, hard pants, muscles locked until they threatened to spasm.

This, he did for Mitchell, and for himself. He sat, making no move, no sound of his own, doing nothing to give them reason to stun him into blissful insensibility. He listened to the torment of a friend, making the only offering he could—he stayed.

There were never understandable words. The inspector's voice was too soft, too high-pitched to carry across the corridor. Mitchell's wordless voice not only carried, it echoed—it must have been audible throughout the deck and, by rights, should have penetrated the hull—a desperate yet proud incoherence Lefebvre judged the bravest thing he'd ever heard.

Then, nothing. Lefebvre opened his fists, unsurprised that he'd driven bloody holes into the palms with his fingernails. He held his breath.

The silence was shattered by the thudding of booted feet, moving rapidly. Lefebvre lunged up and hurried to the servo door, craning to see. A body on a grav sled sped by, heading toward the med room, surrounded by guards and followed by Inspector Logan. Logan paused in front of the opening to look down at Lefebvre.

Lefebvre couldn't help himself. He spat, watching the

liquid flash to steam as it was intercepted by the servo door's automatics. "You won't get away with this, Logan! You hear me? If you've killed him, I'll make sure you pay!"

"Do you enjoy irony, my good Captain Lefebvre?" the giant Human said mildly, as though they engaged in polite, dinner conversation. "I don't, as a rule. It so rarely lives up to its potential. But in your case?" Logan's lips thinned in a satisfied smile. "The irony is so rich, it's almost—painful. Sleep well."

"What about—?" Lefebvre couldn't finish. He sagged, every muscle burning.

"A foolish, stubborn individual. Don't worry, Captain. I have scheduled my next appointment with your—friend— for tomorrow morning. I'm sure the med-techs will have him ready to join me. Again, good night." The inspector turned and walked away down the corridor, his back easily as wide as any two of the guards who preceded him. *He would have been intimidating at any size,* Lefebvre admitted to himself. *Evil usually was.*

He slammed his palms against the sides of the opening, leaving tiny red streaks, then turned away. Although every mouthful sickened him, Lefebvre forced himself to finish the meal tray brought earlier. There was nothing to be gained by weakening himself.

Mitchell hadn't told him what he wanted done—but Lefebvre knew he would do it. There was something about Mitchell Kane that made him the kind of leader you would die for, the kind Lefebvre had believed didn't really exist, the kind beings like Kearn couldn't begin to imagine.

Lefebvre made himself think coolly, drawing on years of experience assessing vague and disconnected clues. Mitchell wasn't dead—not yet. And there was something going on. Earlier, the intership had broadcast a child's voice, singing a pretty little tune, something unfamiliar to Lefebvre, but which elicited a great deal of reaction from the Tly in Mitchell's cell. One guard had apparently been dismissed, and Lefebvre had watched him running down the corridor—an expression of horror on his face. *From a song?*

The air quality had continued to diminish. The Tly must have noticed by now, but there hadn't been any improvement. He and Mitchell had talked about this ship, about the possibility it was undercrewed for its size. Perhaps there were other problems on board—mechanical ones—problems he could use. *If he could walk through walls.*

They'd talked a long time before Logan's return, in spite of the state of Mitchell's throat, an easy conversation that wound its way around places they'd both seen, amusing stories, childhood dreams. They'd surprised each other: Mitchell had confessed to grand visions of a multispecies' library, a collection of languages and cultures designed for use by anyone, not just experts—inspiring Lefebvre's own admission of hoping to be an alien contact specialist, of joining one of the teams pushing the borders of Human knowledge about others.

He'd left the academy to join the Botharis patrol instead—to learn how to hunt other Humans. The conversation had faltered there, Lefebvre uncomfortable revealing more than the name of his target, until Mitchell changed the subject to his children, a grown daughter and son of whom he was obviously proud.

They'd never talked about his friend, Lefebvre remembered, both wary of the vids.

Yawning, he pushed the tray toward the opening, ready for the servo to retrieve on its rounds. There was nothing on it to use for a weapon, the tray itself being a spongy material about as dangerous as the mashed vegetables it had held. Lefebvre lay down on the blanketless cot, shivering in the damp chill, and threw an arm over his eyes to keep out the dimmed light.

The song was sweet, not so much because of the lyrics but because of the voice lifted in its melody. Lefebvre thought he was dreaming at first, then, as the song grew perceptibly louder, he took his arm from his eyes and realized the music was coming from the corridor.

He got to his feet quietly, making the movement casual for any Tly guard watching the vid, and walked over to the servo door.

She was there, almost floating down the night-dimmed corridor, a young Human, a girl dressed in what looked like bloodstained rags—*which couldn't be right,* Lefebvre told himself numbly. There was nothing suggesting injury in her soft voice or the way her slim hand supported a bag over her shoulder. Her other held a long-handled broom she was using to gently mark time with her song.

He felt something cold slide down his spine, as if part of his mind tried to warn him this wasn't real, that he saw an apparition or created one in his drug-abused thoughts.

She looked right at him.

Nothing prepared him for her eyes. Meeting them was like drowning in some bottomless ocean, like falling through aeons of time. He couldn't have told their color or shape. He did know the emotion filling them—he shared it.

Desperation.

Without wondering how he knew this tiny slip of a being was the friend Mitchell protected, Lefebvre said quickly, "He's alive. They took him to the med room." Then he glanced meaningfully at the vid just behind her.

Still singing, she nodded her head, placing her bag on the floor. She began walking down the corridor, waving her arms about as though reaching for some invisible support. Lefebvre moved so he could watch her, again wondering if she was real or hallucination.

Then, she calmly drove the broom handle through the protective grate, into the nearest vid, destroying it with a hot shower of sparks that danced past her hair—a tactic she repeated until the corridor was monitor free.

Definitely, Lefebvre thought with relief, *not a ghost.*

23: Brig Night; Flight Deck Night

I BRUSHED sparks from my hair and shoulders as the last vid in range exploded overhead. *This should allay any lingering doubts a ghost was on board,* I sighed, but the disguise was wearing thin anyway. I wished I could say the same for the now-dried liquid I'd poured over my clothes and skin, scratching at my arm as I headed back to Lefebvre's cell.

The lock was mechanical—perhaps a safety feature in case this outermost deck lost power during battle. I used the broom to help lever it open, grumbling to myself about the lack of strength in my current hands, but not prepared to do anything about it at the moment. Not with who was standing in front of me in the now-open door.

Lefebvre looked the worse for wear and definitely smelled it. Despite this, and his avowed task of hunting for Paul, I found his attempted smile the most encouraging thing I'd seen all day. He bent in order to look me in the eyes, then nodded to himself. "You're Mitchell's friend, aren't you. So am I."

I blinked at this, somehow finding it completely feasible Paul could charm even an archenemy, and nodded. "You said he'd been taken to the meds. Where?" *Why?* I kept to myself, able to guess and having enough to do keeping my temperature within Human norms.

Lefebvre didn't bother pointing; he took the broom from me, which looked almost weaponlike in his larger hands, and led the way down the corridor. Given we had no time for explanations, this was fine by me. Given he was obviously hurrying for his own reasons, my mouth dried with fear and I snatched my bag to follow quickly.

"Wait," I hissed, grabbing his arm as we turned the corner and I could see brighter light washing the floor ahead of us. "Let me go first."

When the Human looked inclined to argue, I gave him my best glare. *He'd better not,* I said to myself, *start treating me like a child.* But Lefebvre closed his mouth and waved me ahead, taking up a position against the wall beside the open door to the med room. *Perhaps,* I thought, momentarily amused, *he'd remembered in time who'd let him out of his cell.*

Heart pounding, I started humming the song, promising myself I'd never sing it again once off this ship, and walked right into the med room.

I should have considered letting Lefebvre go first.

There were two things wrong with my entrance. First, I hadn't thought of how I'd react to seeing Paul.

And second, I hadn't thought at all about his seeing me. The Human me.

I froze just inside the door, song forgotten, staring at what only my instincts told me was my friend. He, in turn, was restrained upright in a chairlike bed, sipping liquid through a straw held to his swollen lips, staring back at me through slits between his puffed and blackened eyelids.

Lefebvre told me—later—there had been three Tly in the room. Two had run at the sight of me. The third, the med, whom I presumed was less inclined to believe in ghosts, had gone for the com panel and met the business end of Lefebvre's broom.

I saw nothing of this. I must have stepped forward, since my hands took possession of Paul's wrapped ones before my mind knew it. This close, I still couldn't sense the medallion and my gift. *Stolen.* My lips pulled back from my teeth in what would have been dire threat in another me.

One of Paul's hands freed itself from mine and sought my cheek, the bandaging rough and cold. "I—knew," he whispered hoarsely, oddly triumphant under the circumstances. "I knew this would be you." A flicker within the cavities holding his eyes. "And my friend." His hand left my cheek and raised itself. I felt warmth at my side as Lefebvre stepped up quickly, taking Paul's hand ever so gently in his own, placing his other arm, unexpectedly, around my shoulders and drawing me against him.

This, I admitted to myself in total disbelief, *had not been in my original plan.* I was pleasantly surprised not to explode.

Maybe I was maturing. *Paul needed me intact,* I realized, assessing his condition as he and Lefebvre worked together to remove the bindings holding him to the bed.

"I—" my voice cracked, sounding foolishly young even to my ears. I coughed and made myself continue. "I've made arrangements to get off the ship. Can you walk— Mitchell?"

There was a low mutter that included "dance if I have to," but I couldn't hear the rest. I took that as a positive, grateful not to have to argue with either of them. Lefebvre put his shoulder under Paul's better arm and passed me the broom. I looked up at them both doubtfully, unsure of many things.

Paul's lips made a flinching motion, as if he tried to smile. "Let's go, old lady," he told me. "My friend Rudy and I need to file a complaint."

Still, I paused. "Is there anything here you need?"

Lefebvre answered: "From the dispenser log, they've shot him up with everything available. The only thing more he could use is time in the trauma bed—better yet, a proper Commonwealth med unit. For that, I like your plan. Let's get out of here."

There was something shattered in his brown eyes, I noticed suddenly, and remembered the terse comments of the med to Logan about "the other one" who had succumbed to the drugs. *Perhaps,* I thought with a shudder, *in that same chair.* I touched the back of his hand, lightly, then nodded. "Follow me."

*　　*　　*

The flight deck was directly outward from this one, something which probably explained how we made it to my hiding place before the Tly responded to the unghostlike activities in the brig corridor and med room. Lefebvre tried to ease Paul to where a heap of packing material made a reasonably clean bed. Paul refused, preferring to lean against a crate of heavy machine parts.

"You'll need to find another one of these," I instructed Lefebvre, showing him the space-ready suit I'd prepared for Paul. "Two more," I corrected hastily. *I hadn't planned to need one.*

While the Human began rummaging through the crates, quickly finding an assortment of gear to lay out on the floor, I went to Paul. His face looked even more battered and bruised through the moisture this form kept generating in its eyes. I blinked it away, embarrassed. "Are you damaged?" I asked, trying to hold my voice steady. My hands weren't, trembling as they touched the bandaging covering one arm and shoulder, wrapping his abdomen. They were all he wore above the pants Lefebvre had taken from the unconscious med. I dumped the dying plants from my tablecloth, standing on my toes to wrap it around his semi-bare shoulders.

Paul's lips stretched, an answering drop of blood oozing from one corner. "Only my looks—and they'll improve. I wouldn't have believed—" The lips lost their curve. "My interrogator was quite—accomplished."

I reached up to put a gentle finger over his shattered mouth, shaking. My temperature soared until my heart pounded uncontrollably, this form trying to protect itself by dissipating the heat. "Logan," I managed to say, so full of rage I could barely see, longing for a shape to express my hate. *With teeth. And venom.*

Paul gathered me to him with one arm, making a broken sound as he touched the blazing skin of my arm and knew how I struggled for control. "Careful, Esen," he whispered into my hair. "Careful, please. It's all right."

"What did he want from you?" When Paul shook his

head against mine, denying the question, I insisted. "I need to know."

The words were halting, breathed into my ear. "Logan knew who I was, Es. He knew I was Ragem. Not you. He doesn't know about you. He wanted to know about the attacks—he's after what he thinks is a Kraal weapon. He asked the same questions, over and over again." I shuddered in his grip, and Paul held me tighter. "Don't lose it now. Logan's not worth it—hear me? Es? Esen!" this whispered with a desperate edge to it.

"I hear you," I said.

The deep voice from behind surprised us both. "He'll be all right," Lefebvre said to me, with a quick look at Paul's face. "I've seen worse—mind you, that was following an aircar crash into the side of a mountain, but Carasians can take a fair amount of thumping."

I couldn't help smiling, the urge to destroy something difficult to maintain with the two of them chuckling. *How bizarrely Human, to find humor in this.*

"Did you find the suits?" I asked, stepping away from Paul. The air was increasingly foul; it was hard to catch my breath. *Another good reason for the suits,* I decided, worrying that the flight deck might suffer more from my meddling than the lower ones. Passing out was not going to help matters.

"Even in your size," Lefebvre said proudly. He seemed to be improving with each moment of freedom, perhaps one of those personalities who suffered most when helpless.

I reached out my hand in the Human gesture. "I haven't thanked you—" I waited politely for him to name himself.

"Lefebvre," he said, capturing my fingers in a hand broader and shorter than Paul's. The grip was pleasant, as Humans measured such things, warm and firm yet careful of my smaller hand. "As I recall, I've more to thank you for, Fem. You can call me Rudy, if you like."

"And you may call me Bess," I replied, giving him my best smile and ignoring a certain rigidity in Paul's stance. The Human knew quite well it was traditional to keep the essential sound of one's web-name, although that was less a Rule than the comfort of retaining some identity regardless of shape. *Not that I intended to become used to either.*

"Bess," Lefebvre repeated with a smile. "So, what's with the suits? You aren't proposing we walk off the ship, are you?"

I raised one eyebrow.

"Close," I replied. Then explained.

Elsewhere

"I REGRET you've been inconvenienced, Fem N'Klet—" Kearn began. He'd worn his best uniform for this inevitable and undesired meeting; it always helped his confidence.

"With all respect, Captain Kearn," the Panacian said graciously, as if she hadn't practically blackmailed her way into his office, "I believe you underestimate what I have endured while waiting for your disposition to—improve."

"Have you been mistreated by my crew?" *The note of outraged dignity was perfect,* Kearn told himself, *just perfect.* It paid to rehearse.

She arranged her upper limbs in the position that meant composed determination. Kearn recognized it with dismay. "No, Captain. I have been mistreated by you. Why was I brought along when your ship lifted from D'Dsel? I was a messenger, not a passenger. My absence will distress my family and my Queen."

"A regrettable misunderstanding, Fem N'Klet," Kearn said smoothly, wiping his moist palms on his thighs. "Now, as my officer informed you, we've arranged a stopover at Hixtar Station—"

"I see no purpose in leaving this ship before I have delivered my message, Captain Kearn."

He caught himself before his hands lifted to his scalp, instead, picking up some documents to rustle importantly. "Then, by all means, leave your message with me, Fem N'Klet and I'll get to it as soon as I—"

"It is an oral message, for you only, from the Queen of my family. You had the honor of meeting her before her maturation."

Despite the urgings of the Feneden to avoid any such messages, Kearn couldn't help but be flattered. A Queen had remembered their acquaintance? Not that he could pull the name or face out of his own past to match, but that only proved the impact he must have made upon this individual. Kearn sat up straighter. *Was he not the Captain?* he reminded himself. *Since when did Captains obey the orders of passengers?* "Of course, I remember your magnificent Queen," he said heartily. "Please, give me her message."

"The Human traitor lives," N'Klet stated, her faceted eyes on Kearn as if her instructions included memorizing his reaction to this news. "The individual you told my Queen was the one who brought the Esen Monster to D'Dsel, so it could murder Her Glory Sec-ag Mixs C'Cklet."

"Ragem?" Kearn's eyebrows rose, creasing his hairless forehead. "Impossible! My dear Fem— Your Queen's mistaken—"

"Paul Ragem, the Traitor, stood before my Queen in audience the day before this ship left D'Dsel. He had been known to our kin-group for the past twenty-two standard years as Paul Cameron, a business associate of excellent reputation. He came at our invitation to give his aid, and that of his partner, the noted linguist Esolesy Ki, in our negotiations between the Feneden and the Iftsen. Am I speaking too quickly for you, Captain Kearn?"

Kearn was indeed waving at her to stop talking, but it had nothing to do with N'Klet's measured and capable comspeak, and everything to do with the fact that he was trying not to choke over the name Esolesy Ki.

Esolesy, he thought, wildly. It could be shortened as Es.

Es. Ragem's pet name for Esen.

"We have to go back," Kearn muttered, fumbling for the com panel on his desk. "I have to find them."

"You would be unsuccessful. They have left D'Dsel, Captain Kearn."

"No!" he howled, leaping to his feet and flinging plas sheets everywhere. "No! I can't have been so close and lost them!"

N'Klet tilted her beautiful head to watch him. When Kearn stopped shouting to draw another breath, she said calmly: "The Queen also wanted you to know that Paul Ragem and Esolesy Ki left D'Dsel on an Iftsen ship. According to Port Authority, this ship was bound for Iftsen Secondus."

Kearn felt almost dizzy with joy. *This was it!* "Then we'll catch them there!" He couldn't wait to tell Timri. They'd have to discuss what to do. There had been some general ideas floating about concerning the best containment systems, weapons—but there must have been some new tech developed in the interim—Timri kept up to date on such things. *Then there was that special package, the one from his backer,* Kearn remembered.

N'Klet raised her upper limbs in a gesture of negation. "You have a shipful of Feneden who will not wish to go to Iftsen Secondus. Neither do I, Captain Kearn."

"Ah, but there you are wrong, my dear N'Klet," Kearn crowed. "The Feneden are vitally interested in my hunt. They take it very personally. Very."

"How so?" N'Klet asked, head tilted in curiosity.

"Were you not aware that their term "Shifter" refers to the Esen Monster's species? Oh, yes. The Feneden have been as decimated in the past as I've always warned we may be soon. The Feneden—" Kearn paused, imagining the glory to come, "—they'll want to be in for the kill."

24: Flight Deck Morning; Shuttle Afternoon

IT had been such a good plan.

If I ever had a tombstone, such as some Human cultures erected, that could be the inscription, I said to myself.

All had started so well.

Lefebvre and I had climbed into our suits, then dumped all of the lifepods into space. That was the easy part—the tiny craft were designed for quick, no-questions-asked release.

We'd already helped Paul into his suit; a task made both simpler and more difficult by Paul's fainting as Lefebvre tried to gently slip his injured arm into its sleeve. According to Paul, the arm wasn't broken. The shoulder had merely been repeatedly dislocated and reset. I began shunting these moments into my most private memories, into the cold, dark place that held the final thoughts of my web-kin and the taste of Death.

Timing was critical once the pods left the ship. Klaxons had sounded immediately, heralding the pounding of feet as the Tly shuttle crews hurried to launch their three craft. It was irrelevant to my plan if they were being sent to retrieve the valuable lifepods or to search them for us.

I just wanted them launched—especially the one with the three of us hidden in its belly.

This had been the reason for the suits. Our hiding place was the vacuum hold beneath the pilot's compartment, used for anything from extra fuel to personal effects. There was just enough room for the three of us—given that I was small and folded easily, and both Humans were reasonably compact.

We had oriented ourselves, after some arguing on my part, so Lefebvre would be the first to leap out. I could see his face inside his helmet, lit by the indicators under his chin. It was serene, as though hijacking a shuttle in flight was an everyday part of a captain's life. Paul's face was too swollen to show anything at all, but he'd managed to nod at me. I took that to mean he understood completely that I—as the more resilient life-form here—should have been the one to take any risks, but he appreciated my sacrifice to keep in character.

I didn't have to like it.

The cruiser used a catapult system, firing its shuttles as though they were missiles. I'd known this in theory, but the reality was quite exhilarating. *Well, it was for me,* being lightest, and more or less on top of our pile of flesh. Lefebvre let out a strangled grunting sound for the few seconds of full thrust, which might have had something to do with the juxtaposition of my foot and his throat. Paul remained silent—I hoped because the medications the Tly administered to speed his healing process were finally dulling the pain.

The instant the force on our bodies began to ease up, Lefebvre had fired the opening pins on the hatch, scrambling out through a cloud of condensation. I slid into his spot, careful to avoid pressing on any part of Paul, and followed.

I needn't have hurried; Lefebvre was at the shuttle's controls before I stepped over the nearest body. There were two of them, both male, both—I was relieved to see—still breathing. We hadn't actually covered that point in the plan. I lifted off my helmet and put it to one side, impressed. "You've done this before," I observed, turning to help Paul climb out.

I could make out the corner of a smile as Lefebvre continued to work the panels, by plan setting us a course to casually swing out of range of the cluster of lifepods and the other shuttles before kicking in the translight. "Everyone has talents, Bess," Lefebvre said lightly.

Paul took off his helmet as well, making a soft whistling noise through his teeth. Those, he'd assured me, were intact. "Not everyone can do this," he commented, studying the unconscious Tly. "Handy."

I wondered if Paul was thinking the same thing that I was—how fortunate we'd been that Lefebvre hadn't used this particular talent to its fullest when we'd had our confrontation on D'Dsel. Of course, there had been the small matter of the biodisrupter.

I took a deep breath and began stripping off my suit. It wouldn't fit either of the Humans lying at my feet, but taking it off gave me more room to move as I put them into their own. We had no particular interest in taking crew from *The Black Watch* with us, and it had been Paul who suggested the option of simply suiting up the crew and leaving them behind. This wasn't the callous act it seemed; the suits carried emergency beacons which would guide their shipmates to recover them.

Before we could accomplish this final step, the shuttle's interior lights flickered and died.

The console lights remained, reflecting patterns of gold, red, and blue over Lefebvre's arms and hands as he lifted them slowly from the panels. "Disabler," he hissed. "Everything's knocked out."

A disabler was a pirate's weapon of choice and highly illegal. "Look," Lefebvre said, pointing out the front viewport.

I went to his side.

We had a spectacular view of the ominous, self-illuminated tube that was the *'Watch,* including the sparks of moving light as the pods we'd released tumbled blissfully in every direction. I could spot one of the other two shuttles, busy pursuing a target.

But much closer, and coming closer still, was the silvery sleekness of a ship I knew very well indeed—her grappling arms at the ready. Hands settled on my shoulders as Paul came to stand behind me.

"The *Vegas Lass,*" he said, something in his voice I thought Logan would have enjoyed causing.

I would, I told myself bitterly, *have preferred to be wrong about Captain Janet Chase.*

Elsewhere

"HUNTER Kearn, we have disagreement," Anisco's voice, through her translator, held no emotion, but waves rippled down the cilia from forehead to shoulder as if she stood within a waterfall.

A very pretty effect, Kearn thought, imagining those silken strands between his fingers. It was a fantasy he kept very guarded—the more one knew about alien species, the less likely it was to have such fantasies be anything but dangerous. For all he knew, the cilia were feeding mechanisms that could strip the flesh from his bones in an instant.

"There's no need for concern, Fem Anisco," he said soothingly, unable to resist shooting worried glances between each word at the other Feneden despite the presence of the two largest members of the *Russell*'s crew at his back. "I'm sure we can resolve any disputes."

"I concur," this from the second Feneden carrying a translator, Sidorae. Kearn was still uncertain who led the group—or even if they had a leader—but he had noticed Sidorae and Anisco usually disagreed on every topic. There was no consistency, however, no way Kearn had found to predict which side of any issue each Feneden would choose. It was as if they argued by convention, not conviction.

Regardless, Kearn suspected the two of them of a perverse enjoyment when they could put him in the middle of their debates, as now.

He sighed deeply, pulling his heavy coat more tightly

about himself as he looked around the transformed cabin. It had been Lefebvre's, a choice made in the captain's absence but before he had been declared missing. Timri's choice, in fact. She'd noted—quite reasonably— that Lefebvre's was the largest space available after Kearn's and that the furnishings had been significantly upgraded. She'd been emphatic about how Lefebvre would himself agree. And not only to this, but to her taking the comp system from his room to add to her own.

Kearn doubted this, but was willing to let Timri face the daunting Lefebvre about the loss of his quarters and equipment.

Timri had supervised the refit to suit the Feneden's requirements. They'd liked the huge jelly-bed, but apparently used it for dining, not sleeping. The ceramic tables now graced Kearn's own quarters, as the set of five swings—part of the odd requests they'd had to fill before leaving D'Dsel—required quite a bit of space to use safely. At the moment, the three silent Feneden were rocking back and forth gently, bare feet just touching the floor.

The floor. Kearn sighed again. The Feneden had brought some of their slimy carpeting along. It appeared to grow outward, and with dismaying enthusiasm, from patches they'd fixed at intervals throughout the cabin, already meeting in several spots. He'd insisted that Timri have the crew assigned to the door check regularly to be sure the stuff didn't grow into the rest of the ship.

There weren't chairs. When Kearn suggested he bring his own, Anisco and Sidorae had concurred, amazingly enough, that he must not. Kearn had ventured several times to have their meetings in his office, a place where he felt much more at ease—not to mention significantly warmer.

The Feneden preferred to meet here. In fact, the guard at the door might have been unnecessary, since their guests refused to leave their room at all. *Not that he'd want either the Feneden or their carpet left to their own devices,* Kearn told himself.

"The report I have is most reliable," he said out loud, in his firmest tone. "The Esen Monster—the Shifter," he corrected quickly, having learned by now the word elicited a much stronger reaction from the Feneden, "and her accomplice have accompanied the Iftsen to their home-world. I don't see why you object to following."

"There are no such beings," Anisco said, as she had a truly frustrating number of times already. N'Klet had warned him to expect this response in the Feneden.

Kearn still couldn't fathom it. *How could such reasonable and civilized beings refuse every imaginable evidence?* One thing he did know: there was no point trying to argue with them about the existence of the Iftsen—which was the source of his present state of near-panic.

Sidorae uttered a spate of liquid words which caused the device in Kearn's hand to pause in a crackle of static, as though the translator tried to digest something unfamiliar.

"Sidorae is trying to convey," Anisco interjected, "his disappointment in your source of information, Hunter. He wishes you to know there is much to be gained by examining the ancient ruins of our home. He is in error, of course. The truth is to be uncovered, not under vine and moss, but within the preserved texts and folklore of our people."

Kearn wrung his hands together, wishing he'd brought gloves. "I can't waste time looking for clues from the past when the monster is within reach now!" Then he had a brainstorm. "I believe I was mistaken, Fem Anisco, Hom Sidorae."

"Concerning?" This from Sidorae.

"The Shifter is traveling in a Human ship—yes, a freighter. She is trying to hide in a lifeless system, the one the Panacians call Iftsen."

The cilia of all the Feneden slowly came erect. "This is much more satisfactory information, Hunter Kearn," Anisco said carefully. "We will consult, but I believe we would be eager to accompany your hunt to this place."

"Eager," repeated Sidorae. Indeed, Kearn could see

all of the Feneden looking more alert, as though he'd finally reached them. *Or,* he thought uneasily, *as if they'd finally convinced him of something.*

Sidorae came closer, putting one long-fingered and graceful hand on Kearn's forearm—a feather's touch. Then he gestured to the others, who slipped down from their swings and moved to stand beside Anisco and Sidorae in a line. Afraid to move, Kearn took comfort from the silent, watchful crew behind him.

"We hunt the Shifter," Sidorae said. As one, the Feneden went to their knees, pressing their foreheads deeply into the moist carpet at Kearn's feet.

Kearn was even more grateful he'd thought to bring crew—now, maybe Timri would believe him when he told her the respect the Feneden offered him.

A shame no one else seemed to feel it, he thought bitterly, then smiled slowly. *They would, once he'd tracked down the Shifter. And Ragem.*

25: Freighter Morning

PAUL and I weren't the only ones to meet an old friend.

"If it isn't Able Joe," Lefebvre said, in a voice so completely expressionless it made me nervous.

"Hom Captain," the Ervickian didn't seem affected, although I thought perhaps he should be. From my viewpoint, a step behind Lefebvre and discreetly trying to prop up Paul as we walked through the air lock to board the *'Lass,* the muscles of the Human's neck were doing some interesting contortions, as though he fought to keep himself from punching a certain small someone in all four beady eyes.

Paul pushed me behind him, refusing my help as he stepped over the portal's rim, an attempt, I concluded, to prevent anyone waiting from assuming a connection between us.

I did my best to look every bit the helpless, terrified Human child. *It wasn't hard.*

Lefebvre turned to help Paul, putting an arm around the taller Human. I thought it was also a way for Lefebvre to control his anger; I'd noticed he and Paul had this need for action in common.

"And this is the ghost who terrorized Logan's crew?" the voice, dripping with scorn, could only come from one individual. I looked up into Chase's violet eyes. "Who is she?"

Lefebvre spoke before I could: "My niece. Gloria." He held out his free hand to me. Quickly remembering the appropriate Human custom, I put mine into it. I gazed at Lefebvre, seeing mostly his chin with its outline of dark stubble.

Why was he claiming me as family? I had a feeling it had something to do with Paul.

The ship-to-ship air lock of the *'Lass* was amidships, in an area accessible only during flight, and then by crew wearing gear against the cold. It opened into a large oval space, bisected by a mammoth rack of servo-handling arms used to transfer goods to the holds below. They loomed overhead like the limp arms of something dead, tossed in a tree by a hunter. I could see my breath.

Chase had arranged a welcoming committee. She stood, fists on her hips, the Ervickian shivering in front of her, flanked by four burly, well-armed Humans. I was pleased not to recognize any of them, confirmation she hadn't convinced the crew of a Largas ship to serve the Tly. *Were any of the former crew on board?* I wondered, sure Paul did the same.

Paul. My hand in Lefebvre's seemed all at once to be a betrayal, like the one I expected any moment from Chase as she studied the three of us.

"You must be the Commonweath flunky," she said to Lefebvre, careful not to come too close to any of us. "I hear you had quite the song to sing."

"And who might you be?" Lefebvre replied evenly. "Logan's?"

Chase smiled. "I might be a friend," she said, arching an eyebrow. "Isn't that right—Mitchell?"

I'd held my breath, convinced she'd been about to name Paul and trying to prepare myself for Lefebvre's reaction. I let it out again as inconspicuously as possible. *What was she up to?*

"If you're a friend," Lefebvre said, when it was plain Paul wasn't about to speak, "then you can see he needs a med—now."

Something flickered across Captain Chase's otherwise composed features. I thought her quick look at Paul might have been the first time she'd let herself see the damage done to him. *Fear,* I decided, having had a great deal of experience reading emotions on her face. *No help there.* To be fair, I'd met Logan; hers was the reasonable reaction.

"Even an hour in a med unit could help," Lefebvre urged, possibly misinterpreting her look as reluctant compassion. "Please."

Perhaps seeing this as a safe option to a cell, Chase nodded to her crew. Two of them came and took Paul from Lefebvre. Paul sagged, as though willing to give these strangers more weight to bear than he'd put on Lefebvre's shoulder. I tensed, ready to follow them, only to find my hand trapped in what was now a steel grip. I looked up and met Lefebvre's eyes, seeing both understanding and warning. This form betrayed me again, filling my eyes with moisture that spilled down my cheeks.

Able Joe noticed—those extra oculars rarely missed anything of potential use. "Niece, is it? You didn't have a niece on D'Dsel. Did you forget this niece? Yes?"

"You met me in a bar, remember?" Lefebvre said scornfully.

Chase watched this interchange with what appeared to be sudden boredom, almost as if with Paul having been dealt with she had little use for the two of us. "If you're so interested, Ervickian, take the child and clean her up," she ordered.

Lefebvre's "Wait a minute—" crossed over Able Joe's smug "Of course, Captain Chase." I wrenched my hand free and walked to the Ervickian quite willingly. I glanced over my shoulder and smiled reassuringly at the frowning Human.

Not only could I really use a bath, I thought, following Able Joe, *it was a distinct pleasure to look down at someone for a change.*

Of the three of us, housed temporarily on the *'Lass* as *The Black Watch* worked on her environmental systems, I probably had the best of it.

I ducked my head under the stream of foam one last time, cleaning out the last of the fake blood I'd anointed myself with, and hit the dry cycle. Able Joe's voice still rambled on, easy to hear over the fresher.

"We were watching for that Human—the one going by," a suspicious hiccup "by Kane—Mitchell Kane. What a silly name. Kane, name, Kane, vain name." This went on for a while. Once dry, I stepped out into what was a typical freighter cabin, set up for passengers or extra crew depending on the route and cargo.

Able Joe might have been seeing something of me through what showed of his eyes. *I wouldn't have bet on it.* Their lids were almost closed, and his long thin arms drifted back and forth as if stirred by a breeze. The rest of him had sunk into the cushions of a chair, one foot at an angle that should have hurt, but obviously didn't.

That was, I reminded myself smugly, *just one of the effects of pleal juice on his species.*

I'd known the *'Lass* stocked it. Chase had insisted on having plenty of the revolting stuff on board. What probably only I, and now Able Joe, knew, was the salutary effect of two glasses on the disposition of any Ervickian. Had he been older, he would have had experience enough with the taste to avoid it unless safely in his crèche.

Alas, I had no scruples taking advantage of his youth, especially once Able Joe confirmed certain events and his place in them for me.

I pulled on deliciously clean clothes and nibbled a ration bar.

Nothing, I thought with disgust, *had been a coincidence.* Skalet had been right.

Chase had gone through Paul's mail before leaving Panacia. She'd cued Logan to board her ship on its way back through Tly space—a convenient excuse to exchange information, coupled with the theft of cargo intended for Inhaven. *She'd been a better actor than I'd imagined.* I didn't doubt she'd been the one to slip the tracer into Paul's clothing.

What had made her suspect Paul's real identity? When had she decided to share that suspicion with those interested in finding him? Understandably, Able Joe didn't know the answer to these and other pressing questions.

We'd been unwitting allies. My reaction to her aversion to my Lishcyn-self, while in hindsight well-deserved, had blinded me to what I should have seen. Joel Largas might have picked up on the incongruities surrounding his only non-family Captain, had she not been so obviously enamored of his favorite son-in-law. We'd all tried to slot her within our relationships, ignoring the possibility she had never fit for a reason.

"Where was Chase before she worked for Largas Freight?" I asked, cutting into what sounded like Able Joe's valiant attempt to rhyme the names of all his crèche-mates. To be on the safe side, I pressed another glass of pleal into the hand next time it waved in my direction. The being managed to pour most of the liquid into its second mouth, adding only a portion to the growing stain on its shirt.

"N'ver guess to look at 'er, would you," the Ervickian said, cooperative as ever. It was part of their mind-set to enjoy showing how much more they knew than others. "Quite the accomplis . . . the accomplisss—smart Human. Too smart. Stole her family's fortune and was sent to prison to improve her ways. Didn't stay there long either—joined some mercs—say, did you know that stuff sticking out of your head is a different color now? How'd do that?"

"I washed it," I said, although I knew he didn't really hear my answer. So Chase was a career opportunist, explaining much about her skills and lack of morals, as well as her link with the Tly. It was, regrettably, now the sort of Human society that welcomed both.

"Why did she come to Minas XII?"

The answer was prompt, and somewhat reassuring: "Larga–issh Freight. Tly wants to stop their shippings—ship–ping—to Inhaven Prime. All part of the big picture." Both mouths yawned at once, providing a too-clear view of the otherwise practical Ervickian separation between breathing and digestion. I stared, fascinated by the echoing yellow-greens of mucus and bile. He added, with unexpected clarity, "Nothing like having someone on the inside, y'know."

"Like you?" I suggested. "You were pretty handy on D'Dsel, weren't you?" The eyes blinked, their synchrony off by a few milliseconds. The being was going to pass out on me any second now. "Lefebvre?" I prompted hastily.

"Now, there's a fool for you," the Ervickian declared loudly, arms flinging outward so that I had barely enough warning to snatch the empty glass before it hit me. "The only being who didn't know what that one was doing was Kearn. Now, there's a fool for you."

I didn't try to sort that out—I had a vague impression I'd likely agree, which worried me. "If Lefebvre's a fool, why did Logan want him?"

"Ahhhh," he waggled all eight fingers on one hand at me. "Logan didn't want him. Logan wanted Ragem. But Lefebvre had a key, you see. A key. A key. See me. A key."

"A key," I repeated, feeling as though somewhere along the line I must have lost any control over this conversation. Able Joe blinked again; this time the lower right eye failed to join in at all. "A key to what?" I asked quickly.

"The proof, you see, was in the key—the proof that he— was who she said he'd be." This little rhyme pleased the Ervickian so much, both mouths grinned, all four eyes stared blankly at me, and it gradually tipped to one side, landing with a soft thwump on the floor beside its chair.

I tossed a blanket over Able Joe, as much to hide the somewhat disturbing effect open-eyed sleep had on my Human-self as to keep him comfortable, and mulled over what I'd learned.

There were the Tly, epitomized by Inspector Logan and his ship. It wasn't new—or unique—to humanity, this urge to subjugate an old enemy. As for Logan's belief that the web-being had been some sort of ultimate Kraal weapon? There had been hundreds of similar rumors following Death's attacks along the Fringe. It was as if Humans found a mysterious weapon of mass destruction a more comforting explanation than imagining themselves prey.

My lips twitched. *Maybe it was.* Until living hands held the weapon.

While I didn't have to worry about Logan finding his mythic weapon any time soon—since the only thing comparable was currently sitting on the edge of a bed listening to a drunken Ervickian snore off-key—I did have to worry about his attempts to do so. Whatever this key of Lefebvre's had been, Logan must have already used it to prove Mitchell Kane and Paul Cameron were in fact Paul Ragem. And the name Ragem was inextricably linked to the supposed biological weapon, thanks to Kearn.

Lefebvre. I didn't know what to think or plan about him, and Paul hadn't helped. Paul called him friend—something he never did lightly. It had been a message to me that I was to trust Lefebvre.

Trust him? On D'Dsel, Lefebvre called Paul a traitor, with enough anger in his voice for a hundred Kearns. *Humans were so confusing.*

I did know that an intelligent, resourceful being like Lefebvre was more dangerous to our secret than Kearn could ever be. If Lefebvre ever believed in my existence— I stopped the thought before risking my hold on this form.

Whatever game Logan and Chase were playing with us, pretending Paul was Mitchell, it couldn't last much longer. When it ended, I had to be ready to stand between the two of them. I would never let Lefebvre harm Paul.

Other than that, I told myself sadly, *I might have counted him a friend, too.*

Elsewhere

THE difficulties of treating a prisoner poorly were compounded when all you had to use for a cell was a decent cabin complete with private fresher and someone's belongings. Without compunction, Lefebvre dressed in that someone's clean coveralls after washing.

He went to the cot farthest from the door. A few pillows, a rolled-up blanket or two—he hadn't used this trick since his youth on Botharis, when he'd sneak out to visit the Ragems' farm when their famous son came insystem.

Lefebvre ran one hand to smooth the top cover, no longer seeing the cabin, instead remembering what it had been like before the betrayal, when he and others—cousins mostly—had made their way inside the big kitchen. It had always been filled with the smells of food and the voices of people. A busy, crowded, welcoming place.

And, every so often, the news would spread through the small community that a trader or other starship had brought Paul home for a visit. There were mock fights in the barn among his brothers to see who'd get to pick him up; it took Paul a few hours to become part of Botharis again and, until then, talking to him was like meeting someone from another world, as though something of his travels linked him to the stars so he could bring them home. His mother, the only one at home who had lived in space, would look into his eyes before hugging her son, and nod in complete understanding.

He wasn't the greatest storyteller, but after the greetings ended and the eating was done, the kitchen would steadily absorb more and more people to listen to Paul's latest adventures. There had been something about his voice—eager, fresh, never jaded by what he'd seen—it brought alien worlds to life right there and then, for everyone. Lefebvre could almost hear it now, if he closed his eyes.

Instead, he made himself remember the other voices, the accusing ones who'd arrived before they'd had time to grieve, the ones who questioned everything and everyone. They'd brought with them the final story from Paul's life: how he'd betrayed them by siding with the Monster.

The kitchen had never filled with voices again. The Ragems had locked their doors the very next night and moved away without a word.

Lefebvre shook off memory. It wasn't helpful. Right now, his focus was on Mitchell and the child they both wanted to protect. He gathered up an armload of clothing from the cupboard and made himself a nest behind the door. Then he used someone's lucky coin to access the lighting control panel, plunging the room into darkness.

Hands outstretched, Lefebvre found his nest and made himself comfortable. It might be a matter of minutes, or days, until they came for him.

He'd be ready.

26: Hold Night; Hydroponics Night

THE Ervickian, possibly wary of any Human or, more likely, simply paranoid as were many of its kind, had locked the door. Fortunately, it had locked the door from the inside.

This ship, I knew. Before Chase—who had never made Esolesy Ki welcome on board—the *Vegas Lass* had been in the friendlier hands of Joel's son Denny Largas. Denny, uncle to Paul's children and without offspring of his own, had doted on his niece and nephew and considered me part of his family. He'd died on this ship, victim of a rare disease, slipping away in his sleep as though forgetting how important he was to us all. *I would remember him.*

I could almost hear Denny's voice echoing down the night-dimmed corridors. He wouldn't be happy about what his precious ship was doing. I found a pleasing symmetry in my being the one to do something about it.

This form, while relatively weak and prone to emotion, was remarkably good at moving around noiselessly. I also relished having Human-sized hands for once. They made accessing the secondary com system in the hold so much easier. The system was used when the 'Lass was findown and the hold was a hive of activity, but, as Denny had told me, there was no reason it couldn't be used in space, only spacer habit and the comfort of the primary com on the warm bridge.

The translight burst would be noticed by the bridge crew—you didn't pull that kind of power from the ship without setting off detectors—so it had to be a once-out, no reply kind of message. That meant I needed the most trouble I could rouse with one yell.

Joel Largas.

The moment I hit the switch, I ran from the hold area and headed for hydroponics, my chosen hiding place, a place filled with living mass just ready to become more Esen.

As I ran, I congratulated myself. *This was more like it. Esen the sneak. Esen the clever.*

I turned a corner and ran straight into what felt like a wall. I staggered back, looking up, then up again.

Esen the idiot.

Inspector Logan was definitely larger, seen through these Human eyes.

He wore the medallion. I didn't need to feel the presence of that piece of me; Logan wore it openly, like some trophy. I kept my eyes from it with an effort. Of course, there was very little else to see in the corridor beyond two metal walls and the Human one before me.

Neither of us moved for what began to seem a rather long time, although likely it was a matter of seconds. Finally, I dared lift my eyes to his face.

It was ashen. His lips were pulled back in some horrible rictus and his eyes were as close to bulging as I'd ever seen in a Human. It didn't improve his appearance.

I'd seen that look before, I realized, at first incredulous that this Human monolith could be terrified by the ghost of a child. Then I didn't find it strange at all. *If ever a being should expect to be haunted by vengeful spirits,* I reminded myself, *it was this one.*

All I needed to do was pass Logan while his surely temporary paralysis lasted, get out of range of those extraordinarily long arms, *then run like crazy.* Fearing my voice would crack, I started humming the love song from Garson's World under my breath and moved my right foot forward very slowly.

He shuddered—an awe-inspiring reaction from a Human

who massed enough for six of me—and moved back one step.

I moved forward, always humming, never taking my eyes from his.

Another step back. It was as though we were partners in some bizarre dance in stopped time, *a favorite form of the Urgians,* Ansky-memory unhelpfully added.

Just a few more—

That, of course, was the instant the ship's internal alarm sounded. On the *'Lass,* the deafening shriek warned of imminent disaster, such as fire or hull breach, but I was reasonably sure this was Chase's reply to my message. Logan gave a great shuddering gasp, as though shaking off a nightmare, then lunged at me, those arms I'd planned to avoid sweeping out like immense claws to grab me.

I wasn't there, having thrown myself to the floor the moment his eyes snapped into reason again. I crawled between his legs—for once grateful this particular Human was oversized—scrambled to my feet, and ran.

This form was more agile and I knew exactly where I was going, including being able to hit the door control without breaking stride. Logan was faster than anyone his bulk should have been. His hands met my back, shoving me forward instead of gripping. I wasn't sure whether that had been his intention or not, and didn't care. It accomplished everything I'd hoped.

I ducked and rolled with the force, my body fitting perfectly under the railing around the main floor tank, plunging myself into the thick broth of living plant cells with a relief close to hysteria.

Web-form.

I consumed and shed the inorganics that had been my clothing, sinking to the bottom to become a layer marginally more viscous than that floating over me, giving up the Human senses of touch, hearing, sight, and smell for other, more intimate ways of knowing. Logan, painted now as a cohesive mass of organized chemical structure I recognized as Human—with the arresting glow of my frozen web-mass attached—moved along the railing as if searching. Connecting us were the sweet harmonies of electromagnetism and gravity, beyond, the elegant song of stars and atoms as they spun in and out of pure energy, punctuated by the throbbing power sources of this ship and the others within my inner sight.

Lovely, I admitted to myself, but knew much of the joy I experienced was the relief of being safe from alien eyes.

It was high time I did what my kind did best, I ordered myself sternly.

Wait.

Elsewhere

THE alarm had ended Lefebvre's wait. He'd barely started to react, feeling the roar of adrenaline as his spacer nerves interpreted the sound as trouble with the ship, when the door of his cabin whooshed open.

Lefebvre held absolutely still. It was one of the guards who'd brought him here. The being hesitated, perhaps suspicious of the unmoving figure on the bed when nothing with ears could avoid the alarms. That pause, however brief, was more than enough for Lefebvre.

"Hard head," he commented a second later, rubbing his knuckles contentedly. Then he pulled the unconscious guard into the cabin, closing the door after making sure it wouldn't lock automatically.

A quick search produced a tidy little arsenal, the sort of mayhem one could safely use shipside: a knife, stunner, and, last, but not least, a blister stick. *A common enough weapon,* Lefebvre reminded himself, wincing as the alarm continued to howl.

Maybe something really was wrong with this ship. He hoped so. It would make whatever he could accomplish that much easier.

As long as it didn't kill them all first.

Lefebvre's first thought was that the Ervickian was dead. *Not a loss,* he told himself, then changed his mind as the ungentle nudge of his foot produced a definite twitch from the body stretched out on the floor.

Someone had mercifully killed the alarm, which didn't

explain what Able Joe was doing asleep. Reluctantly, Lefebvre bent closer and sniffed. The still-moist stains around the second mouth were pleal juice.

Able Joe would not knowingly intoxicate itself without others of its crèche in range. *A resourceful young Fem,* Lefebvre thought with approval, as well as considerable relief. He hadn't allowed himself to contemplate what an Ervickian's idea of caring for a Human child might include—everyone knew the rumors about the survival rates in their crèches, but who believed all the interspecies' gossip? Especially when the subject was already held in pretty low esteem.

He took a quick look around, but found no other clues in the cabin, identical to the one he'd just left—in the same corridor, in fact. He'd tried it first as it was the only other locked door. *So Bess had managed to free herself.* Lefebvre's relief faded. *Now what?*

The alarm. He'd hoped for a good old-fashioned hull breach, but that now appeared unlikely. Given the child's handiwork with the environmental systems on the 'Watch, he suspected the alarm had something to do with her freedom and worse, ceased because she'd been recaptured.

Lefebvre's grip on the blister stick tightened. *Surely they wouldn't harm a little girl,* he assured himself, knowing the opposite was true. He'd seen enough in his years as a patroller on Botharis. Then, there was Logan.

He glanced in the mirror. He'd taken time to clean up and shave, but nothing could be done about the shadows under his eyes or the new lines at the corner of his mouth. *Given this crew,* Lefebvre thought wryly, *those would probably help.* He tightened the fastenings on the coveralls he'd found—the guard had worn the same, emblazoned with the Largas Freight logo. The belt he'd taken from the guard wasn't standard spacer issue, having holsters for the stunner and blister stick.

With luck, he'd pass for crew, assuming those on this ship were mostly hired mercs who might not all know each other on sight. Depending on the progress Mitchell had made in the med unit over the past hours, Lefeb-vre thought he could do the same. Once the swelling and bruising were gone, he'd be hard-pressed himself to recognize his new friend. This all assumed Chase had put Mitchell into treatment and that Lefebvre could some-how retrieve him unnoticed—gambles he was prepared to take.

Bess. She was the biggest problem, Lefebvre real-ized grimly. *There was no way to make her inconspicu-ous.*

27: Tank Afternoon

ONE of the many joys of being totally inconspicuous was no longer being interrupted by events or ideas over which I had no control. I let the hydroponics tank dictate my outer edges and let my mind drift through various Esen-saves-Paul scenarios—all of which had a common theme of teeth, Logan's flesh, and a significant amount of screaming. *And,* I added to myself, *chocolate.*

Not that I held with screaming or biting. They were simply therapeutic fantasies, a way to pass the time while part of me raged with impatience to find Paul and be sure he was all right.

The rest of me was more reasonable, knowing my escape and the call for help I'd sent, coupled with my disappearance under Logan's nose, had to be keeping the ship's sapient inhabitants occupied with more than tormenting my Human about a weapon that might not exist.

I was less sure about Logan's reaction to our encounter. Had he admitted seeing me? *Perhaps.* I suspected he hadn't told anyone about my disappearance in this tank: since he'd left, no one else had so much as opened the door. *Which relieved the nagging worry of their flushing the tank to search its depths.* I'd survive it, but I didn't plan to leave the ship without Paul.

Or the other one, I admitted, sloshing back and forth in sudden melancholy. The more time Paul and I spent in Lefebvre's pleasant company, the more likely we'd face a very unpleasant end to our budding friendship. *As usual,* I grumbled, *Humans made my life even more complicated.*

Not that I'd abandon Lefebvre to Logan and Chase. For one thing, I saw no reason why they'd kept Lefebvre alive this long, beyond having forgotten to kill him. Despite an unworthy desire to bend one or two Humans into uncomfortable shapes, I wished no harm to any intelligent being.

Especially, I admitted, *to one who held my hand in front of enemies and claimed to be kin.* That had been brave and unasked, a warm memory I used to keep several other recent ones at bay.

I sampled a bit of the living mass touching me, tasting fresh and vibrant cells, growing at the maximum efficiency this Human technology could sustain. Largas had insisted all of the company's new ships be hydroponics-capable, an expense most other freighters out of Minas refused. Paul and I offered subtle encouragement, planning against such a day as this, but it hadn't been needed. Joel knew first-hand the importance of self-sufficiency in space.

It was certainly important to me, I thought, slightly uncomfortable now, as then, with the knowledge of what Joel would think of this version of his good friend, Esolesy Ki.

Abundant living mass and, so far, privacy. I could cycle into any form in web-memory tolerant of this atmosphere, and I knew a number with significant advantages—including teeth. *Just perfect,* I thought, and would have sighed had I the lungs for it. *How often in my recently hectic life had that combination occurred?*

Of course, Lefebvre would doubtless refuse to leave the ship without the me he knew.

Equally of course, I was not about to show him how flexible that particular identity could be.

So there was really no choice at all. It would be my unimpressive and essentially fangless Human-self to the rescue.

I thought I'd stay in the tank a while longer and enjoy those fantasy triumphs while I could.

Elsewhere

"I SEE he has made a remarkable recovery. Of course I approve, my dear Janet. As always, you anticipate my every need—"

Logan.

Lefebvre kept his head up and his eyes straight ahead as he walked past the open door to the med room, the image of someone following orders. Inside, his guts twisted, as if that snake-soft, high-pitched voice had some power over his body. *What was Logan doing on the 'Lass?*

The next opening led to the galley, empty while the crew searched for the missing child. Lefebvre took a chance and ducked inside to think.

So far, his imposture had passed with flying colors. In fact, the first crewbeing he'd encountered had ordered him to search the lower decks. He'd nodded obediently, somehow keeping a straight face as the Human, apparently the com-tech, vented his justifiable ire about trader brats everyone knew grew up with antique com equipment—so why was it his fault she'd known how to punch out a message?—the incompetence of officers of any ilk, and the general state of a universe that would give any responsibility to an Ervickian.

Now, Lefebvre leaned back against the wall, listening for any sign Logan and Chase were leaving the med room. Bess had sent a message and somehow continued to give a shipload of mercs the slip. *Better than he'd accomplished so far,* he thought, as proud as if she'd been his own flesh and blood and not someone he'd met yesterday.

Whenever he closed his eyes, he saw Bess' face as it had looked when they'd taken Mitchell away and he'd gripped her hand hard enough to hurt, afraid she'd throw herself after her friend and reveal how important he was to her. *He couldn't let them have that weapon to use,* Lefebvre thought grimly. *Mitchell would break.* He'd no doubt Mitchell would agree to anything, do anything, to save the child.

Her pale cheeks had been streaked with tears and dirt; her eyes, locked on his, had been an incredible blue-green, darkened by despair at first, then warming with trust as she must have realized why he held her back.

A trust he planned to deserve.

Footsteps. Lefebvre counted under his breath, estimating how many steps it would take to reach the bend and be out of sight. *There.*

He stepped back out into the corridor, moving swiftly in case someone decided at the last minute to turn back, and entered the med room, closing the door behind him.

"What can I do for you?" the tech hadn't turned around, busy adjusting some controls above an opaque med unit.

"Med-tech," Lefebvre said, moving soundlessly, up on the balls of his feet. "Captain's orders. I'm here to guard her guest."

"I thought we agreed that wouldn't be necessary if I put him in stasis—I mean, how does she think he's going to—" The tech looked over his shoulder with an aggrieved expression in time to see Lefebvre's fist arrive.

"You know officers," Lefebvre said quietly, catching the man as he slumped, and putting him down to one side.

The box was already humming to itself, its interior clouded as the atmosphere within was rapidly being exchanged for the preservatives and sedatives used to hold a body in suspended animation for prolonged periods. Lefebvre had no idea which controls would safely halt the process, so he simply grabbed the nearest metal stool and brought it smashing down on the surface of the box, coughing as the acrid gases mixed with the room air.

There was an echoing cough. Eyes smarting from the fumes, Lefebvre brushed away hunks of plas until he reached something warmer and firmer. *An arm.* As he tugged at it, a hand reached out and fastened on his shoulder, surprising Lefebvre into an involuntary gasp. He felt suddenly dizzy as he inhaled remnants of the sedative, and panicked, grabbing what he hoped was Mitchell and heaving them both away from the box as quickly as he could.

They landed on the floor, Lefebvre trying to take most of the impact and receiving a stinging blow from an elbow in his face for his efforts. He sputtered out a protest and found, to his amazement, the form lying sprawled on top of him was shaking with laughter.

"Quite—the—the—rescue," a voice gasped cheerfully, no longer hoarse with pain, a voice and laughter he *knew* "—thought you were trying to kill me— How's your nose?"

"Who—?" Lefebvre thrust the other away, rolling over so his hands pinned the other Human with brutal force to the floor. He blinked, desperate to clear his eyes, then, suddenly, could see.

Paul Antoni Ragem, his face restored so only the jagged purple outlines of its punishment remained, looked up at him. There wasn't any humor left in his gray eyes—only resignation. "Or are you going to kill me now, Rudy?"

28: Tank Night

LINGERING in web-form wasn't the lazy, danger-avoiding tactic it might seem to any other being. I had a reason—and it paid off much sooner than I'd hoped.

I was waiting for a response to my call.

Without leaving the ship to taste the clarity of *out there,* I couldn't know the direction *The Black Watch* had taken since leaving the *Narcissus.* I had a rough idea of range, which wasn't particularly helpful by itself, but allowed me to invent reasons for continued patience.

So I was relieved to detect the power signature of a ship approaching—a ship I hoped came from Largas, something difficult to tell by the song of its energy alone, and a ship I hoped was capable of standing up to the *'Watch.* My assurances that the Tly cruiser was unarmed had come from a source I now wouldn't trust for the price of marfle tea.

The jets rippling the water ceased abruptly, once-suspended cells sinking until they began coating my upper surface, forming a thick layer I hoped would disguise my unfortunately vivid and beautiful blue. It interfered slightly with my ability to sense what was nearby—which wasn't outstanding at best, fine distinctions not being too necessary in a form originally devoted to harvesting the glowing dust of protostars and other rather easily distinguished food sources. I thinned as much as I could, sending extensions of myself creeping up each corner of the tank until clear of the cell broth but still safely underwater. *Maybe,* I told myself optimistically, *they'll think I'm caulking.*

This did improve my awareness of the tank room. I coupled the information being collected by my web-self with my Human-self memories of the place—a trick Ersh had taught me, since otherwise one had very little chance of making sense of what the movements of cohesive masses meant.

So I knew there were four Humans searching the hydroponics area, concentrating on the deck and areas behind the machinery and tubing. I didn't expect they'd do a particularly thorough job. It was a warm, always damp place, with a tendency to mold and a very unshiplike scent many spacers claimed made them ill. Each took a turn bending over the now-stilled water in the main tank, as well as climbing up and opening the lids on the secondaries. Then they were gone.

The jets kicked back in, freeing me from my living burden. At the same time, Ersh-memory welled up and spun me away from this place . . .

. . . until I rushed through the void as Ersh had done, soaring through the wonder of vacuum, rising and falling in waves of radiation in pursuit of streams of light, spending web-mass as energy until I was more energy than mass, driving forward until space itself dropped away and I moved *aside.*

Freedom.

Others accumulated mass, refusing to use it, hoarding it like some treasure until their movement slowed and they were snagged in orbit around some star or planet. Ersh passed them . . . *scorn.* . . . There had to be more . . .

Curiosity. Leaving the others to the familiar and the safe, seeking the empty spaces . . . spending mass until she was almost gone . . .

. . . I surged up out of the memory, knowing how it ended and having no desire to relive the taste of Feneden or any other life-form.

I did, however, feel a considerable longing to dip back into those memories of flight. I'd done it once, thrown away mass and escaped a planet's gravity, experienced the intense passion of my flesh for vacuum. *It was,* I reminded myself, *something Ersh had wisely forbidden herself and her*

Web. As I forbade myself. Civilized beings, trustworthy, safe beings, used starships; I intended to be one.

Exactly which part of civilized behavior involved lurking at the bottom of a pool of algae was not an issue I cared to examine at the moment.

The approaching ship should be within the range of the sensors on the *'Lass* soon, I judged. Given its past and present, I thought it prudent to assume the corresponding instruments on *The Black Watch* would be even more sensitive.

With every minute, I grew more anxious. *Was this ship our rescue or Logan's reinforcements?* I checked again for signs of Humans—or a hungover Ervickian—within range of this room. None. The web-mass within Paul's medallion sang its forlorn, siren call. By its location, I judged Logan to be on an upper deck.

I pulled myself into the proper teardrop shape of my kind, feeling energized by the condensing of my mass. Then I oozed up onto the platform, not wanting algae on my feet, and cycled.

And shivered. I wrapped my new arms around my bare self and quickly went to the storage locker. There, again through suggestions from Cameron & Ki to the easygoing ear of Largas Freight, was a set of coveralls to be used when cleaning out any contaminated tanks. It was a reasonable precaution against spreading harmful organisms from one tank to another—although that happened so rarely as to be almost unknown. It was also a very reasonable way to insure warm, dry clothing for a visiting web-being without a wardrobe.

I looked down at myself and sighed. *Warm, dry, and only five sizes too large.* I started rolling up the cuffs, then froze.

The door was opening again.

Elsewhere

"WELL, cousin?"

Lefebvre stared down, hardly daring to breathe. The face was older, of course; those fifty years looked back from his mirror, too. The voice was deeper, more resonant. There were fine lines beside the eyes and mouth, some newly etched by pain.

He hadn't thought so much would be the same: the almost fierce intelligence sparkling in the intense eyes, the lean expressive features, the way that lock of hair curled rebelliously over the brow—the despair of Ragem's mother before every family event.

He hadn't imagined what would change, that this face he thought he knew better than his own would mature into something commanding, something compassionate and wise.

This, this wasn't the face he'd hunted. Where was the guilt, the remorse?

Where were all his urgent questions? Now that he could ask them, Lefebvre discovered he couldn't speak, instead choking on an anger so beyond his control that his hands grappled Paul's throat before he could stop them, fingertips digging deep into faded bruises.

Bruises? He felt his thoughts and emotions reel with confusion. *This was Mitchell.* His companion in hell, who'd willingly suffered to hide a child from a monster.

Lefebvre released his death grip, throwing himself up and back until he half-leaned on a desk. "I don't understand," he whispered in horror, feeling the deck ready to open under his feet as he watched Paul take a wheezing breath.

Paul Ragem.

Paul rose as well, every movement cautious and planned as though the outward healing masked inward damage that hadn't been repaired. Or maybe it was the memory of pain—the accelerated healing of a med unit sometimes fooled the mind.

No, realized Lefebvre, *it was to give* him *time to adjust.* Paul had always been good at communicating with others, alien or Human. Now it was as if he'd spent the past years honing that skill, learning to control every part of his body, every expression, even the timbre of his voice. *Why?*

He didn't realize he'd asked that out loud until Paul repeated gently. "Why? Which one, Rudy? I'd think you'd have quite a few for me by now."

Lefebvre shook his head. "For me," he said, faintly surprised by the normal sound of his voice. "I've spent all this time trying to find the truth—trying to clear your name and memory." He faltered. "Why do I—"

"—feel like killing me?" Paul finished, not appearing alarmed, though he gingerly rubbed his neck. "I'd say it was a natural reaction, Rudy. You've every right to be furious. I've deceived you and everyone else. I abandoned you fifty years ago. On D'Dsel, I did it again, leaving you unconscious and so this—" he waved his hand as though indicating the ship, "—happened."

Lefebvre made a short, violent gesture of negation. "Logan would have found some other way to trap me." Even as he said the words, his heart pounded with frustrated rage, rage that seemed all at once to have too many targets, including himself. "He'd have done anything to get at you." Lefebvre's fists clenched. "And I helped, didn't I? He couldn't have known it was you for sure without my key, without what I told him. He wouldn't have—"

"Enough," Paul said sternly. "Nothing would have changed, Rudy." He dipped his head, then raised it, saying somberly: "Logan—and the rest of this—it all comes back to my actions, not yours. I let them spread lies about me—and let you believe them."

"I never did. I knew they were lies," Lefebvre found himself almost tripping over the words to say them quickly enough, as if they could atone for his actions of a moment before. "You'd never endanger your ship, your crewmates."

Paul's face grew pale and determined. "They weren't all lies, Rudy. I didn't harm anyone, but I did have a choice to make. Part of that choice was to let Paul Ragem die—to leave you and everyone else. I made it willingly."

"Why?" Lefebvre breathed. "What could matter to you that much?" *More than your family,* he added to himself, aching with the hurt of that loss as if it were fresh and not buried in their pasts.

Paul slowly reached out his hand. "I had a good reason, Rudy," he said simply. "And I have a good reason now. Trust me."

Lefebvre stretched out his own hand to meet and grip Paul's, then closed his eyes and pulled the other into a rough embrace. "I still think I should kill you," he decided as he let go.

"I think you just did," Paul said, wheezing, but with a feather of a laugh in his voice, one hand keeping hold of Lefebvre's shoulder as though he needed the support. "I wouldn't want to wrestle you these days, cousin."

"So what's changed? You couldn't beat me when I was a kid," Lefebvre retorted, then found his gaze trapped and held by Paul's, his mind caught by memories of a kitchen filled with friendship and wondrous stories. "Trust you, is it?" he said, hearing the ragged edge in his own voice. "Just like that? No explanations."

"Just like that, Rudy," Paul repeated, not pleading, the way Lefebvre imagined some mythical king would demand an oath of loyalty before battle. There was no doubt in Paul's voice or expression: none of himself, none of his right to ask, and, Lefebvre realized with an inner shock, no doubt of Lefebvre's answer.

Lefebvre gave a sigh that felt as if it came from his very soul, shuddering its way through his body until it washed the burn of anger and tension away, leaving something closer to control. "As I said," he offered not-quite-casually, "what's changed?" He took another, steadying breath and felt the universe firm itself around him. "We've been here too long already. You able to move around? Bess will want to see you."

Not quite smiling, Paul nodded once, as if hearing more. His grip on Lefebvre's shoulder tightened briefly before letting go. "Is she all right?" he asked almost lightly, except for the intensity of his gaze. "Do you know where she is?"

"I believe, Homs, I can help in that regard," Logan said from behind them both. Lefebvre whirled, then froze, the biodisrupter in Logan's giant hand looking as familiar and deadly as it had on D'Dsel, if smaller. Noticing his attention, Logan waved the weapon casually. "A gift from my good friend here—Paul Ragem." When Lefebvre didn't react, Logan pretended to scowl. "Not a surprise, I see. And no blood on the floor. How thoroughly disappointing, Captain Lefebvre. You really don't know how to properly hold a grudge, do you?"

"Try me," Lefebvre said, even though he knew better than to bait Logan.

"Perhaps, later, Captain. Right now we are all going to meet a young lady." Logan's attention shifted to Paul. "Who may have had a little accident, I'm afraid."

"If she did, you'd better be, Logan," Paul said, as if oblivious to which hand held sudden death, his face grown so ashen its skin showed fingerprints within the bruises.

Lefebvre remembered that voice, with its utter and convincing undertone of threat, whispering into his own ear. Then, Paul had been protecting his Panacian companion and his own identity from Lefebvre. *It was ironic,* Lefebvre found time to tell himself, *that Paul's act had indirectly brought them back together.* Now, they were both desperate to protect another of Paul's friends.

Some thoughts were the slippery, fish-underbelly sort—the kind that tried to surface at moments when other things, including saving one's life, should have been paramount.

Lefebvre had that kind of thought now, a bizarre thought attempting to coalesce three names into meaning: Ragem. Kearn.

And a young girl Paul was willing to die for, named—Bess.

Lefebvre refused to think it.

It was easy, when Logan began to smile.

29: Hydroponics Morning

TWO of my latest nightmares walked through the open door together: Logan being the one and Lefebvre in the presence of a completely recognizable Paul Ragem being the other.

Interesting how the cosmic gods worked overtime, just for me.

I hid behind the meager protection of the open locker door, and watched through the crack between the hinges.

Paul looked much better, something I would have found vastly more encouraging if there hadn't been a biodisrupter pressed into his cheek. *There were reasons,* I said to myself in frustration, *not to carry lethal weapons when traveling.* I trusted he'd listen to me next time.

The three of them were alone. Logan reached back to close the door and lock it. With anyone else, I would have thought this gave us the advantage.

I trembled.

Paul's eyes were searching; I saw them linger over the hydroponics tank, then move on quickly as though afraid to reveal too much.

Lefebvre's eyes were riveted on Logan, which surprised me. I'd have thought he would focus on his long-sought prey, so close at hand. There was something fragile about him, as though he'd had one too many shocks lately. *I could sympathize.*

All of us jumped when Logan said, "Call her." His precise voice was frayed around the edges. "Now."

Of the three Humans, Paul was the most composed— perhaps the closest to falling flat on his face as well, but he'd always been good at hiding that sort of thing from me. "You know I won't," he answered as if humoring a madman. *Careful,* I said to myself.

"Then I will," Logan said easily, though his sweating face was anything but calm. He tightened his free hand into a fist the size of my head and swung it at Lefebvre. The Human ducked, but not in time to miss all of the blow. It sent him against the railing. He whirled, crouched as if to spring, but stilled as Logan stepped back and waved the biodisrupter between them both.

"Which one, Ghost?" Logan said loudly, the words echoing around the pipes and dampness. "If it's all the same to you, I'd prefer to kill your Paul later—he and I haven't finished our conversations."

"You're talking about a little girl, Logan," Lefebvre objected, his face flushed. "She's no ghost."

"Ah, but only ghosts can disappear. Am I not correct, Hom Ragem?"

Paul was wonderful. "You're the expert on vengeful spirits, Inspector," he said, with just the right touch of sincerity. *Keep him uncertain,* I agreed silently.

"An expert. Perhaps." Logan kept the weapon aimed as he walked over to the tank controls and killed the jets. The water seethed, then calmed. The comparative silence rang in my ears. "I pushed this little girl of yours. She fell into the tank. And disappeared. Is this how a spirit behaves?"

Lefebvre said something incoherent and turned to look frantically into the water. Paul reached out and grabbed his shoulder. "He's baiting us, cousin. She's not in there."

Cousin? I almost fell out of the locker.

"Ghost girl!" Logan called, sweeping the room with his pale eyes. "You'd better show up soon. I won't wait here all night." He pulled out a small stick from his pocket. "Unless I have something to do," he corrected, as if a child offered a new toy.

I couldn't tell from here what the stick might be, but I could read enough in the abrupt way Lefebvre moved to stand in front of Paul to understand it wasn't anything pleasant. *Not that it would be,* I chided myself, *with Logan looking happy about it.*

Logan shook the device. It lengthened and began to make a hissing sound. A blister stick.

Paul tried to shove Lefebvre out of his way. *They had to be related,* I decided. Certainly they showed the same lack of sense when it came to avoiding danger.

Enough was enough. I reached into the locker and threw the main power switch, plunging the room into pitch darkness.

It was a good plan. I heard a tremendous splash as I hurried forward, one hand on the railing so I wouldn't join whoever was already swimming in broth, congratulating myself on my timing.

Then again. The emergency lighting came on at the same moment a wet hand wrapped itself like a band of steel around my leg and dragged me into the tank.

"Welcome, Ghost."

The liquid lapped about Logan's waist; it would have reached my chin, but he'd switched his grip from my leg to my hair to yank me up from under the water. I hung from his hand, tears of pain in my eyes, and thought quite seriously of the living mass now drying on my arms and swirling past my legs.

Paul's "No, Bess!" came right about the moment I'd thought of the ideal form. I rolled my eyes to glare at him.

Perhaps I was being hasty, despite my current discomfort, I decided. The steady aim of the biodisrupter in Lefebvre's hand was a factor I hadn't considered.

"Let her go," Lefebvre ordered. "Now."

In answer, Logan swept me up in his massive arms and held me cradled against his chest in a parody of care that would have been more believable if he hadn't been squeezing the breath out of this form. I glared harder at Paul, wondering how much of this he expected me to put up with, and raised my body temperature to cope. "Shoot me, then," Logan suggested. "Maybe the ghost won't die."

Lefebvre's aim didn't alter. "You aren't leaving with her," he stated.

Logan ignored this, looking down at me, his eyes hard and triumphant. I didn't care much for his breath either. "Real. I knew you had to be real."

"You'd be surprised," I muttered with what little air I had in my lungs.

Most Humans couldn't have done what he did next. Logan waded to the side of the tank and, keeping me against his chest as a shield, climbed out using one of the jet intakes as a step, lifting his leg easily over the rail. I found myself amazed Paul and Lefebvre had managed to throw this behemoth into the tank in the first place. *Perhaps they'd just dodged and Logan tripped himself.*

Paul walked over to the door and stood in front of it, his eyes hard as ice. "Put her down, Logan."

Logan obeyed, setting me down in front of him with his hand curled loosely around my neck. For the first time, I felt a twinge of personal fear and my temperature began soaring out of control. He could conceivably snap my spine before I cycled from this shape. *I could die,* I thought in disbelief and with a certain amount of aggravation. The alternative, to cycle before he tried, meant exposing my webself to his eyes and Lefebvre's.

As if reading my thoughts, Paul said very softly, "Careful, Bess," which probably seemed an odd thing to say, given the situation as Logan and Lefebvre likely saw it.

"You don't need her, Logan," Paul said next. "I'll tell you what you want to know."

At this, Lefebvre—who'd joined Paul in front of the only exit, keeping his weapon aimed at Logan for whatever good he thought it might do in the present standoff—nodded as if unsurprised. "You heard him," he said.

Logan shifted his hand to my shoulder, engulfing most of it and my upper arm. I swallowed tentatively, resisting the impulse to feel my throat. "All right, Ragem. Where is the Kraal's living weapon? You took it, didn't you?"

"Yes. I was working with the Kraal." I took comfort from Paul's expression, there being something in the combination of intent gaze and deliberate calm reminiscent of several instances in which his gifts had exploded in my face. "What you want is on an asteroid in the Iftsen System."

Logan laughed, a chilling derisive sound. "You'll have to lie better than that, Ragem. The Iftsen have no weapons. Or need for them."

"They do now. You know about the Feneden—Rudy would have told you." I saw Lefebvre's lips press into an even grimmer line at this reminder. "They've been raiding Iftsen Secondus. Why do you think Kearn is so ready to deal with the Feneden?" Paul continued. "He's not after me—he's after what he thinks is his monster." A dramatic pause. "We both know what it really is. A biological weapon of unheard-of power. And the Iftsen have it. The Feneden— and Kearn—are going to try and get it."

"The Iftsen." Logan rolled the name over his tongue. "You're telling me you no longer have this weapon. They do?"

"They needed something deadly—and now—to deal with the Feneden's attacks. That's why they brought me to their ship—to arrange delivery." Paul paused. "Let her go. I'll give you the exact coordinates."

Logan's hand slipped caressingly down my arm, making me shudder. "Hom Ragem. Really, you remain such a fool."

"He can't let her go, Paul," Lefebvre said angrily. "Don't you see? How else can he control us?"

Since I was reasonably sure Paul was more worried about controlling me, I didn't view this as much of a concern, although I found myself quite warmed by Lefebvre's inclusion of himself.

Then, with the sort of artless symmetry many species called luck, the *Vegas Lass* chose that moment to remind us we were not, in fact, alone.

A shrill, doubled whistle sounded, accompanied by a strobelike increase in the lighting intensity: the proximity warning, usually a signal to the freight handlers to head midships to prepare for the exchange of cargo with an incoming ship. I presumed, in this case, it signaled the arrival of the ship I'd sensed earlier. Such a routine docking did not bode well for it being rescue.

Logan, who perhaps knew more about this than I, picked me up, wrenching my arm painfully in the process. At my cry, Paul rushed forward and Lefebvre looked torn between guarding the door and helping us.

I blew up.

It wasn't my fault. I'd done my utmost to control the urge to cycle, but the stress of the conflict was too much to bear. All the energy building up as my molecules resisted their imprisonment in this shape released simultaneously.

Feeling much better, I scrounged enough living mass from the puddles on the floor to return to Human form within a heartbeat and peered around to see what had happened.

Logan wasn't dead. *Thank Ersh.* I had no wish to see him live, but I also had no intention of becoming a murderer. He appeared somewhat bent, hanging unconscious over the railing. *A little discomfort served him right.*

I went to check on the other two. Paul must have had some inkling—he'd managed to cover his face and duck, so only his clothing and arms were blackened. He shook his head at the sight of me, then shrugged off his shirt with a wince and tossed it into my hands. I took it, putting it on as I waited for the groaning, sooty lump that was Lefebvre to look up.

There were several ways this could go, I thought uneasily. It didn't make me feel any more confident to see how Paul's hand snaked out and surreptitiously recaptured his weapon from the floor.

Lefebvre blinked like an owl, the whites of his eyes startling against the ring of black coating his face. He rolled to his feet and faced me in a lithe movement that brought Paul to attention, his own eyes narrowing dangerously. *Another of those pivotal moments,* I noted, wishing to have avoided this one altogether.

"Kearn's Monster," Lefebvre named me, breathing heavily and teeth flashing in an unidentifiable grimace. "You're Kearn's Monster. The Esen Monster."

"I'm no such thing," I answered primly, still trying to

do up the shirt. "I'm a sensible, civilized being." I ignored a choking sound from Paul.

Lefebvre appeared to consider this statement for a moment, then tilted his head, still staring at me. "Do you—explode often?" he ventured, as if fearing a repeat performance.

I felt my face heat up, blushing being another Human inconvenience. Beside Lefebvre, Paul visibly relaxed, a smile starting at one corner of his mouth. I glared at him. "Of course not," I snapped. "That was an unfortunate accident. I was a little stressed at the time, if you remember?"

Like someone in a dream, the Human walked over and reached out his hand as though to touch me, then dropped it to his side. "I didn't believe in you," he admitted, appearing as embarrassed by this as I felt about my indiscretion.

Paul's voice had definite laughter under it. "Rudy Lefebvre," he said formally. "Meet the remarkable and utterly unique Esen-alit-Quar."

"Es," I informed my new Human friend, "for short." I held out my hand and, after a brief pause, Lefebvre took it in the warmth of his larger one and began to smile broadly—a striking effect on his soot-streaked face.

"Now," I said briskly, relieved to have passed this hurdle without further mayhem but knowing the next lay beyond the locked door. "May I have your belt, please?"

Elsewhere

WITH any luck, he'd soon face the Esen Monster.

At the thought, Kearn rolled over and keyed up the light in his cabin. He pulled the blankets higher on his shoulders, a cold sweat having broken out all over his body. It wasn't easy getting to sleep these shipnights. It wasn't easy waking up either, so he'd had to stop using the sedatives.

Fifty years of searching and failure—of mockery. Victory and vindication in one!

So why was he terrified?

Timri assured him the *Russell III* was armed and ready. Sas was quivering with delight—and allergy medication. His Kraal backer had confirmed the Monster's vulnerability. *They could kill it,* Kearn reminded himself, curling his body into a miserable ball.

But no. He had to risk his life and catch the damned thing.

His mysterious backer had been most—adamant.

The Feneden, Kearn knew, weren't going to like this modification to their common goals. They'd responded to the idea of confronting and destroying their culture's legendary demon with what amounted to religious fervor.

The ship would land on Iftsen Secondus in the morning. N'Klet had locked herself in her cabin, citing a lack of guidance from her Queen and her determination to avoid participating in anything Kearn had planned. There would be Panacian ships in the Iftsen system to take her home. Kearn looked forward to that.

The Esen Monster was a different story. He whimpered and pulled the blanket right over his head, leaving on the light. He'd spent fifty years chasing down the creature.

He just knew their meeting was not going to go well. Not well at all.

30: Hydroponics Afternoon

NATURALLY, the belt was too long. *My next form would be one that considered an earring or two to be well-dressed,* I promised myself. Paul helped me loop the ends so I wouldn't trip, while Lefebvre stood with his ear to the door. None of us expected a very long reprieve.

The Humans had cleaned themselves, after a fashion. The cells had again settled to the bottom of the tank, so they'd been able to splash relatively clear water over themselves. Lefebvre had found some cabling in a locker to tie up Logan. I glanced over to where the giant lay against one wall. Considering it had taken both Paul and Lefebvre straining at their limit to haul him off the railing and secure the cables around his arms and body, I was just as happy Logan remained unconscious.

Paul stood, looking down at his former tormentor. I watched him, understanding all too well the rage and revulsion making the muscles on his bruised arms and back shudder. He reached down to unclasp his medallion, careful not to touch the other Human at all, as though any contact between them would snap Paul's mastery over himself. I doubted any other Human I knew, including Lefebvre, could have succeeded as well.

"Es?" he handed me the medallion, stooping so I could put it back around his neck, soot stains and all. "Thanks, old friend."

Old friend. Is that what he still thought of me? Despite our situation, and the real need to do something about it, I put my hands on Paul's forearms to keep him close. "How long have you know this was me?" I asked him.

"Known? Not long." He smiled, then bent his head to press his lips gently on my forehead. "I've suspected for many years, Esen. You told me you would be yourself, no matter what your shape. But you kept finding valid reasons not to use certain forms, so I started keeping track, just out of curiosity."

Excessive curiosity, I grumbled to myself, but kept listening. Lefebvre was paying attention, too, looking fascinated and appalled at the same time. I felt much the same.

"All of them had one thing in common: visibly distinct younger stages," Paul continued. "That didn't quite answer the question, until I had some experience with my own youngsters and began to notice some—behavioral signs," he said with a chuckle that invited me to share, rather than mocking me. "I confess, I wasn't sure you were this young until it was plain you'd never molted as a Panacian before."

"My age is relative," I said stiffly, lifting my hands from his arms.

"I know," he answered quickly, as if concerned about my reaction. *And so you should be,* I thought, *once I know what it is.*

Lefebvre started to say something, then stopped, shaking his head as if he'd decided he didn't want to know.

I frowned warningly. "I'm not a little girl." *Well, to be technical, I was,* I reminded myself honestly, but that wasn't the point. *Or rather, it was.*

"You are almost six hundred years old and not Human," Paul said. "I understand that—"

"Really?" I asked. "As a Human—and an adult—you have biological imperatives hardwired into your very being. Trust me, Paul, I know about such things. I never wanted to be Human with you—to have those instincts affect our Web, our friendship." This last came out past a lower lip that had started trembling. My eyes were filling up with moisture again. "See!" I complained bitterly. "This form is—" my voice broke in frustration.

Paul nodded. "I don't deny I feel protective. And proud.

But that's not biology alone—you know I feel those things all of the time, whether you have fangs, fur, or scales." His eyes gleamed. "Not to mention aggravated, confused, impatient—"

My lips stretched into a smile, as he'd meant them to. There was that about both of us being Human—this cell-deep connection between us that couldn't exist when I wore any other form. It was seductively like sharing.

It was so much less. I was suddenly more alone than I'd ever been, a desolation so piercing I almost cycled to try and find my own kind. I'd understood the dying Ganthor too well.

Whatever Paul read in my face, it made him wrap me tightly in his arms. "I know, Es," he murmured into my hair. "It isn't enough. I'm sorry."

"If you know that much, my Human friend," I said, bearing the embrace because it comforted him and my Human-self. *Perhaps,* I confessed to myself, *it comforted something in Esen as well.* "If you know that, you know how much I wish it were."

There was a knocking sound.

"While I hate to interrupt," Lefebvre said dryly. "We do have some problems a little more pressing."

"Yes, of course," Paul replied, ruffling my hair as he released me and went over to stand by Lefebvre at the door. "Esen?"

"It's Largas, or it isn't," I said with a shrug.

"There's only one way to find out," Lefebvre said briskly. He held the blister stick with what looked like expertise, while Paul stood ready with his unfortunately permanent form of persuasion. I moved to stand so I couldn't be seen immediately by someone entering, but didn't bother hiding. *It wasn't as though I could hide the others with me,* I told myself.

Paul unlocked the door.

Meony-ro, looking every bit Kraal military and not at all the happy-go-lucky party goer of my more recent acquaintance, took a long step inside, sweeping the muzzle of a very unpleasant-looking example of the latest in nonprojectile rifles with a smooth twist of his body. The muzzle settled itself pointing toward Logan.

Even his speech patterns seemed to have undergone this metamorphosis, becoming clipped and curt: "Received your message, Hom Cameron." I thought Meony-ro paled ever so slightly as he looked at Paul and saw the abundant signs of abuse marring his face, neck, and upper body. His voice hardened. "We have this ship."

Lefebvre didn't even blink on hearing yet another name for his infamous cousin. "What about the *'Watch*?"

Meony-ro looked to Paul, waiting for a nod before answering: "The Tly cruiser has remained a nonparticipant." He paused. "Sir, we have not been able to locate Fem Esolesy Ki. Do you know if she's all right?"

Paul gave a great sigh, staggering and then catching himself. "The Fem was never involved in all this, Meony-ro, thank you for your concern. She's safe and waiting for me on Iftsen Secondus. This is Captain Rudy Lefebvre of the *Russell III*," he indicated Lefebvre, who'd wisely put away his stick. The Kraal's weapon began to lift, and Paul added hastily: "A fellow captive and friend. I owe him Clan Debt."

Meony-ro let his rifle rest on its shoulder sling, aiming it with his left hand while pressing the fingers of his right hand to the faded tattoos on each of his cheeks—the indelible marks that linked Clan to Clan among the family-conscious Kraal. Clan Debt was something that maintained itself through successive generations, had frequently spawned wars, and was considered by the Kraal to be the only meaningful currency between individuals of honor. By invoking it, in Meony-ro's eyes Paul had basically adopted Lefebvre and any offspring he might have—or had—into his family.

Considering what Lefebvre knew, I thought practically, *we might as well.*

The Kraal looked interrogatively in my direction. I waved. "My niece Gloria," Lefebvre volunteered, impressively quick on the uptake. "And that's the one responsible for Hom Cameron's present state," he added, pointing at Logan.

From Paul's immediate frown, I knew he hadn't planned to tell Meony-ro for reasons that were abundantly clear as the Kraal went over to the unconscious Tly and rammed the mouth of his weapon into the approximate area of Logan's stomach.

"No!" Paul ordered. "We may need him." Meony-ro's expression was definitely doubtful, but he listened.

"First things first," Paul went on, looking more and more like a being on the verge of collapse. "Let's get out of here, get Logan locked up, and see what our status is. Then we need to head to Iftsen Secondus as quickly as possible."

As Meony-ro spoke into a wrist com, another piece of military-issue gear not typically found in the storerooms of Cameron & Ki Exports, I met Paul's eyes and knew what he now saw in mine.

Questions.

Starting with how our desk clerk had responded—and so effectively—to a distress call I'd tight-beamed to Joel Largas on Minas XII.

And ending with why Paul hadn't been in the least surprised to see him.

Elsewhere

LEFEBVRE opened his eyes, then yawned. "Quite the dream," he told himself out loud, sitting up. Then he looked around, disoriented.

This wasn't the *Russell III.* And it certainly wasn't his Latasian jelly-bed.

He dropped his head back onto the pillow. *It hadn't been a dream, then.*

In the space of a day—a mere day!—he'd found both Paul Ragem and Kearn's Monster.

Among the many scenarios he'd imagined over the last few years, none had included friendship with the one nor the reality of the other.

He couldn't help grinning, feeling as though he'd awakened from a much longer sleep than a night. *Esen.* What an amazing creature. Lefebvre's mind brimmed with questions. From what little Paul had been able to tell him in private before disappearing into the healing sleep of the *'Lass'* intact med unit, she could become any intelligent life-form in the blink of an eye. It was wonderful. It was—

Kearn's Monster. Lefebvre sat up again, leaning forward as an entirely new set of thoughts thrust themselves into his mind, destroying any sense of ease.

He hadn't needed Paul's reminder that only the two of them could know the truth of Esen's existence or abilities. The message had been clear enough in her ocean-deep eyes. She trusted him, because she had no choice.

She trusted Paul because the two of them were as

close as living things could be, Lefebvre thought, somewhat surprised to feel a twinge of envy.

The Esen Monster, he reminded himself, as though the name he'd secretly scoffed at would put some different look in those eyes, make that small face live up to its reputation as a killer. It didn't seem possible to reconcile the evidence Kearn trotted out at the least sign of interest—or lack of it—with the reality of Esen. A tendency to explode into a practically harmless puff of smoke hardly qualified her to tear apart ships in space and consume their crews. Lefebvre shook his head. There had been no time for the really important answers—and little privacy—since their rescue.

The Kraal—Lefebvre recognized the tattoos if not the face—had indeed made short work of the *Vegas Lass.* There had apparently been fake ident codes and keys to overcome a last-minute attempt to lock out the approaching ship. All preparations that had to have been ready long before Esen's plea for help hit translight.

And she'd noticed, too. That face, childish as it might seem, could assume very adult expressions indeed, including the long, considered look Esen had given Paul as he'd fallen asleep in the med unit.

Lefebvre thought back to his childhood dreams of being an alien specialist, of working on a First Contact Team, of being the one to meet a totally new species.

He hadn't expected it to come true quite like this.

31: Hold Morning; Galley Afternoon

IFTSEN Secondus.

The wonder, I thought, as I usually did on approaching this planet, *was that the Panacians had bothered to look here for life.* It couldn't have been easy for them. They detested wearing spacesuits or e-rigs and, until this place, had happily left exploring poisonous atmospheres to others.

Paul stood beside me, looking out the viewport. "You'd never know they were here," he said thoughtfully.

I nodded agreement. It wasn't as though the Iftsen had gone out of their way to attract attention, as other species had done—particularly Humans, who maintained an extensive number of ships devoted to nothing but making themselves known to the rest of the universe. *Not a shy bunch,* I smiled to myself. Not that the Iftsen were shy, they were just too busy to reach outward.

Like the Panacians, the Iftsen built. Unlike the Panacians, the Iftsen didn't alter what had been done before, but kept everything, incorporating the old into the new, building their cities into towering mazes of evolving styles. Scholars didn't need to dig into ruins on Iftsen. There were none. They only needed to take a perfectly functional lift system down through the various aeons of construction, all maintained with care.

The same went for their other art forms, especially epic song. The Iftsen's oral history was one of the most intact of any species within web-memory. They almost didn't need us. *Almost.* As Ersh had said, it was our responsibility to preserve the Iftsens' accomplishments against disaster, as long as they existed only on this one fragile rock in space.

A rock perpetually shrouded in heavy, multilayered clouds, seasoned by photochemical reactions my web-self found thoroughly fascinating, Iftsen Secondus was a rusty beacon below us. Light reached her surface as a faint, diffuse presence—encouraging the growth of plants with immense flat leaves, outstretched to starve their neighbors. It was a place insulated from the climatic fluctuations that charged the evolutionary changes pushing life elsewhere. Intelligence had arisen here, several times, in no hurry and with no need to impress anything else.

The Iftsen maintained two shipcities: Upperside and Underside. Upperside, as its name implied, was an orbital station, Human-operated, and received most of the traffic to and from their world—a practical concession to the majority of trading species, who couldn't survive the Iftsens' chemical-rich atmosphere and would prefer not to strain their ships' scrubbers either.

The other, Underside, had been tacked on to Brakistem, a city-state growing in the lee of the low mountains which constituted the western shore of the famed Bridklestet Sea. According to several Iftsen sagas, their species had originated in its depths. As there weren't, and had never been, depths greater than a meter anywhere in the Bridklestet, and its waters were acidic enough to keep even the Iftsen from wading, this seemed less than likely. But creamy foam trailed across its calm darkness in intricate ribbons of fluorescence and I remembered long nights seaside spent listening to the haunting, whistling call of the Bridklestet cranes. *A lifeform,* I reminded myself, *with nothing whatsoever in common with a bird and a fair similarity to mobile bamboo.* Ephemerals cared so deeply about naming; I frequently found I had to hold my tongue—or whatever—when someone proudly recited the name of something and the word brought to mind something quite different.

The *'Lass* would leave us at Upperside. This was, according to Paul, where he expected to meet Esolesy Ki. It was also where Lefebvre would catch a transport to Panacia and his supposed niece would be safely on her way home. *A suitably vague home.* As I'd feared, being a visibly young Human induced parental instincts in the most unlikely individuals of the species, and it was becoming painfully obvious my Human-self would have great difficulty vanishing unnoticed.

"We'd better get ready," Paul told me. "Unless you want to stay and watch the docking?"

I shuddered. "There's nothing appealing in witnessing Meony-ro's attempt to ram one end of this ship into a hole. I've seen him drive a grav sled through the warehouse, remember?" I drummed my fingers against the rim of the viewport. "Paul, explain again why you have to come with me."

"No."

I slid a glance his way, pretending to keep looking out the port. Paul knew how much I loved watching the approach to a planet—it had been his idea to visit this window beside the massive cargo door. "That's not particularly reasonable. We'll both need e-rigs, there's nothing you can do that I—"

"No." This time, the word issued through tightly-set lips. *As if growling impressed me,* I told myself, but desisted.

"Hom Cameron? May I have a word?"

We turned as one to greet Meony-ro. *Who was piloting?* I thought with some alarm, then was more alarmed by the look of what had to be mortification on the Kraal's face.

So was Paul, asking quickly, "What's happened?"

Meony-ro hesitated, then looked pointedly at me. "Perhaps Fem Gloria would care to join her uncle on the bridge and watch the docking procedure?"

She would not.

Paul put his hand on my back and pushed firmly enough to send me forward a step. "Fine idea. Off you go." I pulled my lips back from my teeth in what probably didn't pass as a smile and went. Logically, Paul would tell me what was going on as soon as he could. He was remembering to keep in character, better than I.

Just one more reason why I had to cycle out of this child-form as soon as possible.

As if I needed more encouragement, Lefebvre's enthusiastic approach to our invented relationship provided it. He greeted me with such an air of pleased surprise I wanted to dodge back into the lift. *Our interactions,* I decided, *should improve substantially once he'd spent time with me as something with warts and pungent body odor.*

In the meantime, there was no doubt I was the favored young niece, invited to perch in the captain's chair and learn all about docking.

I endured, accepting my role for the sake of camouflage and remembering every detail. *Pungent body odor,* I reminded myself as I nodded cheerfully to Lefebvre, *and slime.*

The erstwhile captain of the *Russell III* did know what he was doing, ordering last minute adjustments which Skalet-memory told me would nudge us perfectly into Upperside's assigned parking spot—somewhat of a relief as the five crewmembers following Lefebvre's commands were unknown to me. Chase had left ten of the *Vegas Lass'* regular crew of fifteen back on Minas XII, under the cover of their being investigated by Port Authority, a reasonable indication they weren't part of her scheming. She'd filled key stations with hired mercs on Panacia, taking Able Joe and the unconscious Lefebvre as her only passengers.

Meony-ro, obstinately closemouthed about the ship he'd used to follow Chase from Minas—for that was what he must have done, no matter that Paul shrugged away the notion when I broached it—had nonetheless been able to carry enough crew with him to provide a skeleton crew for the *'Lass* while leaving sufficient to escort Chase and her accomplices back to Joel Largas.

And Logan, I thought, as Lefebvre ordered the lockdown of ship's systems and a switch to station air. They'd taken him as well, a clear provocation to the Tly I found exceptionally dangerous, no matter how unpalatable it would have been to let Paul and Lefebvre's tormentor go free. I hadn't tried to argue, knowing the futility of the attempt. *Humans rarely saw the bigger picture when personal grievances were involved.*

"It had been a risk—"

At a loss for words, I simply locked gazes with Paul. He blinked first. "So they're all free now," I said then.

He shook his head, a lock of black hair tumbling over his forehead. "The Tly weren't interested in any disputes between traders from the Fringe," he corrected. "They only took the person who mattered to them."

This had been the source of Meony-ro's urgent need to talk with Paul back in the cargo hold—news from his other ship, well on its way to Minas XII before being intercepted by *The Black Watch*. Which was, no surprise to anyone, armed after all.

Paul and I were sitting across from one another in the *'Lass'* galley, Lefebvre leaning, as seemed to be his habit, beside the closed door. I considered them both, schooling the expression of this form with exceptional care. It was a distinct handicap, knowing how well they could read this face.

I hadn't succeeded. "You think it's for the best," Lefebvre accused me angrily, keeping his voice low. "Didn't you see what that fiend did to Paul? Or doesn't a web-being care about pain and suffering?"

I wasn't sure which shocked me most—his accusation or the name of my kind casually on the lips of someone I'd only known for a handful of days.

Paul turned on Lefebvre, a rare fury in his own voice. "Never speak to Esen about pain and suffering. You have no idea what she's been through to save my life and the lives of countless others. You have no idea what price she's paid."

I raised my hands appeasingly, and Paul subsided. Lefebvre stood looking at us, red spots on his pale cheeks, unconvinced. "I care, Captain Lefebvre," I told him as evenly as I could. "I care a great deal. But it is the way of my kind to care for more than individuals. We dare not give

the Tly an excuse to back Logan's ambitions against Inhaven. We must not invite retaliation against Minas XII and
those who survived Garson's World. You're right. I do think
having Logan return to his own kind is the best of bad
choices." I couldn't help reaching out for Paul's hand, feeling it take mine and squeeze. "There will be," I surprised
myself by adding coldly, "other opportunities for justice."

Paul's fingers became a vise and there was a clear warning in his look to me, as if what I'd said disturbed him.
"The Tly remain within the legal system of the Commonwealth, do they not?" I reminded them both, tugging my
hand free. *What did he think I meant?*

"Barely," Lefebvre countered, as if deliberately oblivious to the conflict between Paul and I. The former patroller
had already expressed several graphic—and physiologically
unlikely—views on how to deal with Logan. "Depends on
whether you ask the Tly Deputy Minister or their neighbors."

Paul stood, pacing around the table as though he felt it
was time for action. Since customs and other officialese
would take a while yet, I hardly saw much reason to ex-
pend energy. *Well,* I told myself philosophically, *it was a
sign my impetuous Human was feeling himself again.* "The
main thing is to get Esen back to a more—"

I saw Paul struggling for some tactful word and cheerfully inserted: "—useful, practical, less embarrassing, and,"
why not, "definitely something bigger."

That brought a chuckle from Paul and a look of doubt
from Lefebvre. "All those things, my dear Es," my friend
agreed. "I don't want to be recorded as arriving with you,
if I can avoid it. Meony-ro has some ideas about that." He
paused, stopping to gaze at Lefebvre. The two Humans regarded each other silently for a moment. I had no idea what
they were doing, but Paul nodded suddenly. "Rudy will escort you on-station."

Where I'll get rid of this form, I added to myself, suspecting both Humans were in danger of becoming down-
right sentimental concerning the present version of Esen.

Elsewhere

"YOU promised we would destroy the Esen Shifter. We want to destroy the Shifter."

Kearn could feel Sas' hot breath on his neck. He didn't need the reminder that the Modoren shared the Feneden's intense feelings on this subject. *Insubordinate creature.* "We will," he promised. "This is the first step. It's the best way—the most sure way—"

"This is merely a trap," Anisco said with enough scorn in her tone to almost come through the translator near Kearn's ear. "It will not kill the Shifter. The Feneden will remain vulnerable. This is not acceptable, Hunter Kearn. We have disagreement."

He mopped sweat from his brow, in spite of the chill in the room. "The trap keeps the Shifter where we can kill her. I assure you, Fem Anisco—"

She snapped off the translator to consult with the others. Kearn used the moment to gingerly survey the room. The carpet had grown to cover the entire floor, glistening tendrils making attempts to climb up the walls but thankfully sagging back under their own weight. The three Feneden who did not use the translators remained on their swings, eyes flashing red as they blinked. Kearn tried to avoid looking at the cilia rippling down the back of Anisco's head. He no longer entertained any fantasies it was simply attractive and exotic hair.

Despite the translators, communication was becoming more and more difficult. *Almost hostile,* Kearn fussed to himself. The Panacian, N'Klet, now safely awaiting her transport on the orbital shipcity, had been right. *There was something wrong here.*

The Feneden claimed the Iftsen didn't exist, yet were uncannily familiar with Iftsen Secondus, insisting the *Russell III,* which was capable of independent liftoff, land at their chosen location—a wide strip of beach in sight of the Underside shipcity and Brakistem, places the Feneden refused to discuss. Kearn hadn't known what else to do, so he'd given the order—wishing Lefebvre were at the helm instead of the less experienced Timri. The landing had been mercifully uneventful, in part due to the glassing of the beach under what had to have been multiple landings in the recent past.

Kearn wasn't sure anymore if he dealt with legitimate representatives of a government or dangerous lunatics. Timri had sent numerous incomprehensible messages for the Feneden directed at their home system. The *Russell III* hadn't received a single reply.

All that seemed to make sense was their desire to kill the Esen Monster. A desire that now seemed greater than his own.

32: Station Afternoon

"I'M fine."

Lefebvre raised an eyebrow at me. I moderated my tone to something approximating sweet and told the med-tech again, "Thank you. I'm fine."

The med, a grumpy, overweight Odarian who looked as though he should be cooking prawlies in some diner—or perhaps be an entrée himself—wasn't impressed. "I have standards against which my sensitive and modern equipment measures your parameters, young Human. You are a bit short."

I am a civilized, intelligent being capable of dealing with other cultures in a civilized, intelligent manner, I reminded myself, counting under my breath and really wanting to kick the appendage within reach of my foot. "That's because I am a young Human," I said sweetly.

"I wish to make new measurements—"

"I haven't grown in twenty minutes," I almost shouted. *So much for sweet.*

"Gloria," Lefebvre said, finally stirring from his post by the door. I suspected he'd been enjoying my discomfiture—or else was fascinated by how this version of me was passing, or rather not passing, the examination Upperside chose to inflict on its visitors. *The med hadn't measured him,* I grumbled to myself. Human children were apparently uncommon fodder for this med-tech and he was determined to make the most of me.

"I'm going to miss my transport, Uncle Rudy," I used a rising tonal variant I'd seen make Human parents wince and observed a similar effect on Lefebvre. *Interesting.*

He made a show of checking his wrist chrono. "Why, you're right." Lefebvre's hitherto friendly tone developed a captain's snap. "Med-tech Vidbruk, while I appreciate your—zeal—I have to insist. If you haven't found any medical problems, my niece and I need to be on our way."

The Odarian sputtered—quite effectively, since this involved the expulsion of moist air through its trunk. "There are no specific identifiable problems, Hom Lefebvre. But your companion does not fit within the standards set by my sensitive and modern—"

Lefebvre managed to nod an acknowledgment, press what looked suspiciously like a credit chip into the med-tech's elbow pouch, and sweep me from the med bench all in one smooth series of movements that were impressively irresistible.

"Short," I muttered when we were out in the main shipway. "I am not short."

Lefebvre coughed; I looked up at him, suspecting Human humor. *It hadn't,* I assured myself, *been funny.*

His face was reassuringly serious. "Thanks," I offered. "I thought he'd keep me in there until I somehow stretched."

"Can you?"

We were isolated within a busy crowd, mostly spacers, some tourists and art critics—the usual assortment that disembarked at Upperside and milled around waiting for room on a planet-bound shuttle bus, most lining up to rent e-rigs. It still didn't seem private enough, but this Human had been remarkably helpful for someone running on trust. "I am always Esen," I informed him quietly. "This is the Human version. This—me—will grow taller as my true self ages. Eventually I'll fit into his standard parameters for adulthood." *Although not soon enough to look you in the eyes,* I calculated, but didn't think Lefebvre needed to know that particular detail. I was striving for the respect due my age as Eldest of the Web of Esen; emphasizing my youth was unlikely to help.

Paul, in what I could only assume was another of those inexplicable moments of prescience he'd been increasingly exhibiting, had booked temp quarters using one of our more secret accounts while we were still on Panacia. I hadn't been part of all of the planning—this form demanding more sleep than either Paul or Lefebvre seemed to require now that they'd recovered from Logan's ill-treatment—but I knew Paul was to look after the e-rigs. We were to meet him there.

Upperside might not be as large as Hixtar or other ship-city stations, but it took time to walk its girth. All was fine, and I was enjoying the chance to stretch my legs, until we passed the posting board for ship arrivals and departures.

There were too many assorted backs, shoulders, heads, and carapaces for me to read it. Lefebvre, veteran spacer, automatically craned his neck to see, then muttered something that sounded anatomically impossible under his breath and began moving much faster through the crowd.

"We could," I suggested after a few minutes of a decidedly ungraceful series of hopping steps, Lefebvre's lengthening strides covering the equivalent of one and a half of mine, "take a taxi if there's a rush."

"It's only a third spinward," he said, slowing for at least ten paces before speeding up again.

I hauled on his arm, making him stop. "Short," I reminded him sternly. "What's the hurry? What did you see on the board?"

Lefebvre kept looking around us, rather than at me. I could see he was frowning in concentration, surveying the continuously noisy bustle of strangers around us as though seeking one face in particular. *Not good,* I realized. *Not good at all.*

"What's wrong?" I demanded.

"Let's keep going, Es. Okay?"

Humans. "Not," I said imperiously, not an easy thing to do with my current voice, "until you tell me what's happening."

Perhaps anticipating my reaction, Lefebvre wrapped his fingers around my arm, gently tugging me forward as he said, "The *Russ'* docked yesterday. Kearn's here, Es."

As if that was a surprise, I told myself, wondering, as I often did lately, why the cosmic fates so enjoyed complicating my life. "Kearn does get around," I replied calmly, more for Lefebvre's sake than mine. After all, the Human had been living with my secret for a couple of days—he didn't have the perspective of almost six hundred years of hiding in plain sight, not to mention fifty dealing with this particular nuisance. "Given all you know about Kearn and his search for me, Lefebvre, do you honestly expect him to pick me—this me?—out of the crowd just like that?"

"He might not be not alone this time. Can the Feneden recognize you in other forms?"

I blinked. Ersh-memory, which usually roused unpleasantly at that name, remained uncommonly silent—*not*, I decided, *a good sign either.* She'd lived among the Feneden and hunted them for hundreds of their generations. Had some of those who survived her done so because they'd sensed her presence? Could Ersh have influenced their evolution? "Impossible," I told him, this time more for my sake than his. "The med scans read me as Human. I am Human—at the moment," I added truthfully.

"So am I—and recognizable to anyone from the crew. I'd rather not try out my story in the middle of this concourse—especially with you to explain away as well."

A valid concern, I agreed, finally extending my legs as far and fast as they would go without breaking out into a gallop. I wasn't at all fond of Lefebvre's planned explanation. It made sense, *of a Human sort,* to claim he'd found a clue to the infamous Paul Ragem on Panacia and desperately jumped the first available freighter—the *Vegas Lass*—to follow it. Kearn, understanding obsession as well as he did, should fall for that one. As to the fine details of their supposed pursuit, including how the *'Lass* mysteriously changed captain and crew in deep space, Lefebvre had shrugged, saying he'd come up with something if asked. Since the truth drugs were gone from Lefebvre's system, and neither Janet Chase nor Able Joe was available to testify differently, it was a simple enough fabrication.

The trouble with his story was how close it came to the truth, I warned myself, not as ready as Paul to completely trust a being who, until recently, spent every waking moment trying to uncover our secrets.

*   *   *

There were times when the virtue of self-sufficiency paled beside the proof of how nice it was to know someone truly thoughtful.

A silk caftan and trousers, in my favorite bronze tone, lay across the table, the ensemble completed by a beaded bag for anything I might choose to carry and already loaded with a portable lamp. Beside it was a broad deep box, filled past its brim with soft, artificial grass. A lightbox stood guard atop a tray of lush, growing duras plants.

I knew, without having to ask, that this room and the ones attached to it had been scanned for eavesdroppers and recording devices—likely before we docked at Upperside and undoubtedly since Paul's arrival. *With the most modern tech available here.*

I went to the mirrored surface of the fresher stall to say good-bye to my Human-self. She looked back at me, hair tumbled out of order already, eyes spilling moisture for no reason I could name—unless it was the fleeting, unguarded look I'd surprised on Paul's face as he watched me enter this room. He'd worn the same expression of inevitable loss as the ship carrying his son and daughter sliced upward into the clouds over Minas XII those many years ago.

I rubbed my eyes and strode almost angrily to the plants, sweeping up the two nearest pots in my arms even as I loosed my hold on this treacherous form, assimilating their mass into more of the true Esen, the real Esen. *The Esen,* I told myself, *perilously close to forgetting who and what she was in order to please one ephemeral.*

I put such thoughts behind me as I rediscovered my Lishcyn-self, concentrating on the delightful slipperiness of clean silk along my hairy scales, and assessing my physical state. A bit hungry, a little overtired. *Nothing a snack and nap wouldn't cure,* I thought wistfully, knowing they'd both have to wait.

It was time to find out what was happening on Iftsen Secondus.

Elsewhere

"ACTING Captain Kearn. Captain."

Kearn added another folded strip of plas to the top of the delicate tower on his desk. *Steady,* he told himself. *Steady.*

"Captain!"

There. He held his breath as the structure almost toppled, then steadied. He selected another urgent message and creased it into a v-shape.

The nagging voice went away. Kearn sighed, closing his eyes for a moment. Then he opened them wide, staring at the door which had begun to glow around one edge. "What do you think you're—" he shouted, spilling the entire mass to the floor as he leaped to his feet.

Before he could finish objecting, the door whooshed open as far as it could, sticking on the white-hot remnants of its locking mechanism. Timri stood in the opening and tucked her blaster into its holster. They'd been issued lethal weapons in anticipation of their capture of the Esen Monster, *not to use against his door,* Kearn thought apprehensively.

"Ah," she said calmly, stepping forward and giving a light salute. "There you are, Captain." Her dark eyes narrowed slightly as they took in the collapsed stack of folded plas. "Busy?"

"Which p–part of 'Do Not Disturb' escaped you, Officer Timri?" Kearn hadn't been able to come up with a suitable title for his comp-tech since assigning her virtual control of the *Russell III.*

"I thought you'd like to know, sir, that the Feneden have taken the e-rigs you provided and left the *Russ'*."

Kearn settled back down into his chair, feeling every bone in his body relax until he couldn't help but smile. "Why didn't you say so, instead of breaking down my door? Which will come out of your pay, Timri, make no mistake about—"

"The Feneden left the *Russ'*, sir," Timri continued as if she hadn't heard him at all, "to board the Feneden starship which landed an hour ago. It set down close enough to scorch our fins. Security Chief Sas has kept watch and reports a considerable amount of activity. Several beings have left the ship."

Kearn's smile struggled to stay in place. "Maybe they have business with the Iftsen," he suggested.

"They don't believe in the Iftsen. Sir." She took another step toward him; Kearn tried not to cringe, but lost the smile completely. *Timri was such a very—imposing person when agitated.* "It is our opinion that the Feneden have taken the search for the Esen Monster into their own hands."

Letting him off the hook, Kearn thought immediately, and wondered if the scornful look on her face meant she had read it in his expression. He put his hands together, lacing the fingers to keep them still. "Officer Timri. This is very serious. We must inform the Iftsen that they may have armed and dangerous aliens—yes, very dangerous aliens—entering Brakistem."

"It's the Festival of Living Art, sir. There won't be more than a handful of sober Iftsen in the city."

"Well, if the Feneden don't believe in the Iftsen, and the Iftsen are too drunk to be offended by the Feneden—we should have no problems, right, Officer Timri? Perhaps," Kearn added pompously, quite impressed with his own reasoning, "you could arrange for repairs to my door."

Timri, her mouth hanging open as though whatever she'd imagined couldn't come close to this piece of brilliant deduction, was shoved to one side as Com-tech

Resdick, usually a very placid, reserved individual, came careening into Kearn's office at a full run.

"Is my door wide open to everyone now, Timri?" Kearn snapped, aggrieved beyond measure.

Resdick saluted, the effect spoiled as he used Kearn's desk to stop his forward momentum. "Sir, Sir. He's back. The Captain!"

"Lefebvre?" Timri almost shouted, grabbing the other by his nearest shoulder as if she had to look into his face. "What do you mean—back?"

"He means," said the deep, commanding voice Kearn remembered all too well, "I'm back and reporting for duty. Sir." Lefebvre had lost none of his ability to look and act totally respectful, while immediately conveying the opposite.

Kearn closed his eyes. If he did it long enough, maybe this would turn out to have all been another nightmare.

33: Festival Afternoon; Gallery Night

ALWAYS look a gift horse in the mouth was one of Paul's favorite expressions. Although the original Human axiom, as held in Ersh-memory, urged the recipient of a free equine to politely refrain from checking its true age as determined by its teeth—at least until out of range of the giver—Paul's version was more along the lines of exercising caution before accepting the unexpected. It was a sensible paranoia, I'd found, especially when preparing to open one of Paul's little surprises.

So, I told myself in disgust, *why hadn't I learned by now that the unexpected gift was rarely to be trusted?*

In this case the gift had been an unexpected chance to leave Paul behind on the shipcity. *Well, here I was. Alone.* I loosened the belt of my e-rig, wondering why I'd ever thought this was a good idea. This was also something rapidly becoming habit.

The original plan—Paul's plan—had been for us to take the seventh hour shuttle to Brakistem. There wasn't much choice in destination or time: all shuttles went from Upperside to Underside, and from there to Brakistem's shipcity; anything earlier had been booked. It was, we were informed by amused shipcity staff, the opening day of the Festival. We'd considered taking the *Vegas Lass* down, but it seemed cruel and unusual punishment to Largas Freight to subject their lovely ship to Iftsen Secondus' challenging atmosphere. *She had,* I'd remarked, *enough to live down already.* Paul hadn't taken my comment well.

What he did take remarkably well was the news that the *Russell III* was already findown—for some mysterious reason, outside the shipcity. Obviously, this wasn't the revelation to Paul that Lefebvre and I thought it might be. Lefebvre had used a significant number of our credits to purchase an off-schedule flight down. He was, by a bizarre twist of fate I had yet to reconcile with our usual luck, to act as our being on the inside.

I looked at the chrono's green gleam within the helmet, below and to the left of the tip of my broad nose. Lefebvre should have made Kearn's day about three hours ago.

Paul had had the e-rigs ready and our tickets purchased. He'd introduced the new me, Esolesy Ki, to Lefebvre with every look of a being delighted to see an old friend. Lefebvre, I'd noticed, had a certain amount of difficulty adjusting—prone to taking second glances at me, as if to surprise me cycling into something else.

There was movement ahead. I crouched lower, longing to switch on the lamps on either shoulder.

So it was supposed to have been Paul and I, just like old times, ready to investigate the Feneden together. *Which, as any being realized, was a needless duplication and a significant risk to him.* I'd persisted in my arguments with him, as Lishcyn having gained both confidence and a more impressive voice with which to present my case. Paul, completely unaffected by either reasoned argument or bellowing, had said he didn't care if the rig pinched my ears, there was no way I was going down to the planet without him, and would I stop spitting.

I watched the next group of Feneden enter and did my best to look like a lumpy sculpture.

My golden opportunity had come when we were leaving our rooms. An incoming message had chimed for attention. Paul had frowned at me, *as if it were my fault,* then went back inside to answer it. He'd pointed out the door, indicating I was to go ahead to the shuttle.

It had probably been a ploy to stop my arguments. But

when Paul hadn't arrived by the time the shuttle conductors were busy asking for last minute boarders, I'd seized the opportunity. My ticket having two seats on it, I'd simply smiled and grabbed the nearest Human waiting in the line for the next shuttle. She hadn't argued.

So here I was: on Iftsen Secondus, without Paul—which was about the only part of my scheme working properly. I was still in the e-rig, because I'd had no chance to cycle into Iftsen form. It was now distressingly dark outside. And I was surrounded by Feneden thieves.

Next time, I promised myself, *I would not only look the proverbial gift horse in the mouth, I'd dissect it first.*

I'd visited Brakistem during other Festivals—the Iftsen, not surprisingly, found innumerable reasons to celebrate— and knew what to expect when I'd arrived in the late afternoon. The living towers of stacked Iftsen were everywhere, busy doing what they enjoyed most. As usual, those subspecies with incompatible frills found this a little tricky, resorting to artificial wedges to help their mixed stacks stay vertical. I walked past these quickly, knowing such stacks were about as stable as the mind-set of their members and not planning to spend time under a pile of happily squirming Iftsen as the flattened beings sorted themselves out.

Those not so occupied were milling around food carts. In pretech days, the serving of food and drink during any gathering required a large number of First Citizens delegated to miss the fun; needless to say the Iftsen had adopted Human servos in as many capacities as possible and there were almost no First Citizens in sight. Among its other virtues, my e-rig insulated me, and more accurately my tender stomachs, from any interaction with food odors I remembered as rivaling the poisonous nature of Iftsen Secondus' atmosphere.

During the Festival of Living Art, there were always singers. *Actually, there were singers for every festival.* This particular event, the streets and courtyards hosted meandering choirs, mostly Nabreda, attempting to convince any being who would listen that they had completed a worthy new stanza for the epic song commemorating the history and significant events of First Citizens' Gallery of Brakistem.

My magnificent and highly sensitive ears had to be folded in order to fit within the helmet. Listening, especially through the indignity of an external com pickup, was no way to do any song, epic or otherwise, justice. But I lingered beside the singers, making sure I caught every word. It wasn't pleasant.

Epic song, for the Iftsen, was the equivalent of Human newsmags, political debate, and historical record rolled into one. The Nabreda were singing with intense passion about the pillaging of their magnificent Gallery by aliens. Depending on the choral group, these aliens were portrayed as evil and stupid, incomprehensible and stupid, or simply art thieves with really bad taste. The climax of this particular stanza hadn't been completed—the singers would wait for a consensus from the crowd to help decide that—but that wouldn't take long. The most enthusiastic response I heard from those Iftsen currently paying attention had been to a straightforward set of rhymes with a haunting undertone of regret and a thrillingly triumphant fanfare.

The lyrics, unfortunately, sang of the need to eradicate this scourge by destroying the aliens' birthplace.

Any non-Iftsen I'd encountered as I passed through the throng had looked decidedly uncomfortable by this point, and there were eddies here and there as the more alarmed individuals decided to head back to Underside—presumably to leave before anything more hostile than emphatic rhyming took place.

I, on the other hand, had cleverly decided to head to the Gallery and confirm the singers' complaints for myself.

They'd been justified, I now sighed, very quietly, watching from my post inside the main public entrance to the Gallery.

Amber lights made swaths through the murky air, pinpointing rare works so they seemed to float before one's eyes. Not all of the art was comprehensible, even to the Iftsen, and several of the illuminated pieces weren't technically art at all, being exposed parts of the Gallery's cooling and plumbing systems. No matter: the Gallery's mandate was to be inclusive and it contentedly accepted any and all works to exhibit, explaining why this building would have been visible from Upperside's orbit, had the cloud cover ever broken.

There were some local clouds indoors, particularly here in the entrance, where the warm humid night air puffed inside with each upward swing of the doors. As each puff met the cooler air of the Gallery, drops of acid condensed and ran down almost every surface, including the outer skin of my e-rig. The surface of the sculpture forming part of my hiding place was succumbing to corrosion. There were schools of art here in which this effect contributed to a deliberate, somewhat shocking impermanence, but most of the damaged works were contributions from offworld artists who hadn't done their research.

There were no visitors in sight, at least within my Lishcyn-self's sight. This might have been due to the attraction of the Festival outside, to the time of day, *or the simple fact that a fifth of the planet's population could hide in this maze of floors, hallways, and viewing rooms,* I reminded myself, remembering an interesting week spent lost somewhere between the three hundred and thirteenth and three hundred and fiftieth subfloors because Lesy decided to explore Iftsen cave art.

I thought it more likely the visitors chose not to enter, given the steady procession of Feneden streaming in and out through this door.

No trouble spotting them. E-rigs, especially the rented sort available at the Upperside shipcity, tended to a certain flexibility of design. The basic shape was humanoid, most renters being Human, but, to accommodate a broader clientele, the suits had zips running up the dorsal, ventral, and sides sealing various pouches. The pouches in turn contained your choice of extra sleeves for those body parts that just wouldn't tuck inside a round, expandable torso. Rented suits turned offworlders into a uniform lumpiness that I'd heard occasionally confused younger Iftsen into believing they were all one species. Reasonable guess, given the rigs muffled a wide variety of alien shapes into something much less varied than the Iftsen themselves.

The Feneden, however, had brought their own e-rigs. They were skintight, shiny affairs—whether intentionally or not—amply displaying all of the slender grace I remembered. The helmets were even more unusual, being completely transparent although illuminated from within. I could see the rhythmic waving of cilia as each Feneden passed my hiding place. Having a clear view where one didn't have eyes seemed unnecessary, but I was reluctant to summon Ersh's past to enlighten my present.

They were clearly robbing the place by any definition—the ones marching from the depths of the gallery and emerging from the lifts across from me were burdened with bags and crates, while the ones entering were empty-handed save for what looked very much like the handle of some type of weapon being carried by every other one.

Not bad, I congratulated myself. I'd confirmed that the Feneden were stealing from the Iftsen along with very vocal proof the usually easygoing Iftsen weren't planning to take much more of it. Other species might have confronted the Feneden here and now, and once in a while I did notice an Iftsen peering in the doorway, but then other species had invented locks along the way. Theft was unknown here—since everything was created by all living Iftsen, everything belonged to all living Iftsen. Lesy had run head-on into that aspect of their philosophy, discovering Iftsen artists routinely adding to her work in the years following its display. Ersh had wisely advised the rest of her Web not to look at the changes, probably fearing they'd been improvements and we'd inadvertently share that with Lesy.

Time for the part of my plan Paul hadn't liked. I eased farther into the shadows and cycled, assimilated the mass from the plants I'd stuck into the generous allowance of the rig as well as the rig's inorganics. I automatically shed the latter on the floor in a stencil of myself as I hurried from web-form and became Iftsen.

The Gallery was immediately brighter, the air sweetly

thick, and the arrangement of walls, roof, and flooring made complete sense to the paired echo-locatory organs in my rump. *A magnificent and vibrant building.* I filtered appreciatively through my bladder, detecting a lovely metallic tang that likely came from some aromatic delicacy being cooked outside. *Bridklestet flounder roe!* I was halfway back out the door before remembering the Feneden and my mission here.

There were, I could hear Ersh now, *some disadvantages to this form.* The only way to keep my present brain on track was to convince myself I was the assigned First Citizen here. Being the only Iftsen here didn't help much. I recited the First Citizen's litany to myself: *I am responsible. I am the designate. The safe joy of others depends on me. It's my turn next time.*

That last bit wasn't part of the official mantra, but I'd always found it helped.

I felt my urge to join the Festival fading to manageable levels. At the same time, and not by coincidence, most of the enthusiastic protrusions along my outer edge sagged unhappily back into themselves.

I rotated until I faced the line of Feneden and moved from the shadows. They didn't react to my sudden appearance or somehow sense my split-second in web-form, *the latter a new nightmare I owed to Lefebvre's imagination.*

Time to get some answers. I rocked myself back and forth until I was completely blocking the path of the next Feneden attempting to leave the Gallery with a bag.

The Feneden stepped around me and continued on his way.

I rubbed my forehead pensively, having found it located around my midriff. An improvement over my first time in this form, when I'd stared at my knees for months and had to lie flat to eat anything.

I took a deep, satisfying breath, refilling my bladder, and put myself in the way of another Feneden. Before this one, female by the shape, could go around me, I greeted her, saying: "Greetings, far traveler. Ease and comfort to you." The language was as close to colloquial as my brief experience with modern Feneden allowed, meaning my accent was likely as archaic as the phrase itself. Considered ventrally, it was the best I could come up with on short notice. All I wanted was to have at least one Feneden acknowledge the existence of one Iftsen. It would be the first step to a diplomatic solution. Paul would be so proud.

What I didn't want, I thought numbly, was to see every Feneden within range of my voice run screaming in any direction that took them away from me as quickly as possible, including one who managed to climb *The Transformation of Joy*—the famous, intricate, and decidedly erotic sculpture which formed the centerpiece of the entranceway.

I changed my mind. I was very glad Paul wasn't here. He hadn't liked my plan at all.

I hated it when he was right.

Elsewhere

"THERE'S a priority call for you, Captain Lefebvre. You'll—" Com-tech Resdick paused as he came up beside Lefebvre and joined him in surveying what was left of his quarters, finishing lamely: "I guess you'll have to take it somewhere else, sir."

Lefebvre nodded. "Thank you, Resdick. I'll be up to the bridge in a moment." Once the com-tech hurried away, Lefebvre gingerly stepped inside the door.

The carpeting, whether it had been alive before or not, was definitely dead now. The ship's scrubbers were hitting overtime attempting to clear the results from the air. A crew detail had been about to remove the stuff, but Lefebvre had asked them to wait until he'd had a chance to inspect what the Feneden had left behind.

Not much, he said to himself. Kearn had almost climbed into his lap in his eagerness to unburden himself about the Feneden, their plots, their attempts to take over his ship, their evil influence, their—about the only thing Kearn hadn't accused the Feneden of was disbelief. They'd believed all too well in the Esen Monster.

So, of course, did he—now, Lefebvre thought with a wry grin, pushing a swing out of his way as he continued his examination. *Which he couldn't exactly tell Kearn.* Lefebvre had listened to his commander's babble with unusual patience, reevaluating everything from his own preconceptions to the desperate, glazed look in those close-set eyes.

Strange as it seemed, Lefebvre now recognized some-

thing heroic in how Kearn, despite his flaws and weaknesses, had kept up his quest to save the universe for
so long, alone and disbelieved.

And tragic, Lefebvre thought. Kearn had wasted a career and much of his life because he so feared and misunderstood Esen, an Esen Lefebvre couldn't seem to
picture as other than that mere slip of a girl, with faded
freckles and infectious smile. This, despite knowing she
was the literal personification of everything alien.

He walked as lightly as possible, but each footfall
threw up more of the putrid smell. Lefebvre put his hand
over his nose in self-defense and kept looking. At one
point, something crunched under his foot: something that,
on closer examination, looked alarmingly like the de-
composing haunch of a rat.

In the end, it wasn't what the Feneden had taken or
the condition of his quarters that made Lefebvre's heart
start pounding, although he knew they'd stolen e-rigs
and some device Kearn ranted was crucial to trapping
his monster.

It was what they'd left behind.

Their translators.

34: Gallery Night

PERHAPS *the phrase lost something in the translation,* I theorized, standing alone in the midst of discarded bags, crates, and weapons. The Feneden climbing the sculpture had slipped and dropped to the floor—I assumed unhurt, from the way he scampered after the others.

Just wonderful. I had succeeded in drawing the Feneden's attention to a member of the hitherto-invisible Iftsen. I was reasonably sure Paul would agree the result was an abysmal failure.

As if responding to my mood, a deep vibration suddenly coursed through the floor, as though the mass of voices singing outside had coincided on a bass note. *Now what?* Intrigued, but still muttering *It's my turn next time,* under my breath, I rocked over to the doorway and looked out.

It wasn't singing, I discovered. It was the tortured sound of a huge aircar never designed for Iftsen Secondus coping with this atmosphere. As the aircar touched the tiles in front of the Gallery, a side door opened and a Herd of e-rigged Ganthor mercenaries charged out.

There are moments when I seriously doubt the senses of a given form, having an innate distrust of other biologies. *This was definitely one of them.*

I rotated to orient my dorsal side toward what I doubted, preferring echo-location over what could be fooled by holos and projections.

The Ganthor didn't cooperatively disappear or—another thought I'd had—turn into costumed Feneden.

I rotated to face them again, concentrating on presenting a noncombative silhouette. *Never run from stampeding Ganthor* was a useful piece of Skalet-memory under the circumstances.

Don't stand in their way, was another I remembered in time to roll myself to one side, barely escaping their booted feet. The Ganthor, a smallish Herd of thirteen, crowded and bumped behind a larger individual who had to be their Matriarch as she led them up the steps of the Gallery. They thundered past me to disappear inside.

I winced at the sound of breaking glass and snapping wood, among other things. The Herd must have run right through the art the Feneden had dropped in the entrance-way.

Not sure what I could do to either improve or worsen the situation, I opted for trying to understand it. *Knowledge,* as Ersh never tired of reminding me, *was the only thing separating rocks from sentience.* Mind you, she used the same expression to refer to the continuing debate among the crystalline Tumblers over the morality of selling their excretions to offworlders as gemstones. I dropped to my slick ventral surface and coasted down the stairs to the side of the aircar.

Only it wasn't one. I added Human interpretations to my Iftsen vision and knew what stretched in front of me, engines self-destructing at the end of its mission. A 'crasher— identical to those I'd lately seen on *The Black Watch.*

Logan? I asked myself, wondering if the heady atmosphere was generating a few extra reactions in my bladder. *What in the seventeen icy hells of Urgia was he doing dropping mercs on an art gallery?*

This was beyond curious. I rocked my way back up the stairs, mumbling dark things about Moberan designers who thought only of appearances and made stairs to impress offworlders with their fancy knees and other joints.

The Ganthor stood back-to-back in the middle of the huge opening hallway, a position I judged had more to do with their need to exchange scent-information through the u-shaped connectors on their e-rigs than defense, since they, and I, were the only beings presently occupying what had been the most magnificent room in the most magnificent building on Iftsen Secondus. I felt my serpentine hearts triple their beats in dismay, this being one of the few emotions an Iftsen designated as First Citizen was allowed to indulge.

Not that Ganthor were big on defense at the best of times, being suited by temperament to a rather blunt, straight-at-the-enemy approach.

Clang!

I fell flat on my dorsal surface in surprise as this new sound reverberated through every cell of this form. *Now what?*

The Ganthor must have known—they remained in their positions like some new piece of art added to the Gallery's collection, the glitter from the huge disrupter rifles each carried at the ready simply part of the illusion.

I got up and went to the door again, almost afraid to look out this time.

The 'crasher had disassembled itself, revealing what else it had brought to the Festival of Living Art: a Ganthor All-Terrain Assault Vehicle, known by refugees from various conflicts as a hog-hauler and more politely—or safely, depending on company—referred to as a gravedigger.

Organized warfare was a blight of too many intelligences, I reminded myself, as always finding it difficult to imagine the mind-set that would trap the formidable natural armament of a Herd into a metal box on treads.

Four huge treads that were, I noticed in horror, starting to move. Those on this side clanked and creaked themselves backward—the others must have moved in the opposite direction, because the gravedigger ponderously spun on its axis. The machine paused as though sniffing for direction, then headed for the staircase. The first few stairs were crushed into sand beneath its treads, then the 'digger caught hold and began its slow climb, tilting its beard of weapon barrels upward in anticipation of the width of the doorway.

My Iftsen-self responded with debilitating confusion, both at the destruction and at the Esen-based anger I couldn't help but feel, a confusion demonstrating itself in the appearance and retraction of various appendages, most pointed or clawed. I drove up my temperature to maintain control, careful of the very limited range acceptable to this body. I'd have to cycle into something sturdier as soon as possible.

Sturdier, yet still able to breathe here, I reminded myself. That was going to be a neat trick, since nothing suggested itself with the exception of web-form. *Not my preference.*

I rocked myself behind *The Transformation of Joy,* standing sideways to be as small and inconspicuous an Esen as possible. Some of the Iftsen in the streets would definitely notice the immense machine currently ramming itself through what had been an elegantly arched doorway. Only the First Citizens among them would pay any attention and, among those, it was doubtful any would bother to react. They were very philosophical when it came to accepting that others were larger and meaner.

Unless, I thought with a rise in internal temperature that blurred my vision and produced a very unfortunate reaction in my gas bladder, *unless the Iftsen had more than one planet-killing Messenger ready to send.* This entire episode was getting out-of-appendage translight. The Ganthor's homeworld was hardly vulnerable, being girdled by a defensive system paid for by their many offworld clients—in particular the Kraal. This didn't make me feel any better about the possibility of the peace-loving Iftsen becoming murderers in retaliation for petty theft, property destruction, and bad manners.

I'd been ready to bury in memory what Logan had done to Paul, accustomed to considering species' needs over those of individuals, however dear to me. Of course, I would have enjoyed seriously annoying the Tly sometime in the future, when the source of that annoyance was less easily deduced.

I wasn't prepared to put up with one lunatic's disruption of entire worlds.

So. Why assault the First Citizens' Art Gallery of Brakistem?

Elsewhere

PAUL'S message had been cryptic. Lefebvre read it out loud to himself to see if there was more to be gleaned from it than the terse: "Been delayed. Our friend went to the Festival on her own. Will follow as quickly as possible. Looking forward to that beer you promised. Mitchell."

Delayed how? Lefebvre, having spent so much time hunting Ragem, had a great respect for how effectively his cousin had preserved his secrets while living a fairly exposed life. Since coming back on the ship—and retrieving his comp system from an unrepentant and curious Timri—Lefebvre had done some checking. The *Russell III* had even used the reputable firm of Cameron & Ki Exports to broker supplies out on the Fringe, no one the wiser.

Or was that the case? Lefebvre's patroller instincts had been aroused. *How had he managed to miss Ragem all these years?* He could understand missing Esen— her "disguise" as the Lishcyn trader was so perfect as to have him still shaking his head in disbelief. He could understand Kearn's failure as well, since, until Panacia, Kearn had adamantly believed Ragem dead.

But once he'd *started looking?* Lefebvre shook his head, amazed he'd been so blind. It wasn't vanity to know your own skills. Ragem should have tripped across any number of traps and trip lines Lefebvre had left for him all through this edge of the Commonwealth, but hadn't. At the very least, the fact of his still being alive should have come up before D'Dsel. The conclusion was plain: *Ragem had had help.*

And, Lefebvre told himself grimly, there was only one individual who could have sent out warning; only one on the *Russell III* with both training and access to interfere with him.

Holding Paul's message, with its unspoken plea for help, tightly in his fist, Lefebvre looked up at the person he'd summoned to his temporary office.

"Ah, Comp-tech Timri," he said easily, almost lightly. "I'd like your assistance with something that's just come up."

"Of course, Captain."

Lefebvre studied her, remembering the first time they'd met. She had been a welcome breath of expertise and credibility on this ship of fools, living up to every one of Kearn's extravagant claims about her ability to make sense out of seemingly unconnected data, to dig stubbornly resistant patterns out of what appeared random events.

She'd also been as personally welcoming as a chill, winter wind. There was no denying Timri would have turned heads when younger—even now, she had the high cheekbones, long bones, and fine skin that defined many Human perceptions of beauty, regardless of age. Unfortunately, her customary expression whenever forced to communicate with anyone or anything but her comp system was a forbidding combination of impatience and disdain.

"Close the door, please," he ordered, seeing that expression now as she obviously tallied the time wasted by his not coming right to the point.

Sure enough, she closed the door and turned to say: "Will this take long, sir? I have—"

"Something I believe you want to tell me, Comp-tech." Lefebvre used his iciest tone.

Her eyes darted to the system hastily patched together on the table serving him for a desk. "If it's about your comp, sir, I did explain to you why it had to be removed before the Feneden took over your quarters. It seemed reasonable to put it with mine. Was I in error?" There was a hint of anxiety in her voice.

She was good, Lefebvre thought, even more convinced he was right about her. "No. After all, none of you knew if I'd be back. This is about something else," he began, switching to a more casual tone that brought a confused frown to her face. "I met someone during my time away from the *Russ'* who has—changed—some of my opinions about our search."

"Did you find some evidence, sir?" This with visible eagerness. "You do remember our bet," Timri continued boldly, before he could respond. "If anything came up while you were on leave, you said you'd put through my promotion. Sir."

Damn good. He had to smile at that, but hid it behind one hand while pretending to cough. "We'll discuss that later, Timri," Lefebvre said. "Have a seat."

"If it's nothing immediate, sir, I—"

"Sit."

Her lips tightened as she obeyed, her posture managing to convey an impression of enduring what she must.

Lefebvre had thought very carefully how to approach this; the risk he was about to take wasn't his alone. "You know I've had my own interests since coming aboard the *Russ'* as Captain, Timri, and you've quite capably spied on them." He raised a hand to silence her protest before it was more than an indrawn breath and a look of righteous wrath. "I'm not concerned. We are on the same side, aren't we?" She subsided, but her eyes narrowed.

"Or are we?" Lefebvre stood up and walked around to her side of his desk, propping one hip on an edge. He leaned forward. "I think we both know that Paul Ragem faked his own death in order to escape with the Kraal's Nightstalker weapon. And we both know he's been living in the Fringe under an assumed identity ever since."

"If you are implying I have some secret source of information about Ragem, you are mistaken, Captain," she said flatly. "I knew nothing of his—survival—until the Panacians informed Acting Captain Kearn and he saw fit to tell me. I would be interested to know if you have corroborating evidence to back up that claim." She glared. "I certainly don't see why you think I've been spying on you—or why you think I would—"

"Come now, Timri," Lefebvre said with a patroller's scathing cynicism; remarkable how easily the bearing and attitude of a professional interrogator came back to him after all these years. *Or maybe it had been more recent events.* "You must realize I discovered your searches through my comp."

"As I traced yours long ago!" Timri snapped. Her wide nostrils flared. "Did you consider me a fool, Captain? Or were you like Kearn—so terrified of what we hunted that you couldn't even trust those under your command?"

"I've never trusted you," Lefebvre replied comfortably. "Or anyone else on the *Russ'*. Why should I? I'm here because the Commonwealth saw fit to pay me to follow a madman."

"You're here for blood—Ragem's blood," she disagreed, then closed her mouth tightly as if that had been more than she'd meant to say.

"There's that," Lefebvre agreed. He sat back on his hip, letting one leg swing, adding a little triumphant smile. "And now I have it." Lefebvre spoke this last with the heartfelt satisfaction of someone seeing the end of a quarter lifetime's quest. *No need to tell her his quest had never been to harm Ragem.* Not yet.

He could see she believed him. "What do you mean?" Caution in her eyes, no matter how Timri's expression altered to one of pleased expectation. "You've found Ragem," she breathed. "How? Where is he?"

"Here. More exactly—" Lefebvre pointed a blunt forefinger upward. He made a show of consulting his chrono. "I should hear from Port Authority any time now. Why don't you wait here with me and we can share the moment together?"

"What about Kearn?"

No, "sir," Lefebvre noticed. "What about him?" he replied. "Once we have Ragem, he will take us to his weapon. There's no such thing as Kearn's Esen Monster."

"There is," she said with an edge to her voice. "I saw what it did."

"With all respect, Comp-tech, what you claim to have witnessed—" Lefebvre tapped his comp system to remind Timri her testimony was on record, "—what you saw bears no relationship to anything caused by a living organism. There is nothing in your statement to prove what attacked your ships wasn't simply an unfamiliar and devastating weapon. You don't mention seeing any living thing. Come on. I would have thought someone of your intelligence would have admitted this to herself long before now."

She didn't look convinced, but he hadn't expected her to—it was his own belief Lefebvre wanted to establish. "What makes you think Ragem will just tell you what you want to know?" Timri asked, an odd note to her voice. Her eyes were fastened on him now, no doubt of their expression. She was alarmed.

Lefebvre reached into his pocket and pulled out the blister stick, activating it with a snap of his wrist. Even now, the angry buzz drew sympathetic flashes of pain along his cheek, a reflex he turned into what he hoped was a look of vengeful anticipation. "He'll talk."

Timri's lips tightened into a thoroughly disapproving line. "Torture, Captain Lefebvre? This is a Commonwealth research vessel; we aren't some band of criminals."

"What Ragem has done puts him outside the protection of law. His crimes demand retribution, not delays in the courts."

Timri stood.

"Where do you think you're going?"

"To tell Kearn," she said defiantly, but stopped as if held by his tone.

Lefebvre considered the tip of the blister stick. "Funny. I thought you might be going to make another call to Upperside. To our mutual friend Mitchell—or should I say Ragem? That is who you called after my—unexpected—return to the *Russell III,* isn't it? The logs were quite clear," he said, looking up at her. "Careless or in a hurry, Timri? My guess is the latter, since you've never been careless before."

Timri no longer looked impatient or disdainful. She retraced the step she'd taken toward the door, taking another in order to stand so close he felt warmth from her body. There was none in her voice. "'Mutual friend,'" she repeated, disbelief plain on her face. She had height on him, and used it to glare down. "Are you implying I'm somehow in league with Ragem? That I warned him? Captain or not, you'll answer for that—"

Lefebvre closed the blister stick. "I have many things to answer for, Timri, but being wrong about you? I don't think so. Being wrong about Paul Ragem? Yes. Being unable to stop the slander about a good, decent being? Absolutely."

With her rich complexion, it was impossible to tell if she paled, but he saw her swallow before saying: "You've changed your mind about the Traitor? Why? What's happened?"

Lefebvre met her eyes and told her the truth. "I met him—and discovered the Traitor never existed except as a lie. Ragem has never meant harm to any living thing."

Her hands fastened on his arm with unexpected strength, as if to pin him in place. "Why are you telling me this, Lefebvre?" she almost whispered, her words fast and furious. "Don't you realize I can go straight to Kearn? I've proof you've been snooping through my research for him. Now you admit to meeting Ragem? That he's convinced you—as easy as that—to take his side? Did that blister stick to the head unravel something?"

Lefebvre kept himself perfectly still. "Paul needs our

help," he said quietly, aware he might be wrong about her, sincerely hoping he wasn't. *There weren't,* he thought darkly, *too many options if he was.*

Timri thrust herself away from him, as if the force helped distance them more than physically. "Help him? Sure. If he tells us where the Esen Monster is. Or have you conveniently forgotten why we are all here?"

Lefebvre sensed his opening. "Forgotten? How could I? At least now I know what we've been chasing. Not fables. Not some superweapon. And not a beast."

If he'd ever seen utter stillness in a living thing, he saw it now. Timri might have been carved from stone. "What do you think Esen is, Captain Lefebvre?" she asked, a question posed almost as if she were simply curious, except for that air of listening to more than his words.

What had Esen said to him? Lefebvre remembered exactly. "A sensible, civilized being."

"Sensible." The lines at the corners of her generous mouth deepened. *Mirth or scorn?* he wondered anxiously. Then Timri's face creased in a broad smile, redefining her into someone not only relieved but welcoming. "That had to be Esen's opinion."

Lefebvre let go the breath he'd unconsciously held, beginning to smile back. "As a matter of fact," he admitted, "it was."

Kearn toggled off the device and sat without seeing for a long moment. He'd expected to use this, and the other recorders hidden throughout the *Russell III,* as evidence to allay any future doubts of what had happened during their pursuit and hopeful capture of the Monster.

Even at his most paranoid, he'd never expected to hear his two most senior officers conspiring against everything he believed.

35: Subbasement Night

THE arrival of the 'digger had shaken my belief in myself and my ability to cope with the situation. I'd almost left the Gallery and headed for the nearest com link to contact Paul.

Almost. Just in time, I gathered the tatters of my pride. I was the Eldest of the Web of Esen. What kind of Eldest ran to an ephemeral for advice?

A scared one, I admitted, watching the Ganthor. The Herd was now larger than the original thirteen I'd managed to avoid. Those must have come ahead to scout safe passage for their armored transport through the deadly maze of modern and postmodern sculpture, and the occasional bench.

Now that it was here, those in the 'digger lost no time making contact with the others. *Literally.* The side doors dropped down, allowing the five mercs who'd been operating the machine to rush out. I winced at the considerable amount of body contact which ensued as the Herd reestablished the comfort of who was allowed to knock whom to the floor. In a bunch of young Humans, it would have been sport. In an edgy bunch of hair-trigger mercenaries, this habit of urgent violence was another reason why Ganthor often won battles for their clients by simply showing up.

They were quick about it; the Matriarch, through her Seconds, stamped orders and the entire group squeezed back inside the 'digger. The doors thudded shut.

What were they up to now? I leaned forward.

A hammer's blow threw me backward along with a whirl of dust and debris, to land flat against the nearest wall. Undamaged, if startled, I rocked back to where my former protective statue had stood.

The statue was gone. More significantly, so was the 'digger. In its place gaped a huge, glowing hole in the floor. I rocked cautiously to its edge and looked down.

I could see the top of the 'digger below, quite intact. *They were cutting their way down through the subbasements.* There was another blast as the next floor gave way and the 'digger dropped with it. I had to admit, it was a novel way around the problem of fitting their oversized transport into a lift.

The Ganthor were searching for something. *What?*

If Logan had believed Paul about the Kraal superweapon now belonging to the Iftsen, this literally mythical Nightstalker, he could have sent the Ganthor to retrieve it. *In an Art Gallery?*

I rocked as quickly as I could to the lifts, then into the first one that opened, cuing it to descend. The only thing Ganthor were good at finding on their own were living things—being scent-driven, much of their technology dealt with enhancing their ability to trail and interpret biochemical traces.

Which living things were of this much interest to Logan? They'd gone right past me, an Iftsen.

Who else was in the Gallery tonight? I asked myself. *And also making nuisances of themselves?* The Feneden.

It made some sort of logic, especially in Human terms. They were prone to seek alliances to gain numbers and strength. If Logan was on his own, with one ship, he might well seek such allies to help him find this weapon and take it once found. The Feneden, being the supposed target, seemed the obvious choice. *To those who didn't know them better,* I said to myself. And if those allies were impossible to contact discreetly, he might well choose this somewhat forthright approach to arrange a meeting.

It was the type of devious scheming Skalet always loved. *She probably would have preferred the giant, twisted Human as a student,* I grumbled to myself, keeping my right appendages pressed against the door of the moving lift. When the door shook violently, indicating the floor presently receiving its visit from the 'digger, I went to the next one down and stopped the lift to look out. Everything looked normal: no cowering Feneden or signs of theft.

I repeated, checking three more floors before I found what I expected.

The Feneden, Sidorae, had tried to sell me Iftsen pretech art. This floor and the ones below were jammed to the ceiling with the stuff, along with an assortment of bags, crates, and other thieves' paraphernalia. My Iftsen-self paused to admire a nearby bench, clearly made by some more recent talent by welding together several pieces—*definitely the kind of thing that had troubled Lesy.*

There they were. The Feneden were huddled in a far corner, staring up at the ceiling. I felt sorry for them until one caught sight of me and they all started screaming and running again. This was decidedly counterproductive with Ganthor literally overhead.

"I mean you no harm!" I shouted, trying to be heard over their combined bedlam. An Iftsen's bladder has properties in common with a Human instrument known as a bagpipe, so there was no doubt I'd succeed.

I succeeded a little too well. They bolted through the nearest open doorway just as the ceiling began raining down little bits of itself in preparation for dropping great, jagged hunks.

Then I spied something I thought could potentially solve almost every problem at once, a conclusion I later came to thoroughly regret.

It was a spare Feneden e-rig.

Elsewhere

LEFEBVRE leaned back in his chair, putting his hands behind his head. On the surface, and if one could disregard the somewhat aggressively clean smell, his quarters and life were back to where they'd been before going insystem at Panacia.

The real change was inside. Used to keeping his own counsel, and his own secrets, Lefebvre found himself burning with the desire to shout out what he'd learned, to clear Paul Ragem's name, to let everyone—especially Kearn—know about the wondrously strange Esen.

"I felt that way at first," Timri said quietly. "Dying to tell someone—anyone." The Feneden's eating habits had ruined Lefebvre's jelly-bed, so she was lying on her stomach on a standard issue cot, chin supported by her hands as she watched him. Her long dark eyes were still guarded, despite her relaxed position. He wasn't sure she trusted him at all, even after admitting she knew Paul Ragem and had conspired to keep his new identity secret all this time.

"But you didn't."

"No." Her lips tightened. "After that moment passed, I realized what I owed them both and it was a non-issue."

What she owed them, Lefebvre repeated to himself, *Paul and Esen.* There were remarkably few lies in Timri's past—merely a convenient omission or two. She had been part of the Tly blockade and witnessed firsthand the attacks of a monster. He'd heard her descriptions before, but this time they meant more since he finally understood she was talking about a real, living creature.

A creature that ripped into the side of starships as if biting into fruit, consuming everyone aboard before moving on; able to move translight or cling motionless to asteroid or ship. It stalked living beings as intelligently and remorselessly as any predator had ever stalked its prey but, by the end, had *enjoyed* the hunt.

This time, however, Timri went beyond the horror of those days and completed the story. Esen, at terrible risk, had lured the monster after her. Together with Paul, she'd planned an ambush—for the creature could be hurt, the Tly had proved that. Esen had used her own body as bait, holding the creature long enough for Kraal heavy cruisers to find and destroy it.

Timri had been there. She'd used her contacts and talents to hunt the monster after it attacked the Tly, determined to enact vengeance and end its threat. She and her companions had almost been its prey instead. The monster had chased them, almost caught them, before inexplicably changing course. Timri had followed, and they'd hung at the limits of their sensor range. They'd observed a single ship leaving before the monster's arrival, and noted its designation.

Then they'd witnessed what happened, wondering at what they couldn't interpret. One thing Timri had been sure of—the creature had attacked another of its kind, and in so doing, had been destroyed itself.

But there had been no way for Esen to prove herself innocent of being the very monster they'd destroyed. It had been a renegade of her kind, another web-being. With it gone, and she the last of her kind, her only wish had been to flee scrutiny and hide herself away in peace.

Esen had done her best to lose Paul as well, giving him an opportunity to clear his name and return to his ship. He'd known she shouldn't be alone, that she needed and deserved a friend. It had been during his determined search for Esen that Timri's equally determined search had found him.

"You followed the freighter back to Minas XII and tracked down the stranger who'd been on the Inhaven colony," Lefebvre repeated wonderingly. "Why didn't you turn him over to the Commonwealth then and there?"

Timri raised an eyebrow. "You've met him," as though this would be sufficient explanation. *It was,* Lefebvre thought. "Anyway, I can't say I found Paul. He didn't wait for that. He found me first. I already knew the rumors about some weapon were lies. What he told me, however wild, had to be the truth." She twisted up to a sitting position. "Are you sure the call went straight out? I don't like how long this is taking."

"I'm sure," Lefebvre said, but he began wondering himself. Paul should have sent a reply by now, letting them know which shuttle he was catching. Their meeting place was prearranged—the "beer" of Paul's earlier message had referred to the All Sapients' Tavern on the main road into Brakistem, a popular open-air facility overlooking the sea. Since enjoying the view meant staying in one's e-rig, it was as anonymous as could be imagined.

Lefebvre reached for the com on his desk, one finger pressing the button to connect to the bridge. Nothing happened.

He sat straighter, pressing more firmly. *Nothing.*

Timri, who'd watched, hurried to the cabin door. It didn't open as she approached. She slammed her hand on the control panel. *Nothing.* She turned to face him, mouthing one word: Kearn.

It was, Lefebvre told himself savagely, *a little late to worry about being overheard.*

36: 'Digger Night

WAIT here without movement.

I clicked my wholehearted agreement, having no intention of testing this remarkably fragile body against even a courteous prodding from a Ganthor. The Ganthor, oddly less formidable in its e-rig—an opinion which probably constituted wishful thinking from my Feneden-self—took up a station where it could watch me. Since my back was against one wall of the 'digger and I was literally squeezed in between the other Ganthor sharing this bench with me, I thought the precaution overdone. I doubted I could move if I tried.

The Ganthor were cautious but obviously delighted. There had been a considerable amount of thumping—fortunately not including me—in response to my arrival among them. Skalet-memory made it quite clear that the Ganthor and their ungainly machine were vulnerable as long as they were hemmed inside this building, a condition the Ganthor were hardwired to dislike intensely.

They were also a species that was rarely if ever surprised, and so hadn't shown any reaction at all to my being fluent in their percussive language. *Mind you,* I thought, *they were also a species that didn't talk a great deal at the best of times,* making do with the plentiful information usually detected by scent. The sense-constraining e-rigs, despite their hookups to allow individuals to exchange air, were another reason the Herd was more than ready to declare their mission a success. They'd been after, as I'd surmised, a Feneden to speak to their commander.

I didn't think I'd bother trying to explain their chosen representative had only been Feneden for approximately fifteen standard minutes.

I still wasn't used to my new self and could only be thankful the Ganthor wouldn't notice any mistakes I made. Every other form I'd assumed until now had been first assimilated and tried by the other, older, members of the Web. This form hadn't been shared within the Web by Ersh—understandably—and the memories of it she had given me were not all helpful. *They were certainly incomplete.*

The first surprise had been the truly painful experience of feeling the atmosphere of Iftsen Secondus eating at my new skin, prompting me to set a record donning the Feneden e-rig. *Or had it swallowed me?* I recalled, amused now by what had been somewhat alarming a few minutes ago. The instant I'd inserted my feet and hands, the fabric had softened and stretched as though an active participant, climbing of its own accord over every inch of my skin. Only the helmet had behaved like it should, requiring me to lift it into place as my eyes watered and my nose stung. The immediate relief of fresh, breathable air went a long way toward reassuring me I'd made the right decision.

In hindsight, I should have expected some period of adjustment. What actually happened was that I stood paralyzed while my Esen-self tried in vain to correlate what I urgently needed to know about my surroundings with the barrage of input the Feneden-me was providing. The Feneden, for all they looked humanoid, were definitely anything but.

At least I hadn't provoked the Ganthor by running, I reminded myself, prepared to look for anything positive at this point.

Once I began sorting out my perceptions, things became clearer. *Not quite clear, but better.* The room flashed bluegreen each time I blinked, reminding me of the red translucent lid. I realized the cilia wrapping my head and shoulders were infrared sensitive as well as expressive of my mood, making the 'digger and the damaged ceiling glow almost painfully bright. I now possessed a pair of flat, oddly unfocused ocular organs on the top of my head, and spent a few moments worrying if my Feneden-self needed corrective lenses. There was a sense of smell, currently suffering from its brief exposure to the fragrances of the Gallery, touch through the quite delicate lining of the e-rig, and, I licked something caustic from my lips, taste. Hearing appeared to be without a definitive location at the moment— I blamed the e-rig—so I wasn't sure where or what my ears were.

I'd achieved this much accommodation with my Feneden-self at about the same instant the main doors of the 'digger clanged open and the Herd thundered out, most in my direction. I was flooded by a rush of hormones, all intended to enable me to run for my life—the sooner the better. *Well,* I thought, *this certainly explained a few things.*

I held still, my brain definitely aware how unhealthy running from armed Ganthor was likely to be, but my limbs trembled with the effort required and cilia lashed around my face.

Just what I needed, I told myself with disgust, *another cowardly body.*

So now I sat, lurching from Ganthor to Ganthor in the dark claustrophobic machine, as the 'digger winched its way back up, floor by floor, and hoped I knew what I was doing.

Not, I realized, *that there was much I could do about it at the moment.*

Confidence is something you feel before you truly understand the situation. Ersh had drilled that into me during innumerable attempts to instill the requisite caution of a Web observer among aliens into my thought processes. As observer, I was to do exactly nothing, while remembering everything. It's not that she thought I was stupid. Far from it. Her greatest fear was that I would think for myself.

So I wisely distrusted any sense of growing confidence, knowing from past experience it was a chancy feeling at best. As for being inventive—I'd grown to disagree with Ersh. Sometimes, thinking quickly could be a vast im-

provement over hiding and hoping the situation would resolve itself.

To be fair, I told myself, *Ersh had expected all members
of her Web to simply outlive ephemeral situations. Another
case of confidence lacking facts.*

The 'digger had pulled itself back to ground level and
left the Gallery, negotiating the stairs—or what was left of
them—with a combination of jolts and jerks that drove my
small teeth into my thick, raspy tongue if I wasn't careful.
Since then, we'd maintained what I guessed to be a steady
pace out of the city, mainly on roads judging from the
smoothness of our travel. As we'd done more than enough
damage to local architecture already, I was just as pleased.

The Ganthor around me kept nodding into a light sleep,
obviously unconcerned about my Feneden-self. Even my
guard was leaning back against the wall, rifle hung on a
sling, and looked about to snore. *Good,* I thought, and
squirmed until I could free one numb shoulder and then the
next from the Ganthor now using them as pillows. I might
not know much about this form, including the annoying
fuzziness of the image I was getting from overhead, but I
did know Ganthor. It was time for a female-to-female conversation.

Waste of effort. The Ganthor Matriarch paused to vent
mucus from her helmet. Judging from the gloss over the
floor, she'd been doing a lot of it. It was a sign of her personal distress at not being able to scent the members of her
Herd directly. If this had been a longer campaign, they
would have used a pressurized 'digger, shedding the e-rigs
in its air lock. As it was, they would need to leave the 'rigs
as soon as possible. No wonder they were delighted to have
found their target so quickly, although the Matriarch wrinkled her snout at me through her misted helmet in distaste.
Not at me. At their client.

Sends down a Battle Herd to fetch a spy, she complained, clicking with one hoof. The Ganthor hoof spread
into two capable digits, opposed by a third, longer one extending from the back of the wrist. The inner surface of
each digit was spongelike and sensitive, the outer, a bony

shell ideal for their clicking speech. Her e-rig, as those of all the Ganthor, came equipped with small metal disks at the tip of each digit, so their clickspeech was a disarming tinkle of tiny bells. Coming from a creature who massed at least three of me and whose e-rig was wrapped in bandoliers studded with shells and explosives, this was a little disconcerting.

I was tapping the blades of two rather formidable knives to hold up my end of the conversation, knives belonging to the Matriarch's Second. He stood right at my shoulder, close enough that his breathing kept sending the nozzle of his rifle into my back. *Inadvertently,* I hoped.

I am honored to have such an escort, I clicked respectfully, *while appreciating this is a waste of your Herd's bravery and skill, Matriarch.*

There were pleased thumps from all present, including the remaining six Ganthor in the 'digger's control room: the Matriarch's other Second, three taciturn individuals seated on a bench who wore sufficient land mines strung over their bulk to take out most of the city—probably the Herd's more experienced officers, inherited by default when this Matriarch assumed control—and the two operating the controls.

Well-spoken, spy. This click from the Second lurking behind me. There was a plop of mucus and something oozed between my feet. *Stressed, was he?*

I couldn't stamp in my soft-soled boots, but I brought the knives together as loudly as I could. *!!No* *I am not a spy,* I clicked firmly. *I am the greatest military strategist of my kind.* *Had Skalet been in a grave,* I grinned to myself, *she should now roll over in it, as Paul would say.*

Mind you, it was a gamble. Ganthor usually had one of two reactions to the concept of strategy: they ignored it completely or they nursed deep grudges against those not-so-brilliant planners responsible for their losses on the battlefield.

I judged this Matriarch as too clever for either. Her plan to find the Feneden with the 'digger, while typically destructive of the landscape, had been nonetheless effective and quick. Such a being should comprehend the value of the knowledge I pretended to possess.

The Tly need advice, she clicked, her tense body posture signaling an underlying meaning.

I thought I could guess, and felt sudden anger. This form didn't care for the emotion—my cilia distracted me by coursing across the back of my neck in draft-causing waves. I was careful in phrasing my question: *There has been waste?*

!!Too much!! stamped the Matriarch. She smacked the Second nearest her.

He clicked what dignity would not permit her to tell me. *Two Herds have been lost. Every member. The Tly Commander, Logan, says this is due to poor strategy by Ganthor.* *There's an oxymoron,* I thought, but squashed it guiltily. We were talking about lives. *This is,* he clicked morosely, chiming in almost a minor key, *difficult to accept.*

!!Retribution!! The *Matriarch's* opinion of the matter was plain.

I had worse news for them, convinced Logan would repeat his tricks and eliminate this Herd as well, once their usefulness ended. The last clicks of the dying Ganthor on Minas XII haunted me. *The Matriarch was betrayed. Abandoned. No Herd.* That tactic wouldn't work on Iftsen Secondus—the Iftsen wouldn't harm them. But, unless he was ready to be exposed, Logan couldn't risk having them questioned by Port Authority or Commonwealth officials. Ganthor were constitutionally incapable of holding in the truth. *It was,* I thought, *a significant part of their charm.*

The hard part was going to be warning this Herd without sending them into a vengeance-fueled frenzy or winding up a blue smear on the floor before I could explain how I knew.

Confidence, I told myself, *was something you needed to show others before revealing how wrong they'd been.* Especially really large, well-armed, hot-tempered, others.

Elsewhere

"SIRS?"

The tentative and worried voice on the formerly dead com system was not the one Lefebvre had expected. He turned and met Timri's glance. She shrugged, but took a stance to one side of his door.

"Yes, Com-tech Resdick?" Lefebvre snapped in his best, don't-bother-me tone. He had no idea what Kearn might have said to the crew to explain why the captain and comp-tech were locked in the captain's quarters. *Knowing Kearn,* Lefebvre reminded himself, *he might not have said anything at all, fearing a mutiny.*

The worry deepened. "We have a—situation on the bridge, sir."

Lefebvre forgot all about Kearn, sitting up straight. "What kind of situation?"

"Port Authority is on the com, sir. They want to speak to a senior officer. You, sir."

"Did they say what it's about?"

There was a slight pause, as though Resdick—only two years from retirement—was considering exactly what might get him in the least trouble. Then, when he spoke, Lefebvre realized he'd misjudged the being. Resdick had merely hesitated to find the words: "Sir, there's a Gan-thor assault vehicle approaching the shipcity, Underside. It's already attacked the—the Brakistem Art Gallery. Sir."

"Where's Kearn? Security Head Sas?"

"They've left the ship, sir. A half an hour ago. I'm not

getting a response to my calls. I believe they were try-ing to catch the next Upperside shuttle."

Timri spat out a quiet curse.

Lefebvre drew a long, slow breath in through his nos-trils, letting it out again slowly, feeling his mind and body settle into the calm readiness he knew he'd need more than any adrenaline.

First things first.

"My door's jammed, Resdick," he said calmly. "Send someone down here to open it."

37: Shipcity Morning

I MIGHT have been masquerading as a strategist—*somewhat of a trend, since I'd already been a diplomat, ghost, spy, and any number of things I was not*—in order to gain the Matriarch's confidence. That hadn't let me avoid a difficult choice. The easy part had been convincing the Ganthor her current employer was a bad risk. The account I'd accessed through the 'digger's com system had perhaps softened the blow of dropping a supposedly lucrative contract, although I thought it probable this exceptionally worldly Matriarch recognized Logan could be killing his mercs—at least in part—as a cost-cutting method. It did nothing to moderate their reaction to my disclosures.

Once they'd calmed, and I could descend from the precarious safety of an upper shelf, we discussed—more or less without bruising—what to do next. Understandably, the Seconds were all for a frontal assault. Unfortunately, all they had was a location to meet their transport offworld. I didn't see Logan risking himself in person, however convenient. Nor did I expect he'd really send a transport capable of retrieving the Herd, in case they attempted to commandeer it—a detail confirmed by the simple expedient of having two of the Herd exit the 'digger, shoot a climbing rig up the nearest tall structure with the necessary orientation, and launch a servoscope from the top. It was illegal, intrusive, and broke any number of regulations about how Commonwealth species acted toward one another.

It also improved my credibility with the Ganthor a thousandfold when the 'scope panned the seashore in the di-

rection of the so-called transport and found only an automated one-person shuttle.

So the next move was up to me. The Herd dealt with its
inner turmoil by lining up so they could connect each in
turn to the Matriarch's e-rig, a reassurance I could have
used myself. My Feneden-self apparently craved the company of its own species as well, a craving my cilia tried to
satisfy by sampling heat signatures from the e-rigged bodies near me. Needless to say, that instinctive searching
merely confirmed I was the only one here without a thick
hide and even thicker layer of insulating body fat.

If I'd had mass, and an expandable e-rig, I could have
cycled into my Ganthor-self here in the 'digger. The Ganthor would be so consumed by the presence of a new individual, I doubted they'd register the disappearance of their
Feneden guest for quite some time. *And such a sturdy, brave
form,* I sighed.

But this elegant, timid form was the key, I told myself,
and gathered what courage I could before announcing to
the Second who waited, patiently for a Ganthor, for my
command. *To the shipcity.*

"You're parking—?" the Human repeated.

Since my comspeak was impeccable, I began to wonder
if her hearing was somehow impaired and tried speaking
louder. "Yes. We'd prefer an indefinite duration spot, if you
have it. I'll cover the charges."

The Human leaned farther out of her booth, twisting her
helmet so that she looked left, up, and then right, as if this
was some necessary stage in assessing the dimensions of
the 'digger relative to the available parking spots. I could
see several that would do from here—obviously quite a few
others had left the Festival early.

The Ganthor flanking me were uneasy without their
weapons, no matter that they'd made a valiant effort to look
somewhat more like tourists than troops. Their nervousness
was barely noticeable in the Matriarch's Second, but was
patently a serious matter to the other, a less-experienced and
so more aggressively postured youngster. He'd taken to

thumping me in the back at inopportune moments—an unconscious reflex intended to determine our relative positions within the Herd.

As I had as much chance of returning the gesture with meaningful force as I had of moving the 'digger past this Human without her cooperation, I clicked impatiently at the Second: *!!Settle him!!* The Second reached behind me. The youngster gave a startled grunt but calmed.

This interchange had an effect on the Human gatekeeper. She started closing the gate—a decidedly flimsy affair compared to the heavily armored nose of the Ganthor vehicle.

"You don't want to do that, Fem," I said quickly. "Trust me. We only want to park it. There'll be no trouble. I promise."

She lifted her hand from the control. "Is this the 'digger that was in Brakistem last night?"

As it was barely dawn, I thought that an interesting lengthening of time, but didn't comment. "Oh, you've heard of them?" I said, thinking rapidly. "I'm not surprised, considering the quality and innovation of their art."

"Art?" Both her eyebrows went up, their inlaid feathers twisting with the movement. It wasn't the most flattering adornment I'd seen on a Human face, but then there were as many cultural tastes among that species as there were groups of more than ten.

"Art," I said firmly. "The Ganthor were—guests of the Festival of Living Art." *Which wasn't completely false.* "They were commissioned to produce an interactive piece for the Gallery. I thought everyone knew—this Herd is quite famous."

She actually blushed brightly enough for the color to show through her helmet. "My mistake, Fem—?"

"Tilesen." I'd already chosen the name to give the Ganthor, though having no way to gauge if it was too old-fashioned for today's Feneden. *Some names,* I hoped, *were timeless.*

"Fem Tilesen. Please apologize to your guests for my ignorance. I usually keep up on visiting art groups. It's really quite a passion of mine. You can direct the driver to park your—vehicle—in the fifteenth through seventeenth rows. That should be sufficient space. You know there's a cover charge? And, Fem?" This in a suddenly conspiratorial tone that made the Ganthor stiffen. I smacked them both as hard as I could before they did anything else. "I think it's simply wonderful you've been able to use the art of these talented beings to bridge the gap between your species and the Iftsen. I tell you, a lot of us were getting worried. Any chance of an autograph?"

"I'll see what I can do," I said rather numbly and hurried my escort of talented beings back into their newly christened object d'art.

Having settled the not-so-minor problem of getting rid of the conspicuous 'digger—which included adding the replacement cost of a new one onto the bill—I could then concentrate on what to do with fifteen unemployed Ganthor. The Herd couldn't stay isolated in their e-rigs much longer. I gave this some thought as the driver managed to put the 'digger into a close enough approximation of the rows assigned, the cover arching over us with only a screech as it hit some of the more irregular protrusions out the aft gun ports. We waited until the parking attendant signaled that the air outside the 'digger had been replaced with the oxy-mix standard throughout the shipcity's tunnelways, and then shed our rigs with pleasure.

Well, the Ganthor did. I gave them as much room as possible, anticipating disrobing would necessitate a period of shove and slobber. I hesitated about taking off my own e-rig, then decided that was more Feneden fussing. It would look odd to wear a helmet out there. I felt around for the release, not having bothered to find it earlier. *There.*

With the helmet off, my cilia writhed in delight. It was an automatic and irritating sensation, to have one's hair waving indoors as if windblown. *Get used to it,* I reminded myself, disturbed to find myself making such a trivial judgment of a form's characteristics. *Too much time as Esolesy Ki.* Lishcyns were known for hasty decisions and a fascination with appearances. I was going to have to reconsider how long I remained in a particular form, if I wanted to ensure my thought processes remained Esen-alit-Quar's and so totally my own.

A new and uncomfortable thought. Had my web-kin chosen their favored forms because they enjoyed those more than others? Or had they spent more time in those forms and so begun to change in their very natures? No Ersh-memory, helpful or otherwise, bubbled up cooperatively to reassure me with an answer.

We are ready, Fem Tilesen, clicked one of the Seconds—his personal attention a continuing mark of the Matriarch's favor.

I'd been trying to check my companions for implants, but gave up. It was impossible as long as they kept milling around. *Do any of your Herd have a vocalizing implant?* I clicked, using the fingersnap they'd provided. It was conceivable I was the only other being on Iftsen Secondus at the moment fluent in their speech. I didn't want to leave them without at least one Ganthor who could communicate in comspeak.

My predecessor at the Matriarch's Left. Left wasn't the term he used, just its meaning; the term itself referred to an archaic weapon, somewhat like a battleax, wielded by the Matriarch as a practical symbol of her authority. The other Second would refer to himself as her Right; again, a term referring to a weapon—one with serrated edges able to penetrate a Ganthor's hide. It symbolized her right to their lives and her responsibility for them.

I tugged at his huge, bristle-coated arm until he followed me a little distance from the others. Mucus streamed from his nostrils as he tried in vain to read my intentions. A handsome, not-too-scarred individual. Now that I paid closer attention, he did appear young for his position in the Herd, although he bulked at least twenty-five percent over most of the others. *This may be important,* I clicked. *What happened to your predecessor?* As he lowered his snout in threat, I added quickly: *I mean no offense. This is a matter of Herd safety.*

There was no higher priority for a Ganthor, though he was likely well-enough versed in the ways of other species to suspect I was using it as a ploy to gain his attention. *Explain.* His foot moved as though he had to stop it stamping.

If there was anything—unusual—about your predecessor's death, or if he died while the Herd was employed by Logan, I would see it as a deliberate attempt to reduce your Matriarch's ability to communicate with others.

!! with a whole body shudder that rattled his bandoliers and holstered weapons. This caught the attention of every Ganthor within earshot. I could see snouts wriggling as they picked up on the emotional state of the Second.

Answer. This click came from the Matriarch, who must have kept her ears directed our way after all. As I'd thought, a perceptive individual.

Left was lost to the Herd during an accident as we boarded Logan's transport. A failure within the air lock system.

I didn't need scent to know what rippled through the Herd's consciousness at that moment. It was as well they didn't know Logan's present location or I'd never get their cooperation.

And I was counting on it.

Elsewhere

KEARN looked worriedly down the corridor. Sas was huddled over the stateroom's locking mechanism, looking every bit the burglar if, in Kearn's opinion, acting anything but. *For a security officer with his expertise, you'd think he could break into a room without rousing the dead,* Kearn fumed to himself.

Port Authority on Upperside had not been helpful—not in the least. They seemed to think some scuffle planetside was more important than Kearn's urgent request to examine the quarters of any Human named Mitchell who'd boarded the shipcity within the last week. They'd almost physically removed them from the office.

Kearn would have filed an immediate complaint, but one of the officials had followed them out, slipping them a list of addresses. Kearn planned to combine his complaint with a report against the being for accepting a bribe, the instant he was off this sordid excuse for a station.

Their problems had only begun. Who'd have thought there would be fourteen Humans with some version of Mitchell in their name staying on Upperside? Sas had hissed in disgust.

But he'd agreed, Kearn reminded himself. *They couldn't trust anyone on the ship—not with Lefebvre and Timri against him. They had no one but each other.*

And one clue. That the infamous and dangerous Paul Ragem, the Traitor, was somewhere on Upperside. Port Authority had laughed at his demand they halt downward shuttle traffic and quarantine ships already in dock. This Festival, coupled with some other nonsense about the Feneden and Iftsen, took precedence over his investigation. *Investigation! Hah!*

Kearn wiped his sweaty palms against his pant legs. They'd dressed as tourists to avoid alarming Ragem; Kearn deplored the necessity, convinced the shapeless, soft clothing robbed him of any remaining presence. He should have stayed in uniform. Then they might have taken him seriously. "Aren't you done yet?" he asked the Modoren. "What's taking so long? You've had enough practice." This was the fifth door they'd tried. All the other cabins had been empty except for the furnishings supplied by Upperside.

A suspicious being, Kearn thought, *might believe Ragem had rented multiple rooms under his alias to confuse pursuit.* He didn't like the idea that logically followed: that Ragem knew he was being chased and probably wouldn't use any of those rooms.

"Ashtst!" This satisfied sound from Sas, as the door swung open, coincided perfectly with a shouted "Stop!"

Kearn whirled to find the previously empty corridor now filled by Port Authority in full riot gear, running toward them. He took a couple of steps back from Sas, attempting to look horrified. "Stop!" he echoed loudly. "What do you think you are doing?"

Sas, with the agility of his kind, had already leaped up, lips curled back from his formidable natural armament. He snarled and spat, but the curses didn't render as much more than crackling through the implant in his furred throat. Kearn took the meaning, and backed away even more as Port Authority surrounded them both.

"What is the meaning of this?" he shouted, shaking his arm from the grip of a guardsman. "Don't you know who I am?" Kearn regretted the lack of uniform more than ever.

"Why, yes, sir. We do," came the surprising answer.

"Y-you do?" Then Kearn's blood turned to ice in his

veins as he stared past the dozen or so who'd trapped him to the ring of curious onlookers beyond.

A tall, dark-haired, *familiar* Human sketched a mocking salute before fading into the crowd.

Ragem!

Kearn felt his heart almost stop and his eyes bulge as he tried to look everywhere at once.

Where Ragem was, the Esen Monster was sure to come.

38: Seaside Afternoon; Shuttle Afternoon

I MISSED Paul. I missed the Herd. *Let's face it,* I told myself dolefully, *there were definite reasons why almost all intelligent species were social.* Even the Web had been communal—albeit a deliberate evolution rather than innate. The Human saying: misery loves company, came to mind, but I dismissed it. *I wasn't miserable. I was Esen the diplomat. Esen the daring!*

I couldn't help but add to my list: *Esen who hoped she knew what she was doing.*

I checked the groundcar settings again, needlessly, but compelled by some inner restlessness to constantly verify my location. My Feneden-self appeared instinctively wary of being lost. As this was a sensible concern on a strange planet, I approved.

Not that I could get lost here, I thought, admiring the immense shadows cast by the overarching leaves, each larger than my vehicle. It might be day-dim, but I'd know my way along this road in the dead of night. My own memories of Brakistem and the shore of the lovely, dark Bridklestet were as vivid as if I'd just lived the moments. Away from the changes wrought by the Iftsen, the landscape seemed reassuringly eternal.

Maybe that's where the loneliness came from—remembering. I'd come with Lesy twice, Ansky once, Mixs three times. Skalet never, since she'd been uncomfortable in a culture that valued disorderly behavior. I hadn't come with

Ersh either, but that was a different matter. Ersh traveled, but always alone and in secret—a caution so much a part of her that none of us found it curious, and only I had to endure. I literally matured in Ersh's shadow, knowing at any moment, on any world, if I made a mistake, she'd most likely be somewhere close enough to know. *As if,* I now believed, *she'd sensed from the beginning I was like her,* and could hide certain memories from the others when we shared flesh. So she'd been forced to keep her eye, or whatever, on me as much as possible.

Her subterfuge had, I remembered, rather fondly, *led to my early conviction that no matter how I tried, Ersh could read my most secret misdeeds right out of my mass, so I might as well confess immediately.* It had taken me until my third century to discover her method and know for sure I could have a private self. *As long as Ersh wasn't watching.*

I sighed, feeling not so much grief as a distinct longing for the days when there was someone older and wiser to catch my mistakes. *You never know what you'll miss most,* I thought.

The road wound around small hills, echoing the passage taken by the streams of not-quite water. Those gleamed, unshadowed by foliage. Then again, life at the active interface between Iftsen Secondus' atmosphere and any exposed solvent required adaptations to keep one's body parts from becoming part of the reactions. The skin bits the Iftsen shed everywhere they went made perfect sense here—as well as forming the basis of a not-inconsiderable food web.

All of which would be much more enjoyable if I wasn't sending the groundcar careening around each lazy corner at its maximum speed. The meandering Iftsen road didn't have a shuttle to catch. *Hopefully, I still did.*

Paul should have my message by now, I estimated, proud of this mature and thoughtful gesture on my part. Don't worry, was the gist of it. Of course, there was as much chance of Paul not worrying as there was of my making sense of the fragmented and diffuse images picked up by the oculars on my head.

I'd tried using my hands to push the squirming cilia out of the way. It hadn't made any difference I could detect.

What should make a difference was my arrival at the shuttle. I had thought very carefully this time and hadn't found any reason why this shouldn't work. After all, I reassured myself, Logan had wanted to meet a Feneden.

He didn't have to know I wasn't one.

I made the last turn, relieved to see the plain and ugly lines of a Tly personal transport shuttle caught among the dappled shadows, then alarmed to notice the shoreline mere steps beyond it. The shoreline had undoubtedly been much farther away when they'd landed the craft here. The Bridklestet might be shallow, but it had tides nonetheless. I hurried to pull the groundcar alongside the shuttle.

So far, so good. The Black Watch was unlikely to be in orbit. The Iftsen might ignore starships landing on their world, but, unlike Minas XII's, Upperside's Port Authority took traffic control quite seriously. So this shuttle was the only way I could find the *'Watch* and the repulsive Logan. *Who,* I said to myself quite cheerfully, *was a being definitely both able and motivated to find the Iftsens' planet-killing weapon,* especially when accompanied by his new ally—an ally who had a reasonably accurate idea of where, in the sunward asteroid belt, the Iftsen had hidden their ultimate defense.

What I could do about the weapon once we found it was something I intended to leave up to Skalet's ample memories of such devices. *As for what I could do about Logan?* I smiled with anticipation.

I keyed open the groundcar's roof and sat looking around, exhibiting a reasonable amount of caution. Logan had to be watching this area. He would have expected a 'digger full of Ganthor to bring me; a 'digger full of surprised and displeased Ganthor once they realized they were about to be left behind on Iftsen Secondus by their employer. So what had he planned? To talk them into heading back to the ship-city and buying tickets home? That didn't seem Logan's style.

There had to be a trap. Reluctantly, I laid Skalet-memories of less honorable tactics over my Feneden-perceptions of this peaceful setting. As I did, the Bridklestet lapped a little closer to the landing gear, a gentle background hiss as her acidic waters etched the salt-crusted shoreline. *Deception on all sides,* I thought, gazing along the lines of froth repeating the curve of shore in both directions.

I shut down the groundcar, listening. Other than its fading hiss, and a faint susurration as hundreds of huge leaves slowly twisted to steal more of the cloud-filtered light from the neighbors, all was quiet. Too quiet. There should have been cranes whistling like giddy lunatics in the distance. At the very least, once the machine had stilled, the air should have hummed with the ever-present droning of griffids—tiny herbivores who lived out their lives attached to a single leaf until it died and fell to the ground, giving them the opportunity to lay their eggs at the tree base before scampering up to fasten on a fresh feeding ground.

The griffids were here. I could see dozens hanging above me, their bodies suspended from feeding appendages drilled into the massive ribs of the leaf, rows of beady eyes fixed on me. Their bladders were collapsed within their lower limbs as they held their breath, becoming as inconspicuous as possible. Something had scared them, recently and badly.

My hands had difficulty with the door latch, trembling in a reflex I did my best to ignore. Although I didn't see anything I could identify as alarming, this form was strangely on edge, as though something was hiding behind me, ready to spring.

If being Feneden wasn't an essential part of my plan, by now I'd have gladly cycled into just about anything else. Even my Ket-self had been steadier, *which was,* I thought, *saying a lot.*

My body temperature rose involuntarily, the dump of energy helping me control my instincts to change. This had the surprising effect of sending my cilia flailing wildly about, responding to the heat rising from my skin: a conclusion I arrived at somewhat later. My first reaction was to thump the side of my helmet to settle them down.

While that didn't happen, something else did. The helmet, formerly completely transparent, suddenly displayed an arc of tiny, brilliant specks over my head. *Stars,* I realized, completely distracted by finally receiving a meaningful image through my upper oculars. It blended within my awareness of my surroundings as the rumble of distant thunder could be recognized while listening to music. *Polarized light,* recited something that tasted of Ersh in my thoughts. Other memories floated past: this was how the Feneden oriented themselves on their world, a sense so vital to their awareness of place and self that I guessed the e-rig's helmet was preset to display stars where none could be seen.

Where none could be seen. I tucked the thought away, aware of connections making themselves in my innermost memories, not ready to be distracted.

I did feel better, I admitted. As I cooled, the currents through my cilia eased as well. There were other displays, starting to fade. I tapped the helmet again, very lightly, and the depictions of various gauges and controls brightened immediately. I shook my head, chagrined at this proof of one of Ersh's many rules, namely: Never use unfamiliar technology. *As if there'd been an owner's manual,* I grumbled, but took a moment to examine what the suit was telling me. Other than the stars, which only showed to my upper eyes, the rest was reasonably standard stuff. One thing relieved me. This e-rig appeared to have been serviced recently, implying I didn't need to worry about running out of breathable air.

Because the air outside the suit was anything but, and getting worse. It was growing darker—something this form apparently didn't mind, now that I could show it some fake starlight—and the corrosive evening mists were beginning to drift down from the treetops. The forest was ready, the edges of each huge leaf already perceptibly curling into their protective night roll, inadvertently protecting their parasitic house guests along with their own tender undersides.

I climbed out of the groundcar and headed for the shuttle, examining the ground carefully before each step. I hadn't yet spotted Logan's welcome for the Herd, which didn't re-assure me at all.

In unnecessary confirmation I was being watched, the shuttle's engines powered up, startling in the silence, and the door whooshed open. Given the proximity of the rising water to the craft, and the approaching nightfall, I got the hint. They wanted me to hurry. *Fine,* I thought, but kept to my deliberate pace. *If they wanted a Feneden this badly, they could wait.*

My care paid off. As I stepped on the ramp, my cilia collected a burst of heat energy. I paused, looking upward, my Feneden-sense revealing a ring of hovering warm objects my eyes couldn't see. *Antipersonnel mines,* Skalet-memory cataloged and explained. *Hidden when dormant. Deadly when activated.*

They could, I remembered with a shudder, *be set to hunt by species.* Had the Ganthor refused to listen to me and come along— I stopped my imagination in its tracks.

As I entered Logan's shuttle and the door closed behind me, I began to seriously doubt my ability to deal with such a being.

It was, of course, too late to change my mind.

Elsewhere

"YOU!"

Of all the beings who might have interceded with Port Authority, not that he'd expected any rescue, Kearn had never imagined N'Klet. Yet he'd been freed from the holding brig almost immediately, whisked through procedures with a speed that implied very high level interference indeed. The Port Jellies hadn't been pleased, but they'd been disturbingly cooperative.

And there the Panacian stood in the waiting room, her limbs primly folded. "My dear Fem N'Klet," Kearn began after his initial hesitation, hurrying forward. "This is most embarrassing. How ever did you—?"

She inclined her head graciously. "Upperside Shipcity has obligations to the Hive as well as the Iftsen, Hom Kearn. It is Port Authority's pleasure to serve. Now, we have urgent matters to discuss, Hom Kearn." This suggestion came more softly. "Please come with me." She gestured to the exit.

Kearn stared at her glistening blue form, wondering why he found it impossible to move his feet, wondering how he could be afraid of this small, courteous being. They'd had their disagreements, but there was no reason to suddenly think her more a threat than the ominous figure of a still-alive Paul Ragem—who had certainly been the one to arrange their arrest.

But his apprehension was real enough to make him ask: "Fem N'Klet? My officer, Sas? Has he been released as well?"

A wave of an upper claw indicating agreement. "He demanded a shuttle to Underside, Hom Kearn, apparently to rejoin your starship. I assumed this was on your orders and made the arrangements. Was this incorrect?"

Was this a lie? Kearn asked himself, finding no clues in her impeccable comspeak or polite body language. *Or,* the horrifying thought occurred to him, *was Sas in league with Lefebvre—gone to free his co-conspirator and act while he couldn't protect himself?* Kearn felt short of breath.

N'Klet bowed, passing him a plas sack. "Your belongings, Hom Kearn."

Kearn took the bag and opened it, trying unsuccessfully not to sag with relief. He'd brought his precious recordings with him, as well as the Kraal knife—not daring to leave them anywhere else. *All here.* His weapon as well. Surely if she intended him harm, she wouldn't return it.

And if she wanted his secrets, she hardly needed to talk to him with these in her possession, he realized, closing the bag with numb fingers. "What do you want from me, Fem N'Klet?" Kearn asked.

Her compound eyes caught the light as she inclined her head toward the office door, opening and closing as a variety of beings, official and otherwise, conducted their business. "Not here."

Kearn swallowed. He had no choice.

N'Klet had austere quarters for a Panacian representing a Queen, almost bare. Kearn knew the Ambassador caste prided themselves on suiting their meeting areas to make the best impression on their guests, whatever the species. *This didn't feel right,* he fussed to himself as he took the only other chair in the room and faced her across a thin, plas-topped table. The interrogation room at Port Authority had been more welcoming.

N'Klet had arranged herself on a Human-suited chair with effortless grace, her every movement flawless and supple. Kearn felt all of his clumsiness as he watched her. The scarring along her side was almost completely gone now, leaving no more than faint impressions. *What could have happened?* he wondered, distracted. She'd never said.

N'Klet tilted her head as if following his gaze and looked down at herself, then back up at him. "An accident, Hom Kearn," she offered unexpectedly, as though sharing a confidence to put him at ease. "I am actually not a member of the Family which operates the Ambassador's School on D'Dsel. Rather, I'm attached to the Iftsen delegation. Their well-being during their visit to D'Dsel and the School was a responsibility I assumed gladly for the Hive. There was a regrettable—incident—during our arrival on D'Dsel in which I was exposed to their atmosphere for a time."

Kearn winced. Had it been a long enough exposure, N'Klet's entire carapace would have dissolved, costing her life. *An agonizing death.* "My sympathy, Fem N'Klet."

"Her Radiance was most gracious," N'Klet continued, bowing an acknowledgment. "I had been damaged and, of course, suffered a distressing loss of my former Queen's scent. But, as you see, I am fully recovered— which is fortunate, as this desperate situation requires someone familiar with the Iftsen as well as yourself."

"I don't understand. I'm here to find Paul Ragem—"

"Ah." She made the gesture of extreme mortification, then passed a message cube across the table to him. "That is the first matter we must discuss, Hom Kearn. My most gracious and honorable Queen has sent this message of apology to you as well as to the offices of Cameron & Ki Exports. She wishes you to know she was in error. The Human known as Paul Cameron is not Paul Ragem."

Kearn dropped the cube. "What did you say?" he blurted. "What's this nonsense? Of course he is. I—" he closed his mouth, somehow not wanting to say: *I saw him with my own eyes.*

The Panacian stiffened. "There is no nonsense here,

Hom Kearn. My Queen regrets any confusion her misidentification may have caused. She has reviewed the tapes as well as genetic information I obtained from Paul Cameron's quarters. There is no doubt. The resemblance is striking, but Cameron is not Ragem. Please understand that you Humans are a very uniform species to us, and identifying individuals is fraught with uncertainty. My Queen anticipates you will accept her apology. And cause no further disruptions on Upperside."

Kearn felt his face grow hot and knew he was likely glowing red from his neck to the top of his head. Somehow he managed to grind out, "Please inform your Queen that I accept her apology and understand completely." He paused to collect himself. "This is very disappointing and embarrassing news, Fem N'Klet."

She put the fine tips of two marblelike claws together. "I have ensured that Port Authority has purged your arrest record. The Hive is prepared to further compensate you for this misunderstanding, Hom Kearn, beginning with the—damages—incurred during your pursuit of Ragem on this station."

She doesn't know, Kearn realized suddenly, lowering his eyes to hide the glee he feared would be readable even to this non-Human. *Somehow, Ragem had succeeded in tricking P'Lka, but the Panacians didn't know about Timri and Lefebvre, the evidence he had gained. Meaning N'Klet hadn't played his tapes.* He clutched the bag on his lap, with its still-secure secrets. "You said 'beginning with the damages,' Fem N'Klet," Kearn acknowledged, suddenly bold. "Is the Hive prepared to assist my search for the Esen Monster? The *Russell III* is badly in need of updated equipment and supplies."

His pulse raced as she nodded. "Of course. Funds will be made available to you. I believe you will find them adequate. Should you need additional support, you have only to contact us." When he started to thank her, N'Klet interrupted. "First, we need your help."

Kearn had been waiting for the catch. "Help?"

N'Klet's limbs folded inward, an expression of grief

and sadness. *Sometimes,* Kearn remembered uncomfortably, *it was how Panacians requested forgiveness for bearing ill news.* "Hom Kearn, you represent the military might of the Commonwealth in the Iftsen System."

Kearn shook his head almost frantically. "No, no, Fem N'Klet. You overestimate my position. I'm the project leader on a research vessel—not even her Captain." *Especially at the moment,* he thought miserably. "There's a Commonwealth Deputy Minister at Engulla Terce and surely at least one cruiser within a day translight." He stopped and asked very slowly. "Why do you want the military?"

"There is a crisis here. The Iftsen are about to destroy Fened Prime."

Kearn couldn't help laughing out loud. "The Iftsen? My dear N'Klet. Aside from the dangers of their atmosphere, the Iftsen are the most inoffensive and harmless of creatures—you should know that."

"What I know," N'Klet said coldly, her tone wiping any laughter from Kearn's lips, "is what the Iftsen have revealed to my Queen. These harmless creatures own a planet-killing weapon they call The Messenger. They have sent three warnings to the Feneden and received no satisfaction. You know the Feneden do not believe in the Iftsen. They refuse to acknowledge any and all communication, while continuing to take whatever they wish from Iftsen Secondus. As of this afternoon, Brakistem time, The Messenger has been armed and a final ultimatum delivered."

"Wh-what have the Feneden done?" They were unpleasant—and Kearn feared he'd always have nightmares about their carpet—but hardly offensive. *Besides, they'd only just met the Iftsen.*

"There has been a report they've hired Ganthor mercenaries to pillage Brakistem and disrupt the Festival. So far, I've been able to stop the Iftsen from sending a similar ultimatum to the Ganthor—you and I both know how that would be received."

Ganthor? Kearn was grateful to be sitting down. *Gan-*

thor! "Where is this weapon?" he asked numbly. "Have they told you?"

"Not directly." N'Klet's head tilted. "You must realize that such a matter between our Treaty-partner and another species is of paramount concern to the Hive. Should the Iftsen destroy the Feneden, we would have to assume some of their guilt. Should the Iftsen fail to destroy the Feneden, and the Feneden defend themselves, we would be embroiled in the conflict." She unfolded her limbs. "There were Panacian contractors and ships involved in constructing The Messenger's asteroid facility. They, of course, serve the Hive in all things."

"Good," Kearn heard himself say. Any other time, he would have been surprised at the sudden ring of authority in his voice, but not now, not when his mind was filled with visions of dead and dying Feneden, of worlds at war. "I'll need the location of this weapon. We can't allow the Iftsen to launch it under any circumstances." He stood, pushing his chair back roughly. "Fem N'Klet, I would also ask you to send for the Deputy Minister, and arrange for additional support."

"Of course." N'Klet stood also. "Where are you going, Hom Kearn?"

Kearn drew in a deep breath, not quite believing what he was doing, but finding a certain reckless freedom in knowing he was absolutely right. "To contact Captain Lefebvre. I'm going to need my ship."

There would be time to find Paul Ragem, Kearn assured himself, *and to pursue and end the threat of the Esen Monster—later.*

39: Shuttle Night; Lounge Night

THE trip up on the shuttle had been inspiring. My Feneden-self relished being freed from the e-rig almost as much as being able to see stars on the vid screen. There wasn't a polarized light source within the cabin, so my upper eyes were again distressingly blind. But now that I understood the reason for the lack of image, I found it quite easy to ignore. *It was merely a reminder,* I told myself, *of how simple a thing could separate cultures from understanding.* But first, there was the little matter of disarming the Iftsen.

The com had been silent. I hadn't tried to use it, knowing it would be monitored even if they allowed me to transmit. I judged the lack of communication due to Logan's need to control the conversation. There wasn't much bullying or bribing to be accomplished by remote, especially when he couldn't know what to expect from me. *On many levels,* I thought, with some relish.

I was making an effort to be unemotional and logical—for the most part succeeding quite well—except that, every so often, I'd pull out my perfect memory of the bruises and cuts on Paul's skin.

My Feneden fingers were slim, long, and delicate. I ran them over the lightly pebbled skin of my face, enjoying the tactile sensation on both fingertip and cheek, but was unable to suppress the sudden flare of gruesome memory telling me how this skull crushed so easily between my web-form's jagged teeth, how delicious the taste of bone and tissue would be as I assimilated it into more of me.

Oh, I knew the danger. Paul hadn't needed to warn me during our confrontation with Logan. Ephemeral cultures could overcome their darker natures, forgive their own cruelties, as simply as the birth of a new generation. I didn't have that luxury. Today's Esen was tomorrow's Esen. If I ever crossed the line and harmed others, it would be a stain I carried always. *As had Ersh.*

Seek my revenge on Logan for the harm he did my webkin? If it brought me a breath closer to becoming what Ersh had been, I was better off dead myself.

"Do you understand comspeak?"

Logan had dressed for the occasion in what I guessed to be a uniform from one of the original officers from *Tly Defender*—or he'd been one, since the uniform fit his immense frame as though tailored to it. I would have thought him too young for that, but a great deal was possible with the right medical staff and sufficient motivation.

The lounge of the *'Watch* was dressed for the occasion as well. He'd done his homework, or had bribed someone. The climate control was set almost cool enough to please this form. There were two swings set up over a patch of the slimy carpet the Feneden on D'Dsel had in their quarters. He probably didn't realize the carpet was carnivorous and used to keep small pests out of homes; the swings kept one's feet and furnishings from prolonged contact with it. The Feneden, I'd discovered, were very fastidious beings, especially when staying in strange locations with hosts of unknown habits.

There were guards, twenty of them, leading me to wonder what unknown habits Logan suspected me to have. As they were arranged as if in my honor, it was difficult to take offense.

So I inclined my head to Logan, seeing little of him through my upper eyes but gaining a fair bit of information about his emotional state through my cilia. Flushed, warm, all indications of excitement and stress. I felt some of that myself as I said: "Yes, Human. I can converse with you in this language. I would like to begin by asking why you had me captured by those terrifying creatures. They threatened my life if I didn't obey them and come here." I had no intention of revealing to Logan that this particular Herd of terrifying creatures knew all about his ambush. *Let him worry about the change in plan,* I thought contentedly.

Logan gestured to one of the swings. He was too large to safely take the other, no matter how I privately hoped he'd try, settling his bulk into one of the chairs arranged nearby. One of the other Humans, a grim-faced older female I assumed to be the captain of the *'Watch,* took another seat but didn't speak. Her ship orbited one of Iftsen Secondus' three icy moons, carefully avoiding the direct gaze of Upperside Shipcity and its Port Authority. I thought it quite likely they'd used this tactic many times before to scout departing ships.

There were tables, set with trays of delicacies likely stolen from such other ships. *Probably the trays as well as the food,* I decided, noting the quality. None of the porcelains recently shipped by Cameron & Ki, but then I wouldn't have the stuff on my own table.

"My intermediaries had instructions not to harm or alarm you in the least, Fem—?"

"Tilesen, Inspector Logan," I told him, staring right into Logan's glacier-blue eyes. *Find the truth in the name,* I dared him, but just to myself. "There was harm done in interrupting me, in taking me from my—kin-group. I trust you will explain yourself?"

"Fem Tilesen, I brought you here because of a vastly urgent matter of concern to both your people and mine." Logan leaned forward, intimidating even when seated. I kicked my long legs to start the swing moving. Once each swing we were farther apart; at the other end of my arc he visibly restrained himself from flinching back, so altogether I was pleased.

"And this matter would be?"

"The Iftsen weapon."

How very odd, I told myself, hearing the words and yet

almost not understanding them. It was as if this form resisted wrapping its thoughts around the reality of the Iftsen. Merely thinking about them, which I realized abruptly
I hadn't done for some time, was difficult. *What was going
on?* Suddenly I felt oddly trapped, imprisoned by flesh that
wasn't being reasonable, and my rising heat sent my cilia
outward until I must have looked to be wearing spines instead of hair. *Iftsen. Iftsen. Iftsen.* I kept up the litany until
I found it comfortable to say. *Iftsen.*

"What about this weapon, Inspector Logan?" I managed
to ask. "Why is it of concern to me?"

"If I were you," he said bluntly, although his eyes strayed
to my cilia with a somewhat puzzled look, "I'd be concerned about something threatening my homeworld."

I slowed the swing. "Why would there be this threat to
Fened Prime, Inspector? Is this your threat?" *Iftsen,* I reminded my Feneden-self.

"No. Of course not. It's the Iftsen who have the weapon
aimed your way, Fem Tilesen. I represent the Commonwealth." Rather than choke on that claim, I pumped the
swing again. Logan, not noticing, continued: "As you know,
our government, while predominantly Human, is responsible for keeping peace between signatory species, as well as
protecting the rights of newly-met species such as yourselves. Mistakes happen," he said with commendable hu-
mility, shaking his massive head from side to side like some
Ganthor testing for scent. "We do our best to prevent them."

"Most reassuring," I said with an effort.

"I wouldn't be reassured, Fem Tilesen. While we are
doing our utmost to negotiate a truce with the Iftsen concerning your people, they are being unusually resistant to
a diplomatic solution. I fear your world is in the gravest
and most immediate danger. We have to act."

Time to show a little emotion, I decided, and arranged
my Feneden-face into a Human-similar expression of growing dread. "What can we do?"

Logan was too good to let his own satisfaction show, but
I caught a glimmer of it in the captain's face. "We must

find and remove the Iftsen's weapon of destruction before they can use it against Fened Prime."

Finders, keepers, I recited to myself, knowing exactly what Logan hoped to accomplish. I was more than willing to help, as long as our purposes coincided with saving the Feneden and Iftsen. Out loud I asked, "Do you know where to find it?"

The captain spoke for the first time, her voice rough-edged as though worn from bellowing at fools. I looked at her, assessing her stony features and downturned mouth. This was doubtless one of the career military abandoned and reviled by the Tly as they sought to erase their past, ripe for Logan's approach to diplomacy. "The Iftsen are not used to keeping secrets, Fem Tilesen," she informed me. "We have a very good idea, yes."

"Why do you require me, then, if this is your responsibility?" I demanded, stopping the swing and touching my toes to the floor. "I am an art dealer. I have no desire to be on a military mission."

"We need your ship, Fem Tilesen, to accompany us," Logan said, trying to lower his high-pitched voice to something persuasive. *It wasn't working.* "That way, the Iftsen will realize this is not an action by the Commonwealth alone, but that you are taking justifiable steps to protect yourselves from a preemptive strike."

Thus making that strike ourselves and starting a war. How much did Logan know about the Feneden? Did he truly expect me to be that gullible? I had a sudden feeling of caution. He wasn't a being to suffer fools for long. I stood, and so did they. "Inspector Logan. Unless you can assure my people that these—aggressors—" I couldn't form the word *Iftsen* without obvious effort, "have no other means of attacking us, I will not cooperate in any scheme to involve us directly. That is an open invitation to disaster. For all I know," I ranted, warming up to my point nicely, "for all I know, these beings have allies surrounding our system, ready to attack us from many points, not just this one. Do you expect me to believe there is only one weapon aimed our way? Do you take me for a fool?"

Logan flushed, but his look down at me was sharper, more intent. Almost respectful. "Of course not," he said. "But we know there is only one of these weapons in their possession. It's an appalling device, capable of destroying ships, colonies, and most likely entire worlds. It's independently mobile and self-directing—you won't see it coming—you won't be able to defend against it." He smiled and I felt a chill run down my spine. "Wouldn't it be safer for the Feneden if you owned it, rather than your avowed enemy?"

Definitely, I told myself, keeping any triumph from my face. I sat back on the swing, kicking out to start it moving again. "Tell me, Inspector, more about your plan to ensure the safety of the Feneden."

Elsewhere

"WHO?"

"It's Project Leader Kearn, sir. He's on a secure channel."

No one turned from their posts, but he knew they were listening. The bridge crew had been wound tight since he had reappeared; tighter still since his upping their ready status to a preflight alert. They'd all received military training, despite their posting to a research and contact ship. There was a different feel to the air, knowing Ganthor were involved. *They were hard enough to handle as tourists,* Lefebvre thought glumly.

He tapped the arms of his chair, once, twice.

"Comp-tech Timri." Lefebvre didn't look behind to where he knew she stood waiting, a reassuring aura of competence about her. "Take over here. I'll receive the call in my quarters."

"Yessir."

Once in his quarters, safely alone, Lefebvre accepted the call. "Lefebvre here." *Maybe Kearn would assume he was still locked up.*

"Kearn," said an unfamiliar voice. "I know you are in command, Lefebvre. You can stay there. Just get the *Russell III* up here. Now. Port Authority has a priority docking arranged for you."

"Sir?" The word was involuntary. Lefebvre realized why. It was the first time he could recall Kearn snapping an order at him.

"We have a problem," the voice continued. "What are the Feneden doing?"

Lefebvre hadn't paid much attention to their neighbor. "All quiet. There's been no activity since a large group arrived back at the ship. What's wrong?"

"I'll brief you when you are here." As if Kearn could sense Lefebvre's immediate resistance, he continued, his tone suddenly dropping into something filled with foreboding: "We don't have much time to save them, Lefebvre. And we have to. Hurry."

The docking was priority one, as Kearn promised. The station didn't clamp holds on the hull, leaving them free to leave without notice. A wartime precaution Lefebvre didn't like in the least. *What was going on?*

Lefebvre stopped pacing by the com station. "Any more from Port Authority on Underside, Com-tech?"

"They say—well, this has to be wrong, sir." Resdick's voice hadn't lost its note of strain. "I've requested confirmation."

Lefebvre braced himself with one hand on the back of Resdick's chair. "Let's hear it."

Resdick swiveled his head to look up at his captain, obviously more puzzled than alarmed. Lefebvre relaxed slightly. "It's the Ganthor, sir. They've parked their 'digger in a shipcity lot. Apparently, sir—apparently they're claiming to be artists, participating in the Festival of Living Art. The Iftsen are raving about their contribution to the Gallery. There's a reception underway."

Lefebvre had one thought. *Esen.* He didn't know why he saw her hand in this and he certainly couldn't imagine how she'd done it, but he laughed out loud, clapping Resdick on the back. "Get that confirmed, Com-tech. But if it's verified, I want clearance from Port Authority to return to Underside immediately."

"Belay that, Captain."

Lefebvre whirled, again not recognizing the stern voice. It was Kearn, dressed in what had to be the most garish assortment of ill-fitting casual wear he'd ever seen, rushing in from the lift with Timri in tow. He'd sent her to meet Kearn at the entry port, knowing she could handle him if necessary. Her expression was one of absolute amazement, and she waved her hands at him as if trying to convey helplessness.

The clothes and Timri's waving faded from Lefebvre's sight as he met Kearn's eyes. For the first time, Kearn didn't glance away or become defensive. Instead, Lefebvre saw confidence there, the look of someone victorious. *Paul,* he thought with sudden, heart-stopping dread. *Kearn caught him.*

"This has nothing to do with our search or—personal differences, Captain," Kearn said with startling accuracy. He held out a trip tape. "Set this course. Then I'd like you, Comp-tech Timri, and Engineering Specialist Warner to join me for a briefing."

No one seemed to breathe, except Kearn, who stood waiting for obedience with unusual patience. Lefebvre studied him, trying to figure out how a person could change so completely, or if he'd somehow missed this Kearn all those years. The worried look was still there, only deeper, more concerned. The receding forehead gleamed with sweat, and the hands trembled. But there was a certainty of purpose, a steadiness Lefebvre had never seen before. *This Kearn,* he realized, *could be worth hearing.* "Aye, sir." He took the tape and handed it to the nav officer. "Get us moving, Nav. We'll be in the Project Leader's quarters."

"Yessir."

"Sir?" This from Resdick just as they entered the lift. "You asked to be notified about any change in the Feneden."

Kearn pushed past him. "What is it?" he demanded. "What are they doing? How do you know?"

"We left a remote vid," Lefebvre explained, moving with Kearn to the com-tech's post. "Report?"

"Here, sir," Resdick cued the vid on the small screen set into the upper right of his control panel. The ship's surveillance gear went via the security station on the next level down from the bridge. "See? They've had a visitor."

Lefebvre saw. A private shuttle, one of the expensive sort, sat to one side. Its occupant, a lone e-rigged figure impossible to identify by species, let alone as an individual, walked to the Feneden ship and headed up the ramp as though expected. Then the picture went black.

"They launched, sir," Resdick explained, then added unnecessarily: "Guess it fried the vid."

Lefebvre turned his head and met Kearn's eyes. "Is this good news, sir?" he asked.

Kearn rubbed one hand over his face. When it came away, he looked like someone seeing the odds mounting against him, but determined nonetheless. "I don't know, Captain," he said flatly. "But I find it hard to imagine it is. For anyone. Let's get underway."

Lefebvre nodded, wondering to himself: *who had left with the Feneden?*

And why?

40: Lounge Morning

THERE were times when the fates smiled so broadly, I confidently anticipated disaster; cosmic cooperation like this had to have a price.

Logan knew where to find The Messenger and was taking me to it as his honored guest. He had the equipment to remove the weapon before it could be used against the Feneden. *Safely,* I hoped.

Paul was on Upperside, his cover intact and with Lefebvre in place on the *Russell III* to keep Kearn occupied. My friend might be furious with me for striking off on my own, but he knew what I was doing—*well,* I added honestly, *he knew what I'd planned to do until the moment the Ganthor dropped in and forced some on-the-spot modifications.* Anyway, at least I knew he was safe.

I'd taken advantage of the encounter with the parking attendant to forestall any lingering problems between the Ganthor and the Iftsen. By now, the art reviews I'd sent out under various names would have hit the newsmags on and off Iftsen, praising the adventurous and bold new exhibit by the Ganthor, a species finally showing their creative side to an admiring universe. *I did like that one.*

All of which meant far too many parts of my life were going far too smoothly for comfort, I reminded myself. Of course, it was like watching the majestic slide of a newly-birthed iceberg into the ocean. There wasn't much one could do to alter the event except get out of the way.

I'd contacted the Feneden ship, as Logan requested. They'd been somewhat surprised to receive a call from someone fluent in their own language, but once I'd begun passing along Logan's information—carefully, and all too easily, avoiding any reference to the Iftsen—that surprise had turned to outright panic. It was a response I'd expected—had counted on, in fact. Any calm consideration would lead to inconveniences, such as contacting Fened Prime for reinforcements or, worse, involving the local authorities and so alerting the Iftsen.

The Feneden, to Logan's delight, had been ready to lift almost immediately, a speed suggesting plans already made—a point I didn't make with Logan.

Meanwhile, I was experiencing a slight problem, which I hoped balanced the fates: one of those "owner's manual" events that I should have considered. My Feneden-self was starving. *The Black Watch* had a marvelous galley, if an unhappy cook, but I didn't dare try anything they offered, claiming a period of fasting—always a convenient excuse with aliens.

The truth was, I had no idea what was safe on the Human ship for my Feneden-self. Ersh's memories were regrettably lacking in details beyond local delicacies currently out of reach. This form, despite its outward resemblance to theta-class humanoids, was anything but similar in physiology. For one thing, a large amount of my appetite seemed centered in the clusters of cilia bunched under my clothes, the ones forming lumps that, on a Human, would be substantial breasts.

I had a sense this form could withstand a reasonable amount of fasting; it would have to, because if I tried something poisonous to this body, I'd have to cycle to save myself. *Not the ideal choice, given present company.* I was never left alone, which ruled out trying for another rezt.

"Fem Tilesen. May I join you?" Logan bowed from the open doorway of the lounge, pausing in a polite fiction that my answer would make any difference.

"Certainly, Inspector," I said, looking up from the reader they'd given me. It contained a series of travelogues from systems more or less neighboring the Feneden's, implying Logan was being very careful with the information made available to me. They weren't boring; I was always happy to collect any new data on living cultures, even when packaged for family fun. "These have been fascinating. Thank you."

He looked nonplussed for a moment, then recovered. "My pleasure. Just let one of the crew know if you need anything."

Since I doubted either of the burly, armed Humans standing at attention to either side of the door would dash off in search of my next whim, I didn't bother to answer that. "How long until we reach the weapon?" I asked, kicking the swing into motion as though unconcerned.

"We're there. I've come to ask you to accompany me to the facility."

I'd had better invitations, I decided, fancying I heard the cold winds of disaster starting to test my ears. But this had been the target I'd aimed Logan toward; *again, so far, so good.* "Are there no—guards?" I ventured, trying not to sound eager. *It was distressingly easy.*

He came and sat, crossing his long legs and stretching his misproportioned arms over his head with a chilling bulge of muscle. Regardless of his intelligence and scheming, I suddenly realized, this was a being who defined himself in physical terms and preferred his battles that way. Perhaps that was why he discarded his Ganthor Herds after each use—their inborn strength might seem a direct threat to his own.

His thready, high voice always took me by surprise. "They appear to have relied on camouflage rather than defense, Fem Tilesen. There are no living guards we can detect. To our scans, the construction appears Panacian— which makes sense. The Iftsen adapt or buy Panacian tech for everything off-planet. It also makes our little visit easier. Since they used Panacian materials, they'd have to worry about corrosion. There's a breathable atmosphere in place."

"Where is our transport?" I'd fallen into the Human habit of naming ships, especially as Esolesy Ki, and found the Feneden lack of one for their starship almost as disconcerting as my growing hunger pangs. "Will we rendezvous with them before going to the asteroid?"

Logan's brow rose. "I don't think that would be wise, Fem Tilesen. Disarming an unknown weapon is fraught with uncertainties. We shouldn't risk more than ourselves. Once we are back on the *'Watch* with the weapon safely disarmed, you can instruct your ship to dock with us to receive the weapon."

Once we were back, it would be a quick departure with the Feneden left to do any explaining—or to take the blame. I'd thought he was clever.

It remained to be proved if I was, too.

Elsewhere

THE vid tape hadn't been helpful. Neither had Sas, their expert in interpreting the remote feeds, currently unavailable as he languished in a Port Authority holding cell on burglary charges. *Kearn had been badly surprised by that,* Lefebvre remembered, as though he'd expected the Modoren to beat him back to the *Russ'*. That part of the story he hadn't bothered to explain.

Lefebvre had rerun the tape several times, telling himself it was his imagination trying to convince him this was Paul Ragem. There had been no replies to his messages for Mitchell—but that might just be Paul's common sense. *Why would Paul go to the Feneden?* On the other hand, if Human, the figure was half again taller than Esen as Bess.

That much he could be sure of, and, unlikely as it would have seemed a few brief hours ago, he could be sure of Kearn. The transformation had been startling to say the least and Timri, for one, stubbornly refused to credit it. But strangely, Lefebvre did. Kearn's obsession with Esen welled from his fear—he truly believed she posed a danger to innocent beings. Faced with a more immediate threat—the Iftsen's planet-killer—Kearn couldn't help but turn from his hunt in order to protect the billions on Feneden.

In many ways, Kearn's had always been the more noble chase, Lefebvre confessed to himself, feeling a burning shame each time he remembered his own obsession. He'd thought he'd been after the truth, to restore the tarnished reputation of his childhood hero, doing something worthy. Perhaps, in part, but once he'd found Paul, Lefebvre had seen the ugly thing inside himself, the need to make Paul pay for his desertion. It had been for that anger's sake, not the truth, that Lefebvre had left his family behind, warded away friendships. He'd been lucky enough to find both again. *With,* he thought ruefully, *the knowledge of how little he'd known about what he'd chased.*

It was an experience he didn't envy Kearn.

Lefebvre sipped his cooling sombay, loath to leave the bridge even to grab some breakfast. The information Kearn had about the asteroid was precise. Fuzzy-haired, young, and altogether shy, Engineering Specialist Warner, bewildered by the sudden attention, turned out to have made a hobby of exotic weaponry. He wasn't an expert, but he was more qualified than anyone else on the *Russ'*. Kearn, it seemed, had extensive background information on everyone on board. For once, his paranoia had been useful.

For now, they were on the same side. Lefebvre knew Timri was right, that they had to be prepared to run for it, or somehow defend themselves from the recordings Kearn must have of their conversation. She'd offered to search for them, an offer he hadn't outright rejected, instead convincing her to wait. Kearn had been right about one thing, this situation was theirs to handle until the Commonwealth could send help.

Then, it could get very interesting, Lefebvre thought, taking another slow sip.

41: Asteroid Afternoon

LOGAN had called this Panacian. I gazed around me and thought I recognized several Human touches as well. *There were always congruencies,* Mixs-memory reminded me. Keeping in atmosphere and heat on an asteroid usually produced some version of a dome. Body mass and machinery determined door shapes and sizes. *There were,* I sighed to myself, *very few concessions to aesthetics in such utilitarian buildings by any species.*

The air locks had been secured by a code. Logan had ordered one of his crew to burn out the lock—simple and effective, if extraordinarily dangerous. The builders could easily have left a surprise or two. Any alarm would be delayed in its impact by the time a response would take—but a booby trap, that would be immediate. *So,* I thought to myself, *this Human sought to risk his own life.* I wasn't surprised, although I'd been poised to run for it.

There might have been an alarm shattering the peace of some Iftsen First Citizen, but no traps showed themselves as we—Logan, ten of his larger crew, and I—entered what could have been any smallish mining dome, an unmaintained, older dome at that. We removed our helmets, leaving on the rest of the bulky space gear as a precaution. The air was breathable, but left a dead, metallic taste on my tongue.

I stepped thoughtfully over the remains of construction debris no one had bothered to collect, looking around with my forward-facing eyes like the Humans, processing star patterns with my upper eyes—the incoming light polarized nicely by the dome's plas layer. I derived an intense and pleasant feeling of placement, a knowledge of where I was and where I was going that had nothing at all to do with rational thought about my situation.

The Messenger wasn't hidden. It stood beneath the highest reach of the dome, a tall, ugly, and thoroughly odd-looking device festooned with curls of pipe and wires. I blinked as we came closer, trying to determine exactly what type of weapon it was. There were no matches within my assimilated memories. *I needed to get out more,* I fussed to myself.

Logan's crew knew their jobs, most hurrying forward with tools and hand sensors, while a pair drew the grav cart closer. There wasn't much gravity to speak of here—without the extra mass around our waists, we would bounce off the clear ceiling with each step—but The Messenger appeared massive enough to have significant inertia. I stood back, quite happy to let others disturb what looked implacably dangerous sitting still.

Still, I was curious. There was some text down one side of the weapon. *Why?* Instructions on its use? I eased over that way, keeping my distance, and started reading. It was an obscure Iftsen dialect, probably Peoteran, and, typically, set in rhyme.

There was simply, I decided with sudden, deep contentment, *nothing better than a good education.*

"There." Logan grunted with effort as he helped heave the weapon on to the grav cart, keeping one hand on it as though the hideous thing was a treasure beyond price. "You might not be the Kraal Nightstalker or even the Esen," he murmured to it soothingly, "but you'll do. You'll certainly do." It was just as well his attention was on The Messenger, as I had no control over my startled expression when I heard my name.

"Get her loaded!" Logan ordered, before coming to loom over me. "Now, Fem Tilesen. I have one last task for you."

Before I could so much as blink in surprise, Logan's long arm reached past my head and I felt a sharp tug. His hand came away with my reserve air tank. "You won't need this," he said in that cheerful voice I remembered disliking intensely. He kept my helmet tucked under one arm, adding, "I'll keep this, too, if you don't mind. A souvenir of our time together."

"What are you doing?" I protested. I knew perfectly well, but predictable villains such as Logan expected victims to follow protocol.

"Your fellow Feneden are almost in range of the asteroid, my dear Fem," Logan explained, ripping the gauge off the top of the tank with a wasteful display of strength. "I'd like you to stay and welcome them."

"You want them to enter the dome and be caught as thieves. I could warn them. I can prove it was you. Why not just kill me?" I really hadn't meant to say that, but, Ersh knew, my curiosity sometimes got the better of me.

He ran a finger along my chin, sending shivers of heat through neighboring cilia. "Do you think I mind if you tell them the Commonwealth took this amazing weapon? You go right ahead. As I told you, it's our job to take care of new species."

Fortunately, I did know better than to answer that. There was no benefit whatsoever in having Logan know I knew exactly who he was—especially if it cast any doubt on who, or rather what, he thought I was.

I sat back down, slumping as though he'd won, watching the triumphant smile spread across his face while restraining my own with difficulty.

Assured I wasn't going to present a problem—which I was sure would have resulted in an uncomfortable and potentially awkward attempt to actually kill me—the Tly made quick work of removing themselves and their prize from the dome. I spotted the flash of reflection from their shuttle as it left the asteroid's shadow and was caught by the Iftsen sun. Then it was gone, presumably to dock with *The Black Watch.*

Being alone was fine with me, especially when the alone part removed Logan from my life. I settled myself where I could see the dome's port and thought wistfully of foods

I'd enjoyed in other forms and in other places. *With any luck*— I sat up straighter. Another flash in the black sky.

It had to be the Feneden. I had two fond hopes for this meeting. One, I could straighten out the confusion about the Iftsen.

And two, they'd bring lunch.

So it wasn't surprising I was standing, almost trembling with anticipation, by the time I spotted suited figures marching toward the dome. I went over my planned speech, really hoping there wouldn't be any complications from my being a stranger to them—some species were incredibly awkward about introductions, including the Ganthor who were simply incredibly painful about it—and held my breath as the inner door of the air lock swung open.

I hadn't expected the first individual through the door to be Paul. He went to his knees as though pushed from behind.

And I certainly didn't expect the next two individuals through to throw some sort of scintillating membrane over my head before I could so much as complain.

I kept very still, waiting for the next surprise with some fatalism.

This definitely implied no lunch.

Elsewhere

"HOLD our position, Captain. She said we had to wait."

"She. N'Klet." *Enough was enough.* Lefebvre paced away, then back again, putting his fists knuckle-down on the top of Kearn's desk and leaning on them. "N'Klet lied to you about Sas. I don't see why we should trust anything else she told you."

To Lefebvre's surprise, Kearn didn't flinch. He merely nodded as if weary. "Yes, she did. I can't tell you why. But she sent us here, where we had to come—"

"Conveniently leaving Upperside on the next transport."

"What more could we ask her? You know I've verified the situation with Port Authority and the Deputy Minister. This is where the Iftsen weapon is hidden. N'Klet told us the truth about that."

Lefebvre pushed himself back with an oath. "The Feneden are already findown on the asteroid. They beat us here."

"Another reason to wait," Kearn urged, wringing his hands absently. "The *Russell III* isn't armed. Who knows what they're capable of?"

"That's another thing," Lefebvre shot back at Kearn. "What's with the Iftsen? They want us to simply observe the situation? They forbid hostile action within their system? Are these the same beings advertising how they are going to blow a planetful of beings into atoms over some stolen art?" He paused to collect himself. "What are we missing from this picture, Kearn? Who's lying to us the most?"

Kearn put his chubby fingertips together, appearing to consider them thoughtfully. "Who indeed, Captain?" he said as if to himself, then looked up. "Strike that. I promised to put aside that other business until this situation was resolved. And you've been—" he paused, as if knowing what he wanted to say, but unsure.

Lefebvre took a deep breath and dropped back into the seat he'd exploded from moments before. "And I've been acting like a captain for the first time since boarding the *Russ'*," he said, completing Kearn's sentence. "You can say it, Kearn. It's the truth." Lefebvre hesitated, then realized he owed some truth of his own. "I'm not proud of it."

Kearn stared at Lefebvre for a long time, his expression caught between anguish and decision. Decision seemed to win as he unlocked a drawer in his desk and began pulling out record cubes. The pile grew until half of his desk was covered, then Kearn stopped, sorted out twelve, and shoved them toward Lefebvre. "These are the ones from—from your quarters. And Comp-tech Timri's. And from the crew areas." Without meeting Lefebvre's quizzical gaze, Kearn swept the rest back into his drawer and locked it. His voice defensive, he added: "I'm keeping the records from my cabin and the bridge. I'll need them one day, when my search is successful. There will be a need for clear records, for corroboration."

"Yes, sir," Lefebvre said very quietly, picking up the cubes. "I do understand, sir."

"That will be all, Captain. Please notify me of any change."

"Yessir," Lefebvre repeated. He stood to leave, then looked down at the smaller Human, still dressed in his rumpled tourist clothes. Kearn looked up, a frown growing between his eyes.

"Yes?"

Lefebvre drew himself up and saluted smartly with his free hand. "Thank you, sir."

42: Asteroid Afternoon

IT could have been a comical exhibit of living art for the Iftsen Festival. None of us moved for a truly astonishing amount of time, a tableau of crouched Human and erect Feneden, facing one another under a starry dome. It might have gone on longer, but the unusual membrane the Feneden had tossed over me, although air-light and transparent, interfered with my upper eyes, causing a touch of disorientation. I estimated it would feel worse to a true Feneden and began to sway as if becoming mildly dizzy.

I desperately wanted to go to Paul, make sure he was all right, then return one of his scathing lectures about being in the wrong place at the wrong time—preferably over a cold beer. But that wouldn't have been the reaction of a true Feneden.

My reaction must have reassured them, for suddenly the two Feneden who had covered me, and the three behind them, removed their helmets. Their noses twitched at the smell of the air.

"Greetings," I said in Feneden, cautiously leaving out the rest of the salutation. *It hadn't,* I recalled, *been well-received in the Art Gallery.* "Is this necessary?" I continued, pushing with one finger at the membrane.

"Are you a shifter?" The word came out with intonations of demon and baby-killer.

"Are you a shifter? Or you?" I repeated back, keeping to my role but making my tone more polite—suited to a modern, practical Feneden who didn't believe in me.

"We are not shifters." The assurance came from one of

the Feneden standing behind the first two. *Anisco. Without her translator,* I noticed, wondering how they'd managed to communicate with Paul. After my one quick glance at him, I'd deliberately kept my eyes away. I doubted he could recognize me in this form, although I was sure he suspected. *Who else could manage to be stranded on a secret weapon's base, without a helmet, com link, or air supply?* Outwardly, my Feneden-self looked remarkably like Anisco, the relative age difference, if one existed, perhaps marked by my slightly lesser height.

Paul and I had arranged codes between us long ago, so I could confirm my identity—none, however, in Feneden. *An outburst in an alien language,* I reminded myself, *was unlikely to help right now.*

What I hoped would help was this form, despite my inexperience with it, but knew I could be wrong. I could sense their emotional states through my cilia. Two had body heat patterns indicating they were conflicted, perhaps puzzled but not obviously fearful. Unfortunately, the other three, including Anisco, flared to my inner sight as beacons of terror and anger, a reaction I didn't understand or expect.

Perhaps some good news, I thought. "Fened Prime is safe from—the aggressors." I found the word *Iftsen* stuck in my throat again. "If you check out the center of this place, you'll find the weapon has been removed."

As if the word "weapon" had been a cue, all five pointed something at me that looked distressingly like Paul's biodisrupter, although much smaller. They blinked in unison as well, eyes flashing that disconcerting red. My Feneden-self followed suit, why I didn't know.

"We have no interest in more lies about weapons and threats to Fened Prime," Anisco said, her soft voice almost harsh. "We knew you lived, Shifter, from the moment your servant arrived at our ship on the demon planet." She held up her free hand, then tossed Paul's medallion at my feet.

Since I had good reason, I took the chance and looked at Paul. He'd removed his helmet, but had stayed on his knees, gloved hands on the rock floor. *He knew me,* I decided. His eyes burned beneath that rebellious lock of hair, and there was no mistaking the meaning of his tense posture or tightly compressed lips.

We were in very, very big trouble.

And it was my fault, I sighed to myself. *Again.*

I ignored the medallion, with its betraying flesh. "I'm not a shifter; I'm an art critic," I said, keeping my voice polite but firm, with an underlying humor as if dealing with the mentally feeble. "I don't have a servant—let alone one of these untrustworthy aliens. My name is Tilesen. I've been kidnapped by hideous creatures, left here without supplies, all to supposedly save our world from destruction." When they didn't respond, I snapped: "I'm tired. I'm hungry. Can we go to your ship and contact Fened Prime?" I took a step in that direction.

"Stop!" Anisco's hand shook as she raised her weapon higher. I stopped instantly. "Do not try to attack us! You cannot change form in Kearn's trap, Shifter."

Cycling was the last thing I planned to do, so it didn't matter if her threat was some of Kearn's wishful thinking or the flimsy membrane might actually have some real effect on me. "Change form?" I said with disdain. "Of course I can't. Nothing can. You've been tricked by children's fables. I'm ashamed of you all—chasing a legend when our world has been threatened."

"Legend?" said a Feneden I didn't know, an older male at Anisco's shoulder. His body patterns were almost painfully hot; it had an effect like a strong wind blowing through all of our cilia at once. "Tell me this, Legend," he growled. "How did you leave Fened Prime, when only we were permitted to do so?"

Anisco jumped in: "And where are your life-companions? No true Feneden would be alone, whether they believe or not. That custom is too deeply ingrained in all of us—we learn it from birth. To be alone is to tempt the Shifter." Her eyelids flashed red twice. "Any Feneden alone, any Stranger among us, is the Shifter. You."

Thanks, Ersh, I told her memory, tasting the bitterness of it. An entire civilization primed to weed out imposters. *No wonder she'd left.*

"I swear to you," I said in complete honesty. "I am not the Shifter. You are making a terrible mistake. There really is a weapon—"

"We are saving ourselves and our people from the only true threat," countered the male, waving a signal to the others. They backed to the air lock, one pausing to tear the helmet from Paul's fingers, another stopping at the air lock control panel for a moment before joining the others.

This didn't look good at all. "Wait, Anisco," I pleaded quickly, careful not to move as my knowing her identity apparently startled them. "There's no reason to leave the Human here. You know who he is. This is Paul Cameron. The translator the Panacians brought to you." I thought feverishly. *They were a nervous bunch.* "He's important. He'd be missed. You'd be asked questions."

She hesitated and might have listened to more, but Paul, somehow perceiving what I was up to, chose that moment to sabotage anything I'd gained. He surged to his feet, scooping up his medallion on the way, then came to stand, stiff and straight, at my side.

Anisco spat out a name that translated somewhat literally as "picker of scraps" and urged the rest of the Feneden out. She turned back at the last minute to say in a terrible voice: "Then he can be your final prey, Shifter."

The air lock closed with a rather final-sounding clang of metal to metal.

In the following silence, I could hear a faint hissing over the dual, mismatched sounds of our breathing.

They were venting the dome.

Elsewhere

"I HAVE a call for Project Leader Kearn," Com-tech Resdick told Lefebvre. "It's from the Feneden ship."

Finally. "Patch it through," Lefebvre ordered briskly. When the com-tech hesitated, Lefebvre raised one brow. "Now."

"Yessir."

A high-pitched squeal arched through the com, making everyone cover their ears until Resdick switched off the speakers. "I've recorded it, sir," he said hurriedly.

"What was that?" Lefebvre asked, still hearing a painful echo ringing in his ears.

Timri spoke from her post. "The Feneden abandoned their mechanical translators. I presume this is whatever they used to make contact with the Commonwealth in the first place. I'll see if I have any information on it."

"Quickly," Lefebvre said, staring at the vid display of the asteroid and its single, glittering dome. Any more delays, and he was taking the *Russ'* down, no matter who told him to stay put.

"Captain?"

"Yes?"

Resdick was definitely thriving at the formerly quiet com station. "There's a message from Iftsen Secondus, sir, to the *Russell III.* Did you want to take it here or in your quarters?" At Lefebvre's impatient nod, Resdick brought up the com.

The voice spoke comspeak with a soft burring around the consonants. *Iftsen, for sure,* Lefebvre identified, sitting up straighter. "This is the present First Citizen of Brakistem, *Russell III.* Am I speaking with the being in charge of this ship?"

"This is Captain Lefebvre, First Citizen."

There was a long pause. "Are you in charge of this ship?" the Iftsen asked, sounding cautious. "Are you the decision maker?"

"I am."

"You are near our asteroid?"

Lefebvre frowned. "Yes, First Citizen. As you requested, the *Russell III* has not yet taken any action toward the asteroid or the Feneden ship which landed there. But I must tell you, on behalf of the Commonwealth, we are prepared to forestall any attack—"

"There can be no attack, Captain. Our instruments record that The Messenger has been taken from its place. We are now—" a definitely melancholy sigh, "—quite defenseless. I invite you and your crew to return and share our Festival, Captain Lefebvre. I can offer personal introductions to our most honored and innovative artists."

Timri touched his elbow. "The Feneden just left the asteroid," she whispered.

Lefebvre took a deep breath. "Thank you for informing us, First Citizen. And the invitation. I'll keep you posted." He drew a finger across his throat, and Resdick cut their transmission.

"I never thought I'd say this," Lefebvre announced grimly. He stood, rising up a little on the balls of his feet as though preparing to rush forward.

"Follow that ship."

43: Asteroid Night

"KEEP still, Es," Paul ordered, tight-lipped and obviously angry. He ignored the departure of the Feneden. Instead, he stood, fists on his hips, surveying the membrane they'd called Kearn's trap. "First things first."

"It wasn't my fault—" I began, then closed my lips as he shook his head.

"Keep still," my friend repeated. "What did they tell you about this thing?"

I rolled my eyes, including the distorted ones on top of my head. "They got it from Kearn. They made some ridiculous claim it would stop me from changing form. I can't imagine how this could do anything but cause claustrophobia. I'd like to take it off, if you don't mind. It's bothering my oculars."

"Just wait a minute." He prowled around me, using a piece of broken plas from the floor to gently prod at the glimmering stuff. "Patience, Es."

I obeyed, more because I hadn't done much of that lately, than because I saw any sense to it, but fumed. *We had a few more problems than my having a bag over my head.* I reminded him of at least one. "They're venting the dome. Shouldn't we be looking after that?"

"I noticed. But we can't take chances with this," Paul said. He'd moved around in front of me again, looking worried. "Es, this didn't come from Kearn—not directly. He doesn't have access to this type of tech. Might be Kraal; it's similar to their stealth cloaks."

I went almost cross-eyed trying to see the stuff, then

shrugged. It was so light, my cilia could ripple beneath the top. "I don't really care who cheated Kearn into buying it. It's just a bag, and I for one have had enough of it." My next move might have been due to my empty stomach, a Feneden dislike of having my upper eyes clouded, or simply impatience.

Paul shouted "No!" at the same split second I reached out and grabbed handfuls of the stuff in order to throw it off.

There was a blinding flash.

"Esen."

It wasn't morning. *There hadn't been night,* I assured myself smugly, *so it definitely wasn't morning.*

"Es. Esen. Please?" The quiet, annoying voice became suddenly much louder: "Esen-alit-Quar!"

Confused by memories of others using that tone, I opened my eyes, seeing Paul's face looking oddly pale and out of focus. Then I blinked, and his face became clear, with bright red spots on either cheek. "Morning?" I said doubtfully.

Ouch. Everything hurt.

His strong hands slid under my shoulders. *Ah,* I thought cleverly, *I had shoulders.* After a few uncomfortable tugs, I found myself more or less supported by one of Paul's arms, my cheek on his chest. *Not every Esen had cheeks,* I remembered.

Which Esen was I?

More to the point, why was I semicollapsed and semiconscious? "Wassh, what's happened?" I said, finding my mouth very stubborn about moving properly.

Instead of answering, which would have been helpful, this evidence I was more or less awake apparently compelled the Human to crush me against the hard edges of his space suit with his other arm and start rocking back and forth.

I mumbled a protest into a mouthful of flexible tubing.

He was too busy talking to hear. As for what he was saying—I woke up the rest of the way realizing Ersh would never have used such language when scolding me. *Humans.*

"I'll be okay," I gasped, when Paul stopped to take a breath. "Let me up."

His ferocious grip loosened, so I lay back again, but he didn't let go. "You—"

"I believe you've adequately covered that, my friend," I said, finding it easier to move my lips now, as though all of my muscles were shaking off some type of paralysis. "What happened? What—am I—?" I struggled to see myself, not feeling anything from this form that made sense yet. He helped me sit up.

I knew those long legs. I was still Feneden. *And hungry.*

"You touched the membrane," Paul explained, hoarsely. "It turned opaque, then disappeared. You—you dropped to the ground. Are you hurt?"

"Stiff," I informed him. "Help me up, please." I clung to his shoulder once on my feet, needing his stability as the dome spun around uncooperatively for a few seconds. "How long was I out? How's the air?"

"Long enough to scare me half to death," he said, under his breath. Louder: "The pressure alarms haven't sounded yet. Must be a pretty slow venting rate. The Feneden took the control rods with them. We can't repair it."

I resisted the urge to start breathing more deeply, knowing it was purely psychological. *Time for that later,* I decided.

Paul had other priorities as well, which including a typically stubborn desire for details. "Esen, the membrane, Kearn's trap, it worked, didn't it? You couldn't cycle to escape."

Pulling free, I scowled up at him, feeling the cilia on my head lay flat as well. "I didn't have time," I corrected. "There was a flash of energy—something that overloaded the nerves and senses of this form. Maybe it would do the same to any form. I don't plan to test it again."

"In other words," Paul said doggedly, "it did work as they intended. You couldn't cycle."

"I didn't try," I objected, not sure why this mattered so much to him. "I see no reason the membrane alone would have stopped me. Now that I know its properties, I would simply cycle into web-form. As myself, I could absorb the energy. Why?"

Paul's eyes were dark and somber. "Because, old friend, this means someone, somewhere, knows enough about a web-being to design a trap capable of subduing you—if only this once."

"And gave it to Kearn," I added uncomfortably, thinking it through. "Kraal tech." There wasn't much doubt in my mind, and I could see echoing agreement on his face. *Well, this couldn't get much worse,* I told myself.

"What else do they have?" Paul speculated, immediately proving me wrong.

Elsewhere

LEFEBVRE'S eyes snapped open. There weren't too many things that could rouse him like this from an exhausted sleep, but a footstep in his supposedly empty cabin was one of them. He lay still, breathing easily, trying to identify the location of the intruder.

There!

He lunged over the side of his bed, sweeping out both arms. The unseen figure gave a sharp cry of pain as Lefebvre's momentum drove them both to the floor in a pile of covers and limbs. He kept one hand wrapped around what felt like a neck, reaching back with the other to snap on the light.

Then Lefebvre let go. "Sir?" he exclaimed, squinting down at Kearn. "Are you all right? What are you doing in my quarters?"

Kearn's eyes were watering, his mouth working without words coming out. Lefebvre offered his hand, but the other Human refused, pushing free of the tangle of covers as he stood up unsteadily. "I w—wanted," Kearn began, then rubbed his throat as though it helped. "I needed to talk to you, Captain. Privately." With a familiar trace of affronted dignity in his voice, he added: "I hardly expected to be assaulted trying to wake you up. That's a nasty habit. You could have killed me."

"Sorry, sir," Lefebvre said, hiding a smile. He offered Kearn his desk chair, then, on a whim, grabbed two glasses and the half-bottle of Brillian brandy Timri had kept from the Feneden for him, before taking the remaining chair. "Drink, sir?"

Kearn blinked slowly. Lefebvre took in the puffy, shadowed eyes, and sallow skin. Kearn looked pasty at the best of times, but now it was as if he hadn't slept for weeks. Without waiting for a reply, Lefebvre poured a generous dollop of brandy into each glass and pressed one into Kearn's unresisting hand.

"Cheers, sir." Lefebvre tossed back his own drink in one gulp, welcoming the soothing burn on the back of his throat. Kearn followed suit, coughing as the alcohol hit, but keeping it down. Lefebvre refilled both glasses before asking: "What can I do for you, sir?"

"Sir?" Kearn stared at the glass in his hand like someone suspecting poison, then downed the next shot in two quick swallows, barely wincing this time. "Sir." He gave a bitter laugh. "As my commission is unlikely to continue once our current mission ends, Captain Lefebvre," he said, matter-of-factly, "you might as well call me Lionel."

Lefebvre didn't argue the point. *As if my career will last any longer,* he reminded himself, toasting the person most likely to destroy it. "Rudy," he invited, before draining his glass.

"Rudy. Thank you." This as Lefebvre filled their glasses a third time. "Rudy, I have a question to ask you," Kearn continued. "Off the record. Just you and me."

Lefebvre kept his face open and neutral, despite the alarm bells ringing in his head. "That's fine, Lionel," he said, "as long as 'off the record' means you aren't recording this."

"This isn't a conversation I want recorded either." Kearn thumped his empty glass rather hard on the desk. "I dream about the Esen Monster every night, you know," he began slowly, heavily. "Fifty years, I've dreamed Her. Sometimes, I win—and everyone believes me. Sometimes," his pudgy fingers reached out into the air, "I almost catch Her, but she escapes, running away. But since I found out Ragem was alive, I've been losing,

Rudy. I've been losing to Her—and She destroys every-thing." *There was,* Lefebvre decided, *something appalling about the haunted look on Kearn's face.* It was the look of a being who has faced his own death over and over again. *No one deserved that.*

"Ask your question," Lefebvre said, knowing he was being a fool, but pitying Kearn nonetheless. He shared the last of the bottle, sucking out the dregs before toss-ing it behind him. "After all, this is just the two of us, Rudy and Lionel, chatting in the dark, having a few drinks." *Fair warning,* Lefebvre decided. *He wouldn't promise the truth or future verification.*

Kearn nodded, as if acknowledging what was unsaid. "I thought She'd killed him, you know," he began, keep-ing his eyes on the glass in his hand, tilting it so the amber liquid flowed from side to side. "Ragem was like you—he didn't take orders, my orders, well. He was bright, smart, ambitious. A gifted linguist, mind you. Truly gifted. He was my second, but I knew he'd outrank me within a few years; less with luck. He seemed to have that, too." Kearn paused, then went on as if the brandy or Lefebvre's attentive silence was a goad. "I didn't like him, but I depended on him. Like you.

"Then our Captain was murdered, and I was pushed into command. I needed Ragem more than ever, but that's when he brought Her aboard. It all changed. I could see it, we all could. She—this Esen—was every-thing to him. We were nothing." Kearn paused, taking a huge mouthful of brandy before going on. "He insisted She was harmless, innocent, well-meaning—even after the killings started. There was nothing I could say to convince him and, then, She killed him."

"But she didn't," Lefebvre said very quietly, remem-bering a delicate, green-eyed face. "You know that now."

"No," Kearn agreed. "She didn't. She's protected him, hasn't She? All these years." He looked up, straight at Lefebvre, a mute demand for the truth.

Lefebvre nodded, once.

Kearn squeezed his eyes shut for several seconds.

Lefebvre waited, more curious than concerned. *Maybe it was the brandy,* he warned himself. *Or the lack of sleep.* He hadn't had much lately either.

Kearn's eyes snapped open. "Has Ragem been Her pet?" he sounded bitter. "A plaything?"

"You knew him," Lefebvre countered. "Do you believe that?"

"Yes." The smaller Human rubbed his gleaming forehead, then sighed. "No, I don't. Ragem told me Esen was his friend. I thought, all this time, She'd betrayed him."

"That's not what happened, is it?" Lefebvre's temper flared. "You're the one who betrayed him, Kearn. You branded Ragem a traitor, cost his family the memory of their son. You're the one who tried to charge him with crimes he didn't commit and, when that failed, spread rumors until no one could separate the truth from your lies."

His outburst brought only a shrug from Kearn, deep in his contemplation of a now-empty glass. "Ragem could have defended himself," he said almost mildly, but his hands were perceptibly shaking. "He could have returned to his family. Instead, he chose to hide, to leave everything—for Her. Why?"

"I don't know," Lefebvre said, hearing the truth in it. Paul hadn't explained, not yet, maybe not ever. A tiny flicker of anger burned at that thought, then faded to resignation. "He had his reasons."

"Does She control his mind? Does She rule him by fear?"

"Those must be quite the dreams you've been having," Lefebvre snorted.

"I don't recommend them," Kearn replied, without irony. "Then what is it? What is it about the Esen Monster that could draw such loyalty from someone like Ragem? That's my nightmare, Captain Lefebvre. That I—that I—" Kearn seemed to lose his voice.

"That you've been wrong for fifty years?" Lefebvre finished for him, unsure what was more dangerous: Kearn's vulnerability or his.

Again the urgent glance, this time from eyes filling with tears. "Can you tell me that, Captain—Rudy?" Kearn pleaded. "Have I been wrong? Or is Esen a monster? I'm going to catch her. What will I be facing when I do? My destruction? Do you know?"

"What I know—what I know is that we're both over-tired and need to be fit to deal with the Feneden in the morning. Anything else, you'll have to find out for yourself. Sir." Lefebvre took back the glass, hating himself as he watched the desperate hope on Kearn's face fade to despair alone.

Paul warned there'd be a price for keeping Esen's secret, Lefebvre reminded himself.

He hadn't expected it to be Kearn.

44: Asteroid Midnight

WE'D explored the entire dome and taken turns staring gloomily at the sabotaged vent control. All we had to show for our efforts was a pile of packing material to sit on and, certainly on my part, a greater appetite for what was not present—lunch.

We'd caught up on some news, most of it deteriorating into arguments about which of us should have listened to the other before leaping into situations alone. *On the whole, I decided, we were remarkably even.*

Now we sat, grateful for the warmth of our helmetless suits, although mine was set appropriately cooler than Paul's, and contemplated the lovely spray of stars overhead. There wasn't much else to be done. I was of the opinion the Iftsen would come to check on their asteroid. Paul had doubts, especially once I told him about the inscription I'd seen on the side of The Messenger.

" 'Messenger of Peace and Harmony, donated by the First Citizens' Art Gallery of Brakistem, a work in mixed media,' " he repeated for what had to be the fifth time. "I thought you said it rhymed."

I chuckled. "It has a very nice rhyme in the original dialect. You want me to say it for you?"

"No, I believe you." His gray eyes sparkled with grim amusement. "So Inspector Logan stole a work of art."

"And was very pleased with it, I might add," I said pompously. "Sometimes, there is symmetry, my friend."

He shook his head in amazement. "As long as you're sure the thing's harmless."

"Totally. Except to the backs of anyone trying to lift it. And," I grinned, "to the reputations of those who try to use it."

"Which leaves us with three problems."

We were sitting side by side. At the sudden seriousness in his voice, I turned to face him. "Three?" *When had our troubles multiplied?*

My friend gestured at the view. "Getting out of here. Reconciling the Feneden and Iftsen."

"That's two," I tallied suspiciously.

"Our friend Logan. He may not have his superweapon, but he's still a threat to Inhaven—and to Largas Freight."

I tapped a slender finger against the medallion hanging outside his suit. "I've taken a step or two in that direction," I confessed, peeking up at him through a flash of red eyelids.

Paul raised one brow. "Why am I not surprised?"

Fortunately, my Feneden-self was spared a Human-like blush. "Nothing you'd object to," I hastened to assure him. "I merely—clicked—a bit of information into the right ears."

My friend had a wide, generous mouth, one that smiled particularly well, I'd always thought, with an infectious, warm quality. It was smiling now. "You told the Herd."

"Oh, not just the Herd Logan dropped on Iftsen Secondus," I corrected, smiling back. "I informed the Ganthor Homeworld."

If I'd thought he smiled before, I was dazzled by the warmth in his face now. "That's just—that's just—"

When Paul appeared at a loss for words, I supplied: "That's just brilliant, Esen?"

He shook his head. "I was thinking poetic, but brilliant? Definitely, old friend. Logan's biggest misjudgment. No one deceives the Ganthor on the battlefield." His smile softened, and he put one hand on my shoulder. "That lonely soldier on Minas XII would have appreciated this, Esen."

His praise made me uneasy. *Why was my solution to the least of our problems so important to him?* I asked myself. Of course, it was an ephemeral trait, one Paul had in full measure, to ignore the life-threatening in favor of the emotionally satisfying. *It was a good thing I was here,* I decided, *to make sure he had the right priorities.* "The air is getting thinner," I reminded him, waving one arm at the dome. The venting air was freezing as it escaped, snowing on the rocks and forming a rim of frost along the lower third of that area of the dome's surface, occluding the stars. I'd hoped it would jam up the vent, but the mechanism had a servo heater to maintain an opening. "We have a few hours left before the pressure drops too low for—comfort."

"I know," Paul said, too calmly. I narrowed my eyes, blinking red once or twice before turning my back on him.

"See if you can pry that tank off my suit," I suggested. "We can rig something to keep the pressure up in yours— won't be pretty, but—"

"Esen, we have to talk about what might happen."

I froze, not turning to look at him. *Ersh. I hated that note in his voice.* "I don't need the air," I went on. "Let's get working on this."

I felt his hands on my suit, but they didn't start working on the fastenings of the air tank. Instead, they pulled me around.

"Just listen," Paul insisted.

"This is a good idea. I can—"

"Shut up, Esen." Paul's smile was gone. In its place were deep lines drawn around his eyes and mouth, lines I'd never noticed as prominent before. "If the air keeps venting, I'm going to die." He stifled my involuntary protest with a hand over my mouth. "Listen to me! We both know it could happen. And I've something I want you to do for me."

I nodded, licking blood from my lip as Paul removed his grip: my Feneden teeth were sharper than Human norm. "Anything," I said despondently. "You know that. But you aren't going—"

"Shh," gently. "I want you to use my mass. To assimilate—isn't that the word?—my body into yours."

Whatever I'd expected, it wasn't this. I stared at my friend. "It won't preserve you," I told him, feeling the truth as a sharp wound. "Your flesh would be altered into web-mass. Nothing Human, nothing of you, would be left. No transfer of memory. No remnant of self. Believe me, Paul. I would give anything if that could be, if I could take you into me and—and save you."

Wonder of wonders, he smiled. "I know, Es. I think I understand the process as well as it's possible for an alien to do so. But this is what I want you to do for me. You'll know the moment."

Oh, yes, I told myself bitterly. *I was very good at detecting the imminent death of cells, of the cessation of life,* if not restoring it. "You are my friend," the last came out past a hiccup I couldn't help. "I will do whatever you want. But why this?"

His fingers fluffed the soft, sensory cilia under my skin. I savored the warmth of his touch and the patterns of heat from his face. "I want you to have my mass, Esen-alit-Quar," Paul Ragem said. "And I want you to use it to fly."

I lurched back from the gentle-voiced Human and his horrifying vision. "I won't leave you," I snarled, knowing even as I spoke that he was right, that if we were here long enough to cost him his life, I could escape by spending his mass for propulsion. In web-form I could easily break free of this dome, and soar into space. His body might be enough to take me translight to safety, to a future, to a new life.

Alone.

"There will be," I promised him with utter and complete conviction, "another option, Paul. I don't want to hear this wish of yours again."

"I'll stop if you promise me." *He could be as rock-solid, immovable, and depressingly irresistible as Ersh.* "Promise, Esen."

I dropped my face into my hands, admitting the inconceivable with a nod.

"Good," I heard him say, but with a little break in the word as though he'd been sure I'd argue longer.

I didn't bother telling him he didn't have the air or time for it.

Obviously, Paul knew that as well as I.

Elsewhere

"WE'VE decoded the Feneden transmission, Captain."

Lefebvre ran a hand through his hair, wishing he'd had time to stick his head under the 'fresher. Kearn looked worse than he felt—something Lefebvre attributed more to last night's conversation than the brandy or few minutes of sleep they'd had before this urgent summons to the bridge. Timri stood with the message in her hand, immaculate as always, and looked from one to the other of her superiors as if wanting to ask, but knowing better.

"I'll take that, Comp-tech," Kearn said before Lefebvre could reach for it, almost snatching the sheet of plas. Lefebvre settled one hip against the railing behind navigation, waiting to be enlightened, and stifled a yawn.

Kearn, already pale, looked about to faint as he read. Lefebvre glanced at Timri. Her lips were tightly pressed together and her look was a warning. "Sir?" Lefebvre prompted. "Is it about the weapon?"

"Take it." Kearn's voice was reed-thin, and his hand shook as he held out the message. Then he threw back his shoulders and raised his head to look Lefebvre in the eyes. "I told you this day would come, Captain," Kearn said before turning on his heel and leaving the bridge.

Lefebvre read: "Our congratulations to the Shifter Hunter. Your glorious trap has worked. We have imprisoned the Esen Monster and her Human slave within the asteroid dome, awaiting your arrival. This has been a victory for all of Fened Prime and your Commonwealth. Glory to the Shifter Hunter!"

45: Asteroid Morning

HAVING a painfully empty stomach did offer one advantage I'd never considered. It made a fine distraction from the difficulty I was beginning to experience whenever I exerted my Feneden-self and had to gasp for air.

Not that exerting myself was a problem, I thought, looking over at Paul. There wasn't much room and no reason to move anyway. We'd managed to coax the inner air lock door into opening, then made a snug nest inside from whatever was portable. With the door closed again, we had a bubble of air that wouldn't be vented, although it was mountaintop-thin by the time this plan had occurred to us. Our air tanks raised the oxygen levels near our faces whenever we allowed some to escape. There was nothing we could do about the accumulation of carbon dioxide within this space except refrain, as Paul quipped, from dancing.

In lieu of dancing, the Human might have been meditating, so shallow and slow was the rise of his chest with each breath, but his eyes never left me. Each time I made to speak, he'd close his eyes briefly, *No.*

I didn't dream, but this was nightmare enough for any being. I went through every form assimilated in my memory, searching for anything that could help Paul survive until help came. *If it came.*

There was nothing. I was locked as living flesh, flesh that, with the exception of web-form, was as vulnerable to vacuum as the flesh encompassing the spirit of my friend. I wondered how terrifying I would be to Kearn now.

Soon, I knew, I'd have to assume my natural form. I

could scrub some of the carbon dioxide from our pocket of air before it poisoned his blood, grant Paul an hour or so more of life, while robbing him of whatever comfort my companionship provided. *There wasn't,* I had to admit, *much a blob of corrosive blue jelly could offer in that regard.*

My promise was another reason not to cycle—not until he lost consciousness. I couldn't bear to see fear in his eyes, to be the proof he was about to end.

Memory overwhelmed my sight for a moment, painting his dear face with marks of pain and abuse, merging with the despair of the present. "This is Logan's doing," I said, as unable to save my breath any more than I could keep rage from my voice and thoughts. I felt cilia writhing as my temperature rose with my anguish.

Paul's gaze intensified, his eyes darkening as if he heard more than I said aloud. "Es, when we met, you spoke to me of how each species, each individual, has its limits, that point beyond which none of us can go because of our very natures. I told you mine, as a condition to our friendship. Do you remember?"

Of course I did. "You won't endanger innocent lives."

"Then tell me, Esen, because I must know. Was I wrong to befriend you? Are you capable of killing someone? Will you hunt and kill Logan if I die here?"

"Your definition of innocent appalls me," I said, trying hard to be angry instead of simply terrified.

Paul was implacable. His eyes burned into me like coals. "What will you do? Tell me, Esen. And I want the absolute truth."

I studied his face, needlessly memorizing it, endlessly fascinated by the curve of his eyelashes and the shape of his nose, knowing to each cell how fragile a being formed the other half of my Web. *Fragile in form, yet so much stronger,* I told myself. "The absolute truth, my friend?" I looked up at the stars, imagining where I might go, what I might do. "I will remember you. Always."

His voice was relentless, if gentle. "What will you do?"

I looked back at him, understanding what he needed to know. "Do not fear my grief, Paul Ragem. I would never taint my memory of you with revenge or rage." *As if,* a darker thought intruded, *there could be enough blood to pay for your life, in Logan's flesh or on all the inhabited worlds.*

"Will you go home?"

I flicked a finger at our surroundings, inviting him to share the joke. "Home is where the Web gathers."

"I meant Minas XII."

"When you are gone?" I paused for breath, then shook my head. "I will be alone. I don't think I will be able to stay among your kind for some time." *Seeing echoes of your face, but never you.* I lightened my voice—a difficult feat as my Feneden-self was already gasping slightly. "There are places I may go. Perhaps I will visit the Iberili and sleep with them for a while. Ersh did, once. There's a lot to be said for resting."

Paul was frowning. "Esen, the Iberili hibernate three hundred years at a stretch. You can't disappear that long—you'd lose track of languages, you won't know the cultures—you won't be safe."

"I can relearn what I need," I reminded him. "It just takes time and patience. I have the one and am learning the other. You shouldn't talk so much," I continued, worried about the blue tinge to his lips. "Have a bit of air."

He obeyed, but only so he had the strength to demand almost harshly, "What of the Web of Esen? What about protecting this sector? I thought it was your chosen task. How can you abandon it?"

I shook my head. "As you said, there are those with enough knowledge of my kind to be dangerous. They can deal with any web-being who misbehaves—perhaps better than I could." *My only success in that area having involved far more luck and discomfort than skill.*

"You think we can trust them?" His lips twisted, as if on a bitter taste. *I'd settle for any taste at all, right now,* I thought, inclined to focus on the hollow space down one side as a far more comforting topic than this one. Still, if Paul wanted to spend our air in conversation, he had the right. "We don't even know who it is. Why leave, Esen?"

he asked, as though driven. "Esolesy Ki has a good life, a family—"

He wanted the truth? "It's your family, Paul. Not mine. There would be no belonging," I shook my head, unsure how to help him understand what I knew to my core. "You are the only web-kin. The only one with whom I am truly Esen-alit-Quar. You are all I have."

"Esen." Paul seemed to make some decision, because his voice suddenly firmed. "I am not all you have."

"Lefebvre?" I would have laughed, had I not thought it more likely another sound would come out.

"No."

What was he saying? I surged to my feet, a regrettably silly action as I immediately fell to my knees with dizziness, in control of the need to cycle from this failing form only because of the fresh air from the tank Paul held under my nose. He held me as well, and dropped his face into the air to control his own whooping gasps. I put my hands on his shoulders and pressed my forehead against his.

"What have you done?" I whispered urgently, staring into the one gray eye I could see.

"Esen," Paul told me, his breath warm on my lips, "the faces I gave you in your gift. They are more than my past."

I pushed back so I could see all of him. What I saw wasn't reassuring. There was a hardness there, a determination that had more in common with a doctor about to set a broken leg, than a friend's caring last moments. "What are you saying?" I asked.

"As part of your Web," the Human said with a strange edge to his voice, "it was my role to gather information and prepare it for you. By all I know of you, that makes me the Senior Assimilator."

There was a notion to roll Ersh right off her rocky mountain, I thought, but couldn't argue.

Paul took my silence for agreement. "As Senior Assimilator, I decided our Web needed more."

"More?"

"I knew you'd outlive me. I knew before I chose to return to you, fifty years ago, that whatever we accomplished together had to last longer than I could. Esen—you can't exist alone. And I couldn't allow you to exist in secret." *The air had to be fouler than I thought,* I decided, trying to make sense of what Paul was saying so passionately. "I knew you were young—too young," he went on. "You make mistakes, potentially dangerous ones to you and those around you. You have enemies we don't even know yet. Do you understand? I had to make sure others would be there to protect you—when I was gone. That others would know what I do." He gripped my arms, tightening his fingers as if afraid I was about to run. "Esen, those faces in my gift, are my gift. They all know you. They know all about you. Web-kin, Esen. You aren't alone."

Had I been Human more often, maybe I would have seen Paul's frequent trips away from Minas XII, his network of beings on many worlds, his occasional secrecy, for what they were. *Had I been Human more often,* I told myself grimly, *maybe he wouldn't have done this at all.*

It was never easy, changing vision to see through another's eyes and mind, making the accommodation necessary when my thought processes had to deal with a different set of interpretations once I cycled. The most familiar aspects of one's life took on completely new meanings.

Only this time, I had a choice how to see: *was Paul's gift to me a glorious extension of my Web? Or were those faces a list of spies—a threat I'd have to avoid?*

If I could have refused to see either, to step back to what I'd been, what we'd been together—*the wish of a child.*

From safely unknown among those I knew, the Human had made me known to those I didn't—surrounded by those who might, or might not—my most secret and safest self a fractured and uncertain thing.

Ersh. I wrapped my arms around my torso, rocking back and forth in a reflex this form found comforting, feeling cold inside and out. "What have you done to me, my friend?" I whispered. "What have you done?"

Elsewhere

KEARN was looking at himself in the mirrored tiles of the 'fresher in his cabin when the expected knock on his door came. He closed his eyes tightly for an instant before saying: "Come in, Captain."

Lefebvre entered. Kearn could see his face over his shoulder in the mirror, but didn't detect anything there but respectful attention and a touch of anxiety. "The Feneden have been intercepted by the Commonwealth cruiser, the *Vigilant,* sir. I believe that's the ship you contacted from Upperside?"

It had been N'Klet, but Kearn didn't plan to tell Lefebvre that detail. He brushed a nonexistent piece of fluff from the polished strip of silver topping his left epaulette. "Thank you, Captain. I'll be up to the bridge shortly. Be ready to change course once I confer with the Feneden and the *Vigilant.*"

Lefebvre shut the door, but stayed inside the cabin. Kearn felt his pulse begin to race but clamped his lips together as he turned. "What is it, Captain?" he snapped, quite pleased with the firm sound of his voice. *There was,* he firmly believed, *great benefit in a full dress uniform on important occasions.* It didn't hurt to know a secret or two.

Unfortunately for Kearn's confidence, Lefebvre didn't look like a someone intimidated by gilt or guilty secrets. "Sir. I'd like to know what you're planning to do."

"About you? And Comp-tech Timri?" Kearn asked, sitting behind his desk and hiding a wince as he did. There were, alas, disadvantages to a uniform donned once every decade or so.

Lefebvre shook his head, then pulled up a chair of his own. Kearn stiffened. "About Esen," Lefebvre said. "And Paul."

Kearn wove his fingers together, controlling the urge to run them over his scalp. "Are you going to provide me with any useful information, Captain Lefebvre? Information that has a bearing on my disposition toward either—individual?"

Lefebvre's eyes glinted warningly. "I've always provided you with whatever credible information is in my possession, sir. You know that."

"Yes. Yes, of course you have. Then," Kearn pulled open the desk drawer and brought out the Kraal knife, not needing to watch Lefebvre to sense his sudden attention on the deadly, ornate thing, "then we have nothing more to discuss at this time. I really do think, Lefebvre, that you would learn not to waste my valuable time." As Kearn continued to ramble along, slipping into the familiar phrases of the lecture he'd given to every new arrival to the *Russ'*, his hands were busy twisting the handle from the blade.

He slid both pieces across the desk, soundlessly, and looked at Lefebvre. "So you see, Captain. I'm much too busy for these little chats of yours right now. I'd like you to think for yourself on occasion."

Kearn's mouth was dry. *Would Lefebvre understand what he couldn't say out loud?* They didn't know one another, not in ways that could help now. He heard himself continue babbling, saying the usual meaningless drivel he'd always used to build a safe wall of regulation and rank between them. All the while, Kearn—as fearful and fascinated as when he was forced to watch an Urgian snake handler dance with sixteen cloud vipers amid its tentacles—watched as Lefebvre's blunt, competent fingers lifted the handle, turning it slowly so he could look inside.

Lefebvre immediately glanced up at Kearn, meeting

his eyes with an expression of shock and dismay. He pantomimed tossing the handle over his shoulder, obviously believing, as now did Kearn, that the device within was some type of recorder and transmitter.

"I'm glad you are paying attention, Captain," Kearn continued, while he brought together both fists, then snapped them apart. *Destroy it, but keep the evidence,* he tried to say with his eyes alone. "Now, I think you'd best let me get back to my work, and you look after your end."

Lefebvre's brisk, approving nod was the friendliest gesture Kearn could remember seeing in a long time. He sagged with relief, covering his face with his hands for a moment.

Kearn might have imagined it, but he thought Lefebvre's hand brushed his shoulder before the captain left with the knife handle.

46: Asteroid Afternoon

PAUL was asleep, his head cradled on some filthy material I'd folded into a pillow on my lap. *It was sleep,* I reassured myself, thoughts heavy and slow, running my gloved fingers lightly across his hair. I wasn't entirely sure I could wake him up; on the other hand, remaining conscious held little that was attractive.

It was growing harder to hold form. I'd opened the fasteners on the arms, thighs, and front of my Human-fitted space suit to allow some of my heat to escape. My Fenedenself, while a nuisance in many ways, was considerably more tolerant of a raging fever than most.

Under those conditions, I wasn't surprised to have a hallucination or two. Still, the figure waving at me through the frosted air lock did appear more substantial than I'd been told such things would be.

Paul would know best, I told myself, nudging the sleeping Human. When he didn't stir, and the figure began pounding on the door with a rock, I reached for the control on Paul's suit that would pump out another short burst from the little remaining in his reserve tank.

The air—or the banging—did more than my physical approach. "What? Es?" Paul coughed, then drew three deep breaths from the fresher air rising from the neck of his suit. Awareness flooded back into his eyes and he climbed to his feet, pulling me with him.

This seemed to relieve the hallucination, who stopped pounding and began pointing at something behind me. I looked around, but saw nothing but the other door. Then, I understood and, grabbing Paul's arm, tried to tug him toward the inner air lock control. "They can't come in, Paul, until we get out of here," I explained, surprised when my Human resisted my urging, standing like a statue.

"Who are they?" he said, hoarsely, breaking free of my grip and taking my arm instead. *Who was holding up whom?* I thought, as we both staggered. "I'm not leaving until we know, Es. If they break in—"

"If they break in, you'll die in the vacuum!" I said in horror. The hallucination had started pounding again.

"If they are willing to break in, they don't plan to let me live, do they?" Paul looked down at me, eyes sunken and blue-tinged, cheeks almost hollowed, lips already losing the pink tinge provided by the burst of suit air, and smiled faintly. "Sweet Esen. You know what to do then."

"I won't leave you."

He ignored my protest. "I want you to go to any of the faces—there's contact information in our system. Please, Es. The pass phrase is: 'Ersh wouldn't approve.' It's also the code to identify yourself to them. Remember that."

Remember it? In spite of everything, my friend could make me laugh. I must have said that a thousand times, only to him, only in private. *As for going to one of my so-called Web? That,* I decided, *was something I couldn't promise. Not yet and certainly not in the grip of emotion.*

"How do we find out who this is, beyond dying in front of them?" I asked practically. The helmets had our com equipment; the dome appeared to have very little working gear except the venting system and some lighting. Of course, it had only been a warehouse for a planet-destroying work of art, not a shelter.

The question was answered, not by Paul, but by the hallucination outside. The suited figure's pounding changed to something varied in tempo and force.

It wasn't click speech, I decided, puzzling a moment. Then I recognized a pattern. "Paul, isn't that—?"

He didn't waste time discussing the message, for that's what it had been, nor bother telling me what it meant. "Hurry, Es!" was all Paul spared breath to say as he urged us both to the inner door. *Well,* I thought, *this was a positive sign.*

Paul rested his hand on the control, then put one arm around my slender, Feneden shoulders. "You know—"

"It's likely almost vacuum in the dome?" I finished, and nodded grimly. If the being who'd tapped in a Commonwealth code was a friend—or a rescuer intending to succeed in that profession—I hoped they knew as well.

There was no point in taking a deep breath; the atmosphere in the air lock was almost poisonous now. We pulled sheets of packaging over our heads against the cold and to keep in what breath we took with us, and plunged through as Paul keyed the door open. He whirled to shut it behind us.

We lay flat, hoping what air remained was cold enough to be dense and settle to the floor I waited as long as I could bear before trying to breathe. When I couldn't help but gasp, the air seemed to be leaving my lungs rather than entering it. My heart hammered in my ears, ready to burst with effort. I could feel Paul shuddering against me. Shunting my fear and grief to where I would feel them later— and forever—I prepared to cycle, readying myself to wait for the cessation of his life so I could accept Paul's final gift—and leave this place of death.

Before I could relax my hold on this form and free myself, a large, warm mask covered my face. I hadn't thought air could seem as thick, rich, and absolutely intoxicating as hot spurl, but this was. I heaved in as much as I could hold, feeling new life circulating throughout this form.

Paul? I clung to the mask, pressing my hand over what felt like someone else's, and sat up.

My friend was sitting beside me, his face obscured behind another mask, his hand groping in my direction. I caught it with my free one, and only then looked up to see what trouble we'd traded death to meet.

There were four figures, in Commonwealth issue 'rigs, Human from the way those suits molded to their forms. I could see the face of the nearest one through his helmet as he held the mask on Paul. He was looking at me, smiling broadly, and, when he saw I was aware of him, winked.

I hadn't seen Paul's friend and former crewmate from the *Rigus II* in fifty years. What was Tomas doing on the Iftsen's asteroid?

And why was he winking at me?

Elsewhere

WHILE it made no sense at all, Lefebvre wanted to get out and push—*anything,* he decided, *to make the* Russell III *go a little faster.* Not that it wasn't a fast ship. When Kearn's project had started, he'd insisted on it, citing the astonishing abilities of the Esen Monster in space. But even translight could be too slow when friends were dying.

Still, Lefebvre thought, they'd done what they could. They were retracing their path to the Iftsen asteroid at better than best speed, and they weren't alone. If he glanced toward the proximity monitor, it would be bright red. He'd ordered the piercing alarm shut down, but the visual display couldn't be stopped. Lefebvre shook his head, quite impressed with the gutsy captain of the *Vigilant.* She'd been the one to suggest they link ships, combining their engines for a more than theoretical gain in speed—although they could well be ripped apart in the process. He'd heard Lawrenk Jen had worked up through the ranks as an engineer and sincerely hoped this meant she knew what they were doing.

How long would it take for the dome to vent—how long before the air thinned to uselessness, before the beings trapped within lapsed into unconsciousness and then—? Lefebvre relaxed his grip on the railing. It was only hurting his hand and making his impatience obvious to crew who didn't know Paul Ragem and Esen, who thought this was a rescue of strangers caught in a tragic misunderstanding with the Feneden.

Five of the Feneden were on the *Russell III* right now, confined—politely—to the upper crew galley. Two had eagerly strapped on the translators they'd left behind in order to share their almost hysterical joy, insisting on cheering Kearn as the hero of their kind. The Iftsen weapon was a subject they bluntly refused to discuss. *Vigilant* crew had already boarded and searched their vessel without success before the *Russell III* had arrived—a case of interspecies diplomacy taking a definite second to which ship had the greater armament.

It was painfully clear the Feneden were close to irrational on the subject of the Shifter. The only reason the *Russ'* and *Vigilant* were on their way was because the Feneden had confessed what they'd done—not out of guilt but because they weren't sure a lack of air would kill their monster, and demanded Kearn finish the job.

The lift opened, and Timri stepped onto the bridge. Lefebvre summoned her to his side with a look. She'd been studying Kearn's Kraal device; *another piece of the puzzle,* Lefebvre thought. "Well?" he asked quietly, trusting the busyness of the crew to give them privacy.

"It's beyond anything I've seen or heard of," she told him, her dark eyes troubled. "At a minimum, it was a location tracer. I think Kearn was right to suspect it also eavesdropped, but for the life of me, I can't tell you how something so small could transmit—without our detecting it—let alone send translight bursts. Quite the knife."

"Were you able to disable it?" Lefebvre kept scanning the bridge, checking on each station in turn, making no effort to look casual about it. There was nothing casual about the situation or destination.

When she didn't answer immediately, he turned his head. Timri's face wore a permanent frown these days, as well as new creases at the corners of her eyes. That frown had deepened. "Too risky," she admitted. "I took a thorough scan, then melted it down before we went translight."

Lefebvre's lips twitched. "I believe our good Project Leader was hoping to keep the pretty thing, Comp-tech."

"Then he's still a fool," she snorted. "If I'd made something like that, I would have built in either a trigger to warn me the device was compromised or some sort of destruct mechanism. Or both."

"Dropping out of translight, sir," the nav-tech called in warning.

"Understood. Call Project Leader Kearn to the bridge, Com-tech."

Lefebvre whispered a rusty prayer as the *Russ'* settled herself into real time with an unusual whine. He hadn't quite believed Jen's assurances this would work.

"Status," he snapped, hearing the lift and waving one hand to acknowledge Kearn's arrival.

The reports came in order.

"We've arrived at the asteroid, sir," nav asserted promptly.

Resdick chimed in. "*Vigilant* signals disconnection complete, sir. And, ah, mentions something about setting a record. Sir."

Not that they could claim it, if either captain wanted to keep their posts, Lefebvre thought distractedly, waiting for what mattered. "Scan-tech?"

"Sir, I have the dome. It's—there's no atmosphere registering inside, sir."

They hadn't had helmets, Lefebvre thought numbly. Esen would survive—perhaps she'd already escaped somehow. *Who knew what she could do?* But Paul? Lefebvre felt a sudden helpless anger. Couldn't she have helped him—protected him from the Feneden? *What good was her ability to change form if she couldn't save her friend?*

"We have a ship on the surface, sir."

"Com-tech?" Lefebvre asked, keeping his voice level and calm.

"Yessir." Resdick huddled over his panel, then straightened. "It's a freighter, sir. They've identified themselves as *Vegas Lass.* Largas Freight Lines." Kearn stepped forward, but didn't speak. "They have two survivors, sir."

"Send our congratulations," Lefebvre ordered. Kearn

was quivering—whether from eagerness or in fear, Lefebvre could only guess. *Keep it by the book,* he decided,
knowing the situation was anything but. "Ask if they need
medical assistance."

Kearn had his Monster in reach, witnesses on board,
and a warship standing by. Lefebvre met Timri's look
and understood its meaning completely.

This was it.

47: Med Room Afternoon

THIS was everything I'd feared: a clear sign of Paul's tampering with my secret, an even clearer sign that I had no way to control it. We'd been rescued by the *Vegas Lass,* although I'd yet to see Meony-ro. Tomas, who didn't belong on the *'Lass* any more than my erstwhile office clerk, was back in my life—*or was he?*

Beyond the wink—a commonplace gesture from this easygoing, friendly Human, one I recognized from our shared past—I had no proof Tomas knew who or, more to the point, what I was. That he was here argued collusion with Paul, *since,* I thought wryly, *even the cosmic fates weren't this obvious when meddling.* And how much had Paul told Meony-ro? It wasn't something I could just ask. *Excuse me, but do you belong to the Web of Esen?*

My Web, I thought with significant self-pity, *was supposed to have defined me, to be a sustained sharing between beings of total trust, to be my accomplishment over time. It was definitely not to be dropped piecemeal into my lap, or to contain beings whose very belonging was a mystery.*

Paul, as befitted someone so thoroughly and deliberately devious, had come with me to the *'Lass'* med room, then abandoned me without a word to the tentative ministrations of a crewbeing who had never seen a Feneden, never heard of a Feneden, and was patently terrified I'd turn green and die if he did anything wrong. At least I was reasonably certain this person wasn't in my Web. *If he was,* I decided after five minutes of indecision over an oxygen feed I certainly didn't need, *I didn't want him.*

Finally, I couldn't stand it any longer. "What I really need," I told the Human as kindly as possible, "is something to eat. Please. I'm starving."

He stopped dithering over a selection of stimulants, and looked at me in surprise. "Fem? I'm so sorry. No one—"

"Told you," I completed. "Yes, I'm aware of that. If I could just go to the galley?"

"I'll have a tray brought—right away." He turned as if to run out the door, then stopped and came back. "Ah, diet?"

Not again. I blinked twice, seeing him start each time at the sight of the red lids. "I don't know what's compatible," I admitted with a long, slow sigh. "My physiology doesn't fit within the parameters of what you refer to as theta-class beings. But I'm very, very, very hungry." I didn't think that was adequate to describe the gulf encompassing the left side of my body. "Very."

His face went an interestingly mottled color, as though he saw his first bona fide famous patient dying beneath his hands. "I've done a prelim blood workup. I'll bring a selection that looks safe. But—"

"That would be fine. Right now," I admitted, "even you are starting to look appetizing." My cilia waved as if in agreement, detecting a sudden drop in the temperature of his face and extremities.

"Oh, my," he said faintly, then literally ran out the door.

I started counting under my breath, reaching three before Paul Ragem walked in and shut the door behind him.

"Fem Tilesen. In all the commotion, I don't believe we were introduced. I'm Paul Cameron, of Cameron & Ki Exports."

I narrowed my eyes, lids flickering with stress. *So, like that was it?* I glanced around the med room, as though I could pick out a listening device that easily.

"Hom Cameron," I acknowledged, modeling my voice and expression on the cool, noncommittal grace of a real Feneden. "I trust you have recovered?"

My Human looked better, his skin so pink I assumed the

med had shot him up with everything in the cabinet. *Quick, if likely to cause a metabolic crash later.* "Fully, Fem. And yourself?"

"I will expire within seconds," I informed him, "unless I get something to eat."

His generous mouth lifted at one corner. "Try this," he said, offering me a small, yellowish bar. I took it in my fingers. It looked as appetizing as soap. "Go on. Take a bite. Trust me."

At those words, I put the bar back in his hand.

Had I struck him, I thought coldly, there might have been a similar look of hurt on his face. Since, at the moment, I would have preferred the blow to come from a larger, stronger me, I wasn't sympathetic. "I'll wait for the med, thank you, Hom Cameron," I said, politely.

"Of course, Fem Tilesen. My mistake." Paul's level, controlled voice was so at odds with his stricken look, I was certain he believed we were overheard. "I only hoped to help you get ready for our visitors."

Visitors? I stared at him, wishing—not for the first time— that I could nibble a bit of him and learn what I needed to know. *There were some advantages to how web-beings shared information.*

The opening door made us both jump, but it was only the med, balancing a tray loaded with more of the small, yellow bars and several full glasses of what appeared to be beer. "I was told these were safe, Fem, so I brought as many as we had," the little Human said cheerfully. "These are Engullan crabcakes. There's quite a bit of protein in them. I can't say much about the taste." This last somewhat doubtfully as he put the tray beside me on the examining bench. "Have you eaten, Hom Cameron?" the med asked worriedly.

I dipped one of the cakes into what appeared to be beer, judging they had to taste better that way. Both Humans watched me; the med with a look of anxious anticipation. Paul? He'd schooled his face back to neutral interest, an expression familiar from countless negotiations with greedy traders and entrepreneurs. I knew him well enough to recognize impatience and growing temper, emotions I could match quite easily.

Relying on Ersh-memory—*and making a mental note to never be this ignorant about a form before using it again*—I ran my fingers down the front of the e-rig to expose the mounds of feeding cilia where a Human had breasts. The med made a funny noise in the back of his throat, and I glanced up. "I said I wasn't theta-class," I reminded him, breaking off a piece of the dampened cake and offering to my left mound. The cilia reached out greedily, like the warm fingers of a hungry child, collecting every crumb to convey to my feeding mouth. As I'd feared, the cakes were foul-tasting and dry, while the beer was warm and, to this form, had a heavy aftertaste. Regardless, I shoved a glass of beer as deeply into my right mound as I could manage without spilling it—Human containers leaving a great deal to be desired—and absorbent cilia slipped reluctantly into the liquid.

It was probably the worst meal I'd ever had, but I felt my Feneden-self strengthening with each morsel and sip, so I kept at it with the grim determination of a soldier on the march. Paul, realizing I wasn't about to talk to him anymore, and so without reason to stay, watched my gluttony for a few moments before running a hand through his thick hair like a being driven to distraction and took his leave.

The med, visibly distressed by my eating habits, was even worse company. I sent him on an errand to find fresh clothing, leaving me alone to finish the remaining three dozen crabcakes and four glasses of warm beer.

I waited, giving both Humans ample time to clear the corridor, then put aside the tray with relief and stood up. Before I closed my suit, I shoved a handful of cakes inside the front for my feeding cilia to worry at—this body being far from satisfied. I was ready to go.

Of course, I hadn't thought at all about who else might be outside the door.

Elsewhere

KEARN hesitated, surprised by the being who seemed to just appear in his way. The bedraggled Feneden was as lovely, or more so, than Anisco, despite wearing the remains of what looked to be an e-rig more appropriate for strolling around Iftsen Secondus' market street than a starship's corridors. He hadn't known any of the species was on board the freighter.

She was shorter than the others, peering directly at him through clouds of reddish-brown cilia, and appeared charmingly shy. *A nice change,* he thought, *from other, somewhat difficult members of this species.* He bowed, a bit stiff in his dress uniform, and smiled reassuringly.

The Feneden's eyelids flashed red, then she bowed as well, rising with a smile. "Greetings, Hom Kearn," she said in accent-free comspeak, her tone low and soft.

"Greetings—" Kearn stopped. *She had no translation machine.* "I didn't know any Feneden could—"

She made the universal gesture for quiet, one slender finger over her lips, and slipped her other hand beneath his elbow. Numbly, he let her draw him down the corridor. After taking a look inside, she pulled him into the next room, a storage space barely large enough for them both. "Hom Kearn," she whispered quickly. "The Feneden—my people—need your help."

He sighed theatrically, oddly disappointed. "Please don't start, my dear Fem. I haven't even confirmed if the survivors are who your people say they are. And I've heard enough from Fem Anisco about how much you want me to make sure the Shifter is finally dead."

She seemed to stop breathing for a moment. "And this is why you are here?" she asked finally, her face inexplicably troubled. His arm felt warm under her small hand.

"The Shifter is important and dangerous," Kearn began, tired of the argument and claustrophobic in the tiny room, then, suddenly, released his pent frustration. *If only he could get one of them to understand!* "But the Shifter isn't as important or dangerous as a war. I'm here to make sure the Iftsen—why can't you hear the name!—stop a terrible mistake. You people have to start listening."

Her other hand crept to his arm, resting there lightly, as if a tiny bird dared to trust him. "The Iftsen," she said, her mouth working as though the word burned her lips. "I am listening, Hom Kearn."

His head whirled with relief. "Thank goodness. You have to tell the others. You can't keep robbing the Iftsen. You have to communicate with them. You must stop immediately—and return what you've taken—before the Iftsen find another weapon to threaten Fened Prime." He put one hand over hers, feeling its warmth and the subtle pebbling of subcutaneous scales. "Please. The Iftsen have never been warlike. You—the actions of a few of your people—are driving them to this. There have even been Ganthor involved!" Kearn searched her face, trying to impose some meaning to her thoughtful expression.

"I hadn't thought to find someone so—impassioned—among your kind, Hom Kearn. I believe you are the one I have sought."

Kearn hardly breathed. "Me?" he said faintly.

"You. Did you know, Hom Kearn, that my species sees polarized light?" the strange Feneden asked him. "We see the night stars in the sky, and literally sense our place on our world and within our communities."

Kearn was confused. "What does that—?"

"This ability separates the sentient species of our world from the nonsentient, Hom Kearn. It is the basis of many of our legends. You know of the—Shifter, but do you know of the older beliefs? That all demons come from a land without stars—void of obligations to each other, outside of rules, because they can never feel where they are or where they belong. It is our Hell, Hom Kearn. And one must never talk about demons or admit they exist, lest they hear and take you there."

Kearn felt his eyes widening. "The Iftsen," he breathed, playing the ramifications over in his mind. *The smallest things,* he thought, remembering innumerable such mistakes between species, though none as intense as this. Impulsively, he grabbed the strange Feneden and hugged her. "This is marvelous. This is—"

"A little uncomfortable," she said, easing out of his hold.

"My apologies, Fem. I must go. I must arrange a meeting—Upperside would be best, don't you think?" Kearn rambled, not really expecting an answer. "Somewhere neutral, but with stars. Yes. Lots of stars. But through an atmosphere. A projection, perhaps."

"There's that Iftsen saga about the constellations," she suggested. "The one the Moberans use at their Birthing Moon Festival. That should help prove the Iftsen know astronomy."

"Ideal. Yes, ideal. Part of a formal occasion. It will have to be planned very carefully so the Feneden feel safe." Then, it was as if the universe had shifted on every axis possible. *What Feneden would be familiar with Iftsen sagas?* Kearn could sense the blood draining out of his face and head as he looked into her impossibly blue eyes and knew.

He was in a closet with his worst nightmare.

"Thank you, Lionel," his Monster said ever so gently. Everything went black.

48: Storeroom Afternoon; Hydroponics Afternoon

I LEFT the storeroom door ajar, having no wish to see the poor Human suffocate while he recovered from what I hoped was a simple fainting spell and not a major failure of some body part.

It was, I hummed to myself, *another pleasing symmetry*—a state of balance I always attempted in my life, but rarely managed. *The fates were so seldom cooperative.*

Walking right into Kearn had been a serious shock, not to mention I hadn't been overly pleased to find the Feneden had sent him to kill me, if they hadn't already. But I'd always regretted becoming Kearn's personal demon. *Likely I still was*, I thought rather sadly.

That didn't matter. Kearn had redeemed himself in my eyes the moment he showed he would leave the chase when a true crisis arose. With any luck at all, he would now be able to redeem himself to his superiors and any doubters by finding a solution to the dispute between the Iftsen and their starry-eyed Feneden thieves. *A pleasing symmetry, indeed.*

Ah. The central freight lift was empty. I slipped inside and sent it down. One level. Two. Three. I hit the stop and stood to one side as the doors opened. *All clear.*

The hydroponics room. I almost ran, eager to shed this form and return to Esen, to be invisible, hidden, safe. To be where I could gain the mass I needed without sacrificing a friend.

I keyed open the door, looking over my shoulder. The corridors were conveniently empty. If it hadn't been for the lighting, I'd have assumed it was shipnight and most of the crew were off-station. *Perhaps,* I thought with a shudder, *they were gathered on the bridge discussing what to do with their Shifter.*

Or, I realized numbly as I entered the tank room and listened to the door close behind me, *they could all be here.*

Elsewhere

"I SAID, wake him up!"

Lefebvre waved aside the mutely protesting med—from the look of him, more likely an engine-room-tech on temp assignment, *typical trader economy*—and shook Kearn's shoulders, careful not to bend the silver epaulettes. "Sir?"

Kearn's eyes cracked open. Almost instantly, his hands fastened like claws above Lefebvre's elbows and he pulled hard, drawing Lefebvre down so their faces almost touched. "I saw her!" he whispered desperately. "I saw her!"

That certainly explained finding the Project Leader in a dead faint in a storeroom, Lefebvre thought with some disgust. *What had Esen been thinking?* He broke Kearn's hold with an easy motion, nodding at the med. "Leave us. And close the door, please."

"Are you all right, sir?" Lefebvre then asked, keeping his voice neutral. "I found you passed out in the hallway. Has this happened before?"

"Yes, I'm fine. No. It wasn't the hallway," Kearn said roughly, struggling up. Lefebvre helped him sit, then stand. "And no, of course it hasn't happened before. Help me up!"

"Are you sure you should—so soon?"

Kearn scowled furiously at him. "Are you deaf, Lefebvre? Didn't you hear what I said? I saw her! Esen's on this ship! Now!" He began walking to the door, then staggered; Lefebvre steadied him before he toppled to the floor.

"Now, sir," Lefebvre said in his most persuasive voice, "you know that's impossible. She's not here."

"Not here?" Kearn looked ready to faint again. "Of course she's here. They found her—they found Ragem in the dome—"

"No, sir," Lefebvre said in his most reasonable voice. "The *Vega Lass* came after two of her own crew—they'd been on Iftsen Secondus for the Festival and were caught up by the Feneden. The crewmen aren't pressing any charges. Timri's looking into why the Feneden would have mistaken them for—"

"No!"

"Please calm yourself, sir. I spoke to them just now. They're a bit shaken, but none the worse for the experience. I was on my way to inform you when I found you unconscious." Lefebvre paused. "Maybe you were dreaming."

"I was not! The Esen Monster was as close to me as—as you are now! She took me into the storeroom."

"The storeroom? Sir, you were in the hallway." Lefebvre almost choked. *Esen!*

Kearn frowned. "I was?" He shook his head, looking troubled. "I remember. I was in the hallway, then she led me into the storeroom."

"Why would she do that, sir?"

"Do what?"

Lefebvre began easing Kearn back to the cot. "Why would she take you into the storeroom, sir? Are you quite sure that's what happened? After all, I found you lying in the hallway, alone. You gave me a scare, sir."

"The hallway?" Kearn seemed numb as he acquiesced, his hands fluttering about as though he'd forgotten them. Lefebvre wondered guiltily if he should call back the med. "It—it all seemed so real—" Kearn's voice trailed away. "And She was a Feneden, Captain. A beautiful Feneden, with tiny hands and eyes the bluest blue."

"Such things can appear very real," Lefebvre said

soothingly. "I think you should rest, sir. Perhaps the med can give you a sedative. Things might seem clearer if you relax."

Kearn nodded, lying back and closing his eyes. His pursed lips moved in and out, as though he was re-playing something said in his sleep. Suddenly, his eyes opened wide and he lunged up, grabbing Lefebvre by the front of his uniform.

"No time! We have to hurry!" Kearn said almost fran-tically. "I must arrange an immediate meeting on Up-perside between the Feneden and the Iftsen. I've learned what's causing the difficulty between their cultures. It's imperative they be dealt with promptly."

"Learned? How?"

Kearn's expression worked its way from pride to shame and settled on deeply perplexed. "My dream," he admitted. "In my dream, the Esen Monster spoke to me. She had unique insights into the—the physical nature of the Feneden and why it was preventing them from deal-ing with the Iftsen." He paused and shook his head, then looked at Lefebvre pleadingly. "I—I don't understand how or what happened. Why would she tell me—me, of all beings? Why would she do that?"

"Anything can happen in a dream, or hallucination," Lefebvre told him, both amazed and appalled by the risk Esen had taken. "Maybe your subconscious used this—image—to pull the facts together from your research. No matter how you've done it, sir, this could be the break-through in understanding we've all been waiting for. Con-gratulations."

"Congratulations?" *It was as if a new person was climbing out of the shell of Lionel Kearn,* Lefebvre thought, watching the transformation with awe. Kearn sat up, his shoulders rose and straightened, his head lifted. "Captain Lefebvre."

"Yessir."

"Have the Feneden meet me on the *Vigilant,*" Kearn ordered sternly. "We'll be going directly to Iftsen Secon-dus to get to the bottom of this mess. Meanwhile," he hesitated, then went on, "meanwhile, I want an immediate and complete search of this ship and the dome for the Esen Monster and her accomplice. I know. I know," Kearn said, forestalling Lefebvre's protest. "It had to be some sort of hallucination—I've been under a lot of stress, lately. Too much for any one being to bear. But we have to satisfy the Feneden and find out what's been happening here. You'll be in charge of it, Captain, until I'm finished with my diplomatic duties. Then I'll be back on the *Russ'*." There was a definite gleam in Kearn's eye. "Count on it, Captain."

"Yes, sir," Lefebvre said, saluting crisply, hardly daring to hope it was going to work, abruptly wondering if it was like this all the time for Esen and Paul.

Kearn took a couple of steadying breaths, then stood. Gathering himself, he went to the door. Lefebvre opened it for him and stood to one side. As Kearn passed, he slowed, then stopped. "On occasion," he said very quietly, not looking at Lefebvre, "I have received messages—information—from an unknown supporter in my search. This information has always been very accurate."

Explaining a few things, Lefebvre thought. "Should I be watching for more of these in your absence, sir?" he ventured.

Kearn shook his head, once. "With the—theft—of my supporter's 'gift,' I imagine those messages will stop. But I thought you should know, Captain, just in case. I leave how you deal with any future contact to your discretion." He rose to his full height. "I have a war to prevent."

49: Hydroponics Afternoon

THERE were five Humans waiting for me in the hydroponics room of the *Vegas Lass*. Those to my left had faces
which swam up from my memories of Paul's gift. One was
an older male, lean, with the look of a working spacer despite being dressed like a diplomat or politician about to
greet royalty. The other was female, perhaps the same age,
tall and dark, wearing a Commonwealth uniform with comp
specialist bars on sleeves and legs, and inscribed on one
pocket: *Russell III*. I found myself pitying Lefebvre and
Kearn, carrying a spy with them. I wondered, among so
many questions, if either knew.

Two more stood to my right, these faces from my own
past: Tomas and Lawrenk Jen, crewmates from Paul's original ship, the *Rigus III*. Tomas wore civilian garb as if planning a night out in some insystem bar. His face matched
my memory almost perfectly, though its cheerfulness was
suggested only by the creases that usually marked dimples.
Lawrenk Jen was now a captain, Commonwealth military,
with the *Vigilant* written in small silver script along her collar. Her hair had silvered along both sides and her face
looked less open than I remembered, as though more than
my secret had burdened her heart.

Centered, and I doubted by accident, was the director of
this play, Paul Ragem, friend, and *now,* I realized with a
sense of despair, *my keeper.* He'd taken the time to change,
wearing a dark blue shirt against which my medallion shone
as though on display.

Being the worst-dressed being here was not helping my mood.

I took a step closer, then halted. The tanks were stilled; perhaps to check their depths. *All of these Humans,* I thought with a sudden, intense shame, *would know what to look for.*

Paul opened his mouth and then closed it again, as if, having planned all this, he couldn't remember the script. The older Human shot a glance in his direction, then took a half step toward me. "Ersh wouldn't approve," he intoned, as if he could have any idea what he was saying.

Or how it insulted my memories and hers to hear her name in his Human mouth. I glared at Paul.

The words, my icy look, or both stirred Paul from whatever reluctance or outright paralysis had gripped him. He took a matching step forward and nodded brusquely at me before gesturing to the Human who had spoken. "Esen, I'd like you to meet Councillor Sandner, member from Inhaven Prime, Comp-tech Mesa Timri from the *Russell III*," the woman, "and you know Tomas and Lawrenk."

There followed one of those deadly silences in which no one knew what to say that wouldn't be catastrophic. I certainly didn't, never having imagined facing a group of aliens who knew the real me.

Tomas suddenly grinned, complete with dimples. "Quite an improvement over Old Fang Face," he said slyly.

I couldn't quite smile, but I saw Paul's grateful look to Tomas. The Human referred to a night I treasured and remembered often, even if I'd never learned to relish the nickname he'd given me on our way to celebrate Christmas. "Less than you'd imagine," I admitted frankly. "Fussy eater and prone to hysterics."

Something eased in Lawrenk's face. "It's you, Es?" she breathed, a reassuring hope in her voice.

Paul was trying to get my attention. I gave it to him and saw his lips form the word "please." His eyes were almost desperate.

I nodded, feeling there was very little left to lose anyway, being heartily tired of this form and these filthy clothes, especially since gaining a trail of itchy crabcake crumbs down my torso and leg. Releasing my hold, I cycled, passing through web-form quickly enough they should see only a flash of blue . . .

And stretched to my less-than-considerable height in my birth-form, the Lanivarian. *Fortunately*, I thought, *this stomach was empty.* I shouldn't get seriously spacesick for a few moments at least.

Paul's companions handled it well. *Probably better than I,* I thought, gripping this form tightly. No outright fainting, very little in the way of shocked looks. In fact, Tomas and Lawrenk looked openly delighted, like children shown a magic trick.

I relaxed slightly, by no means pleased to perform for strangers, but happier in a form physically braver and far better at growling. And one I understood thoroughly. I looked cross-eyed down my muzzle. I needed a shave; then again, I needed clothing. *Nothing was perfect.*

The thought repeated itself as I looked steadfastly into the eyes of the one being I'd admitted into the Web of Esen, the one I'd trusted to the limits I was capable. My lip lifted over a fang and stayed that way. It wasn't a smile.

"Why are you here?" I asked, not working hard at sounding pleasant. *They,* I reminded myself, *had more to prove than I.*

Sandner, not Paul, answered promptly. "We came to meet you, Esen-alit-Quar. We've been working on your behalf for many years. When the chance came to greet you in person—"

This arrangement of Paul's would never be a Web, I thought wildly, taking an involuntary step back. *This Human wasn't sharing with me; he was lying.*

Paul knew. He put up a hand to silence the other, then offered it to me. "Easy, Es," he said quickly. "Give them a chance. Please." To the other Human, he snapped: "Esen is older than your grandparents—she's spent that time living in secret from us. Do you think it's a pleasure to meet you? Get to the point, or she'll leave."

I cocked my head to one side, just a bit, listening to Paul's voice. Controlled, smooth, but defensive. I sniffed.

Under various perfumes and the cloying green from the tank, I could detect the scent of stress. Not fear. I flared my nostrils slightly, dipping my snout toward his hand. *Anger.*

So, I thought, schooling my face into something more patient. Paul wasn't totally in charge here. There was a threat to me—and a threat to him. I dropped my jaw in an almost smile. *This, I could understand.*

"Forgive any misunderstandings, Fem." Sandner, without benefit of my senses, still appeared perceptive. "If you would prefer me to be blunt, I will. We came here to observe you. We hadn't planned our observations to—interfere with you in any way."

"You were spying on me," I corrected. "You took advantage of my leaving Minas XII. But you didn't expect to get caught."

Paul smiled that smile I knew gave our competitors nightmares. "The *Vegas Lass* was tracking me," he explained. "It was near the asteroid the entire time. They could have pulled us out of the dome the minute I gave the word."

"Gave the word—how?" I asked, struggling to put that horrid experience together with what Paul was trying to tell me. Nothing in the combination made sense.

Paul flipped over his medallion. I remembered him showing me the tiny scrambler device he'd said was to keep a Kraal sensor from detecting the web-mass within. *He'd never said that was all it was.* "They were listening, Esen," explained the person who always swept our rooms for eavesdropping devices. *Who better to plant one?* I thought.

I curled my lips back in full threat and would have gladly nipped him if Paul had left his hand in range. "Them, I understand."

Sandner looked embarrassed. "Don't blame Paul, Esen. We—those in this room—gave him an ultimatum. We knew what your kind could do if you wanted to. Paul's belief in you—after a while, it wasn't enough."

"We had to know for ourselves that you were safe," Timri went on. "We had to know we were doing the right thing by helping you."

"Safe," I snarled. "As in ways to destroy me. As in testing your trap."

"No!" This came from more than one. Paul stopped them with an upraised hand, saying, "Esen, I swear to you, that had nothing to do with anyone here. There was no intent to harm you in any way. It really was Kearn's trap. Timri says it came from a Kraal backer, someone with the technology to follow the *Russell III* and obtain Kearn's results."

"So what was the point?" One disadvantage to my Lanavarian-self, in addition to the minor complaints beginning in my stomach in response to the artificial gravity, was a need to pace when emotional. I made it appear relaxed, walking to the railing as though contemplating the smelly, green-stained water. Then I turned, my paws wrapped around the railing so I could lean back comfortably. I could see Paul's eyes narrow in understanding, and he shook his head the tiniest amount. I agreed. I didn't want to cycle again, but this form would soon become a nuisance. It seemed wise to stay close to living mass that didn't have a name. "You listened to us in the dome instead of helping us. Why?"

"The Web—" Sandner started to say.

I interrupted him, my ears flat to my skull in full threat. "Don't ever use that word to refer to this group. The Web of Esen does not contain you. My Web—" I glanced at Paul. He gazed back at me with the oddest look of hopelessness on his face. *Foolish Human,* I thought with exasperation. *I'd rarely agreed with my former web-kin twice in the same day. Did he not know by now the strands of the Web are severed only in death?* "The Web of Esen consists of two," I finished, rewarded by the flash of gratitude in his eyes. I kept my ears back, not done glaring at him.

"The Group," Sandner continued, the smoothness of this transition likely more to do with his years in politics rather than space, "thought if you were placed in a situation where Paul's life appeared to be threatened, and you had a clear target, it would show us—"

"Show you what?" I interrupted again, completely exasperated. "For all you knew, my species might not have had comparable emotions to yours at all. An Ervickian in a life-threatening situation with beloved crèche-mates will eat them, and they're civilized! How humanocentric are you?"

"It wasn't that, Es," Paul said carefully. "I had to prove to them once and for all that you were incapable of violence against others. The Feneden's trap was the perfect opportunity." Paul seemed to become oblivious of the others, stepping forward until he could reach out and run his hand along the side of my jaw. I growled warningly, but permitted it. "Esen, it wasn't fair. But it wasn't a trick. I was prepared to die if that's what it took. I knew you'd show them your true nature—and you did."

"However," Paul continued with a measuring look at the others, "You weren't the only one being tested. And I believe I failed."

"Of course you did," I said. *Sometimes*, I thought almost happily, *the universe could suddenly rearrange itself into something reasonable.* I licked my friend's hand. "I wasn't to know about them—was I? They were supposed to remain a secret from me. That's why Tomas came so quickly to our rescue."

"I came as soon as I realized he was going too far," Tomas protested, his normally ruddy complexion pale with the memory. "We were convinced, Paul. You didn't need to keep going like that."

"No," I said gently. "You may be Paul's friend, Tomas, but you didn't come because you thought Paul was about to die. You came because you heard Paul start to tell me about you, about all of you." None of them appeared to even breathe. Paul's hand was on my shoulder, firmly aligning himself with me. *And I with him, as it should be, I thought almost contentedly.*

"You didn't know until you overheard us that he'd given me your faces," I went on, seeing it clearly, "so I'd recognize you before you could recognize me. Paul gave you to me in case I needed you—or you turned on me."

"I don't see why any of you were surprised," Paul said to them, looking from one to the other. He didn't sound angry, only disappointed. *Like Ersh*, I thought, *the Human had sufficient personal charisma to turn that into something completely devastating to the recipient.* "I warned you when this started, if you ever threatened Esen, if this Group of ours began to turn from support and help to anything else, I'd stop you. No matter what it took."

To their credit, all four looked ashamed. My stomach lurched, an unnecessary reminder my time in this form was limited. I surveyed the unhappy Humans, perceiving the Web-like bonds between them. None had meant any harm to me or to Paul. All, like Kearn, believed they were protecting others.

No wonder Paul had been angry when I mistrusted the source of his gift, I thought, replaying that scene. But it hadn't been anger at me. It had been anger at those he had trusted, who'd forced him to take this step against them. *And,* I thought, *it was anger at himself, for taking my side against his own.*

It was, I growled to myself, *a typically Human mess.*

As the most civilized being present, I would have to do something about it. I took my paws from the railing, thinking wistfully of the restful depths of the tank, and stepped forward. "Allowing Paul to know my true nature was the most difficult thing I had ever done," I told them. "If it hadn't been a matter of life or death, I wouldn't have been able to take that risk.

"Since then, I've learned to value Paul as part of my Web: a relationship closer than your family groupings or life pairings. Within a Web is the sharing of—" I stopped before saying flesh, "—essence, of one's true nature. That is what Paul is to me and I to him. This is why I cannot accept you into my Web, although I value your help." I drew in a breath and said what I'd never dreamed I'd say. "It is possible, one day, I will. I need to understand you, and you, me. Starting with why."

Sandner spoke first. "We each have our reasons for helping Paul—and you—and our own ways of doing it. I've used my position in government to discourage those hunting for you, with Tomas' help. Timri, here," she nodded, "has done the same on the *Russell III.* Kearn was the obvious threat to your identities, but there have grown to be others, less easy to detect. Captain Jen routinely patrols the edges of Kraal space, and uses her position to listen for rumors there. There are more of us—some involved in funding Paul's network, some more active."

Funding? I kept my tail low with an effort. Paul had access to virtually limitless funds. If he had his contacts generating their own, that could only mean he'd deliberately kept this from them. I couldn't help but glance at him. His face had that innocent look, the one that accompanied exploding presents. *Perhaps,* I told myself with a depth of relief that was almost unnerving, *there were still secrets.*

"There are three levels of contacts, Esen," Paul elaborated. "The first are the ones you already know: they gather data for us but have no idea who we are or what we do with the information. The second are those like Meony-ro. He's trusted and knows we guard against a recurrence of what happened when Death came through this sector. He doesn't know about web-beings or you, Es.

"The third are those faces I've shown you, plus Tomas and Lawrenk. If I'd put their faces in the list, you would have known what I was doing before I was prepared to tell you." Timri's gaze slid his way at the same time as I thought: *what of Lefebvre? And she knows you've left him out. Interesting.*

Secrets inside secrets. I had the feeling it was going to be a long time before Paul completely trusted these individuals again, if ever.

"Why you, Sandner?" I asked.

"I was on Hixtar Station when that—that thing began attacking shipping in the Fringe," he answered. "I lost—people I cared about." Something in the abrupt words reminded me of Joel Largas, whenever memories of Death's attack on his convoy came back to haunt him. "You saved a lot of lives, Fem Esen-alit-Quar, when you killed it."

"Esen, please," I said impulsively. "The full name—well, it makes me feel I'm in trouble."

Sandner looked startled, then half-smiled. It warmed his eyes nicely. "Esen."

"I was on the Tly blockade when this Death creature attacked us. Later, I saw you help kill it." This surprising comment came from the woman named Timri. She raised her chin. "I was the first one Paul trusted with your secret. I'd tracked him to Minas XII, when he was still searching for you. He found me, instead."

Tomas grinned. "I found Paul. We accidentally took the same transport to Ultari. When I spotted him in the lounge, I couldn't believe my eyes. Then I pestered until he had to trust me or put me out of my misery." I didn't look at Paul, but I found it singularly unlikely my very cautious Human would actually take any transport carrying an old acquaintance, let alone spend time sitting in a public area. There was a definite pattern here, whether these Humans noticed it or not.

It was as though they were drawn to confessions. Lawrenk Jen spoke next: "I'd helped Kearn convince Joel Largas to send a ship to the ag-colony. I was hoping Paul was the one signaling. When the Largas ship didn't find him, I was—angry." She looked suddenly ashamed. "I took leave and chased down Char Largas, ready to accuse her of cheating us and abandoning Paul. You can imagine how I felt when Paul met me at the door of their home."

They all fell silent. From their expressions, they were awaiting some pronouncement of doom. While I appreciated the irony of being on the other side of this type of worry for a change, I didn't know what they expected me to do. Then Paul winked at me, and pointed with his chin to the tank.

I shuddered, a movement that brought up the fur along my spine. "Are you sure about this?" I asked Paul outright. "You've seen me. I'm not exactly—" I reached for a word, settling for a lame: "comfortable."

Sandner turned pale as a ghost, Timri shivered as though seeing one, while Lawrenk and Tomas looked determined. Paul collected nods from them one by one.

"Show them, Es. Then hide. I'll look after things here."

Another test, my friend, I thought. *Do you realize it?* I met his earnest, intense eyes and knew he did. I didn't blame him. This was a Human need: to ask me to demonstrate my utter trust, not of these relative strangers, but of him.

As I cycled into the perfection of my web-form, losing sight, sound, and gaining all else, I gave it without hesitation.

Elsewhere

LEFEBVRE put his feet on his desk and pulled up the file on his comp. The messages Kearn had received from his mysterious Kraal friend had disappeared from every record; in the process, they'd tunneled their way through nearby data like Kita worms in wood.

Still, like worms, the messages had left holes. There wasn't a detectable pattern, yet, but it was just the type of thing Timri enjoyed working on by the hour. When she came back from visiting Paul, he'd set her on it.

Lefebvre was disappointed not to see Esen or Paul again. His search of the *'Lass* hadn't turned them up on the corridor to the lift, on the lift itself, or in the air lock to the *Russell*'s shuttle. That was perhaps to be expected, but that was as much searching as he'd been prepared to do.

This file, on the other hand, contained a great deal that was interesting and extensive. Lefebvre gave a sigh of pure delight.

Here, he told himself smugly, *was a monster worth chasing.*

50: Office Morning; Dump Afternoon

THE thing about vacations, I decided, *was that when you returned home, it seemed as though you hadn't left.*

I walked into the office of Cameron & Ki Exports unsure what I expected to find, but it wasn't a desk piled head-high with work which anyone else surely could have done, and a staff who said hello, then plunged into detailed descriptions of their problems without one question about our trip.

It was absolutely and wonderfully normal.

There were a few changes and surprises. I had to promote Meony-ro immediately, finding it distinctly unnerving to watch him twirl a stylus when I'd seen the same move with a blaster rifle. It worked out well. Paul and I had never bothered with a driver before and, given the traffic rules on Minas XII, it was reassuring to have one capable of hijacking a starship.

The Panacians had, inexplicably, sent a long formal letter of apology to Paul Cameron. It had confused the staff, as the letter never did say what the apology was for, but, as it included a generous renewal of several contracts, they took it as a sign we'd done something odd but positive during our vacation.

Janet Chase was gone. She and her mercs had arrived in the shipcity, but their transport had been jumped as it passed over the far edge of the Dump. Joel Largas had a reward out—and expressed his personal interest in her capture. Paul and I thought it most likely the combination drove her out-system immediately. Even the Dump didn't have that many hiding places.

As for things hidden, most of our luggage, including the dreadful hats, returned piece by piece from wherever it had traveled without us. There were several odd stamps on the outsides, and a streak of purple slime on the inside of my largest trunk. I sent it all to be cleaned and settled into picking up the threads of my life as Esolesy Ki.

It was on the fourth day, when the events of the past weeks might have seemed like a dream to anyone with a lesser memory, that Paul came into my office and closed the door behind him.

"It's been done," he said, dropping into the chair across from my desk. It was one of his favorites, lumpy and with a fuzzy texture even a Ket might find obnoxious. "All we have to do is visit Diales and set things in motion." Paul yawned, stretching both arms over his head, and slouched deeper into the chair. "Had a great dream last night," he announced, grinning at me. There appeared to be very little of the executive, father, or deep, dark conspirator in him this morning. *Humans back in their own beds,* I thought affectionately, feeling quite rested and inclined to be cheerful myself.

I showed a tusk. "What about?"

The grin widened. "There was a lab—a really dirty, smelly lab—hidden on a really dirty, smelly planet so far off the beaten track you probably couldn't get spurl if you tried. And in that lab, our good friends Chase and Logan were feverishly trying to get The Messenger to work, full of evil plots to take over the universe and corner the market for those hideous porcelains. Needless to say, they weren't having much luck."

"Porcelains?" I repeated doubtfully.

"Dreams are like that," Paul explained unhelpfully. *This entire dreaming business was confusing.*

"I like it," I decided after some consideration. The Ganthor were certainly looking for Logan—and would make a considerable noise when they found him, having every in-

tention, I knew, of both celebrating and letting other employers know the penalties for betrayal.

"I have news—it isn't from a dream," I told him contentedly, "but you'll like it. Sandner and Joel Largas have
been invited to meet with the Tly Deputy Minister." Joel
had described it as a long-overdue bootlicking and, from
the look in his eyes, planned some blackmail as well. "High-
level negotiations about shipping and Inhaven," I tempo-
rized. "It's a start."

Not fooled for an instant, Paul's eyes twinkled. "Joel will
have them cleaning freighter holds by the time he's done.
I'd love to be there."

"You could go," I said, flicking my ears in his direction.

"Not," he slapped the arms of the chair and rose abruptly,
"not until I'm satisfied things have settled. You ready? Diales is skittish about clients being late."

I put an unbeaded bag around my neck, a suitably plain
accessory for a visit to the Dump. It had to be in person,
given the inconvenient issue of having Diales set the idents
to my Lishcyn eyeballs, blood, and bone. Later, Paul would
have to reset the system to obey several other biological
Esens, something the notorious but respected Diales didn't
need to know.

Just then, the com on my desk buzzed. I glanced at the
code. "It's for you—from the warehouse."

Paul looked at his chrono and muttered under his breath,
but came anyway. There had been several—interesting—
occurrences during his absence, including the, to him, mysterious return of some fleeceless Rillian sheep, and I knew
he'd be unable to resist finding out what else might have
gone awry.

I casually strolled to the office door to give him privacy,
then paused to check the fall of my least favorite silks. I
flicked one ear. Whatever the call was about, the voice on
the other end was certainly excited about something. I
watched Paul throw out his arms in exasperation.

I slipped out the door altogether.

*   *   *

While my Lishcyn-self's platter-sized feet weren't good for sneaking, they could cover a fair amount of distance in a dignified hurry. I waved good-bye to the staff, who barely noticed me, and made record time reaching the lift to the aircar parking. No sign of Meony-ro. *Even better.* His Kraal training seemed to be coming out more and more lately, so I'd anticipated some difficulty avoiding his company. *Definitely,* I thought again with some satisfaction, *not an office clerk.* One day, after a large amount of wine, I might ask him why his tattoos were so faded, and why he was in the Fringe.

The Kraal popped his head out of the aircar. *Fates and the laughter of cosmic gods,* I muttered to myself, *was nothing going to work today?* I didn't have time to argue with him.

"Meony-ro, I'd like to leave immediately—" I began. "Nothing's wrong," I puffed hurriedly as the Kraal looked alarmed. I supposed my running was a bit out of character, although you'd have to know Lishcyns well to recognize this shambling gait as a run. *Ersh, this form was slow.* "I don't want to be late."

"'Bout time you got here," said Paul, coming out from behind the aircar.

How'd he—? Then I noticed the door to the stairs was still open. I managed to slow my momentum in time to stop before running into either of them. "Paul," I said intelligently. "I thought there was some crisis in the warehouse."

He waved me courteously into the aircar, smiling for Meony-ro's benefit, then said for my ears only, "Nice try."

Wel, it had worked once, I thought, tempted to be petulant, but aware I had about as much chance now of getting Paul to stay behind as I had of getting my unhappy first stomach to settle. *But I'd tried.* There hadn't exactly been a lot of time to prepare. *Around ephemerals,* I noticed, *events seemed to happen considerably faster than anticipated.*

As Meony-ro drove us from Cameron & Ki to our meeting place, I thought about last night. Paul and I had shared concerning the Group, as they now seemed to be called. *Anything,* I'd decided, *was better than thinking of that conglomeration of strangers as members of my Web.* It had been Human-style sharing, a long, slow conversation over more than one bottle of Inhaven wine, free of apologies. *What was done, was done,* as Ersh had been overly fond of saying.

And, we'd decided, what was done had to be dealt with. First, a new security system, hence today's appointment in the Dump. Paul couldn't be sure what might have been compromised by those members of his Group who'd felt driven to test my limits, and agreed with my somewhat hysterical wish for privacy. It would have to be state-of-the-art, he warned me. Some of the Group were quite expert in such matters—including those responsible for the definitely illegal treatment Paul had received to protect our secret from truth drugs. *Not news I'd taken well,* I recalled. He'd tried to reassure me by revealing that every member of the Group had undergone the treatment.

That hadn't worked. I'd felt all of my centuries bearing down as I'd realized how this turned responsibility for their brief lives back upon me. *If they'd risk themselves to keep our secret, it was up to me to ensure they never were forced into that position.* The Web of Esen protected what lived and thought. To that extent, Paul's Group was part of me now, whether I'd wanted them or not.

Hence the next step. If these individuals were to be the friends and helpers Paul had intended, rather than terrified keepers or worse, I would need to introduce them to Esen, one at a time. Paul, needless to say, hated this idea, but I'd brought him around to my point of view. *Taking most of the night—and the wine.* He'd been most unhappy. After all, thanks to his betrayal of the rest, their faces were safely in my memory. Paul had carefully ensured that, with the exception of Esolesy Ki's handsome visage and my Ket-, Feneden-, and Lanivarian-selves, the Group did not know mine.

It protected my identity in thousands of forms, but it was a perilous ignorance. No matter how much they believed

Paul—who was, beyond doubt, exceptionally persuasive—I knew each needed to see me in order to believe, to understand. It was the unknown that bred nightmares in ephemeral species; I'd had enough of being a monster. It wouldn't be necessary or wise to show all I could do or become. *I wasn't,* I'd argued relentlessly, *being foolish.*

In the end, to convince Paul, I'd cycled into my Human-self. He'd stared at me for a long time, as if I were some apparition, ultimately forced by his own innate honesty to admit that it was this form, this Esen, that no Human could fear. *Underestimate, yes. Become annoyingly overprotective, quite possibly.* But these were judgments I could live with, if it meant those who knew my secret felt safe from me.

Besides, I thought, a good night's sleep later, peering out at the clouds rubbing the shoulders of the Sweet Sisters, *it was going to be a great excuse to travel.* Minas XII, however interesting, no longer felt quite enough.

"So, Esen," Paul said in that dogged tone that meant he was determined to get an answer, "why did you try to leave me behind this time?"

I was surprised he'd waited this long, and showed a tusk in amusement. "Leave you behind?"

"Es." His eyes were darkening. *Not,* I decided, *a good sign.*

A little honesty usually helped. "I don't care to risk others anymore, Paul-friend," I told him, knowing he'd hear the sincerity in that. My ears flicked back and forth. "The Dump isn't a safe place. I'd have left Meony-ro, too, but he's about as easy to shake off as a Carasian sandtick."

His lips tightened. "Since when was the Dump safe for you?"

"For Esolesy Ki?" I shook my head. "But that's not all I am, is it? If I've learned anything from our—vacation—it's that it's easier to look after myself without you." I heard the words fall between us and knew I'd caused him pain. "Paul, I'm—"

"For a being of your advanced years," he said matter-of-factly, "you still have so much to learn, Es." Surprisingly, he didn't look upset. His fingers stroked feather-soft under my chin, settling my stomachs. I leaned into the caress, half-closing my eyes. "You can't leave friends behind, just to keep them safe. It doesn't work that way."

"I've noticed," I sighed.

Paul took his hand away and pulled open his coat to show me the weapon holstered underneath. "Let me take care of myself," he suggested dryly. "Besides, I bargain better than you do."

I blinked. "You do not."

Before Paul could reply, there was a tremendous concussion. I squealed with pain and covered my ears with my hands as the aircar tipped to one side and began to fall, feeling my scales swell and close together in a protective reflex. Paul clawed free of his safety harness and strained forward to slide open the driver's hatch, revealing Meony-ro, thankfully still conscious, fighting the controls.

I looked up for some reason. Where there should have been a roof was now the underbelly of another aircar, a poorly-maintained and rusty one at that, dripping oils on my head. We spiraled down together, a sickening motion that slowed and finally calmed into something resembling flight.

I drew a shuddering breath, only just realizing I was holding on to Paul's arm with all of the considerable strength of my Lishcyn-self. *For comfort,* I told myself, refusing to believe I might have instinctively reached for the nearest living mass, unable, in honesty, to dismiss the thought either. I released him with a muttered and fervent apology.

It wasn't really the time for one. I took back all of my complaints to the fates, overwhelmingly thankful Meony-ro was driving; if we were going to land as anything but a projectile, it would be completely due to his talent. I wiped another drip of oil from my snout and braced myself, holding form with a strength that would surely have impressed Ersh.

What impressed me was how Meony-ro not only brought us down with merely a bouncing lurch to the side that landed Paul on top of me for a strangled minute, but how quickly the Kraal freed himself from his seat to climb up to the other aircar, weapon in his hand. *Humans didn't react to accidents well at all,* I thought, dazedly.

"C'mon, Es," Paul said, hauling at my greater mass without success. *He had,* I realized, *his weapon out as well.*

"Not an accident," I concluded unhappily, stirring myself to move, my body—especially my stomachs—complaining vigorously.

"I seriously doubt it," Paul agreed, looking out before jumping through what had been a viewing window.

Jumping. I sighed, considering my present form's capabilities in that regard, which were nil. The aircar above me chose that instant to sink further with a horrendous grind and screech of metal on metal. I didn't wait to find out if that was a natural settling process or if Meony-ro was bouncing around overhead. I squeezed through to the window, looked down to be sure Paul was out of my flight path, and launched myself.

The drop was no more than my height and half again, however there was something about a massive hunk of scales meeting the already shattered surface of a rooftop that meant something had to give. I pulled my right foot free as Paul hurried to help. "You okay?" he asked, letting me balance against his shoulder while I tugged at my left foot. That one had gone completely through the roofing material, somehow making a hole narrower than the foot itself. I wasn't having much luck.

Meony-ro dropped lightly beside Paul. *Must be their primate heritage,* I grumbled to myself, but accepted his help as well. Between the three of us, we managed to free my foot.

I took a minute to wriggle my toes cautiously, keeping an ear tuned to the Humans' conversation. From their relaxed, but wary stance, we weren't in immediate danger. The aircar that rammed us had been empty.

"It was to bring us down, Hom Cameron," Meony-ro was arguing. "If they wanted you dead, they could have simply packed the aircar with explosives."

At this rate, my scales were going to stay swollen, I thought, envisioning trying to run while my body was wrapped in its version of armor plating. Paul was rubbing his arm absently. I'd likely left some bruises, but at least nothing worse. Under the circumstances, I was rather proud of my self-control.

As for my falling into the roof, shoddy workmanship was definitely a factor—unsurprising, since, once I looked around and noticed, we had crashed almost in the center of the Dump, on one of the long, flat warehouses connecting the grounded starships.

"Why here?" I asked, stepping carefully on a surface that begrudged my mass. The intermittent howls of wind, fortunately dry, seemed frustrated they couldn't push me around as they did the Humans, although what remained of my silks would soon be in tatters. I kept my ears folded to keep out the draft. "If they didn't want us dead—a happy circumstance we owe completely to your skill, Meony-ro— they must have wanted us somewhere."

Meony-ro looked uneasy. *The Dump,* I thought, *did that to reasonable beings.* "The com's functional, Hom Cameron," he offered.

Paul was staring at me. I returned his suspicious look with my most innocent expression. "Let's not put out specifics until we know who's listening," Paul decided. "The crash will be reported anyway." I didn't bother to point out that crashes were reported over Fishertown with remarkable frequency and little result. "There will be someone sent out—if only to check for salvageable parts."

"Like that?" I said, pointing at the sleek, black aircar dropping out of the clouds. I couldn't make out much detail. A cloudy day here was twilight dim to my Lishcyn-eyes. Of course, I really didn't need to see. I'd been expecting something—I'd just planned to meet it on my own.

Paul used some very colorful language. He and Meony-ro armed and raised their weapons with what might have been practiced synchrony. "I take it this isn't good news?" I asked, ducking under the only existing shelter—the tail end of the tangled pair of aircars wedged into the warehouse roof.

"It's Tly," the Kraal grunted as he and Paul joined me.

"So much for your dream of Chase and Logan, my friend," I couldn't help saying.

Paul tore his eyes from the now-hovering vehicle, definitely no aircar but a shuttle identical to those on *The Black Watch,* and glared at me. His expression changed from grim to an interesting mix of speculation and dismay. "You're finding this funny."

"I am not." Still, it was hard to keep my tusk under my lip.

He began to frown. "Esen. What have you done?"

"We have a situation here, Hom Cameron," Meony-ro interrupted testily, patently thinking both his employers were crazy.

Considering the number of uniformed Tly pouring out of the now-landed shuttle and heading in our direction, the Kraal had a point. Paul stiffened as a second group stepped out, one of them head and shoulders taller than the rest. "Logan," he said, in as close to a growl as I'd ever heard from a Human.

I began looking around impatiently. *The difficulty with ephemerals,* I reminded myself, *was their sense of timing. Ah!*

A fresh burst of wind sent some of the Tly tumbling, but it wasn't from Minas XII's incorrigible weather. This wind, I noted with intense satisfaction, came from the two large craft rising from either side of this building as they angled their jets to move inward, flanking the Tly.

"Esen?" Paul sounded as though unsure whether to stomp on my foot or hug me. *It was,* I noted, *a conflict he frequently seemed to experience.* "Who is—" His words were buried by the ear-piercing thrum of the machines as they landed. I hoped the roof could hold them.

I reached out and pulled both Humans farther back, toward me, a precaution against the wind as well as what might occur in a moment. "You aren't the only one with friends, Paul Cameron," I shouted triumphantly into his ear. "And you aren't the only one with gadgets!" I waggled my bag at him.

Meanwhile, the craft—now clearly visible as Ganthor aerial assault carriers—had stopped moving. Their pilots hadn't trusted the roof either, holding just above the surface. Huge doors along the carriers' sides slammed opened, much like those of a 'digger, revealing row upon row of heavily armed, snout-twitching Ganthor.

They didn't move.

The next sound was the Tly dropping their weapons as quickly as they could, some tossing them right off the roof.

I did enjoy a good surprise, I decided, standing up to see better.

"No, Es!" shouted Paul and tackled me. As this had about as much effect as his running into the side of the wrecked aircar, I obligingly fell over in the direction I presumed he wanted me to go. *Humans.* Then I started as a bolt of energy splashed harmlessly overhead, immediately returned by something throatier issuing from Meony-ro's weapon.

"No one was supposed to shoot at us," I complained to Paul. "Who shot at us?"

Paul leaned his elbows on my chest to aim his weapon and fire it. "Not now, Esen," he grunted.

Being flat on my back and unable to see was bad enough, I thought. *But to be a table?* "Get off me," I said, pushing at him.

"No. You—" he bit off the word angrily, then continued, "you just stay down. Logan's wedged himself in and is shooting at us. He knows the Ganthor won't interfere in a private fight and I'm not about to fire at them in order to get them interested. Happy?"

He needn't blame me, I decided, shifting to move my hip out of a growing hole in the roof.

"Paul."

"Not now, Es." Paul returned fire. It didn't sound very successful.

"Paul," I insisted. "This is a lousy roof."

The Human looked down at me, frowning, then a smile spread across his face. "Yes, it is, isn't it. Meony-ro." He moved over to the Kraal, who kept up a return fire as Paul spoke urgently in his ear.

I edged myself up so I could see what the Humans would do. The Tly were either flat on their stomachs or crouched out of the line of fire. The Ganthor were shoving each other in prebattle frenzy, mucus glistening like sweat on their upper bodies. I didn't think the Seconds would be able to hold their Herds much longer—no matter how they disliked interrupting what Paul correctly deduced they'd view as a personal, hierarchical dispute. I did know none of the Ganthor would leave without Logan. After all, there was a hefty bonus, as well as Herd honor, involved. *The Matriarch,* I recalled, *drove a hard bargain.*

Paul and Meony-ro wasted no time redirecting their blasts from where bright flashes marked Logan's position alongside the ramp leading from the *'Watch'*s shuttle, to the section of roof underneath. Almost immediately, the shuttle tilted as it lost support.

Before I could applaud their success, Logan's next blast took out most of the roof in front of me and I tumbled down into the dark.

Elsewhere

PRIVATE messages by translight were hideously expensive. *The com-techs in Upperside Shipcity had seemed very impressed,* Kearn thought.

He himself certainly was, his hands almost shaking as he cued the message cube to play back in the privacy of his quarters on the shipcity. Tonight was the meeting between the Feneden and Iftsen. There had been quite a few messages, as well as art arrangements, offers of temporary liaisons of several types, and assorted wines, all from those hoping he could somehow help settle this conflict. Many were from art dealers whose livelihoods were potentially threatened by the Feneden dumping stolen Iftsen art into a lucrative and expensive market.

But nothing like this, Kearn thought. It would take his year's salary to send this one message. He sat forward, eyes intent.

"Dear Lionel," he read. *Dear Lionel?* From a friend? He couldn't recall any rich ones—at least none he hadn't thoroughly antagonized long ago searching for funds for his quest.

"Dear Lionel, I want to wish you luck. It has always seemed a regrettably necessary part of interspecies' negotiation. I also wish to share something with you. The Iftsen's Messenger was a bluff. They have never built or owned a planet-killing weapon; I do not believe they are capable of doing so. Only you need know this. The Iftsen's false weapon was stolen, but, if they believe its secret remains intact, they will replace it with something equally harmless, and lie about it equally well. And species like the Feneden are young enough to need a reason to respect the rights of others."

Kearn stopped reading, awed by the trust this message implied, excited by its implications. He wondered again who could have sent it. *Perhaps I've been noticed at last by someone high in the government,* he told himself, dizzy with delight. *A Deputy Minister—or better!* With this information, combined with his own dream-driven insights, he had every chance to be successful tonight. *He could save lives.*

It wasn't wrong to want more than that, Kearn assured himself. His superiors had been silent concerning his indiscretion with the *Russell III.* Finding Lefebvre had helped, but he'd known they were simply waiting to pounce. *Maybe this message was a sign that, if he could pull the Feneden and Iftsen together, he could save his career at the same time.*

"I am young as well, Lionel," the message continued, confounding all his hopes and preconceptions at once. *Who was this?* Kearn asked himself, suddenly fearing the answer.

"I make mistakes, but when I do, I do my best to fix them. I believe I have made such a mistake in hiding from you. When you are ready to find me, I will be there. If you ever need me, I will come. Esen-alit-Quar."

Kearn's lips repeated the name without sound as the message faded and disappeared.

It hadn't been a dream, after all.

"Mediator Kearn?"

Kearn started, only then aware he'd been sitting and staring at the now-empty cube long enough to have cramped his back. "Yes?" he said to the steward standing in his doorway, a young Human.

"The facilities await your inspection, Mediator Kearn. May I escort you?"

"I know the way, Steward," Kearn said impatiently, his mind reeling with unexpected possibilities and equally unlooked-for disasters, finding it difficult to focus back on his task. "Let the decorators know I'll be there in a moment."

The steward hesitated. "What is it?" Kearn demanded.

The young Human colored, then smiled shyly. "I wanted to say, sir, I've admired you for years. I've followed your hunt for the Esen Monster in the newsmags—not that I think they'd carry all the real facts, sir. I wanted you to know, sir, that I believe in what you are doing. I hope you find it and kill it. You'll save us all."

It was Kearn's turn to hesitate, overcome by a rush of pleasure as heady and uncontrolled as though some drug had flooded his veins. *Fifty years,* he thought, wildly. *I've waited fifty years for this.* "Thank you, Hom—"

"Cristoffen, sir. Michael Cristoffen."

"I appreciate your zeal, Hom Cristoffen. Perhaps you'd consider applying as crew on my ship when you've completed your apprenticeship here."

Kearn used one finger to tip the empty message cube into the recycle slot on the table.

"I can always," he added, "use more true believers."

51: Warehouse Afternoon

I CYCLED as I fell within the rain of broken tiles and rotting sheets of presswood, a reflex adjustment to conditions totally unsuited to my Lishcyn-self. *Here's hoping it stayed dark,* I warned myself, tightening into a ball before impact.

I struck what was likely the top of a ceiling. It held for barely a heartbeat, then groaned and gave way under me. I dropped again, finally landing on something that gave but didn't break.

Well, I decided, checking out various body parts, *that was fun*—an opinion possible to my Ganthor-self. My current hide was even thicker than my Lishcyn-self's and, although I massed slightly less, my form was more dense and heavily boned. The impact had felt roughly equivalent to a boisterous greeting between Herd mates at a bar.

I tested the air, mucus bubbling from my nostrils as I savored the dissolved aromas. *Herdscent* drifted down to me through the hole in the roof, alluring and almost irresistible. Considering the present state of the Ganthor above me, I had no intention of answering its call. *They wouldn't,* I reminded myself, *take well to a stranger.*

There were other organics. I turned, sampling in every direction: stale Human overlaid everything, including the cinnamon tang of an Engullian and a bitter bouquet of what Ersh-memory labeled as banned drugs of several sorts. *Well, it was the Dump.*

I grunted, catching a fresher, hotter taste in the air. *Human.* Web-memory bubbled up, its molecular discrimination totally precise: *Logan.*

Ganthor were brave and loyal. *They weren't the brightest.* That was my excuse later for what I did next—namely, start running in the almost total darkness toward that scent.

Luckily, there were no holes or walls in my path, since I didn't plunge into the one or run snout-first into the other. The notion of such obstacles did help cool my Ganthor enthusiasm. The thought of who I was running to slowed me even more. But I didn't stop, hearing new sounds from behind that I feared meant Paul had followed me down here, with or without Meony-ro.

I had to reach Logan first.

By rough estimate, I was almost under the shuttle before I tasted blood in the air. It had an interesting effect on my Ganthor-self, being a herbivorous species that instinctively gathered in a group for defense. This blood, though not Ganthor, suggested a predator; my lone Ganthor-self felt the urge to wait for others. I ignored it.

I took two more steps, then heard a click. It wasn't a word in clickspeak, but I knew its meaning. Ahead of me, in the pitch dark, someone had armed a disrupter. I stopped and tried to be quiet, but it wasn't exactly a feature of this form. In the otherwise silent warehouse, I panted and wheezed like a bellows, and there were soft popping noises as my breath passed through the mucus coating my nostrils.

A small light came on, its immediate circle of brightness empty of all but a long arm and a trail of red droplets, casting rays that reached to my legs. Above, the light reflected from the metal of the shuttle. Paul and Meony-ro must have undermined the entire ship.

"A War Hog," said a high-pitched voice I knew too well. "Alone, unarmed, and mute. Well, you certainly aren't of any use to me."

I cycled before Logan could fire, standing before him in Human-form, shedding excess mass as a puddle of water around my small bare feet. "I wouldn't call them that to their snouts," I advised him.

Logan crawled into his own light. He'd been injured, badly, I thought. Blood soaked the neck, shoulder, and chest of his uniform, running down one arm and huge hand to drip over the barrel of the weapon he aimed at me. There was nothing in his glittering blue eyes to show he was anything less than ready to use it; though wounded, the massive Human looked more dangerous than ever. "It appears I face a disturbing choice," he observed calmly, as though we sat across from one another at some dinner table. "I can believe in the dead. Or I can believe in you, shapeshifter. I'd prefer not to believe in either."

"Yet you believe in a mythical weapon. And over the evidence of your own eyes. You wouldn't be here, on Minas XII, otherwise," I said as calmly.

"True, true." Unbelievably, Logan heaved himself up, becoming a silhouette the size of a mountain. I swallowed and stood my ground. *Clothes would have been nice.* "Where's Ragem, little ghost? Such a clever man, with his secrets upon secrets. Too clever. Do you know, he tricked me into stealing a pile of junk? Then he turned the Hogs against me? No matter. You are quite right about what I believe." His voice dropped to a husky whisper, deepened with what I took for excitement as much as pain. *For Logan, maybe they were one and the same.* "I believe your Ragem has the real Kraal superweapon, right here. He or the Kraal with him."

Logan didn't miss much, I thought with disgust. Meonyro's presence on the 'Lass had been just one more confirmation of his pet theory.

Paul could walk in range of this madman's voice at any second. "There is no Kraal weapon," I told Logan. "Everything you think this weapon did—was done by one of my kind. You don't need Paul to find that out." *What I needed was some way to get the Ganthor involved.*

His free hand snaked out after my arm, but his own blood lubricated the grip so his fingers slipped off my skin. I took a step to put myself out of reach, halting as the weapon's tip moved deliberately into the light as a reminder. "I need you, little ghost," Logan disagreed, as if not hearing a word I said. "You are my key to Ragem. He has the Nightstalker. With it, I will take Tly back to her rightful place. With it, I will rule."

Madness was something I'd always found difficult to assess, there being so many different perceptions and patterns of thought between species—let alone the honestly eccentric. Like Ersh and my former web-kin, I considered all ephemerals a little mad, obsessed with hurrying through their lives when they should by rights hoard every minute. But what looked back at me now, blood-streaked and ominous, was the real thing.

So much for talking my way out of this, I thought with disgust. I chanced a step to the right. Logan's weapon tracked the motion with menacing smoothness, implying nothing wrong with his reflexes. Judging by the blood pooling around his feet, I could wait for him to pass out. Since any other Human would have done so by now, I had no idea when that would be.

And it wouldn't be soon enough, I realized. I didn't need to look around to know we were no longer alone.

Logan knew it, too. He smiled, keeping his attention on me, and called out: "Come where I can see you, my friend."

"We've been through all this before, Human," I said with deliberate sarcasm, talking more to the one I couldn't see, than Logan. "I thought you'd learned you can't use me as a hostage. Fire your weapon. You can't harm me—Paul knows it and so do you."

Of course, I wasn't so sure about that, I said to myself, holding my breath. I should be able to cycle before his finger pressed the firing mechanism—and I should be able to thin myself so the burst went through my web-flesh. It was a lot of "should bes" I wasn't planning to test. *If the Iftsen could bluff,* I thought, *so could Esen.*

Logan might have believed me. Unfortunately, it seemed Paul did not. He stepped out of the darkness, empty-handed, his face a mask of dust and sweat.

Three things happened simultaneously. I began to frantically think of something else, Logan smiled with satisfaction, and Paul spoke one word:

"Now."

Lights kicked in from either side, blinding me at first, pinning Logan in their midst. They appeared to confuse him.

He dropped his weapon, putting his better hand up to shade his eyes.

To my left was the Matriarch of the Herd from Iftsen Secondus, flanked by her Seconds, each bearing enough armament to take out the entire building, let alone subdue one Human.

To my right, no less deadly, stood Meony-ro, Rudy Lefebvre, and Joel Largas.

I looked suspiciously at my dear Human friend, whose mask had cracked into an immense grin. *Likely relief,* I thought, then added, less charitably and more honestly, *of course, Paul would know perfectly well how I'd feel standing here wearing gooseflesh and nothing else in front of his father-in-law.*

"Gloria, are you all right?" This from the ever-quick Lefebvre, who rushed forward with his arms open.

I decided it was a very reasonable moment to let myself be hustled away.

After all, Paul had added himself—and half the planet— to what otherwise would have been an excellent and charmingly discreet plan.

It was, I thought, with a pleasant sense of having the shoe, as Humans would say, on the other appendage, *only fair he tidy up the result.*

Elsewhere

LEFEBVRE lifted his glass, then paused, deep in thought. *Strange. It was getting hard to think of a new toast.* "To women!" he exclaimed, sure this one could be repeated indefinitely.

"To women," his drinking companion concurred. "So Rudy. How's your niece?"

Lefebvre peered at Joel Largas. "She's fine, thanks. On her way home."

"Smart work. She's lucky to have you, Rudy. To you!"

Lefebvre accepted the toast, not entirely sure it was deserved. *It had been a satisfying sequence of events,* he thought, but at any point, things could have gone sour. An informant's report on *The Black Watch;* his conviction that Logan was capable of daring an incursion on Minas XII; getting here in time. He shuddered. "We were lucky."

They were interrupted as three newcomers to the bar, working spacers from their look, veered close for no other reason than to clap Largas on the back. One of them bore a remarkable resemblance to the old trader. "Luck? I don't believe in luck," Largas said emphatically, once they were alone again. "I believe in people. Take you and Paul. Great job. Why, if you hadn't warned him, he might never have realized what those Ganthor were doing in the Dump. We could have had a minor war break out—not that I'd mind. There's some who live there we could do without, if you know what I mean."

"How did you know about the Ganthor?" Lefebvre

asked curiously. "They were pretty well hidden—especially for Ganthor."

Largas waved to the bartender, before turning his piercing eyes on Lefebvre. "Information is always the key, Rudy. Remember that. People like to talk. And I listen to every bit that comes my way. You never know what will matter."

The presence of a Ganthor Herd had certainly mattered to Paul. He'd realized immediately what Esen was up to—trying to capture Logan by herself. He'd arranged for Largas, with a vested interest in Logan's activity and his uncanny knowledge of the Dump, to bring Lefebvre to the right place at the right time. Fortunately, the Matriarch had been very reasonable about local talent.

Esen, Lefebvre recalled, *had probably been even more surprised than Logan.* He smiled into his glass as he remembered the look she'd given Paul. *And that blush?* She'd insisted on running for cover as quickly as possible, particularly to avoid Joel Largas.

The more time Lefebvre spent with Largas, the more he liked the being. But Largas was trusted by Esolesy Ki, not Esen. Paul had made that quite clear. So the mysterious young girl being held by Logan was his niece, Gloria, a fiction reinforced by the unwitting Meony-ro.

It had been convincing.

It had been close. *Too close.* Lefebvre put down his drink. No point risking what had been achieved. "I have to get back to my ship," he told Largas. "Nice meeting you, Joel."

Largas' eyes were keen under their bushy brows and he offered Lefebvre his hand. "I happen to have an opening for a Captain," he said as their hands met. "If you're ever tired of working for cruise lines, that is."

Lying to this being wasn't right, Lefebvre knew as he released Largas' hand, not surprised by the firmness of his grip. But Paul had warned him. When Lefebvre had casually brought up the topic of the Monster of the Fringe, to see for himself, Largas had grown unusually tight-lipped, revealing only that the monster was very real and

that Lionel Kearn was a blithering idiot incapable of finding his own nose.

No wonder Esen kept her secret.

"I'll keep that in mind," Lefebvre said quite sincerely.
"I don't know what's ahead, frankly."

If there was anything he could predict about his own
future, it was going to be something he'd never have
imagined before meeting Esen-alit-Quar.

52: Cliff's Edge Night

WINTER was coming. I stood on the porch and watched my breath float upward, looking beyond its faint mist to admire the thick crown of stars overhead. There would be a cold snap tonight, and doubtless a blizzard ready to kill the unwary tomorrow. I fluffed my fur in anticipation. Minas XII was like that. You had to catch its beauty on its terms, not yours. *And be ready to duck.*

Paul should be home soon. The minor distraction in the warehouse I'd arranged to keep Paul from accompanying me to the Dump—doomed to failure, since he'd already outflanked me completely—had turned into something a bit more complicated. All I'd done was open a few cages of pollinating insects. Peaceful, but large and noisy insects. They should have been a harmless-enough nuisance. *How was I to know the things were being shipped pregnant and would vigorously defend their new nesting territories throughout the warehouse?* The importer had kindly supplied antivenom, which hadn't put Paul into a better frame of mind.

His aggravation wouldn't last. *Especially with his favorite supper in a bag on the table,* I thought happily. After picking up my order, I'd left Lefebvre and Largas at the Circle Club, looking as though they planned to drink all night. I had no idea of Lefebvre's capacity, but knowing Joel's, I winced.

Lefebvre had promised to visit: a friend I'd made on my own. I treasured that newest gift, like the starry skies above me.

*   *   *

It had clouded over before Paul's shuttle touched down outside. He'd hurried in to avoid the growing cold, heading straight to the 'fresher to, as he put it, wash off bug guts. I didn't dare ask who'd won the battle of the warehouse. *Some topics,* I knew, *were best left alone.*

This delay gave me time to prepare, so when Paul returned a few moments later, futilely trying to rub some order into his damp hair, I had all the reaction I could have wanted.

The Human stopped dead in the doorway to the kitchen. He wasn't, I was pleased to note, looking at the less-than-artfully arranged meal on the table. Instead, he was looking at me.

I turned completely around, then back again. "Well?" I'd bought the clothing at a children's store on my way home. It had only been a matter of assuming this form to suit. My hair wasn't much better than his at staying tidy, but I'd already become resigned to that.

When Paul didn't speak, my new heart gave an odd and uncomfortable lurch. I studied his face. There was plenty of emotion there—his eyes were glittering as if about to leak, and I saw him swallow—but I was suddenly unsure it was a happy one and lost some of my own joy.

He saw it. "Esen," he said very gently. "You don't have to be Human for me. We've been together all this time without it. I understand your reasons and they're good ones." He paused. "I'm your friend in any form. You know that."

I nodded, feeling my own eyes beginning to fill. *It was,* I told myself sternly, *no worse than oozing mucus as a Ganthor.* "This," I touched my cheek, "is me as well."

Paul leaned his back against the doorframe, folding his arms like someone who'd had a very long, very tiring day. *With bugs.* "What do you want me to say, Esen?" he asked. "I've never asked you to be anything for me and I won't now. Do you want me to admit this version of you is special? Yes. It is. I admit it. That doesn't mean I require it or expect it or even think it's a good idea. You have a purpose and a life beyond our friendship."

Being Human meant lacking so many senses to help me

puzzle out his mood, an insight of itself, I realized, into how very good Paul was at understanding other species as well as his own. *Unless it was something that occurred as this form aged,* I thought. This time, however, he was wrong.

"You misunderstand me, Paul," I said just as gently as he'd spoken to me, moving close and putting one hand on his folded arm. "We share a closeness built from our differences. How could that change? My assuming this form can't change my thoughts into Human thoughts, my viewpoint can never be exactly as yours." I smiled up at him, knowing this face had rather attractive dimples in each cheek. "But when I'm with you, this form returns to me something I was in danger of losing, something you valued in me even when I did not."

Paul's mouth curved up at the corners and his eyes were warm on my face. "And what might that be, old friend?"

"I may be the Eldest in my Web," I informed him. "But I'm also Youngest."

It was after supper, the first meal we'd ever shared as the same species—although I couldn't share Paul's delight in slimy mollusks—that we bundled up and went outside. There was snow tumbling down, a silent heavy drift that coated the mountainside in treacherously soft white. It was hard to discern where the snow ended and the clouds began. *The hail,* I thought philosophically, *would start with the wind.*

"Am I supposed to send you to bed, Youngest?" Paul asked through a pretend yawn, stretching his arms up. One promptly dropped to dump a handful of snow down my neck.

Startled, I glared at him until I saw the mischief in his face. "I'll cycle into Ganthor if you want a snowball fight," I threatened.

His hands went up in mock-surrender. "Cheat."

"Bully," I answered contentedly, digging snow out of the robe I'd thrown on—given it was Paul's, I wasn't too concerned. *'Course, if I was going to wear this form more regularly, I'd have to have a coat. And boots.* "I'm going to have to do some shopping," I reminded Paul. "And we'll have to build another hidden closet. Mine's already full, and I can't imagine explaining a child-sized set of Human clothes to anyone outside the Group."

I'd said it deliberately. Paul knew it, and flashed me a surprised and grateful look. Perhaps he wondered why.

Perhaps one day, I'd tell him.

I used to look ahead and believe I knew the future, that I could predict and become whatever my chosen task demanded.

Now, thanks to Paul and his larger vision, I had absolutely no idea what the next fifty years might hold.

I smiled at my first friend, Paul Ragem, and felt free.

Elsewhere

FIFTY years.

N'Klet examined her carapace critically in the mirrored tiles. The fading pits and scars were still noticeable. She would need more time like this to heal completely. *Inconvenient.*

But expedient. The accident had served its painful purpose. Scentless, she'd gained admittance to the School of Alien Etiquette; scentless, she'd easily taken the identity of the D'Dsellan whose body now drifted in honorable, if anonymous, burial in space. The Iftsen, *worthless clowns,* hadn't even noticed.

The Youngest had been the only risk. Physical contact might have exposed the truth; a suspicious mind might have seen—incongruities. *As expected,* N'Klet nodded to her image, *the distraction provided had been adequate.* Esen was still easily manipulated.

One of the young rezts left its littermates, rubbing its side sleepily against N'Klet's lower limb. Absently, she picked it up with a midlimb and stroked it. *Yes,* she thought, *Esen still followed the Old One's Rules. Significant.*

With a flash of blue, almost faster than the eye could follow, there was no longer a D'Dsellan holding a sleepy rezt, but someone—something—else.

The room was dark, lit only by an antique chandelier. Its circle of light fell partly across an inlaid table, revealing a pair of hands, five-fingered, long, supple, and strong. They toyed with a knife, its handle ornately etched, its blade catching the light in fierce, quick bursts. One of a priceless pair, now solitary.

Two Kraal officers stood within the light as well. "We are grateful for your return, Eminence," said the first Kraal, touching the tattoos on each cheek, bowing deeply. "We regret to have no news."

"The transmissions ceased, Eminence," added the second, with an equally deep bow. "Sooner than predicted."

"No matter," answered a deep, rich voice from the shadows, a voice like velvet. *There were other ways to watch a web-being,* the owner of that voice knew. "Resume course." There was no need to confirm the order. Discipline on a Kraal ship was absolute. The first Kraal left immediately.

"Was there success, Eminence?" this from the second Kraal. "We regret we were unable to confirm her ability to—fly. The test had seemed foolproof."

"Partial success, Holt-ru," replied the shadow. "The Feneden were bait she couldn't resist. It was her response that was—unpredicted."

"Will there be another opportunity, Eminence?"

The hands lifted the knife, turning it upright. One fingertip delicately met the point, anointing it with a single drop of bright, red blood.

"Oh, yes." *The Youngest of the Web of Ersh would share her secrets. It was only a matter of when.*